THE
VANISHING
SEASON

ALSO BY
DOT HUTCHISON

A Wounded Name

The Collector Series

The Butterfly Garden

The Roses of May

The Summer Children

THE
VANISHING
SEASON

Book 4 in the Collector Series

DOT HUTCHISON

Published by Thomas & Mercer, Seattle

www.apub.com

Amazon, the Amazon logo, and Thomas & Mercer are trademarks of Amazon.com, Inc., or its affiliates.

ISBN-13: 9781542040228
ISBN-10: 1542040221

Cover design by Kirk DouPonce, DogEared Design

Printed in the United States of America

To Robert and Stacy—
for answering all the legal questions
I really didn't want to Google.
Thank you for keeping me off lists.

1

"Eliza, help me out here."

I glance at Cass. "With?"

"What is it with Mercedes and sunflowers?"

Our third teammate stops fluffing the arrangement of sunflowers in the vase on the filing cabinet and turns to face my desk, where Cass and I are sitting. "Cass, you've known me for how long now, and you've never asked?"

Cass shrugs, but as with most of her gestures, she does it with her whole body. Even the chair our feet are resting on moves with the full-body ripple. "I guess it never seemed important enough to ask."

"And it is now?"

"No, but now I'm bored and you have a fresh delivery of them."

I tune them out—they've been doing this a lot longer than I've known them—and check the time on my phone, then look to the empty desk set just a bit apart from ours. Bran is late.

Bran is *never* late. He is, in fact, compulsively early for everything.

"I like sunflowers because they reach for the sun, always."

"Oh, God, you and your metaphors."

Okay, so there's a larger-than-average possibility that I'm looking for Bran less out of concern and more out of a wish that his sudden appearance will derail the friendly bickering. Cassondra Kearney and Mercedes Ramirez met at the FBI Academy some thirteen years ago, and both went into the Crimes Against Children division. Until recently, they were on different teams, but not quite a year ago there was a division-wide restructuring to account for the greater workload all the teams were facing, and our unit chief, Vic Hanoverian, decided we'd benefit from a fourth member. He gave us Cass, who'd been loaned to us on a particularly hellish and personal case two years before. Of the various Quantico-based CAC folks, she was the most temperamentally suited to our team, he informed us.

He was clearly trying not to laugh during that little speech. We are, without question, Vic's favorite team, largely because Bran and Mercedes were his partners until his promotion, but loving us doesn't mean he doesn't also enjoy poking us with sticks. Or rather, poking Bran with a stick.

Bran was already outnumbered with just me and Mercedes. Cass makes it a pretty hopeless situation.

"Eliza? Eliza!"

Cass's elbow in my side makes me flinch. "What?"

"What do you think?"

"What do I think? What do I think . . . about . . . the thing I was obviously not paying attention to?"

Both of them snicker, though Mercedes shakes her head. "Situational awareness, Sterling. Try to practice some."

"So what do I think about what?" I ask rather than dignify that with an actual response.

"Is Mercedes a sunflower?" Cass repeats.

"You know, this is exactly the kind of conversation that gives him nightmares."

They look over at Bran's desk and burst into laughter. They don't even have to ask who "him" is. It's comforting, this team dynamic, even if it is still a little terrifying at times. When I graduated the academy, I was sent back to Colorado, to the Denver Field Office. My mother was relieved—if I absolutely *had* to go into such a dangerous, unladylike career, at least it was where she could nag me face-to-face about it—but I was a little disappointed. I'd wanted to go to new places for more than just the seventeen weeks of the academy. Then, four years ago or so, I was offered a transfer to this team. It took a little while for all of us to adjust.

"His bag is here," Mercedes notes. "Look, you can see it poking out from the well of the desk."

Huh. So it is. "In with Vic?"

"Or Yvonne, if something's breaking and she's still pulling all the data down. Is she in her office?"

Cass and I both strain to see Yvonne's office, but the door is closed and the windowless space doesn't give us any hint if the team's technical analyst is in yet or not.

"So Eliza, have you put The Dress up on Craigslist yet?" Cass asks.

"If I give you a fork, will you go play with an electrical socket?"

She grins at me, unrepentant.

Before either of them can offer more suggestions regarding my never-been-used wedding dress, the door to Vic's office—up at the top of a slight ramp that turns toward a conference room a half floor up—opens and Vic steps out to lean against the rail. "Good morning, ladies."

"Good morning, Charlie," all three of us chorus.

Normally he smiles and tells us to save it for Eddison.

Today . . . "You've got a case, local. Richmond."

We share looks between us, then turn back to him. Mercedes says what we're all probably thinking. "Okay?"

"Eddison will join you at the car. Watts's team is taking lead on this one, but you'll be working with them."

Eddison's—Bran's—absence suddenly strikes me in a new, worrying light. "It's a kidnapping, isn't it?" I ask. "A little girl?"

"Yvonne will send you the files in a minute. She's just tagging the last few things sent over."

Which means yes, but he doesn't want anyone else in the bullpen gossiping about it.

I slide off my desk—Cass hops, because she's a little too short to manage the slide with accuracy—and the three of us gather what we need in under thirty seconds. Local, so we don't need our go bags. We do need our coats—hello, late October. None of us like carrying our purses out in the field if we can avoid it, but leaving them in the cars is equally uncomfortable, so what can't hang on our belts gets shifted to the pockets in our pants and coats until they bulge like chipmunk cheeks.

In the elevator, our tablets ding with the incoming file. I flip mine open. "Brooklyn Mercer," I read aloud. "Caucasian, eight years old, blonde hair, blue eyes. Disappeared . . . yesterday."

Cass yelps. "Yesterday? And they're just calling us in now?"

"Disappeared while—shit—walking home from school in the afternoon."

"Mierda."

I reach out and jab the stop button on the console, and the elevator shudders to a halt.

"It's always elevators," Mercedes muses.

"Sterling?"

"Just . . . give me a minute." I smooth a hand over the crown of my head, checking that my hair is still back in its tightly braided, somewhat severe bun.

November 5, just a week and a half away, will be the twenty-fifth anniversary of the day eight-year-old Faith Eddison, with her blonde hair and blue eyes, disappeared while walking home from school and was never seen again. Bran will look at the pictures of Brooklyn Mercer and part of him will, inescapably, see his sister. This time of year, this kind of case, I can't help but wonder how long it took him to stop seeing Faith when he looked at me.

And whether or not it was still happening after we started dating three years ago.

I release the stop and the elevator lurches back into motion. "I guess we know why Watts has lead," I sigh. "Eddison and I will both be banished to fringe work. I look too close and he is too close."

Mercedes nudges my foot with hers. "Vic wouldn't give this to us unless he and Eddison were *both* sure he could handle it. He's got us to back him up."

Cass nods. "We've got him, and Watts isn't going to let him push himself too far."

We'll see, I suppose. Sometimes we only recognize our limits once we've passed them.

2

True to Vic's word, Eddison waits for us at the car. He's Bran off-duty, when he's my boyfriend. But right now, just as Cass and Mercedes become Kearney and Ramirez once we have a case, he's Eddison, the Charlie to our angels, and rather pissed about the entire fucking world, if it's all the same.

Which isn't entirely uncommon for him. He's careful with his anger, works very hard not to lash out except in appropriate or useful directions, but he's had that rage curling under his skin far longer than any of us have known him. Twenty-five years, from what his mother says, and it's not hard to connect those dots back to Faith.

He's already in the driver's seat of the SUV, hands clenched white-knuckled around the wheel. The radio is off instead of turned low. I climb into the front passenger seat, Kearney and Ramirez taking the back. Kearney is the only one who can comfortably sit behind Eddison; she's the only one short enough.

Halfway up the parking level, Watts's team splits into two black SUVs identical to ours. They're actually Cass's old team; this is the first case we've worked with them since Cass came to us. Eddison lets them pull out first, leading the way down the levels of the garage, and he takes up the rear, our own little cavalcade Richmond-bound. For several minutes, uncomfortable silence grips the car.

I wake up my tablet screen again and clear my throat. "Brooklyn Mercer. She and her neighbor usually walk home from school in the company of her neighbor's older brother."

Eddison's hand is so tight around the steering wheel one of his knuckles cracks with the strain.

After a moment, I continue. "The brother, Daniel, had a field trip yesterday, not expected to get back to his school until evening. His sister, Rebecca, went home sick before lunch. Arrangements were made to pick up Brooklyn, but they fell through for some reason. We'll have to ask what happened there."

"Her parents?" Eddison asks, his voice tight.

"Both work. Brooklyn usually either stays with Rebecca until one of her parents gets home or locks her house up tight. There are chain locks on the insides of the doors, so no one else can just walk in when she's home alone."

"When did they notice she was missing?" Kearney asks from the back.

"Eight o'clock. Her parents got home late and realized neither of them had picked up Brooklyn. They checked with the neighbors in case she went there, but she hadn't."

"When did they call the police?"

"Nine-thirty. They did a search first, walking between the house and school to see if she'd fallen or maybe just stayed at the school." I squint at the screen, zooming in on the scan of an officer's scrawled notes. "They called the school's emergency number and got connected to the principal. He and the school's resource officer walk the buildings and grounds together before leaving each day. That was around six, and they didn't see her there."

"Siblings?"

"Only child. Police came out en masse, started a grid search, and joined the family in knocking on doors through the neighborhood and the next ones over. They got Brooklyn's picture out to hospitals, fire stations, malls, and news stations."

Ramirez taps out a note on her screen. "Richmond's only an hour and a half away; why didn't any of us get the AMBER Alert push on our phones?"

"Uuuuuummmm . . ." I swipe through the scant handful of pages in the file.

"They don't always do the push alert to the broader area if they don't have reason to think it went beyond local territory," Eddison answers.

"Actually," I say, fighting against the seat belt so I can twist and better see all three of them, "it doesn't look like there's an AMBER at all. No suspect or vehicle description, so it doesn't fit the criteria of the alert. Not enough information to reasonably assist the public in identification."

"Have they called it into NCMEC?" Ramirez asks.

"And NCIC and VCIN, but not until this morning. Looks like the day-shift captain got in this morning and raised hell."

From the corner of my eye, I can see Kearney open her mouth, glance at the driver's seat, and bite down on whatever she wanted to say. If it's anything like what's running through my head at the moment, it's about the likelihood of the Richmond PD getting heavily retrained on missing kid protocols. There's no real reason for the family to know that you should always call the police before you start searching. The police would rather be irritated by a false alarm than have a kid be missing for hours before they're notified, but most people operate on the instinct to not bother the police until they know for a fact something is wrong. That the Mercers called after an hour and a half is actually not terrible. At least it was *only* an hour and a half.

But there's also not much reason for a family to know that your next call after the police should be to the National Center for Missing and Exploited Children. From the initial call, the police are the ones who should enter the information into the Virginia Criminal Information

Network and the National Crime Information Center, but the family is supposed to call into NCMEC. The faster the child's description and details can be spread through the networks, the better the chance of finding them.

Brooklyn was missing for over twelve hours before anyone thought to get her information beyond Richmond. The night shift screwed this up, and badly.

"Any sign that she did come home?" Kearney asks.

"No. Backpack is gone, a note from her mother is still on the counter, snack is still in the fridge. No signs of attempted entry around any of the doors or windows. Mail still in the box at the end of the driveway. Apparently she usually gets it on her way in."

Eddison's thumbs beat anxious tattoos against the wheel. "Any listed predators in the area?"

"Not sure yet. Yvonne's got a note here that there are a fair number of dings on the registry, but it's going to take her some time to sort it by crime."

The sex offender registry covers a *lot* of ground, from the sick and violent to the drunk and stupid. People learn a neighbor is on the registry and immediately assume the worst, which can be problematic in a case like this. Any time we have to spend convincing a neighborhood that the man who drunkenly pissed in an alley, thereby exposing himself, is probably not the one who kidnapped a kid, is time we should be spending actually looking for the kid.

"Are her parents her biological parents?" asks Ramirez.

"Yes. No prior marriages for either of them, and they're still married and living together."

If Brooklyn was adopted or fostered, or if one of the parents was a step-parent and the other biological parent was still out there somewhere, it would give us specific people to research. There's this mental checklist we all have, going down all the obvious questions so we can figure out what we know and what we don't, what possibilities we can eliminate right off the bat.

Eddison lets go of the wheel long enough to adjust the air-conditioning. Stupidly or not, we're all wearing our coats, which means the heat is a bad option. "Any links to other cases?"

"None obvious. The few other open missing kid cases in Richmond mostly happened a while ago. Suspected runaways, two parental abductions. Only two that have been labeled probable stranger abductions, both several months old. A fifteen-year-old girl and a six-year-old boy."

"Ages don't connect into a pattern," notes Kearney.

"Neither does appearance. The boy is black; the girl is Latina. Different parts of town, different schools, different social circles. Neither had anything in common with the other. Yvonne is running both of them against the Mercers just in case."

"What's the neighborhood like?" Ramirez asks. She has her tablet open to a map of Richmond.

"Pretty solidly middle class, it looks like," I reply. "Mostly families or empty nesters. Yards and driveways, individual mailboxes, maintained streetlights and well-lit roads. Up enough for a homeowners' association, but mostly so they can limit the number of college kids renting out. Must be a hot-button issue, because it's in the officer's notes. A handful of stay-at-home moms, one stay-at-home dad, but otherwise dual-income households or single-earner/single-parent, plus two houses rented to groups of students."

"Do the Mercers have any pets?"

"Two cats, both accounted for. We'll check with the local pet shops and shelters, see if any recent adoptions stand out."

Kearney taps a note into her version of the file. "Is Brooklyn the kind of kid who could be lured with a pet?"

"Don't know; we'll have to ask."

The rest of the way to Richmond, we dissect the scant file, exchanging questions. Kearney writes down the ones we can't answer, which are most of them. A few minutes from our destination, Watts calls my work cell rather than Eddison's. If Eddison is in a car, Eddison is driving. There are very few, and very specific, exceptions to that, because he's a terrible passenger. I flick the Bluetooth connection on.

"Sterling."

"Ready for assignments?" Watts asks, her voice distorted by the car's speakers.

"Yes, ma'am."

"Jesus, Sterling, don't call me ma'am. Ramirez, I want you with the family. You're the best for that on either team. Stay with them, be their focus, explain what the rest of us are doing. To the best of your ability, keep them calm, or at least contained. Eddison, please keep in mind these are Vic's orders, not mine."

Eddison's lips twitch. On a better day, it might be a smirk. "Understood. Where do you want me?"

"You're still second in command on scene, so I want to make sure you meet the day-shift captain and whoever's in charge of the state police contingent. After that, I want you with Sterling. Sterling, you and Kearney are going to start with the neighbors Brooklyn usually stays with after school. After that, Kearney, you're going to pair with Burnside. There's some construction in the back of the neighborhood, an expansion. I want you two to check the sites. You'll have some of the local cops with you. Sterling, Eddison, you'll head to the front of the neighborhood and the school. Map Brooklyn's route, then talk to the administrators and her teachers. The crossing guards are gone for the morning, but they're all coming in early for the afternoon shift so you can talk to them before they need to be at the intersections."

"Roger that," I answer.

"Sterling, you know what I'm going to ask you to do?"

"Not let the Mercers see me?"

"As best you can. Mrs. Mercer is hysterical, and her husband isn't much better. And while I'm not one to assume you look like every

11

blue-eyed blonde in the world, I've got to say you actually do look a lot like this one."

I study Brooklyn's picture on my tablet, then flip the visor down to look in the mirror. Watts is not wrong.

It's one of the things I honestly never anticipated when I decided to join the FBI. I was worried about how I looked, yes, but that's because I'm the kind of blonde and pretty that makes me look *really* young. It's only been in the last year or two that people have stopped asking me if it's Take Your Daughter to Work Day when I walk into a field office, despite the badge and gun at my hip. I was worried about whether or not anyone would take me seriously, if I'd have to be constantly struggling to get people to listen and answer and obey. So, I made myself a list of rules for work and followed them religiously.

Wear only black and white—stark, severe, not remotely girly or young.

Keep my hair in a bun or twist, equally stark and severe, and make sure it's not high enough to be confused for a ballerina bun.

Use minimal makeup, enough to look professional but not enough to look like I'm trying too hard or like I enjoy makeup. (I do. I love eye shadow. And lip stains. And gloss. The shelves next to my vanity look like a Sephora annex.)

In hindsight, I can admit I was entirely too worried about it. Even as my wardrobe and style has shifted, as I've become more comfortable with the feminine creeping in thanks to the excellent example of Ramirez and other female senior agents, I still think about it.

But looking too young used to be my only concern. It never occurred to me that I'd look too much like a victim, that it could cause a family pain.

And then I came to Quantico and learned about Faith Eddison, and saw pictures, and saw the way her parents both had to take a deep breath before they said anything the first time they met me. Faith as a child was blonde and blue-eyed, and maybe her hair would have darkened over time—maybe she wouldn't look remotely like me. While it was one thing to know that, it was another to see your son holding the hand of a woman only three years younger than your daughter would be now, with the same coloring as the child you lost.

I never really wondered why it took so long for me to meet Bran's parents after he and I started dating. The picture on his filing cabinet at the office was enough to warn me.

I flip the visor back up as we pull onto the Mercers' street. It is a zoo, with police cars—marked and unmarked alike—parked everywhere. Neighbors and friends and family members and complete strangers mill around yards and the street. News crews and vans are scattered anywhere there's a space for them that isn't technically on someone's property. One house has a lemonade stand converted to a volunteer sign-up station.

"For fuck's sake," sighs Ramirez. "This is a goddamn mess."

At my side, Eddison scrubs at his jaw with the hand not curled into a fist.

3

We find a spot for the SUV two houses down from where Watts and her team manage to pull in. She taps the first uniformed officer she finds. "FBI. We're looking for Captain Scott."

He turns and points to the Mercers' house and the uniform standing on the porch steps, arms crossed over his chest and a forbidding scowl discouraging anyone from approaching. His stance is just wide enough that he completely blocks access to the front door.

"Thanks."

I'm not sure if it's the air of authority, the walk of purpose, or the look on Eddison's face, but people very quickly move out of our way. There's something a little intimidating about nine armed FBI agents in full strut. One of the neighboring yards is absolutely covered with row after row of hot-pink metal flamingos. The ones closest to the street have a banner looped around their necks that reads SUCK IT, STEVE in large block letters, a level of pettiness surely HOA inspired. There's a sheepish-looking man, though, pulling the flamingos out and stacking them in a wheelbarrow.

That kind of bickering doesn't hold up to a neighborhood-wide tragedy.

Eddison's tan duster flaps as his long legs carry him ahead of the rest of us to the Mercers' porch. He stops just short of introducing himself to the captain, looking back at Watts.

She just gives him a slight smile as she passes him, letting it go. He's been the leader of our team for four years; he's used to being the first contact. "Captain Scott," Watts greets the man standing on the steps, credentials folder already open in her hand. Her tidy, grey-streaked hair bobs around her face with her nod. "SSAIC Kathleen Watts." She introduces us each in turn.

"Frederick Scott," the captain replies, returning the nod. "I'd say welcome, but let's not pretend." He glances at me and almost manages to hide his flinch.

"I won't be dealing directly with the Mercers at this time," I tell him.

"That come up often?"

"Often enough."

"Nelson! Murdock!" Two cops near the end of the driveway turn at the captain's yell. "Stick with these agents. Give 'em what they need. Agent Watts, I'll introduce you to the parents. Detective McAlister is with them; she'll be your point inside."

"Ramirez," says Watts.

Hurrying up the steps after Watts, Ramirez tosses me the small nylon tote she took from the trunk and follows the captain inside. Eddison remains to talk to the captain, while the rest of Watts's team scatter to their own assignments.

Nelson and Murdock are both youngish, probably mid- to late twenties, and have been cops too long to think the FBI coming in is a dick-measuring contest, but not long enough to be disgruntled over past partnerships and territory. It's a surprisingly narrow window, but I get it. Different branches of law enforcement want to be able to work together well; it just doesn't always happen.

Murdock has glasses sliding down a long, narrow nose, and that's about as much of a distinguishing feature as we get with these two at first glance. Kearney introduces us, and they start to offer their hands to

15

shake, then question themselves—probably because we're women—and end up in a sort of awkward half wave in the space between us.

I'm leaning more toward midtwenties after that.

"Which neighbor does she normally walk home with?" I ask them.

"That one," Nelson answers, pointing directly across the street. "Rebecca Copernik. Parents are Eli and Miriam, brother is Daniel. Whole family's home today."

We start walking across the street, and after a moment's hesitation, the officers follow us like startled puppies. Kearney knocks on the door. I've been on the team longer, but she has more experience as an agent. We're not rigidly bound by seniority, but in moments of crisis the expectation reassures people, tells them the chain of command and who they can go to.

Eli Copernik opens the door, looking exhausted. Either he's a generally rumpled sort of person or he's still wearing yesterday's clothes. He leans heavily against the doorway, his fingers rubbing against the blue-and-gold mezuzah on the frame.

Kearney introduces us again, less briskly than she did with the officers. Eli nods slowly and lets us in. The officers dither a bit and decide to stay on the porch for now, in case their captain yells for them. Or at them. It's hard to know where their specific concern is on that.

"I know Rebecca came home sick from school yesterday," I begin once the strained pleasantries are done. "I know she's been through a lot in the past day, but do you think she'd be up for a few questions?"

"My wife is up with her now," he says instead of yes or no.

Kearney meets my eyes, then glances up the stairs. As she settles into the living room with Eli and Daniel—a gangly boy who looks like the kind of fourteen that can almost double in height over a few months—I head up. Rebecca's door isn't hard to find; there's a messily painted wooden sign in the shape of a rainbow. The clouds the arc ends in are covered in glittering unicorn stickers layered over each other. I knock softly in case she's sleeping.

Miriam opens the door, and if anything, she actually looks more exhausted than her husband. "Oh, God," she groans. "No, wait, I'm sorry."

"It's all right, Mrs. Copernik. It's the situation. I don't take it personally." I don't smile—it wouldn't be appropriate—but I do give a friendly nod. "My name is Eliza Sterling, and I'm with the FBI. I'd like to talk to Rebecca, if you think she's up for it."

"She's got a sinus infection. The doctor gave us antibiotics for her yesterday, but . . ."

"I understand. If it's okay, you can stay right here with us, and the second you think it's too much, we'll stop."

She looks at the gold *Magen David* on the thin chain around my neck, her hand rising to brush her fingers against the nearly identical pendant over her shirt. "All right."

Rebecca looks miserable, mostly pale with a splotchy, feverish sort of flush. There's some swelling across the middle of her face, but it's hard to tell how much of that is sinus pressure and how much of it is the amount she's probably been crying. Her mother sits next to her on the far side of the narrow bed and picks up a glass of orange juice with a straw sticking out of it.

I kneel next to the bed so she doesn't have to move or strain to see me. "Hi, Rebecca. My name is Eliza. I'm with the FBI. Do you know what that is?"

She shrugs and tilts her head to one side.

"We're like police, only instead of looking after one city or state, we help look after the whole country. We're here to help look for Brooklyn."

She sniffles and leans into her mother, who rubs her arm comfortingly.

Reaching into the bag Ramirez gave me, I pull out a floppy tan stuffed puppy with darker brown patches over its eyes and on one side of its rump. I place him on the bed next to Rebecca's hand. "This is for you. I know right now everything is a lot. You're scared for your friend, and you don't feel good. If you need to yell or punch or throw something, that's what this guy is for. If you need to hug the stuffing out of something, he's good for that too."

She rubs one finger against the puppy's plush ear. We used to give out teddy bears, but then three years ago . . . well, we shifted over to puppies and cats and monkeys and other things that are distinctly not teddy bears.

"I've got some questions I need to ask you, Rebecca, but before we do that, I need you to listen to me for a moment. Rebecca?"

Reluctantly, she meets my eyes. God, this poor kid.

"This is in no way your fault," I tell her, gently but firmly. "You did not do anything wrong. Brooklyn isn't missing because of anything you did. Brooklyn is missing, and it's sad and it's scary, and I know it's easy to feel guilty. You've probably been up here all night thinking if you hadn't gone home, if you'd walked with her, if, if, if."

Tears streaming down her cheeks, Rebecca nods and curls in closer to her mother.

"But it's not your fault. Someone took her because they wanted to take her, and they are the only one to blame. I need you to keep saying that to yourself, because it's the truth. Can you hold on to that?"

Not moving from the circle of her mother's arms, she reaches for the puppy and hugs it close. Finally, slowly, she nods.

"Okay. Go ahead and have some juice, sweetheart. It's hard to be sick."

"I want to help look," she says, voice raw from coughing, but she does obediently suck down the rest of the juice in the glass. Miriam sets it atop the short bookshelf next to the bed and smooths Rebecca's sweat-damp hair.

"Right now the best thing you can do for Brooklyn is to get better. I know that's hard. But people are going to have questions for you, and that's going to help us look for her. You are helping, sweetheart."

She's unconvinced, but honestly, who wouldn't be? The one day she and Brooklyn don't walk home together, her best friend gets kidnapped.

Whether or not she ultimately accepts that it isn't her fault, that's still a hell of a weight to carry.

"Do you think you can answer some questions now? Or do you need to rest a bit first?"

"Are you going to find her?"

Miriam closes her eyes.

"We're going to do our absolute best." I hold out my hand, and after a moment, Rebecca takes it, squeezing hard. "I wish I could promise you we'll find her, Rebecca, I really do. I wish I could snap my fingers and she'd be right here. But I'm not going to lie to you. Not now and not ever. There are a lot of really smart people who are looking for her, and every single one of us is going to do our best."

She stares at our hands, her eyes pink and puffy. "Okay. What questions?"

4

Almost an hour later, I head back downstairs. There are more questions to ask Rebecca, but she started drifting in and out probably ten minutes before her mother announced it was time for another round of medicine and a nap. Kearney isn't in the living room when I glance in, but Eddison is, perched on the arm of the couch with his hand on Daniel's back. Rebecca's brother is folded nearly in two, his head in his hands. Rather than interrupt, I follow a series of sounds to the kitchen.

Eli is at a long counter with an assembly line of sandwich ingredients. "He's blaming himself," he says, not looking up. "Says he shouldn't have gone on the trip without making sure the girls had a good way to get home. He's fourteen, he shouldn't have to . . . he shouldn't . . ."

"Rebecca tells me he's a very good brother, for a boy."

He huffs out a breath that, on a better day, might be a laugh. At the end of the counter, a serving platter has a mountain of sandwiches already prepared. I suspect he's doing it for something to do, rather than any actual hunger or need. Most of them are probably going to end up in the hands of neighbors and officers. "Miri called Alice yesterday when she checked Rebecca out. Offered to go back and pick Brooklyn up when school let out. Alice told her to focus on getting Rebecca to the doctor, that she and Franklin would figure it out."

"And their wires got crossed?"

"Frank said he'd take care of it, but then he got shoved into an emergency project meeting. He texted Alice, but she was on a conference call for hours and didn't check her phone before heading home. I just . . ." He shakes his head helplessly. "I can't imagine it. How they must be hating themselves right now, and it's . . . we've all been there, with the 'whoops, I forgot something,' but to have your kid go missing because of it . . ."

"My mother once forgot me and left town."

"What?"

"My dad was out of the country for a business trip, so we were going to take the long weekend to go visit her sister a few hours away. Only she drove off without picking me up from school. I ended up spending the whole weekend at my best friend's."

"She didn't come back?"

"Didn't realize I wasn't there until my aunt asked her. She thought I'd just been sulking in the backseat. Decided driving back all those hours was just too stressful, too much for her nerves." I lean against the other side of the counter, watching the steady movements of his hands over the assembly line. "We were lucky my best friend's family wasn't planning to go anywhere. Accidents happen, but we shouldn't have to expect the worst when they do."

He gives me a jaundiced look but doesn't argue.

"As I told your daughter, this is the fault of whoever took Brooklyn. No one else."

"I work the crime desk at the *Times-Dispatch*. I know the odds. Especially with it taking so long to get anything set up."

"Throw the odds out the window."

"But—"

"No, throw them out. Yes, we've faced disappointments, but we've also seen miracles. I'm not going to write Brooklyn off because of odds, and neither are you. Hope is a strong thing."

"The ancient Greeks thought it was the worst evil. The one evil Pandora was able to lock back up."

"Was it? Or was it the thing we kept to help us against the evils?"

His hands still, mustard oozing off the butter knife. "You look so much like her."

Fortunately, Daniel and Eddison join us in the kitchen just then, Daniel red-eyed and tense. His father immediately puts down the knife and bread to hug him, and Daniel sinks into the embrace.

"We'll come back when we have more questions," Eddison says quietly. "My card is on the mantel if you need anything in the meantime. If you need to take Rebecca back to the doctor, let one of the agents or officers know, please."

Nodding, Eli buries his face in his son's messy hair.

We let ourselves out, gently closing the door behind us. Nelson and Murdock are nowhere to be found, but that's fine.

"Rebecca drew me the route they take home from school. Anything we need to do here before we check it out?" I ask.

"No, but text Watts, let her know we're moving."

I report to Watts, who texts back *roger that still with mercers with R.* Must be typing with her off-hand.

Once upon a time, Mercedes was a missing child, sort of. It gives her an exquisite kind of sensitivity atop her usual kindness, the same way Eddison, almost despite himself, is very good with the boys like Daniel, the scared older brothers.

My specialty generally comes later, once we've identified our suspect. I'm the one who's best with the families of the people we're hunting.

I put my phone away and we head down the street. People are milling around, wanting to help but mostly getting in the way.

An older woman stops us several houses down, one hand on my arm. "Oh, dear. Are you Alice's sister?"

Because Brooklyn has her mother's coloring.

I pull back the side of my coat just enough to show the badge and gun at my belt. "No, ma'am. I'm Agent Sterling; this is Agent Eddison. We're here with the FBI."

She snatches her hand back. "Oh, I'm so sorry. I just thought . . . you look so much . . ."

"I understand. You know the Mercers well?"

"Not . . . not *very* well. Brooklyn and Rebecca are in the same Brownie troop as my granddaughter Suzie. They, ah . . ." She laughs self-consciously, absently fluffing her greying hair. "They don't get along, I'm afraid."

We talk to her for a few minutes and then continue down the street, Eddison tapping notes into his tablet. A similar interaction happens four more times before we turn the corner. One sad-eyed man, probably in his late sixties or early seventies, takes a step back when he sees me, clutching a handful of fliers to his chest. When he relaxes a minute or so later, I can see Brooklyn's face printed on the papers.

I catch Eddison eyeing me cautiously. "Just say it."

"It'll be Watts's decision."

"But?"

"But you should probably be prepared to stay at the office from now on. With a resemblance this strong, the effect isn't going to fade as we move away from the neighborhood."

"Couldn't that be useful? Startle whoever has her?"

"If they still have her, and if they're out here to startle."

True.

I sigh and look down the street. "The route is completely open," I note.

He smirks at the none-too-subtle subject change but goes along with the new direction. "No trees overhanging, wide street, lots of lamp posts. She likely went missing in broad daylight, but even so, if you were going to plan a kidnapping, this is not the street most would go for."

"Was it planned, though? Or was it opportunity?"

"What did Rebecca say?" A pained expression flickers across his face. His sister had friends like that, including a best friend she was supposed to always walk home with.

I bump up against him, our arms tangling for a moment, about as much as we can really get away with at work. "She didn't notice anyone odd in the weeks leading up to yesterday. No one who seemed to be paying them unusual attention or asking inappropriate questions. No one outside the neighborhood or school approached them."

From the entrance to the neighborhood, you can actually see the school just down the road. The main entrance is marked with stoplights and wider-than-usual crosswalks for the children. Each corner has a small bench for the crossing guards.

"It's a straightforward route," Eddison says, tugging on his dark green scarf. It's the professional counterpart to the neon green one he uses everywhere else when it's cold enough for scarves. "Predictable but open. No places to hide, nothing suited to letting someone jump out suddenly. Any car that stopped would be in full view and very noticeable. Makes it look more and more like it had to be someone she knew and might have gone off course for."

"We need to map out who was home that afternoon. Find out how long she could have walked unnoticed by someone in a house."

"What could someone have offered her to lure her away?"

"Probably not pet-based. According to Rebecca, Brooklyn hates her mother's cats and has extended that to pets in general."

"To the point that she wouldn't help if someone did the lost- or wounded-pet ruse?"

"I don't know. Rebecca said she's the one who usually wants to stop and look at things or talk to people on the way home, and Brooklyn is the one to keep her on track."

We stand on the corner for a few minutes, assessing the traffic. It's hard to tell what's normal everyday traffic and what's added because of the search. Checking his watch, Eddison tugs my elbow, and we walk the rest of the way to the school. It's a tidy set of buildings, faded red brick and grey stone, not intended to be imposing or impressive. It looks welcoming, comfortable. Except for the line of police cars in the bus circle.

"Extra resource officers?" I ask, indicating the cars.

"Probably. The kids know that Brooklyn is missing. If the administration is smart, they're going to talk to the kids about it rather than let the rumors and fear build up."

A young officer meets us at the front door to the school office. "What's your business here?" he asks sharply.

We just look at him.

After a moment, he blushes slightly. "My apologies. It's just that access to the school has extra restrictions today."

"Understandably," Eddison says mildly. "I'm going to pull back my coat to get my ID, if that's all right."

I follow suit. The officer looks relieved at the sight of our badges, and jots down our names on a clipboard before opening the door for us. A clutch of employees stands or sits behind the reception desk. A muted TV mounted in an upper corner of the room is tuned to the local news and the search for Brooklyn. Most of them are watching.

An older woman looks over at us and gives us a warm, if strained, smile. "The puppy at the gates let you through?"

"At least I'm not the only one who thought he was too young to be there," Eddison agrees.

She walks around the counter and glances at the badges still showing at our waists. "My name is Cynthia; I'm one of the senior secretaries. What can I do for you?"

"We'd like to talk with the principal, if we can. We understand he's busy today—"

"Everybody's busy today," she interrupts gently, "and it's the kind of busy where nothing can get done. We're holding grade assemblies in the cafeteria most of the day. The third-grade classes also have extra resources today. That poor girl."

She has us sign in on another clipboard—the first one, apparently, is just for the police, and this one is for the school records—and leads us back into the school itself. The halls are bright, that strange combination of faded and too-clean that you really only see in schools and official buildings. The doors we pass are all decorated, all sort of grouped around the common theme of Halloween or autumn. Beautifully arranged bulletin boards display information about school events or reading contests. One has safety tips for trick-or-treating.

Cynthia notices me looking at that one. "We're considering opening up the school that night to let kids trick-or-treat through the classrooms. Contained environment, well lit . . . The kids might be a little disappointed, but I can think of a lot of parents who'd be reassured."

"It's not a bad idea," I say, "especially considering how many kids go out in groups or with older siblings, without adults."

The cafeteria is currently home to the fifth-graders, fidgeting in their seats as a resource officer and a woman in a lavender pantsuit trade off talking. It's not a lecture, and not quite a presentation. It's a response. I appreciate that they're not trying to mask it for the kids. Other adults line the sides of the room, teachers and aides and what's probably a good percentage of the front-office administration.

Motioning us to wait where we are, Cynthia eases along the back of the cafeteria to the far wall, stopping by a man in a dark grey suit, a heavy lanyard obscuring the bottom of his yellow tie. He glances at us and nods, then follows her. He waits until we're in the hall again before he speaks.

"Joshua Moore," he says, holding out a hand for us to shake in turn. "I'm the principal here."

"Thank you for speaking with us, Dr. Moore. I'm Agent Eddison, this is Agent Sterling; we're here with the FBI."

I wonder how many times per case we say that.

"Have there been any developments?" Moore asks as we start walking. Cynthia gives us a small wave and power walks in the direction of the office.

"Not yet," Eddison answers. "Obviously we're searching for Brooklyn, but we're also trying to piece together what happened yesterday afternoon."

"Of course. Here, the library will be a bit more comfortable than my office, and we're trying to stay visible for the children. Only essential paperwork is getting done today, I'm afraid."

"How many parents kept their children home today?"

"Maybe thirty percent? Most of our parents work, so staying home with their children impacts their ability to pay the bills. With the children here, they have a support network of friends, teachers, counselors. We'll try to start teaching again on Monday."

The library is a warm, inviting room with mostly open sightlines. Tall bookcases line the walls, but the cases out on the floor are only half the height and broken up at regular intervals by tables, computer terminals, or comfortable chairs. A pentagonal pit in the center has two broad steps like an amphitheater, steps and bottom space alike stuffed with large floor pillows and beanbags. At a cluster of tables in one corner, a group of what looks like college kids are collating and paper-clipping packets of papers.

"They're education majors," Moore explains, following my gaze. "Some of them are volunteers; some are assigned here for their student-teaching quarter. We asked them to put together resource packets to send home with the kids for their families. Some of the parents donated the cost of the copying."

"So they've all had background checks?"

"Yes. Any volunteer who interacts with the children has to pass one before they can begin." He gestures us to one of the tables, set a little apart from the others and on a short platform. It offers a good view of the entire room. He waits for us to seat ourselves before he sits down.

"The same is true for every employee, whether they work directly with the children or not, and any contractors working in the school."

"Have you had to reject any applications because of the background checks?" Eddison pulls his battered Moleskine notebook from his back pocket and opens it, rooting through his coat for a pen. I hand him the one in my hair. He takes notes on the tablet when he has to, but he thinks better when he can actually write it and take the time later to work back through everything as he types it up for the file.

"For this school year? Several. Some drug offenses, some theft. Only one I can think of for any violent offenses. A man applying for a position as a gym coach had an active restraining order against him and several instances of domestic violence in his history. Nothing against children, but we weren't going to put our female employees into a potentially dangerous position with him. I don't recall his name, but his application was pulled and copied for the police this morning."

"You were called last night?"

He nods, smoothing his tie. The motion forces him to resettle the lanyard, which skews the tie again. "We have an after-hours number for the school. Sometimes children forget something that can't wait for the next school day, like medication or inhalers, so we can arrange for a keyholder to meet the parents to retrieve the item. They also take down messages for expected absences if a child or family member has fallen ill. In an actual emergency, whoever is working the after-hours number can put the call through to me or the administrator on duty. For a missing child, the call came to me."

"What time was this?"

"A little after ten. Officer Bernal—the school's main resource officer—and I had walked the buildings and grounds before we left a bit after six. We didn't see anything or anyone out of place. When I got the call, I came back, arriving a little after ten-thirty. Officers met me here and we did another walk-through. No indication that Brooklyn was here after school or that she'd come back."

Eddison nods and jots down the times.

"I understand you have too many students to get to know many of them," I begin, and stop at the principal's smile.

"That's true, but I do try. I rotate through the classrooms in the mornings. All going as it should, I spend a morning with each class twice a quarter. It doesn't let me get to know them well, but it gives me at least a passing familiarity with most of them."

"So you do know Brooklyn."

"A little, yes. Last year, on the first day of school, she came to my office sobbing her little heart out because she and Rebecca Copernik had been placed in different classes. She begged us to put them together."

"Did you?"

"After consulting with the teachers and parents, yes. It turned out that Rebecca's absence was only part of the problem. Another girl in Brooklyn's original class has a history of bullying Brooklyn and Rebecca, and Brooklyn didn't want to be in a class with her."

"This girl's name . . . it wouldn't happen to be Suzie Gray?"

His brows rise. "The very same. The three girls are in the same Brownie troop, as well."

"Suzie's grandmother told us they don't get along."

"I won't try to claim that Brooklyn and Rebecca never do anything wrong, but unfortunately, Suzie is a bully. We have her in weekly sessions with her guidance counselor to address that."

"Any particular cause, do you know?"

"We think it's a response to trouble at home. Her parents seem to be disengaged, at best. Most of our interaction is with her grandmother."

"Has Child Services ever been brought into it?"

"No. Her grandmother is listed as an additional legal guardian, and we've never seen anything to indicate that Suzie is being abused. Her grandmother is involved and active and clearly adores her. The prevailing theory, at least as far as we have information, is that Suzie got jealous of how involved Alice Mercer and Miriam Copernik were with their daughters' troop when they were in Daisies, and started lashing out."

"Dr. Moore?"

All three of us turn to the woman standing a polite distance away. She's either a guidance counselor or a kindergarten teacher, in her long broomstick skirt and chunky cardigan.

"Yes?"

"I've got Suzie Gray in the hall, crying herself sick. She'd like to speak with you."

Moore stands and looks around the room, I assume looking to see if any students are in there. "Go ahead and bring her in. We were just speaking of her."

The woman nods and hurries out, coming back in a moment later with another woman, this one older and somewhat heavyset, and a little brunette girl crying too hard to see where she's going. The girl stumbles over her feet, relying on the women to steer her.

Moore holds out his seat for her, and once she's collapsed into it, kneels next to her. The women take up positions on the edge of the platform. "Suzie?" he says gently. "Tell me what's going on, Miss Suzie."

"It's my fault," she sobs. "It's my fault Brooklyn's missing. I don't want to go to jail!"

5

We all startle at that, but Moore recovers quickly. He takes her hand in his, rubbing his thumb comfortingly against her knuckles. "What do you mean, Suzie? Why do you think this is your fault?"

Suzie gives a great sniff. I pull a travel pack of tissues out of my coat pocket and slide it across the table. The principal accepts it and gives one of the tissues to Suzie to blow her nose.

Eddison and I share a cautious look. In the way of brothers everywhere, Eddison has a tendency to panic when little girls cry around him. It's not that he's unsympathetic or that he's bad with kids, it's just that crying little girls break his heart and he gets very awkward and anxious. Normally, I'd be stepping in here.

But if Suzie thinks it's her fault that Brooklyn is gone, the sight of me may not help.

Eddison twitches an eyebrow. I wrinkle my nose. He tilts his head to one side, nudging.

Fine.

"Suzie? My name is Eliza. I'm one of the people looking for Brooklyn."

She inhales a shuddering breath. Tears still track heavily down her face.

"What happened with Brooklyn, sweetheart?"

"At Brownies on Wednesday . . . ," she starts with another sniffle. The principal silently hands her another tissue. ". . . I took her second cookie. And I pushed her and called her a crybaby when she said she was gonna tell." She cringes, clearly waiting to be scolded.

"Suzie, I'm not here to yell at you. You already know that was wrong; that's why you feel bad about it. What happened next?"

"After the meeting, we went to her house and Mrs. Mercer made us dinner. My grandma had to work late, so Mrs. Mercer offered to watch me. But after dinner, Brooklyn went up to her room and closed the door. So I told Mrs. Mercer that Brooklyn stole my cookies at the meeting. I just wanted her to have to come out, but her mom told her she had to stay in her room and think about what she did. It was hours till Grandma got there. Mrs. Mercer let me watch a movie, but . . ."

"But you were lonely."

She nods and sniffles again. At least she's not using her sleeve. "Rebecca went home early. Yesterday, I mean. Brooklyn was all alone at recess, so I pushed her off the swing and told her no one wanted her around anyway, and she should just go away. I told her . . . I told her . . ."

"It's okay, Suzie. Just talk to us."

"I said her parents were going to send her away, but her grandparents didn't want her either, and that's why they're always fighting. I said she should just run away, and everyone would be happier. And she did. Brooklyn's gone, and everyone's scared, and it's all my fault!" She falls back into full-on, body-shaking sobs.

The older woman hurries around the table, gently pushing the principal out of the way so she can wrap Suzie in a hug. She rocks slowly, making small, meaningless sounds, letting Suzie cry.

I pull out my work cell and text Watts, tagging Ramirez in it as well. *Ask Mercers—has Brooklyn ever tried to run away before? Also, are Mercers and grandparents fighting? Don't know which grandparents.*

Paternal grandparents, Watts replies quickly. *We're looking into it.*

Ramirez's answer takes a little longer, but then, it *is* longer. *Alice says Brooklyn and Rebecca tried to run away to the circus two years ago because they wanted to be acrobats but their parents said not yet to gymnastics lessons. They convinced Daniel to take them. He led them around the back of the neighborhood until they were tired and hungry, brought them home. Only attempt, everyone had a pretty good laugh about it, sounds like.*

Obviously runaway is still a possibility. What brought it up? Watts asks.

Suzie Gray said some mean things yesterday after Rebecca went home. Told Brooklyn it was her fault her parents and grandparents were fighting, and they'd all be happier if she just ran away.

It's almost two full minutes before either of them responds. I'm willing to bet a number of obscenities were typed in and deleted.

The tech analysts are taking the first look at the grandparents. I'll assign the Smiths to it, as well.

Ramirez doesn't respond at all. I'm not surprised.

"What do you think?" Eddison asks too quietly to be heard by the sobbing girl.

"If Brooklyn was going to run away, she wouldn't do it without Rebecca," I reply, matching my tone to his. "I'm sure she was hurt by what Suzie said, but I don't think she ran away. I think she would have wanted to run to Rebecca for comfort, if anything."

He nods and pushes back from the table. I do the same and follow him over to the other guidance counselor. She watches Suzie with concern, her hands clutching her elbows through the sleeves of the chunky heather-green sweater. When we stand in front of her, she blinks and focuses on us.

"I'm sorry," she murmurs. "I'm Hermione Nance."

"You know exactly when kids discover Harry Potter, don't you?"

"Almost the moment," she agrees with a tired smile.

"You're Brooklyn's guidance counselor, aren't you?"

She nods, giving me a thoughtful look. "How did you know?"

"You came inside, leaving your colleague with Suzie. And now she's the one comforting her."

"Yes, I'm Brooklyn's counselor. We decided it would be best that the girls have different counselors so we can be advocates as needed, without a risk of favoritism."

"What can you tell us about Brooklyn?"

"She's a sweet girl. Always willing to help other people. She doesn't like conflict. If it's happening to or around her, she tries to separate herself."

"So if her parents and grandparents are arguing . . ."

Hermione nods. "She's been in my office a lot during recess this school year. She's worried."

"Can you tell us the concern?"

"Normally no, but . . ." She shakes her head, strands of auburn hair escaping a loose, messy bun that tilts to one side. "Her paternal grandparents have never liked Alice. I'm not privy to why. If I were going to guess, I'd say no one was ever going to be good enough for Mrs. Mercer's baby boy. I don't think it's Alice specifically, just the entire notion of another woman coming first in her son's life. After the wedding, they didn't speak for years until Brooklyn was born. Since then, Alice's in-laws have criticized every single thing she's done as a mother. It's constant, and a definite strain on her."

"On Brooklyn, too, it sounds like."

"Oh yes. Sometimes, after her grandparents visit, Brooklyn will ask for an appointment with me just so she can sit quietly in my office. Since school started back up, however, her concerns have been a little more specific."

Eddison straightens, tapping his pen against his notebook. "Specific?"

"Apparently her grandparents have threatened to take her parents to court to try to get custody."

Chas v'sholem.

Well, this case just got simpler or more complicated, only time will tell, but it definitely just did something.

Eddison scratches above one ear with the pen. "I'm surprised you haven't suggested that—"

"—that maybe her grandparents have kidnapped her?" she finishes for him.

"How likely do you think that is?" I ask.

She takes her time with the question, thumb and middle finger plucking at a stray thread in her sleeve. "I don't know," she says finally. "I've never actually met them. Brooklyn doesn't want them at school events. She doesn't want to give them a chance to embarrass her mother around other parents."

"Jesus," mutters Eddison. "Of all the things for a kid to have to worry about."

"My instinct, such as it is, would say that kidnapping her when they're trying to get custody would prove counterproductive. They're not listed as additional guardians on any of her paperwork."

"But?"

"People don't always think things all the way through. Family is messy."

That's God's own truth.

The picture we build through the afternoon, talking to Hermione Nance and to Brooklyn's teachers, is of a friendly, helpful girl who always has a smile for anyone who isn't Suzie Gray, and even with her, she'll still often try. Introverted, but not shy. Both of her main teachers—one for homeroom, language arts, and social studies, the other for math and science—talk about letting Brooklyn quietly recharge after group work or presentations. Rebecca is the more outgoing of the two, but Brooklyn doesn't back away from interacting with the other kids. She just takes some quiet time afterward. Her favorite subject is social studies, history specifically, but art is a close second. Her posters for history projects are always the best.

When the crossing guards arrive, they gather in the bus circle; officers pull their cars around to the parking lot to make room for the buses when they come. The crossing guards all interact with Brooklyn and Rebecca most days. The girls have to take two legs of the intersection in front of the school, and they like to switch it up so they can say hello to all of the guards.

"I asked her where Rebecca was," says the last guard to see her. He's an older man, his face as weathered as shoe leather beneath thinning white hair. He turns his fluorescent-banded hat in his hands as he speaks, fingers worrying the rolled brim. "She said Rebecca had to go home sick and Daniel was on a field trip. She was one of the last kids to leave, just before our shifts ended."

"What time was that?"

"Three-fifteen? Three-twenty? Thereabouts. We're off at three-thirty. She said she thought her parents were going to pick her up, but they weren't there. I suggested she go into the office, have the secretaries call her folks just to be sure, but she walks it every day." He stares down at his large-knuckled hands in their white cotton gloves. "She said she'd be fine. She promised that she'd go straight home, or to Rebecca's. No stops or shortcuts."

"So the last you saw of her . . ."

"She jogged down the road here, on the sidewalk, and turned into her neighborhood."

"Did you notice anyone else who seemed to be watching her?"

"Just Edith here," he says, jerking his head toward one of the other guards. "She had the leg across the pick-up circles yesterday, so she could see her too."

"She seemed fine," Edith offers. "She didn't start jogging until we told her to hurry home. She didn't seem scared, though. Didn't notice anyone else. No cars slowing down or anything. No one turned into the neighborhood just after her."

"Before you left for the day, did you see any cars or people come out of the neighborhood in a hurry?" asks Eddison.

The two guards look at each other, then shake their heads. "No, sir," the man answers. "Not saying there weren't, but not that we noticed."

"Thank you."

"Whenever she and her mother make cookies, she always brings a little bag for each of us," Edith says. "Always says hello and goodbye, and thank you, and nudges Rebecca if she forgets. You're going to find that precious girl."

Eddison swallows hard.

"We're going to do our best," I tell her. I take Eddison's elbow and lead him away. "Come on. Let's head back into the neighborhood, see if anything looks different from this side."

We start retracing our steps, looking for anything that stands out. The ground is a mess from all the previous searches, but there aren't even any hedges or rock piles to duck down behind. There are some fences, but few of them are up to the front property lines. Most block off backyards or form a half boundary between neighbors. The only ones that come up to the front edges are half-height with the kind of open slat-work you can see through. More decorative than functional, except to keep in ankle-biter dogs.

"Car parked in front of one of the houses?" Eddison posits.

"Maybe. Friend of a neighbor, or some kind of repairman. You'd think the owner would be at the house, though. I mean, a house isn't an apartment; there isn't generally a maintenance key."

"Unless you have a regular handyman. Work together long enough, it's not unreasonable to give someone a key or tell them where a spare is."

There are other people on the sidewalks, coming to help or just mingling to stare, even before we get back onto the Mercers' street. Out of habit, I lift the tablet and resume taking pictures of groups and individuals. Sometimes, unsubs will try to be part of the investigation in some way, either to try to derail it or to get off on the fuss and furor. Or, in a community effort like this, to blend in and divert suspicion.

It would be nice if we could just look for someone whose participation seems insincere or disingenuous, but there are a lot of people here who fit that description. There always are. People who are coming just to get the story or have secrets in their pasts, grief-tourists who come to get a contact high off the pain and panic.

Kearney and Agent Burnside join us as we draw close to the Mercers' house. Watts and Captain Scott stand side by side as Watts issues a statement to the gathered reporters. We stop on the edge of the Coperniks' property to watch.

"How was the school?" asks Kearney.

"They did assemblies all day to talk to the kids about what's going on and reinforce Stranger Danger," I tell her.

With a huff, she crosses her arms under her bust. "Stranger Danger. It was a great way to make an entire generation of kids terrified to say hello, and they wonder why we grew up to hate interacting with strangers. You wouldn't remember that; you're too young."

"I'm five years younger, *savta*, not fifty."

She kicks at my ankle, but I slide out of range.

Across the street, Watts says she'll take a few questions, and the reporters all yell over each other. Watts hates speaking to reporters, or to cameras. Frustration flashes across her face before she calls on one of them.

"I have a bad feeling about this case," whispers Kearney.

Eddison leans into me slightly, subtly.

I let my hand drop between us so I can hook my pinky through his. "Me too."

6

We finally pack it in for the day around ten-thirty, because we still have to drive the hour and a half back to Quantico and another half hour after that to Manassas, where most of us live, and about that to Fairfax, where Kearney lives. We get yelled at when we decide sleeping in the office is more practical than going home.

Cass—and this late in the day it is absolutely Cass, even if we are still technically working—drifts over to the Mercers' yard. A few minutes later, Bran and I follow. It would be better—easier—to wait for Mercedes back at the car, but when everyone is up in arms and scared like this, strangers loitering around a large, dark vehicle make people very nervous. We loiter in the area of a street lamp instead, well-lit and as nonalarming as it's possible for a group of armed, exhausted federal agents to be.

While we wait for Mercedes to wrap up inside the house, I pull my hair out of its braided bun and fluff it out, trying to relieve some of the headache that's been building through the day. The concentrated weight of that much hair is definitely a part of that. Without seeming to realize it, Bran reaches over and grips the back of my neck, thumb and forefinger digging into the tense muscle.

Cass sneezes a laugh at my barely contained groan. According to Mercedes, that little sneeze of a laugh is why Cass's nickname at the academy was Kitten. I asked once—*once*—why it was Kitten rather than Cat, and Mercedes barely had time to gasp out that Cass was so adorably pocket-sized before said pocket-sized hellcat started chasing her around the bullpen. Someone on one of the other teams there that evening, and I have no idea who, made a desk plaque that reads "Kitten Kearney (Pocket-Sized for Your Pleasure)." Cass loathes it, but it gets passed around the bullpen to see who can sneak it on her desk and how long it takes her to notice.

"*Debería haber sido una noche de tequila,*" Mercedes sighs as she joins us.

"But it isn't."

"But it isn't," she agrees. "I think—"

"Agent Ramirez!"

All four of us turn toward the house, Bran's hand dropping from my neck. A woman steps down off the porch, heading in our direction.

"Agent Ramirez, I'm sorry, I just wanted to ask—" She stops dead at the sight of me, her trembling hand covering her mouth. Suddenly, with a great wail, she throws herself at me in a hug and starts sobbing.

"Alice Mercer," murmurs Mercedes. Unnecessarily, in my opinion.

I put my arms around the weeping woman and hold tight. I don't even try to say anything. There's nothing to say. *I'm sorry I look just enough like your missing daughter to be terrifying? I'm sorry you see me and wonder if your daughter will get to grow up to be anything? I'm sorry you're going to look at every blonde child and want, so desperately, for your little girl to be home and safe?* There's just nothing to say.

A man—presumably her husband—joins us from the porch and tries to disentangle her, tugging gently at her shoulders. Mercedes helps him, and together they turn Brooklyn's mother back toward the house. She's still crying, stumbling as they guide her up the steps and inside.

Bran and Cass both look at me. So does Watts, watching from a few feet away with the exhausted Captain Scott, who's been getting the night shift up to speed at the end of the driveway.

"Yes, all right, I get it. My being here is a bad idea."

Cass sneezes again, ducking her head to hide the amused gleam in her eyes.

"There'll be more than enough work for you at the office, Sterling," Watts says, at least attempting to seem sympathetic. "We've got a lot of information to go through."

It takes a few minutes for Mercedes to return, looking even more worn than before. "Home?" she asks hopefully.

"Home," Bran replies, and starts shooing us in the direction of the car. He waves at Watts, who nods at him before shaking Captain Scott's hand and trudging off toward her vehicle.

"Mercedes, can I crash with you tonight?" Cass buckles herself in and kicks off her shoes, curling into the seat. "I don't want to drive back to Fairfax."

"Sure. We could probably skip Quantico and go straight to Manassas, shave off the time we'd inevitably spend in the office. Head straight back to Richmond in the morning?"

"Except for Eliza," Cass says, and wrinkles her nose when she catches me sticking my tongue out at her. I know I'll accomplish a lot at the office, but I'd rather be in the field with my team.

"*Mierda*. Is your car at Quantico?" Mercedes asks.

I shake my head.

"It's at the house," Bran tells her.

"You mean The House?" I ask innocently, giving the proper emphasis.

It's been a long, emotionally trying day, which is perhaps why none of us are entirely surprised that Mercedes immediately cracks up. Just fucking loses it, head thumping against the window as she laughs herself to tears. It sets Cass off, but she buries her face in the back of the seat so we can't hear her as clearly.

Bran looks at me, at the way I'm biting my lip to try to keep a straight face, sighs, and starts the car.

Bran's had a handful of addresses in the nineteen years since he was assigned to Quantico, but they've all been apartments. Finally, five months ago, he bought a house. Not just any house, but The House, the one immediately behind Mercedes's cottage. They share a property line. They quibble over joint custody of the firepit attached to his back porch. They can literally hold a conversation back door to back door and barely raise their voices.

When Brandon Eddison finally decided to put down roots, he bought The House immediately behind the teammate he regards as a sister.

Yet he cannot bring himself to call it home. Home is the general area of Manassas, or, more specifically, wherever the majority of his team members happen to be at any particular moment. Home is people, not a place, except when he's planning to face-plant into his mattress and stay there, but a mattress is a little small to refer to as home. He also can't call it his. It's been The House for five months, because he can't even bring himself to say "*my* house."

Mercedes, with her postcard-worthy cottage, and Cass, with the duplex she shares with a cousin, think it's the funniest thing ever.

Even Vic can't keep from chuckling whenever he refers to The House. You can *hear* the capital letters. And this team wouldn't be this team if we didn't give him shit about it.

But because Bran is a wonderful person even when he's a prickly bastard, he's kind enough to ignore the laughter at his expense and pull into a drive-thru so we can get food, as none of us have eaten since breakfast. We were still scattered when Eli Copernik brought out the sandwiches he'd made, and they apparently disappeared very quickly.

We spend the first half of the drive comparing notes; there's depressingly little to compare. Brooklyn Mercer did not simply vanish from the face of the earth while walking home, but for all the information we've got, she might as well have. As the fatigue sets in more heavily, conversation drifts away.

When we get to Bran's, Mercedes and Cass offer sleepy goodbyes and trudge through the back door and across the yard to Mercedes's cottage. Bran and I stand at the back door and watch until the interior lights flick on.

"Are you swinging through the office in the morning or heading straight back to Richmond?" I ask, voice soft in that way that feels obligatory after midnight.

"Office," he replies. "Cass will need clothes from her bag, and Yvonne should have some updates for us."

I lean against him, feeling him slump into the wall, and for a few minutes we just stand together, breathing. Most of his cologne has faded; still, there's a hint of it clinging to his collar, comfortable and familiar and intriguing in a manner not entirely appropriate, given the day we've had. It's simultaneously soothing and thrilling. I've only ever known that feeling with him. One of his hands moves to the back of my neck, kneading the tense muscles there. At this point, my chin digging into his collarbone may be the only thing keeping me upright.

"Staying tonight?" he murmurs.

It takes more effort than it should for me to shake my head. "Not unless you want me to. Thought we might both rest better apart, given . . ."

"Probably true."

Neither of us move, except for his hand still working out the knots in my neck.

"Are you okay-ish?" I whisper into his shirt. Not okay, but okay-ish.

"I'll be fine."

Which isn't the same as yes. It's also one of those lines I'm not comfortable pushing. Three years dating, four years working together, there are still some lines that scream DON'T TOUCH! The problem of Faith is one that none of us bring up if we can help it. He has to, or it doesn't get said. Even in a time like this.

43

"I hate not being able to give them answers," he says after a few minutes. "Last night, today, it's not the worst day of their lives. That's tomorrow, when the initial shock fades just enough for the full weight and fear to settle. One day is terrifying. Two days . . ."

I press my lips to the pulse flickering under his skin, and wait.

"Two days is real."

"Do you think Daniel Copernik will call you?"

"Not yet. If we find her soon, maybe never. He's got Rebecca and his parents to focus on."

"He's never going to be the same, though, is he?"

He doesn't answer. He doesn't have to.

Eventually he pushes himself up to stand straight against the wall, his other hand moving to pet my hair. I let the motion pull me the slightest bit away, the day's stubble on his chin scraping my temple. The kiss that follows is gentler than I would have expected, given . . . well, everything. His hands cradle my head like I'm something precious, fragile, and I can't help but wonder how much rage is clawing under his skin that he feels he has to be this careful.

"Try to get some sleep?" I ask when we have to pull away to breathe.

"You too. And I'm sorry about tomorrow."

"You mean today?"

He smiles slightly, not much more than a twitch of his lips. It's something, though.

"It happens," I say. "Yvonne will have a lot of raw data to parse, and I definitely want to see if the grandparents have filed any legal paperwork regarding Brooklyn. I'm good with the research bits. We don't lose anything for keeping me at the office, and it makes others more comfortable."

"Still. I know you hate when how you look affects the case."

Our section chief—Vic's boss—scolded Bran for looking unprofessional when he grew his hair out a little longer. Not long, not even shaggy, just long enough for the dark curls to have a little more movement, the silver woven through. In other words, the way I like it, because I'm the first to admit I have a thing for his curls. He didn't argue with the section chief. He also didn't cut his hair. His five o'clock shadow starts at six in the morning, and he hates both shaving and the thought of letting it actually grow into something. Bran has spent his whole career walking the careful line between acceptable and unprofessional, but it's only ever been as a career element. How he looks doesn't impact the actual cases.

He gets it, though, why it bothers me. He gets it the same way Mercedes does. Mercedes, who never walks out her door in less-than-perfect makeup, because it covers the two jagged scars down her cheek made with a broken bottle when she was a kid. Because there's a difference between being unashamed of your scars and putting them out for everyone to comment on.

He kisses me again and then walks me to my car, standing in the driveway until I've safely pulled away. I can see him in my rearview mirror until I turn the corner.

Home isn't far, just over fifteen minutes if I obey all the traffic laws. Despite what my team likes to say, I do drive reasonably when we're not on a time-sensitive case. My former team leader, Finney, before his promotion meant he didn't have to be in a car with me anymore, used to turn a bit green when we had to get somewhere five minutes ago. However terrifying it was for him, I also never caused an accident or any damage to vehicle or passengers. I'm allowed to take a certain pride in that, I think.

I check the mail, throwing most of it in the trash can in the mail room, and head upstairs. I don't bother to turn on any lights when I get in the apartment. I come home this kind of exhausted often enough that my bones know the routine; they don't need my eyes to chime in. Bags and keys by the door, gun in the safe disguised as an end table by the couch, timer set on the electric kettle in the kitchen.

After changing into pajamas, I scrub my face and brush my teeth, then head into the closet to pull out clothes for tomorrow—today—and promptly trip over the garment bag that lives in one corner and seems to be growing. I growl and kick at it, but that's predictably unsatisfying. It may be eight million pounds of tulle and satin and it still can't be enough substance.

The Dress.

From the Wedding That Wasn't.

It lives there in the corner of my closet, and every time I've almost figured out how to get rid of it, I chicken out. Every time I'm almost ready to let go of it, something says no, not yet.

I know there's a reason I keep The Dress, I just don't know what it is. Whatever that hesitation is, there's something I need from it. Or maybe it's a ledge, a painful but comfortable reminder of a thing I successfully walked away from, a leash that keeps me from hurtling into the same mistake.

I don't know.

I met Cliff through temple, back when I lived near my parents and let my mother badger me into some of the singles gatherings. A good Jewish boy whose mother is one of the very few people my profoundly overbearing mother can call a friend.

It was the only thing I did that made my mother happy. She hated my major in college, hated my job, hated that I didn't live with her and *aba*. But she was so happy I was dating a good Jewish boy that I stayed with him, even though I wasn't all that sure I actually liked him. I didn't hate him. And then he proposed, both sets of parents at the table with us, him kneeling with a ring and garnering the attention of almost everyone else in the crowded restaurant. We hadn't talked about marriage. We hadn't even been dating a year yet. But he proposed in front of so many people that I honestly couldn't make myself say no. Not with all that attention. Not with all that pressure.

My mother was over the moon. She and Cliff both pushed to get everything decided right away. Choose the venue and the photographer and the caterer, get all the deposits down. Buy the dress.

The Dress.

I wasn't ready, but they pushed and pushed and made me feel like it was impossible to say no. Like I was wrong to not want it, to not be ready for it.

Maybe that's why The Dress stays around. I got steamrolled into buying it before I was ready, so I cling to it until I'm ready to let it go. Until I decide I'm ready, no one else.

Despite the friends gently poking at me to get rid of it.

Muttering curses under my breath, I shove the bag farther into the corner and rifle quickly through my suits and blouses to find a combination for the morning so I won't have to think about it then. As I try to fall asleep, I can't get it out of my head.

Some people have the monster under the bed, the nightmare behind the dresser.

I have The Dress in the Closet and the lingering self-loathing that comes from letting myself be manipulated into something I didn't want. Even when your scars come from escaping something, they're still scars. Brooklyn will learn that, if we can find her in time.

7

I arrive at the office just shy of five in the morning, having finally given up on trying to sleep. I'm not the only one either—the other three roll in twenty minutes later, Bran and Mercedes supporting a zombie-shuffling Cass between them. They look like parents trying to get a kid off to school.

Mercedes lets go so she can grab the bag under Cass's desk. Bran keeps Cass upright until Mercedes can take her back. He slurps down the last of his coffee and puts the empty travel mug on his desk. Knowing him, it had enough espresso in it to kill most healthy people, and it probably wasn't his first of the day. Of all the bad habits I've absorbed since joining the Bureau—or coming to Quantico—replacing my blood with coffee is somehow not yet one of them.

"We'll be back," Mercedes says more cheerfully than should be legal after so little sleep. She starts steering Cass toward the bathroom.

"Métela en la bañera de una vez y abre el agua," Bran grumbles.

"Si no lo hago contigo, no lo haré con ella tampoco."

"Pero a mí sí me lo has hecho."

Mercedes flips Bran off with the hand not keeping Cass balanced.

"You know, being around you two made me learn Spanish so I wouldn't miss out on things." I perch on the edge of my desk and sip my tea. "Sometimes I think I preferred the ignorance."

"But then you wouldn't have been able to send my mother that lovely letter that kept switching between Spanish and Italian."

"I might hate you."

"She framed it and everything."

Bran sorts through the Post-its that have congregated on the edge of his computer monitor since yesterday. Most of them get thrown away. After a moment, he comes over empty-handed and brings me to my feet. He follows it up with a swift hug and a kiss on the cheek, which is more than we usually go for in the office. Partly that's personal preference, and partly that's a strongly worded proactive request from Human Resources when we informed them we'd started dating.

The bullpen is empty except for us, and a look up at the offices shows no lights on, so I touch the bruise-colored shadows under his eyes. "Did you get any sleep?"

He tugs on the end of my too-loose braid, dislodging the elastic. "Did you?"

"No."

"*De cualquier manera, no dormimos mucho.* Turn around."

I scoot back on the desk and swing my legs up to swivel myself around, presenting him with my back. I can hear the slide and squeak of the top drawer opening and closing, and a moment later his fingers shake out the rest of the braid. He combs through it slowly, paying special attention to the knots I was too tired to bother getting out at home. It feels marvelous—not just the slight scrape of the comb's teeth against my scalp, but his fingers moving through my hair or protecting my ears. After a few minutes, the comb drops into my lap, followed by the gentle tug of him sectioning my hair. I don't need a mirror to know that the Dutch braid is tidy and tight, every strand of hair smoothed into place.

He's never forgotten the skills that came from having a sister eight years younger. Her best friends, and almost every woman he's allowed in his life since then, have never let him. Even Mercedes asks for his help with her hair for really important dates.

Mercedes brings Cass back mostly dry, just the hair immediately around her face dark with damp. Probably got shoved face first into a filled sink. I've been on the receiving end of that move after one memorable pub crawl.

Unlike me, Cass does not look particularly enlivened by it.

"I'm probably going to set up in the conference room," I tell them as they get their pockets sorted. "I'll have my cell, but that line should work, too, most of the day."

"Any particular reason?" asks Mercedes.

"It won't stand out as much as being out here. I'm not ashamed or discouraged by staying behind, it just makes good sense, but I know Anderson's stuck doing extra paperwork from the latest harassment seminar he had to attend, so why give him an easy punch line?"

"How have none of you murdered him yet?" sighs Bran. "I'm pretty sure every woman on the floor would alibi you."

"Exactly," Mercedes says with a shrug. "It'll look too suspicious."

Watts walks in carrying a steaming mug and an entire box of protein bars. When she sets down the coffee, she tears open the box and throws a wrapped bar at each of us. "Eat something," she orders.

"Did you get any sleep?" I ask.

"Did anyone? My guys are already on the road to Richmond; I told them to head straight up."

But for some reason, she came here. We all wait for the shoe to drop.

"I got an email from the department shrinks this morning," she mumbles around half a protein bar. "They would prefer Eddison stay here with Sterling and work on the research."

"I'm not compromised," Bran protests immediately.

"You are, a little, but not so much that I would take you off the case, and that's not really what they're asking anyway. But yesterday was hard on you. I saw it. Your team saw it, whether they're willing to admit it or not."

Bran looks at the rest of us. Cass looks him in the eye, unwraps her breakfast, and shoves the entire thing into her mouth so she can't answer.

"The shrinks are not trying to punish you," Watts continues once it's clear none of us are going to say anything. "They are, however, worried about your well-being as the case continues. And I've got to say, if you stay back with Sterling, it makes it look like you two just drew the short straw rather than being ordered to it."

Bran puts up a few half-hearted arguments, more for the sake of form than anything else. He leans against my desk as we watch Cass and Mercedes file off after Watts, Richmond-bound.

Almost at the elevator bank, Watts turns and sticks her head back through the glass doors to the bullpen. "Eddison, don't let Sterling disappear into the void. Force her head up from time to time."

"I'll try my best?"

The three of them disappear from sight, and Bran and I sit on my desk a little while longer in a silence that, while not quite comfortable, is at least familiar. "I'm sorry," I whisper eventually.

He shrugs, his shoulders stiff and tight. "It is what it is. Still want the conference room?"

"Yes. I don't want to be around people not working the case today."

"You do remember that it's Saturday, right?"

"That just means they won't be in until ten or so, mostly."

He concedes the point with a sigh, and we gather our things and head up to the conference room to get to work as Eddison and Sterling.

Yvonne, the team's dedicated technical analyst, comes in around six-thirty with a box of donuts and a haunted expression. She has her own office off the bullpen, keeping the super-powered computers a bit more secure than the ones we have out in the cubbies, but today she walks straight up to the conference room and dumps her things on the table. "Can I work in here today?"

"Sure," I say slowly, pushing my laptop back enough to fold my arms on the table. "Do you need the whole space, or . . ."

"No, I meant with you. Today is a day I need actual human interaction."

"Okay?"

She closes her eyes, taking a deep breath. "She's only a year older than my daughter."

Fuck. Right.

"After the second refill, we steal Vic's Keurig," I inform her, with a pointed glance at her yellow travel mug.

She huffs a laugh in spite of herself and pulls a few things out of the enormous tote bag masquerading as her purse. "I need to grab some stuff from the office. I'll be right back."

Eddison trails after her in order to help carry. About fifteen minutes later, they return with two monitors and a laptop bag that bulges with cables and cords. I help her get them sorted and set up into a comfortable workspace at the end of the table closer to the door. Eddison shifts our things down the side a little to make room. I'm the only one on the team allowed to help her with anything technical, because, as she says, I'm the only one who's not useless with anything more advanced than a smartphone.

Sometimes Eddison is tired enough, or desperate enough, to ask her something genuinely stupid. Her step-by-step instructions are patronizing, insulting, and absolutely gorgeous.

With the last cord in place, she turns everything on. While it's booting up, she digs through the box of donuts and puts two of them on a napkin, handing them to me. "Maple and bacon. Should still be"—she blinks at me—"warm."

I try for a smile, but given that I've got most of a donut shoved in my mouth, it probably doesn't come off too well.

"Chew, Sterling. We chew our food."

"Yes, ma'am," I mumble.

"We also don't talk with our mouths full. He's a bad influence on you."

Eddison looks up from his perusal of the other donuts in the box. "Hey!"

I snicker and make the effort to swallow. "Thank you for the donuts."

"Mm-hmm."

Settling back into my chair, I lick the maple icing off my fingers. It's just a little salty and greasy from the bacon, and I'm in a very good place with that. This is one of the rare occasions in which my love of pork bacon gives me zero guilt.

Giving us both a stink-eye, Eddison plops two chocolate-glazed donuts on a napkin and sits back down.

"Where do you want to start?" Yvonne asks.

"Is there a report from the night-shift captain about last night's work?" he replies.

She glances at her screen before answering. "No, but night shift is still on for another few minutes. I'd guess we get a report in an hour or so, unless Watts patches us through on a verbal report."

"Then we need to sort through the offender registry responses, double-check that the school didn't miss anything in its background checks, and look into Franklin Mercer's parents. I'd like to take the Mercers."

"I'll take the registry," I offer.

"So I've got the school." Yvonne shakes her head, thick locs sliding against her peach silk blouse. "Okay. Why did we choose this job again?"

"So we can help." I lean over Eddison and tap Yvonne's phone, the screen lighting up to show her wallpaper with all four kids grinning, faces smushed together to get them all in frame. "So we can make the world safer."

"Remind me of that a few times a day, will you?"

"Sure thing."

She sets music to play out of one of the monitors, soft enough not to interfere with conversation or phone calls but loud enough to fill the space and the silence that comes of burying your head in your work. A few agents wander into the bullpen to take care of paperwork or do some research. Weekends aren't always a real thing in the Bureau, especially in CAC, so more will come in as the day progresses.

Yvonne separated the Richmond-local pingbacks on the sex offender registry and sorted them by crime. Now it's my turn to sift through the data and put it into context. When a child goes missing, there's no such thing as privacy. Not really. And not just for the parents either. The investigation ripples out through the neighborhood and then beyond, digging into the smallest details of people's lives in the attempt to find the child, hopefully safe and sound.

There were no pings on Brooklyn's street, but there are three within her neighborhood. They're too close to the school for any of them to have child-victim convictions; I dig through them anyway. One man, during a particularly nasty acid flashback, stripped and ran naked laps through the senior assisted living facility where he worked, finally hiding under the bed of an eighty-seven-year-old woman and sobbing about alien ants dissecting him from the inside out. Some of the residents and staff were certainly flustered, but the police interviews make it clear that several of the residents had never been so entertained. Neither had the police officers. Despite the attempts to keep their reports professional, it's obvious they were laughing their asses off the entire time.

The public nudity makes him a sex offender, and this unfortunate streaker lives closest to the Mercers, just two streets over. Sympathetic employers or not, he no longer works at that facility or directly with patients in any capacity. His latest information has him working for an insurance company processing medical claims.

The next street over from him is a woman who got busted for prostitution in one of the states that includes that in the registry, and it carried over when she moved to Virginia. The conviction is old, though, without any indication of recidivism. Sex workers are also far, far likelier to be the victims of sexual offenses rather than the perpetrators.

At what used to be the very back of the neighborhood, though, where the houses were a little more spread out before construction started on the expansion, lives a man who apparently spent most of college raping classmates until he was finally tried, found guilty, and expelled, in that order. He was convicted in two cases, tried in five others, and was a person of interest in *fourteen* others. After serving a partial sentence, he's been arrested twice more in the years since. Once, the charges were dropped because the young woman's employer put pressure on her to keep it out of the news, and once the case was dismissed because the physical evidence was badly handled and largely destroyed.

All of his victims and alleged victims, however, have been in their early twenties, even as he's gotten older. It means he's not a person of interest in Brooklyn's disappearance. I'd still love to burn him to the fucking ground.

Of more relevant interest to the current circumstances, there are literally dozens, if not hundreds, of child-based offenders to go through in the larger Richmond area. Partway through, I thump my forehead against the table, wishing it could knock loose something brilliant. Something that proves to be the key to the whole case, the string that leads us straight to Brooklyn.

"I think I read somewhere that that kind of thing isn't healthy for you."

I sigh and gently thump the table a few more times. "Good morning, Vic."

8

"Head up, Eliza. It's afternoon. Time for lunch."

"Lunch? Really?" I reluctantly sit up, more because of the tantalizing smell of food than the instruction. Soup and sandwiches, it looks like, with a side of stern but gentle Look from Vic.

"Your focus is legendary, but try to maintain a little more situational awareness," he says, passing me a thick paper bowl and a paper-wrapped something. "I checked in on you a few hours ago."

"You did?"

"Eliza, I asked you questions and you answered them."

"Huh."

Yvonne snorts and rolls her chair along the oval table until she's sitting next to me, her food a safe distance away from her equipment. "You were the girl who read through football games, weren't you?"

"No, I was the girl playing the trumpet in the itchy band uniform."

"You play trumpet?"

"Not anymore." I unwrap the sandwich. Ooh, turkey and bacon. "Of course, if you ask my band instructor, I didn't play it back then either."

Eddison swallows a bite of his own sandwich, a bit of lettuce clinging to the corner of his mouth. "Don't worry, Vic. She's gotten snacks and proper hydration."

"I have?"

Yvonne's giggling and not trying all that hard to hide it. "All he has to do is put the cup or piece of food in your hand and you automatically put it in your mouth. It's amazing."

"And frightening."

"Well, yes."

Vic settles across from us with his own meal. It is absolutely unsurprising to see him here on a Saturday. "Anything promising?" he asks.

"Not yet," I reply. "Most of the ones I've gone through so far can be dismissed, either because this kind of crime goes against their progression or they've got different victim preferences. I've got maybe a handful to look into more."

"But?"

"I find it hard to believe that this is nothing more than a crime of opportunity." I bite down into the sandwich, chewing more slowly than necessary to give myself time to think. "From all accounts, Brooklyn is a smart, careful kid. Being alone, she would have been even more careful."

"So you think she knew whoever took her?"

"Well enough to recognize them, maybe even to stop and talk to them. Especially if she was helping someone."

"Which would argue someone in the neighborhood."

"Maybe. Or maybe someone she knew through the school. Or someone through Brownies. Or someone her parents work with who she might have met."

"Or her grandparents," mutters Eddison.

"Have we learned anything on that end?" I ask.

"Not without a warrant," Vic says.

I choke on a bit of crust. "Wait, what?"

"Not quite a warrant. Her grandparents are just up in Delaware, so the Smiths skipped Richmond and drove straight there."

The Smiths, two members of Watts's team, have been partnered up for so long that they have ceased to be individual units. Most of the people in CAC could not tell you their first names with a gun pointed at their heads. On the rare occasions there's a need to differentiate, they're usually described by build.

"Okay?"

"The grandparents wouldn't even let them through the gate. Told them through the intercom that their lawyers would contact the FBI in time."

"Are you serious?"

Eddison just shakes his head. "They have to know that brings them under greater suspicion."

"Brooklyn's father was able to give Watts the names of his parents' lawyers," continues Vic. "She passed them on to the Smiths, who were able to make contact. The lawyers said they'd call on Monday to arrange a suitable time to speak with the senior Mercers."

"Monday?"

"And when the Smiths pointed out that the case was in Richmond, not Delaware, and that they'd driven up—"

"Let me guess. The lawyers told them they could just drive up again."

"Are we labeling them a flight risk?" Yvonne asks, one hand floating over her keyboard. Her other holds both her soup-filled spoon and her cell phone. I need to ask her to teach me how to multi-task.

"We can take them in for questioning as material witnesses, but we can't actually arrest or hold them in custody," Vic explains. "But we can flag their names with TSA. Watts already called and arranged it."

"But that just tells us if they buy tickets anywhere," Yvonne says. "It doesn't prevent them from leaving."

"Have they filed any custody paperwork?" I ask.

"None that I could find," Eddison says. "It could just mean that their lawyers have prepared documents but haven't filed yet."

"So if for some reason our legal team says we can't bring them in as material witnesses, can we threaten them with obstruction of justice? See if that makes them more cooperative?" I ask.

"Bloodthirsty wench," Eddison says fondly.

Yvonne rolls her eyes. "I love how you find that charming."

"You don't?"

"Keep digging into the Mercers, Eddison," Vic says. "Get as much as you can before needing a warrant. Maybe they took Brooklyn, maybe they didn't, but their current actions are unconscionable. If they didn't take Brooklyn, they're forcing us to waste valuable time, time their granddaughter may not have. Eliza, when you were talking to Rebecca, did you get the impression she was keeping secrets?"

"No. She's desperate for Brooklyn to be found. If Brooklyn ran away after telling Rebecca she was going to do it, Rebecca would have told her parents as soon as the police showed up. I'd be willing to believe she knows things she doesn't realize could be significant, but I don't think she's actually keeping any secrets."

"That poor girl," murmurs Yvonne.

"We need to open the registry search past the Richmond area," I sigh. "Virginia, at least, preferably Maryland and North Carolina as well. We also need to dig through ViCAP."

"Abductions with similar victims?"

"And murders."

Vic and Eddison both turn to me gravely. Yvonne draws a sharp breath.

"Obviously it's not the outcome we'd want, but just in case this isn't a one-off, we need to know if there are similar occurrences. We don't know what kind of victim Brooklyn is."

"What do you mean?" ask Yvonne. "What kind of victim?"

"Was she taken because she was easy to grab that day? Was she taken because she fit a mold or preference? Was she taken because she was Brooklyn?"

"I hate approaching the forty-eight-hour mark," mutters Eddison.

It's by no means a rule, but there is a . . . practice? A rule of thumb, rather than a rule of course, that if you don't find a missing person in the first forty-eight hours after their disappearance, the manner of investigation shifts. It has to—the first two days are an all-out mad dash. It isn't sustainable in a longer investigation.

That doesn't keep it from being depressing as hell.

"That's a lot of different systems to start searching." Vic takes a long sip of his sweet tea, a frowning, thoughtful sort of furrow scrunching between his eyes. "Yvonne, who was the analyst you were telling me about last week?"

"I told you about all the new analysts last week, because we were reviewing their transitions."

"The one you said had promise," he clarifies. Sort of. "The apple kid."

About to eat the last of my sandwich, I pause and pull back. "The apple kid?"

"Gala Andriesçu," Yvonne answers. "We took a page out of the CAC survival guide Ramirez wrote for the new agents, started pairing the new CAC analysts with more experienced ones. I've only had her around a few weeks, but she's got a good instinct for the work."

"Can she come in today?"

"I called and asked before I came in. Her fiancé had minor surgery this morning and someone had to be present. Once she gets him home from recovery, one of his friends can sit with him for a few hours. She said she'll be in around one-thirty."

"If Eliza writes up some instructions, do you think she could take over sifting through the expanded registry?"

"Probably. She'll give us a longer list than Eliza, though. That's just a function of experience."

"It will still be a narrower list than the entire registry. Write out your criteria, Eliza, and we'll give that over to Gala. You take ViCAP."

Eddison looks up from his phone. "The Smiths are parked outside the senior Mercers' gate. Right in front of it, too, so if the grandparents are expecting any visitors or deliveries, their guests are going to be told why the FBI agents have to move their car to let them in and out."

"That's legal?" Yvonne asks.

"As long as they don't actually refuse entrance or egress, sure. They're conducting open surveillance on persons of interest in a possible child abduction."

"You people and your loopholes."

"Loopholes are the soul of laws," Eddison manages to say with a straight face.

She gives him the same look she gives her twin boys and gets a sheepish smile in response.

"They have their laptops and a hotspot, so they've offered to take over running background on the senior Mercers."

"Freeing you to do . . . ," prompts Vic.

"Obituaries and death certificates," I suggest.

Eddison ponders that for a moment, then nods. "Not all preferences are sexual. If she fits a mold, it could be someone who's lost a kid."

"All right. I'll update Watts and check in on you in a bit." Vic stands, gathers all of our trash, and heads out of the conference room toward his office.

Yvonne turns to look at us. "He does realize he's not actually working this case, right?"

Eddison just smirks. As unit chief, Vic works any case he feels is important enough for it. He simply ignores the whole not-in-the-field-anymore thing, and anything else that could be considered prohibitive. We're his people; these are his cases. He just takes a less-passively supervisory role in some of them.

Gala, when she comes in, turns out to be a twenty-two-year-old with bright green-and-blue dyed hair, rhinestone-tipped cat-eye glasses, and a thick Georgia drawl that the name Andriescu did not at all prepare me for. "I'd say pleasure to meet y'all . . . ," she starts, and shrugs rather than finishes.

"No worries; that's standard for this division."

As she shakes Eddison's hand, she looks me in the eye and winks. Yvonne and I both turn away to keep from snickering. Oh, I like Gala already.

There's something about Eddison that makes the female baby agents go weak in the knees. Even I don't know what it is, because while he's my personal catnip, he became that gradually over a year of working with him and after two years of hearing our mutual friend, Priya, share stories about him. He's handsome in a roughed-up sort of way, and he's both authoritative and competent, but there are others in the division who can be described that same way. And yet, it is Eddison and only Eddison who makes the brand new agents swoon. Mercedes thinks it's because he projects an air of broody and wounded. Marlene, Vic's mother, pinches Bran's cheek and says it's because he's so respectful of the women in his life.

Maybe it's because she has a fiancé—though that hasn't stopped others—but I like that Gala's immune to the whatever-it-is.

Yvonne helps Gala set up another multi-monitor computer and walks her through the parameters I wrote out on several pages from Yvonne's favorite yellow legal pads. I listen in with half an ear as they review them, in case anything needs to be clarified.

Beside me, Eddison stretches, his vertebrae cracking with a pop that makes him flinch.

Scrubbing at my eyes, I push my chair back from the table. "I'll be back," I tell the others. "I just need to walk a bit."

"It's about damn time," Yvonne says pertly, and ignores Gala's half-worried, half-appreciative look.

Eddison briefly blurs into Bran and takes my hand to press it against his cheek for a moment.

Everything aches from sitting too long, and even as some of my muscles sigh and relax with the movement, I can feel others tightening in protest. We've been trying to convince Bran he should put a hot tub in at The House, but so far he's been too twitchy to do anything to it.

After all, how many changes can you make to a house that doesn't feel like yours?

I walk slowly down the two-wall ramp to the bullpen, sort of lunging into each step to stretch out as much as I can. If it looks half as absurd as it feels, the handful of folks here are getting quite a show. I keep up the weird stretch-lunge-walk thing through the desk-and-quarter-wall cubbies. But just for a few minutes. The case clock in the back of my mind is relentless, punishing. It's easy to feel like every moment you take for yourself is a moment you're taking from that missing child's life. There are a lot of reasons people in this job burn out, and however much anyone else in the Bureau chooses to judge them, they'll never get that from CAC. We understand the job too well to feel anything but sympathy and understanding when people finally have to walk away from it.

Eventually the walk lands me at Eddison's desk. I'm more than a little anal-retentive when it comes to being organized, but his desk unsettles even me on a regular basis. Every file is neatly sorted and stacked, alternating orientation between portrait and landscape to create tidy towers on the back edge of his desk where it meets the row of squat filing cabinets he added when he inherited the space that used to be Vic's. In some ways, it actually makes the workload more intimidating than if it were messy or cluttered.

Bran doesn't keep personal pictures out and accessible at home, whether in his old apartment or The House, but Eddison keeps precisely two pictures out in his workspace here, sitting side by side on the cabinet next to his desk. The newer one is eight or nine years old. In a misty field stands a giant stone bust of President Abraham Lincoln, with an unfortunately placed hole in the back of its head. On one shoulder stands Bran, smirking and pointing at the hole. On the other shoulder stands Priya Sravasti also smirking and pointing. Vic, Bran, and Mercedes met Priya some eleven years ago when her older sister, Chavi, was murdered by a serial killer. The way Priya tells it, she and Eddison bonded after she threw a teddy bear at his head; they were both grieving, pissed at the world, and missing their sisters. I met her six years ago when the man who killed her sister started stalking her. Or resumed stalking her, really. She and her mother, Deshani, were living about an hour or so south of Denver at that point, which brought Finney, and therefore me, into the investigation.

The other picture, a little faded with age where the glass in the frame hasn't always blocked out enough light, is almost exactly twenty-five years old. Sixteen-year-old Bran, dressed in jeans and a long-sleeved Buccaneers shirt, smiles down at the little girl tugging on his hand. She's adorable, her curly blonde hair up in pigtails with a glittery pink tiara. Around her blue eyes is a red fabric mask, and over her Ninja Turtle costume—Raphael, as a joke on her brother's best friend named Rafi—she wears a glittery pink tutu. In her other hand, a Wonder Woman pillowcase bulges at the bottom with candy.

Faith Eddison.

She's grinning up at her brother, the two middle teeth on the bottom either missing or just starting to grow back in. And Bran, whose resting state is a scowl, looks so soft and charmed and fond, it's almost painful to see. It's not that he never looks that way anymore. It's not that he doesn't still have that affection and that bit of softness for the ones he loves. It's that it's just so rare to see it, so well guarded.

He keeps these photos here at his desk because they're his reminder of why he does this painful, difficult job. So that, hopefully, no family has to wait five years to find out who killed their sister and daughter, like Priya and Deshani did. So that, hopefully, no family has to go twenty-five-plus years without knowing what happened to their child.

Like the Eddisons have, and will continue to do.

For someone with over sixty distinct scowls in his repertoire, Bran Eddison lives a life of astonishing hope.

I touch the edge of Faith's frame, that beautiful, happy girl with blonde hair and blue eyes. Then I give one last stretch and head back to the conference room to look for another missing girl.

Brandon Eddison stood at the base of the stairs, draped over the banister in the boneless, sprawling way unique to teenage boys. "Faith!" he called up to the second floor, not for the first time. "Lista?"

"Almost," his little sister yelled back.

"That's what you said ten minutes ago!"

"Almost!"

"Do you need help with something?"

"I'm just . . . just trying . . ." She trailed off into grunts of effort that were audible even downstairs. "This tutu won't stay straight!"

. . . tutu?

Brandon scratched at the back of his head, fingers tangling briefly in his curls. "I didn't know the Teenage Mutant Ninja Turtles wore tutus," he said finally.

"They do when they're princess ballerinas!"

A snack-size candy bar thwacked the back of his head, and he turned to see his mother near the front door, the bowl of candy in her arm and a minatory look in her eyes. "I didn't even say anything!" he protested.

"Don't tease her for this, mijo, *or, as your loving mother, I'll be forced to bring out pictures of Bumblebee the Transformer Cowboy."*

Brandon blushed and turned back to the stairs. "Faith, come on down and let me help you with your tutu. The others will be waiting for us."

A moment later he had to bite the inside of his cheek to keep from laughing as his little sister grumped down the stairs, her curled pigtails bouncing against her shoulders with each step. She wore the superhero turtle costume he was familiar with—Raphael, because Faith adored Brandon's best friend Rafi—complete with the red mask and the twin plastic sai peeking over the edges of her plastic-and-fabric shell. She also had a glittery pink tiara pinned between her pigtails, and an even more glittery pink tutu that kept falling down despite her best efforts to keep it up.

He hitched up the ribbon banding of the tutu and held it against her stomach. "Here, keep that just there," he instructed, and she hugged her arms tightly across her middle, the Wonder Woman pillowcase dangling from one hand. He knelt behind her and got the tutu sorted and tied at her back. Keeping one hand on the ribbon to hold it in place, he pulled a safety pin from the hem of his long-sleeved T-shirt and affixed it.

"Jump twice," he told her.

She obeyed immediately, and while the tutu bounced with her, it didn't slide or pop the pin.

"There we go. Now are you ready?"

"Lista!" she crowed.

Their mamá kissed them both on the cheek as they walked out the door. "Remember the rules," she said sternly. "Faith, you and the girls listen to Brandon. If he tells you to do something or that it's time to come home, you don't argue."

"Sí, Mamá."

"Have fun, both of you."

Brandon led his bouncing, dancing sister across the street and two houses down to her best friend Lissi's, where he could see two other princess ballerina turtle superheroes waiting impatiently on the porch. Lissi had found a lavender tutu and tiara to go with Donatello's purple mask, and Amanda had even found a sort of pale orange for Michelangelo. Unfortunately, Stanzi—their Leonardo—was home with chicken pox.

"*Brandon fixed my tutu,*" *Faith announced as she hopped up onto the porch. "He can fix yours, too, if you need him to.*"

Immediately, two sets of eyes turned pleading looks on him.

Lissi's mamá *laughed at him. "You have enough pins?*"

He turned up the hem of his shirt to show her the rows of safety pins he'd put there half an hour before, which made her laugh again. As he fixed Lissi's and Amanda's skirts in place, he listened to the girls plot out their path like seasoned military strategists. "Listas?" *he asked when he was done.*

"*Listas!*" *they chimed in response.*

He led them over to the next house so they could begin. This one didn't have a porch, so he waited about halfway down the front walk and watched them skip the rest of the way to the door to ring the bell. "Trick or treat, Mrs. Záfron!" *they chorused.*

"*Oh, goodness, don't you all look very brave,*" *the woman greeted them with a grin. "Here we are, then, and Faith, take a couple of pieces for your brother. He's going to need his energy, you know, chasing around superheroes all night.*"

"*Gracias!*"

When Faith handed him the candy meant for him, he slipped it into the plush Crown Royal bag his dad gave him for his pogs and slammers. Mamá had a rule that no candy was allowed to be eaten before inspection. Mostly, he thought, it was so she would know how much they had and could tell if they'd been sneaking any extras. He led the girls over to the next house.

"*Trick or treat, Mr. Davies!*"

"*Trick or treat, Mr. Silvera!*"

"*Trick or treat, Mrs. Chapel!*"

They'd worked through most of the neighborhood when Bran's watch gave them their first warning. "You have forty-five minutes left," *he told them. "We can do another street, maybe two, but then we have to head back.*"

"*Can we head back now?*" *asked Faith.*

"You don't have to, Faith. You have almost an hour left before Mamá said we needed to be home."

"I know, but can we go back now?"

He looked at Lissi and Amanda, who both nodded energetically. "Ay, vámonos," he agreed with a shrug.

But they didn't go to the Eddison house or back to Lissi's or Amanda's. They went to Stanzi's and rang the bell. Her mamá opened the door and let them in with a broad smile. "Shh," she whispered. "The sound carries up the stairs. Hola, Brandon." She kissed him on the cheek and closed the door behind them.

"What's going on?" he asked in a whisper.

"The girls had an idea."

In his experience, "the girls had an idea" was not a sentence to inspire much confidence.

The girls walked into the living room, waving at Stanzi's papá. He sat on the floor counting out paper bowls. He didn't speak, because he had the kind of voice that carried even in a whisper, but he smiled and held his hands out wide over the bowls. The girls knelt near him, unable to sit with the shells on, and emptied their pillowcases into giant mounds of candy in front of them.

Brandon watched as they sorted through their candy, picking out Stanzi's favorites and splitting them across the bowls. Her absolute favorite, he knew, was Sixlets, and Faith and Amanda both pushed all of theirs forward. Lissi sighed—Sixlets were her favorite too—but followed suit.

Faith separated out a little over half of Lissi's and returned them to her. "Everyone's happy or no one's happy," she said as firmly as a whisper could manage.

Lissi beamed at her and pushed forward all of her bite-size Snickers.

Brandon accepted the bowl of candy Faith gave him a few minutes later and let her push him through the downstairs to the kitchen. It was nearly ten minutes before he saw them again, and this time they had their Leonardo with them, her blue mask hiding a stripe of red chicken pox on *her face. Her eyes, he saw, were damp with tears, but she was smiling so broadly her cheeks must be hurting.*

"Trick or treat, Brandon!" Stanzi said breathlessly.

He looked down into the bowl. "You know, I do seem to have some treats, but they're only for princess ballerina Ninja Turtles."

"I'm a princess ballerina Ninja Turtle!"

He tapped a finger against her blue tiara, watching her tutu bounce in place around her with her excited fidgeting. "And so you are. Here we go." He emptied the bowl into her pillowcase, hearing the other girls giggle behind the archway into the hall. "And hold on, I think . . . I just might . . ." He opened his Crown Royal bag and rooted through it. He didn't have anywhere near what the girls did—that wasn't the point of his going out with them—but he had enough that he had to poke through it. "Here we are."

Her eyes were huge behind her mask as he pulled out the three packages of Sixlets he'd been given through the night. "Really?"

He dropped them into her pillowcase. "Really."

She threw her arms around him in a hug, and a moment later he had all four of them crowding him, laughing into his ears as they tried not to hit each other with shells and tiaras and fake weapons.

In the archway, Stanzi's mamá grinned and took a picture.

Faith sighed happily and snuggled into her brother's neck, her tiara tangling in his dark curls. "This is the best Halloween ever," she murmured.

"Just wait until next year," he told her. "Maybe it will be even better."

The girls looked at each other. "I've got an idea for costumes!" Faith crowed, and they all burst back into giggles.

9

Yvonne runs out the door at five forty-three, phone pressed between ear and shoulder as she apologizes profusely to her husband and swears she's on her way to their son's T-ball game. Gala sticks around until seven, at which point she has to return to her mildly drugged-up fiancé to let his friend get to work. Eddison and I use that as a prompt to eat dinner—bless delivery and delicious Thai food—but then he heads out at nine-thirty when Mercedes calls and explains that she somehow managed to leave her keys in Watts's car and could he please come let Mercedes and Cass into the cottage?

"Are you coming?" he asks, shrugging into his coat.

I shake my head. "I'll head out soon. I've just got a couple more things I want to do before I leave."

"You promise soon?"

I smile up at him. "I've got my shortlist of probably similar ViCAP cases, and I just want to tag and pull the full files so I can dive into them in the morning."

"But soon."

"Soon."

Bran gives me a quick kiss and leaves the office. A few minutes later, I have an almost identical conversation with Mercedes via text.

I pull up my messages with Cass, see the bubble that says she's typing, and tap out a quick order not to even start. I get back a wink.

The floor is quiet, still. Unnerving, if I'm being honest. Every time I'm here after standard hours, I'm with my team. I feed my iPod into the speakerphone contraption on the desk and turn on an a cappella playlist. The familiar Hebrew brings me back to my Birthright trip with my best friend, Shira, both of us soaking up music and the food our parents hardly ever made. There are prayers in there, and pop music, and translated covers, a bizarre and eclectic mix that suited us perfectly at nineteen and suits me still. These days, Shira's lucky to listen to anything that doesn't involve counting, the alphabet, or the wheels on the bus.

The research we've been doing all day is valuable, but it also has a glaring problem: we're trying to construct a pattern off of what's essentially a single point of data. Brooklyn's disappearance didn't happen in the midst of a rash of abductions. Her disappearance didn't match known criteria of a case we were already working. Working blind, without any idea if this is a one-off or part of a series, it means we have to treat it as both, without enough information for either, really.

ViCAP is an invaluable resource at this point. It collects specific data from violent crimes, both solved and unsolved, detailing the signatures of cases. It helps link serials from across the country, which was next to impossible before it was up and running.

And it means that I can look for abductions/murders of girls ages seven to ten, and then sort the Caucasian blonde girls onto a separate list. If Brooklyn's abduction was preferential, if this is because of an abductor's particular tastes, then how the child looks is nearly everything. If Brooklyn is blonde, then other victims, if there are any, would likely be as well, and preferential offenders tend to have fairly narrow age windows.

There are so many missing or murdered little blonde girls.

There are so, so many.

Some of it can be connected to fetish, some to profit margins in trafficking, but the number is staggering. And here's the real kicker: white blonde girls aren't necessarily more vulnerable than any other demographics. More vulnerable than some, significantly less so than others. It's simply an ever-present threat.

Once when I was home from college for spring break, my dad and I caught a movie. It was dark when we came out, and the movie theater had a large parking lot that wasn't especially well lit. It was the first time he'd ever noticed how I carried my keys threaded through my fingers to make a punch as painful as possible if anyone tried to grab me. *Aba* asked me about it over milkshakes and fries, the diner's fluorescent lights headache-inducing and bright, and I walked him through the many, many things a girl or woman out on her own does.

He was baffled.

It wasn't that he didn't believe me; it was just that he had absolutely no frame of reference for that kind of caution being a routine. Couldn't understand that it didn't really have anything to do with where you were or what kind of area it was, that this was just good sense if you were a woman walking alone.

When a child gets kidnapped, people wail and point to safe neighborhoods as if that should be protection against opportunity. As if money is the only thing needed to make a child safe.

A lot of the girls on this list lived in safe neighborhoods.

Brooklyn Mercer lives in a safe neighborhood.

I start sorting the list further, separating the blonde files into three groups: solved, found, and missing. Anything that's been solved within the past year can be dismissed out of hand because the perpetrators are either in prison or pre-trial custody. Whatever happened to those girls, whether they were found alive or dead, I'm not reading it. Not now. The people who hurt them have been identified and arrested, and there's only so much I'm willing to torture myself with in the name of compassion.

The girls who were found without their cases being solved get split into two categories: alive and dead. The second list is much longer than the first. Generally when a child is found alive, it's because we've found the kidnapper. They lead us to her. It's uncommon, but not impossible, for it to work the other way around. If a child was sold or traded as part of a trafficking or pedophile ring, they might be found in the hands of someone other than their initial kidnapper as part of a crackdown on the operation. Every now and then a child can be found wandering somewhere, dropped off or escaped, and not know where they are in relation to where they were held. That's rare, though. Anyone who actually kidnaps a child, rather than molesting one they have a connection with, is generally too scared of getting caught to risk leaving the child alive. Their purpose is usually the molestation, but the murder is a safeguard. There are some exceptions, like if the child is taken as a replacement child or if the abductor is punishing the parents or holding the child for ransom. But again, if we find the child, it's nearly always because we've found the person who took them.

As Shira has noted more than once, I stopped being nearly as much fun at parties after I joined the FBI.

Trivia nights, though, everybody wants to be on my team.

The second half of that list, those who were found dead and the cases never solved, gets broken down into a number of subcategories. Where they were taken, how long they were missing, how they were killed . . . whether they were molested or not. Where and how they were found. Details that make me wonder how my eyes aren't bleeding. Brooklyn disappeared on her way home from school, so the ones who were taken from home can be marked off the list. Opportunity, even if it involves stalking, is in an entirely different class than breaking into someone's home. The ones who were only missing a day or two get an asterisk; we've already passed that for Brooklyn. If we find her in the next day or so, those are ones to come back to.

It leaves too many names, and I haven't even touched the third main grouping. Those who've gone missing and have never been found.

Trying to arrange the names in that group into any coherent sub-categories takes even longer than the others, mostly because there's so much less information to work with. So many names and pictures swirling around in my skull.

"Sterling?"

Some of the files have notes, follow-ups from police or FBI that indicate the parents have separated or divorced. There are some things so heinous, so painful, it's difficult for a marriage to survive them. Sometimes other children can keep the parents together, sometimes they're able to stand regardless, but it happens a lot that the pain is a poison and they just can't make it work after.

"Sterling."

Of course, sometimes it's because the marriage was already in trouble. If the official separation or divorce happens very close to an unsolved disappearance, it's generally worth checking deeper into the parents and close family to see if one of them hid the child away to keep them after, to hurt their soon-to-be ex. Desperation, pettiness, possessiveness, fear . . . they can all do nasty things to people.

"ELIZA!"

"What?" I snap, and spin the chair to glare at the door.

Only the rest of the world spins with me, and I pitch forward unsteadily. Hands grab my arms and shoulders to keep me from hitting the floor, easing me back into the seat until my hips touch the chair's back. When things stop spinning, both Mercedes and Cass are standing in front of me, twin expressions of worry on their faces.

"You're back? I thought Bran was meeting you at The House."

"Back . . ." Mercedes leans against the edge of the table, almost sitting on it, and pinches the bridge of her nose. "Eliza, what time did you get in this morning?"

"Uh . . . you saw me this morning."

"You were here all night?"

Through the conference room window, I can see several heads pop up in the bullpen, swiveling to find the sound.

My face feels like it's on fire. "Um. What time is it?"

"Eight o'clock tomorrow morning, apparently."

Cass sneezes a laugh and shrugs unapologetically when I glare at her.

Shaking her head and muttering curses under her breath in Spanish that's a bit too fast for me to follow, Mercedes stalks out the door and plants her fists on her hips as she looks out over the bullpen. Outside of those who are actually supposed to work this weekend, Sunday mornings are popular for devotees of the Church of Paperwork. "By any chance, did any of you feed Sterling last night?"

Amidst the chuckles, Watts, who's just entered the bullpen, shakes her finger up at Mercedes. "Now, Ramirez, I told you: if you're going to have a pet, you have to feed and walk it yourself."

"I'll take her for a walk!"

The "Shut up, Anderson" that follows is resoundingly female and comes from at least ten different desks.

Mercedes comes back into the conference room, still scowling. "You told me you were going home as soon as your list stopped compiling."

"I did."

"You did go home."

"No, I mean I did tell you that."

"You need a keeper, Eliza."

"I thought that was Eddison's job," Cass notes with a grin.

"Oh shit," I groan. "Please don't tell him."

"Why not?"

"Vic has been teaching him the Disappointed Look. I can't get another of those looks in the same twenty-four-hour period. And I told him I was leaving soon."

Mercedes just looks smug, which does not bode well for me.

"Mercedes . . ."

"I'll offer a deal."

"Your deals suck."

"If I don't tell Vic or Eddison, I get to tell Marlene and Jenny."

Vic's mother and wife. That might . . . that might actually be worse. "No deal."

"Then I'm telling Vic and Eddison."

"Telling us what?"

"Nooo," I whine, and Mercedes and Cass snicker at me.

Vic stands in the doorway in the rumpled jeans and faded polo that are his sole concession to coming in on a Sunday, his weathered face both kind and stern. Bran's at his shoulder, and at the sight of me he frowns and eases past Vic to enter the room properly. "Are those yesterday's clothes?" he asks.

"These are today's clothes."

"Because today is still yesterday," Mercedes adds helpfully.

She isn't close enough to kick.

"Eliza . . ." It's hard to tell from that sigh if he's Eddison or Bran right now. When we first decided where the boundaries were, we said being in a Bureau building automatically required Eddison and Sterling, not Bran and Eliza, but over time the boundaries started smudging to actively working, and then started smudging a little more. Kind of like the boundaries between team and family, and this team threw those out the window long before they met me.

"When was the last time you ate?" Vic asks.

"Ooh, I know that one."

He crosses his arms over his chest with an unimpressed look. Then he winces slightly and shifts the position a little lower. His scar must be pulling tighter than usual, which is generally a sign of him being too tired. I am not, however, going to point that out right now, because it will come back at me with added attack power.

"We ate dinner after Gala left. Around seven or eight."

"Did you eat anything after? Drink anything?"

I wheel over to the trash can and look inside. Except apparently I didn't notice the cleaner coming through, so I have no idea if there was snack detritus in there from munching and not paying attention to it.

And the headache starting to demand notice says I probably didn't drink anything, or at least not enough.

I'm starting to understand why Shira insisted on being my roommate through college, even though our scholarships would have let us spring for singles instead. She may be the only way I survived it.

Apparently not answering is answer enough, because all four of them glower at me. "I'm sorry!" I cry. "So sue me if I get a little focused!"

"This is not a *little* focused," Cass points out.

"Lehi lehizdayen."

"E vaffanculo anche tu," she retorts cheerfully.

Mercedes and Bran roll their eyes, as if we don't spend half our lives listening to them bicker in Spanish. As if Priya, who resolutely refuses to learn Spanish purely to tease them, doesn't answer in French when they do it in front of her.

"Ma decided to make breakfast for all of you," Vic says, voice deceptively mild, "but I'm not entirely sure you deserve it if you can't take care of yourself properly."

"You're withholding food to punish me for not eating?"

He blinks at that, then chuckles and shakes his head. "Well, when you put it that way." He picks up the brown paper grocery bag at his knee, moving carefully, and sets it on the table.

Marlene Hanoverian owned her own bakery most of her adult life until she sold it to one of her daughters and retired. Then, bored as hell and incapable of sleeping past four in the morning, she started baking again and relied on her son and granddaughters to get rid of it all. Marlene's baking is amazing. Even after a series of small strokes over the past couple of years have had her reluctantly slowing down and transitioning from a walker to a wheelchair, she's happiest baking.

Along with a tinfoil twist of buttery soft croissants still warm from the oven, there are Tupperware bowls filled with a mixture of scrambled eggs, bacon, sausage, mushrooms, and tiny grilled tomato chunks. I reach for my bowl, but it's intercepted by Bran—and when he does this, he is absolutely Bran, on the clock or not—so he can take my tomatoes and give me his hated mushrooms. It started with him taking things I actually don't like in exchange, but if I like everything in the meal, he'll take what he thinks is the least likely to get him stabbed with a fork.

Attempting to take my bacon would definitely get him stabbed.

Has gotten him stabbed.

Wow, I need to eat.

"So what time did you guys actually get back?" I ask around a mouthful of egg.

"Almost ten-thirty. We just went straight to Manassas."

"Is Cass living out of her go bag for the duration?"

Occupied with trying to shove an entire sausage link in her mouth at once, Cass simply nods.

"Any updates?"

"They're already starting to phase some of the officers out of the search," Mercedes says. "I get it, there are other crimes, but it's hard to explain that to scared parents."

"The grandparents?"

"Legal gave the go-ahead for the Smiths to bring them in for questioning. They'll take the senior Mercers to one of the satellite offices. An agent from the Baltimore Field Office is driving up just in case the lawyers try to get pissy about particulars."

"Okay, but we're the FBI. We are, by definition, federal. Why do they think federal agents from Virginia are going to have less jurisdiction than one from Maryland who's not even working the case?"

"I think their lawyers are going to attack everything they possibly can, even knowing they'll fail, and it's best just to be prepared."

They give me updates through the rest of the quick meal, things too long to consign to text and that I assume they've already told Bran. There's not really a lot to share, and not much new I can tell them either. What do you do when your wheels are spinning but you're not gaining any ground?

If you're this team, it keeps going until you're ordered to stop.

And maybe slightly beyond that.

"I'm going to go change," Cass announces around a jaw-cracking yawn.

"Good idea." Mercedes stands, and it's weird that it's taken me this long to realize she's in full makeup but wearing her navy-and-yellow "Female Body Inspector" running shirt.

I might need to take a nap.

"Eliza?"

"Vic?"

"When you've shown Eddison where your searches stopped last night so he can take them over, you're going to go into my office and get some sleep. This is nonnegotiable."

"Okay."

"It's important that you—what?"

"I said okay." I yawn so widely my face hurts, and shake myself out like a dog. "I'm tired. There's not much I can do in the way of research if my eyes start crossing every time I look at a screen."

"All right then."

He looks a little flummoxed, though.

"Would it make you feel better if I protested so you could use all the arguments you clearly mustered?"

"Hush."

Walking into the conference room, Watts hands a hot chocolate to me, followed by a cup of jet fuel to Bran and a hazelnut latte to Vic, who tries really hard to pretend that he prefers his coffee black. "Eliza Sterling."

"I didn't mean to."

"Eliza Sterling."

"I really didn't! I opened a file while the list was compiling and just . . . sort of . . . got sucked in?"

"Eliza Sterling."

"I'm sorry!"

Vic glances over at Bran. "That was impressive. Does Eliza do that for you?"

Watts tuts. "It is not even nine on a Sunday morning; we are not going to discuss what Eliza does for Eddison, not on the Lord's day."

I cackle as Vic flushes bright red. Bran's blush is a little deeper, with his darker complexion, but every bit as strong.

Watts waggles her eyebrows at me. For someone in her midfifties, she can be surprisingly impish. "Eddison, you going to tuck her in for her nap?"

"Madre de Dios," he mutters, face buried in his hands.

10

Once Watts's team rolls out with Ramirez and Kearney in tow and Vic heads back to his office to make sure there's a clean blanket, I walk Eddison through the results from my accidental overnighter. Afterward, he takes my hand and walks me to Vic's office, our fingers tangled together between us to keep them from the view of others. Vic opens the door, points at me, points at his couch, and then starts whistling as he walks past us with his laptop and a giant stack of case files. He leaves the door to the conference room open, so we can hear the whistling even after he's out of sight.

Bran closes the office door behind us and slumps back against it, his hands sliding over my hips to bring me in close. His expression shifts, dropping the professional mask. He looks wretched. I don't say anything, simply lean into him and bury my face in the side of his neck.

"Vic got a call this morning from Agent Dern," he murmurs into my hair.

"The Dragonmother?"

"That's the one. She said given the type of case and victim and the time of year, IA and HR are considering pulling me off to desk duty for a few weeks."

"But you're already out of the field."

"They mean off the case."

"What do you think?"

He's silent for a long moment, but his arms tighten around me. "I can see the sense in it," he says finally. "I don't like it. As much as this case . . . even with the way this case . . ."

"Better to work this case with its emotional cost than not work it and obsess over both Brooklyn and Faith?"

He flinches at his sister's name. We're so good about not bringing her up, about letting him decide if he wants to talk about her or not. Usually. Sometimes it's simply necessary. After a minute, though, he nods.

"What's going to be the deciding factor?"

"Time. Halloween."

"Halloween, or the end of the month?"

"They're the same thing."

"With completely different contexts."

Faith went missing on the fifth of November, so the end of October makes sense as an arbitrary cut off for Bran's involvement. But Halloween was the last big thing Bran and Faith did together. If I were going to choose a date, I might choose the thirtieth instead, not because a day makes any difference in the level of strain, but because if you're going to cut him loose to drown in memories, at least give him that one good night first.

It's also all of three days away.

"You know we've got you, right? Whichever way it goes?"

"Yeah, I know." His fingers trail along my spine, over my shoulder, to trace along my jaw. "You'll sleep?"

"I hope so. I'll certainly do my best to try."

There's a knock on the window behind the . . . yes, *open* blinds. "If you two just shacked up already, you wouldn't feel the need for any PDA at work," says a female voice.

We both shift enough to aim one-fingered salutes at the window.

Whoever it is just laughs and keeps walking.

Bran and I have been dating long enough that people have . . . expectations, I suppose is the best way to put it. Especially after he bought The House. Popular opinion through the division was that a proposal or invitation to move in had already happened or was imminent.

We haven't once talked about moving in. Or marriage. Or proposals.

I don't think that's only because of me.

I back out of his arms toward Vic's saggy, well-used couch, where two pillows and a blanket are already laid out and waiting. Bran waits until I settle in, then drapes the blanket over me. I'm asleep almost as soon as my head nestles into the pillows, barely noticing that he slides my cell phone into my curled hand.

Precisely at noon, obnoxious German techno blares out of my phone at full volume, scaring me not only awake, but off the couch and onto the floor with a thump and a mess of blanket.

I fucking hate phone alarms.

Granted, that's exactly why I use them, because they're impossible for even me to ignore no matter how focused I am, but fuck.

Standing in the doorway, Vic just laughs at me, the bastard, and laughs harder when I glare at him. "Go freshen up," he orders, still chuckling. "I've got lunch on the way for you, Yvonne, and the apple kid."

"We're supposed to take turns buying the food, you know."

"I know."

Which means I could argue with him about it, but I won't win.

"What about Bran? Not feeding him again today?"

Vic frowns thoughtfully rather than respond, and I pause in straightening my blouse. "He got a call from Detective Matson," he says.

"So why . . . oh. Ian Matson."

He nods.

Retired Tampa Police Department Detective Ian Matson was the lead detective on Faith's disappearance twenty-five years ago. He took

Bran under his wing afterward and was a large influence on Bran's entry into law enforcement. He's a very good friend to Bran despite the age difference.

"Is Ian okay?"

"He was calling from the airport, asking if Eddison could pick him up and bring him to Quantico."

There's a lot in that sentence that doesn't make sense. Ian likes to be a passenger in a car about as much as Bran does, which is to say not at all, so why wouldn't he rent one? And why is he making a surprise visit? And coming to Quantico rather than Manassas?

"Is it . . . about Faith?" I ask hesitantly.

"I'd assume she's somehow connected, but he wants to explain in person. Here."

"That's not promising."

"No, it isn't, but they'll get lunch on the way down from the airport. Go freshen up."

The shower and fresh clothes from my go bag feel better than I expected. It feels so damn good to change clothes, even if it is into another suit. Bran's braid from yesterday looks decent enough still, especially if I throw on a headband to contain the wispy bits breaking free.

"You promised me you'd go home, Eliza," Yvonne says as soon as I walk into the conference room.

"I cannot have this conversation again today."

"If you'd remember the conversations you had yesterday, you wouldn't have to."

Gala giggles and ducks down behind her monitors.

"I hate you all."

With Vic standing over me to enforce his orders, aided by Yvonne's most powerful Glare of Maternal Disapproval, I'm not allowed to open any of the files until after lunch.

I'm honestly not this bad, normally. Focused, yes, but not to the absolute exclusion of all else, except on special occasions. I have the feeling my worry for Bran is sinking me deeper into the research than I probably should be.

When all the trash from lunch is cleared away, I look up at Vic. "May I start now?" I ask, almost politely.

"You may," he answers in the same tone.

Gala giggles again.

I lean over and tap Yvonne's cell phone, the home screen illuminating the picture of her children again. "I'm sorry you have to be away from your kids all weekend," I say.

"It happens," she says easily. "And luckily, this is a weekend where everyone is running all over the place anyway for birthday parties and play dates and such. It was only yesterday's game that I really needed to be present for. My mother-in-law has the kids at a movie this afternoon, and my husband's had dinner in the Crock-Pot since seven this morning. It's one of the few weekends where my absence is barely noticed, much less disruptive. Unlike The Dress in your closet."

I close my eyes and thump my head against the table. "Yvonne, what are you doing to me?"

"I'm killing you, Smalls."

I crack open one eye and glare at her.

Vic chuckles and settles into a chair with his own stack of work.

My lists from yesterday are just as depressing as when I left them this morning, but there's nothing to be done for that. Instead, I keep working, deciphering Eddison's untidy scrawl to see his progress. It's Gala's playlist we're listening to today, something stately and mournful with drums and cellos and one weeping violin.

My work cell beeps with a text from Eddison. *What kind of drink does the apple kid like?*

I wonder how Gala will feel about being renamed once enough people hear Vic and Eddison calling her that.

"Eddison is back or almost back," I report, "and Gala, he'd like to know what kind of drink he can get for you."

"Oh, he doesn't have to—"

Yvonne shakes her head. "Just give the woman your order, Gala. It'll be your turn at some point."

"Oh. Um, caramel macchiato, please."

I confirm that Yvonne wants her usual, and answer Eddison. If I ask Vic, he'll say black coffee, because he's been an agent long enough to be fully indoctrinated into the theory that real agents (real men?) drink their coffee black and bitter. If I say nothing, Eddison will get him the milky hazelnut and French vanilla concoction he actually loves. When I put down my phone without asking Vic his order, he just rolls his eyes.

Maybe twenty minutes later, I can see Eddison crossing the bullpen to the ramp with a cardboard carrier, followed by a man in a worn coat, the dark blue faded with age. The second man also carries several drinks, and a battered leather bag with a patched strap loops across his chest. I save my progress and close my laptop, turning my notepad over so only the plain cardboard shows. It's not out of any distrust for Ian, simply protocol we're supposed to follow for anyone not working the case.

Somehow, Ian looks older than he did just six months ago. The team was ordered to, for the love of God, use some of our accrued vacation time, so Bran and I went down to Tampa to see his parents. It was, all in all, a very strange trip. Being a lapsed Catholic, Easter isn't really Bran's thing. Being Jewish, it *really* isn't mine. But there we were at Easter mass, his mother giving a vicious smile to anyone stupid enough to comment on our not taking Eucharist or going up for a blessing.

And no trip to Tampa happens without spending time with Ian, drinking cold ginger beer out in the studio he built behind his house after retirement. He makes stained glass there, small pieces usually, either commissions or the kinds of things he can sell at local craft fairs. I've bought a few pieces from him for Priya, who adopted her late sister's fascination with stained glass.

Ian is a little shorter than average, around five and a half feet or so, maybe less, but powerfully built. With the fluffy white beard and curly white hair long enough to keep in a ponytail at the base of his neck, Priya likes to call him Bodybuilder Santa, but only if Bran can't hear her; it makes him look a little pained. His face is weathered and tanned, startlingly bright green eyes surrounded by a wealth of wrinkles. It's something in those eyes, though, that makes him look older now. He's a little over seventy, if I remember correctly, but even with the white hair and weathering, he's never looked his age. Now he looks beyond his age.

I stand and greet him with a hug as soon as Bran takes the cups from his hands. "Trip go okay?" I ask.

"Smooth enough," he answers, his accent the kind of watered-down Southern that's so common around Tampa and St. Petersburg. "How are you, Eliza?"

"Exhausted and in trouble," Bran answers for me. "She was here all night after promising me she was leaving soon."

I stick my tongue out at him and pinch the vulnerable ticklish spot on his side, almost at his armpit. He yelps and lurches away, trying not to squeeze the cups and spill the nectar.

Ian smiles, and it lifts nearly ten years off his face.

Which makes me a bit more anxious regarding his reasons for being here so suddenly. Anything that makes him look that worried and old . . .

Lifting one of the drinks from the carrier, Ian squints at the side. "Gala?" he asks, pronouncing it like the event.

"Gala," she corrects. "Like the apple."

"That explains the apple-kid comment, then."

She grins and winks at him, the rhinestones in her glasses winking along with her.

Yvonne accepts her drink with a murmured thank you, and Vic takes his with a glare closely followed by a long, pleased exhalation.

Bran hands me a hot chocolate, which means he's worried about my caffeine intake. He can never remember which teas are caffeinated and which are calming. His apartment had a list on the inside of a cabinet door, but it got lost or ruined during the move. Me being the one member of the team with blood instead of coffee sludge means the others can never remember how much caffeine is too much for me.

At Bran's gesture, Ian shrugs out of his coat and bag and settles into a seat to the left of where Bran spent most of yesterday. He unzips the bag and reaches in, but hesitates before pulling anything out.

"Any update from the Smiths?" I ask Bran, to give Ian a moment.

"They picked up the senior Mercers when they were leaving for church," he answers, absently gathering photos and papers into a neat stack and turning them over to hide the contents.

"And how many seconds did it take them to call their lawyers?"

Vic chuckles. "Apparently one of the Smiths has a cell blocker. They were able to call from a landline at the satellite office."

"So their lawyers had to drive."

"They're rather upset at the moment."

"The senior Mercers, or their lawyers?"

"Yes," Bran says decisively. He's still Bran, somehow, despite the case update. "The Smiths are talking to them now. Or, one of them is talking while the other is in the room texting updates, mostly to make the senior Mercers paranoid."

"You have them both in your phone as Smith, don't you?" sighs Yvonne.

"Who doesn't?"

Cass, who has them labeled Smith the Tall and Smith the Stout.

Ian removes five file folders from his bag and sets them on the table. One of them is thick, bulging with pages and paper clips, Post-its and scraps of paper, even ink-covered napkins sticking out at odd angles. The others are much thinner. He follows them with a battered composition book, the cover patched with electrical tape, thick and ruffled with things added between the pages.

He takes a slow, deep breath. "I know you don't have time to waste on fools' errands," he begins carefully. It sounds rehearsed, and it isn't hard to imagine he spent the plane ride from Tampa going over this again and again in his head. "Brooklyn Mercer is missing, and tangents can cause problems."

"But you have a tangent?" asks Bran.

"I think you all know better than most that there are some cases you just don't let go. You keep trying to solve them, to fix them, long after the department moves on."

Vic stares warily at the thickest file, gaze flicking to Bran and back.

"You kept looking for Faith," I say softly.

Bran flinches minutely, not from shock, I think, so much as reflex. He's known for years, possibly decades, that Ian hasn't given up. Xiomara, Bran's mother, told me as much the first trip I met her.

Ian slides the thickest file out into the center of the table. "Almost every detective has that one case. Maybe more, but there's always at least one they can't let go of. Departments understand that. They look the other way when you copy notes or stay after hours in the archives. Used to pretend not to notice you using the station phones for long distance calls, back when that meant anything. As computers became more widespread, they didn't mind us old-timers coming in for tutorials, running searches, and setting up alerts."

"There are an awful lot of blonde girls who go missing, Ian," I tell him. I'm not trying to be patronizing, and I hope it doesn't come off that way. But it's a fact, and I have a full night's work to prove it.

"Yes."

It's the way he says it: utterly calm despite the tension around his eyes. This man, who knows damn well that every second counts in a child abduction, dropped everything to come here and tell us this.

"Okay. Walk us through it."

Bran glances at me, his shoulders hunching. "Eliza."

I touch his side, my hand hidden under the table. "We can go in Vic's office if you'd rather not hear this. If you want to dig back into yesterday's files."

He shakes his head. "Ian, I don't . . . you know I don't . . ."

"I know you respect me, boy," the detective replies with a small, tired smile. "Maybe I'm past the foul line on this; maybe it's a solid hit. Let me lay it out."

Bran glances at Vic, who nods gravely. "All right."

Ian flips back the cover of the thickest file. Faith's file. Her picture is on the top, an eight-by-ten glossy print with much of the gloss worn away. I've never actually seen this picture of her. Like most missing children, it's her final school picture, because when police are plastering pictures of your missing kid everywhere, you want one that clearly shows their face. This one has a wavy purple background, her broad smile displaying the bottom middle teeth she'd lost by Halloween. Her hair is the same as the picture I'm used to, though, and a handful of other photos I've seen, the blonde pigtails curling down onto the shoulders of her Lisa Frank unicorn tee. Her head is cocked a little to one side, like the photographer said something she didn't quite understand, but she knew she had to keep the smile. It's adorably confused, and, oh, God, I've seen Bran with almost the exact same expression minus the smile. A thin chain drapes around her neck, leading to a pendant that rests just beside the unicorn's horn. It's the kind of glittery enamel pendant that kids love regardless of decade, the kind where you look at it and automatically wonder if it also glows in the dark—a pink, yellow, and blue rainbow that arcs into two white stars rather than clouds.

Bran gave her that their last Christmas together. She made him help her put it on that morning, and never took it off. Their mother told me that.

"Twenty-five years ago," Ian says. "Almost exactly. Heard about Brooklyn on the national news last night. Eight-year-old girl, white, curly blonde hair, blue eyes, disappears walking home from school in the afternoon."

Gala looks at the photo of Faith, at Bran, at the large picture of Brooklyn clipped to the whiteboard wall behind her, and loops around again. She swallows hard but doesn't comment.

"When you were at the academy, Brandon, you told me about a friend in your cohort. When he was a kid, his little sister's best friend went missing."

"Sachin Karwan," Bran whispers.

Sliding a second file to the center of the table, Ian opens it to show another little girl who bears a more-than-passing resemblance to both Faith and Brooklyn. "Her name was Erin Bailey. Eight years old, white, curly blonde hair, blue eyes, disappeared walking home from a tutor's. She went missing in Chicago twenty-seven years ago tomorrow."

Shifting the papers off my laptop to the counter behind me, I wake up the computer. I have to log back into the various systems, but a couple of minutes later there's Erin's face on my screen, already tagged to one of my lists.

Unsolved, never found.

Another file joins Faith and Erin in the center of the table. "Twenty-one years ago come November 3. Her name was Caitlyn Glau, from Atlanta."

Her complexion is ruddier than the other girls', patchy with pink and red, and her hair has a tighter, bushier curl, but not enough to pull her out of the line of photos. Vic picks up the printed picture by its edges, handling it carefully. He looks up at me.

Caitlyn's name isn't on my ViCAP list, but I run her name through NCMEC and she pops up, classified as a runaway. The last update to her profile is over a decade old.

"How did you find her name?" I ask.

"One of the officers on the initial search transferred to Tampa nine years ago. Around nine, I think. Manny keeps a photo of Faith on his desk at work, right next to his kids."

"Rafi's younger brother." Rafi and Manuel—Manny, as he goes by now, when he can convince his family not to call him Manuelito still— were Bran's best friends growing up. They're still family.

"New guy noticed the picture," Ian continues with a nod, "they got to talking. Neither of them seemed to think it was anything but coincidence, but Manny mentioned it to me not long after." He pulls the next file out and opens it. "Fifteen years ago, Emma Coenen, Nashville."

Emma is on my ViCAP list.

"There's a nonprofit group in Nashville that haunts around old cases like this. A few years ago they worked with artists to recreate what the missing kids might look like now, ran them on television. Emma was eight years old, white, with curly blonde hair and blue eyes. She disappeared walking home from her aunt's house on November 7."

Unsolved, never found.

"Seven years ago"—Ian opens the last file—"Andrea Buchanan from Baltimore vanished walking home from her voice lesson. Ordinarily, your team might have been called in, but it was the same day Keely Rudolph was kidnapped from a mall in Sharpsburg."

Vic looks suddenly exhausted, and the heel of his hand presses against the gunshot scar on his chest. Bran drops his face into his hands.

Expression a little frightened, Gala delicately clears her throat. "I'm sorry, I don't . . . what's the connection to Keely? Is she another blonde girl?"

Yvonne shakes her head. "Keely was twelve. She was kidnapped by a man whose family kept teenage girls prisoner in a garden complex on his estate. She was rescued, but the Garden . . ." She closes her eyes momentarily. "It was a mess of a case. A lot of girls died when the building exploded. That was before we learned how many had died over the years preceding it."

"I remember the Garden case," Gala whispers, hands hovering around her mouth like she wants to cover it but doesn't want to risk muffling her words. "I was in high school, and after the news broke, they pulled all of us girls into a safety lecture. It was all anyone could talk about for weeks."

"The explosion was on Halloween," Yvonne says. "The next day was my first back at work after giving birth to my oldest daughter."

"Keely and Andrea both went missing on the twenty-ninth of October." Ian's stubby fingers, square and thick with callus, poke the edges of Andrea's picture to where we can all see it. "Andrea was never found."

Andrea has a cheerleader's smile, wide and toothy and fixed in place like she could hold it for hours at a time. Her hair, a slightly redder blonde than the other girls in the line, is up in two high pigtails and done in tight, sprayed-fast spirals bound with starched ribbon twists. Cheerleader pigtails. Around her face, though, the wispy curls are soft and loose.

"They all went missing in the same two-week span. All in the last week of October or the first week of November." He sits back, gaze traveling around the table to study each of us. "Two might be a coincidence, but six? Six eight-year-old white, blonde, blue-eyed girls who all disappeared at the same time of year? I think they were taken by the same person or people. And I think there are probably others."

I close my laptop again, leaning over it to flick through the printed pages in the files. Not to read them, exactly. Just to see what they are.

"They're not full files," notes Vic.

"No, just what I could pull from online, except for Faith's. Corbero, the transfer from Atlanta, didn't think they were connected. I couldn't get a copy of Caitlyn's file from him. The rest, I didn't have someone with access."

"Eliza," Vic asks quietly, "what are you thinking?"

Interesting that he's asking me. But then . . . well, I suppose it's not fair to ask Bran. It's a compelling story, certainly. That doesn't mean they aren't coincidences. We've seen stranger. Hell, we've solved cases by stranger coincidences. Still . . . I rub my finger against the date on the bottom of one of the printouts in Caitlyn's file. Ian heard about her nine years ago, but he only put this folder together recently.

"Ian?" I say. "What's your diagnosis?"

11

Bran flinches again, full body, and scowls at me. It only takes a moment, though, for him to realize that Ian hasn't corrected me, hasn't refuted that there is a diagnosis of some sort. He turns in his chair, the blood draining from his face. "Ian?"

His friend, his first mentor, the man who saved his life in very important ways, gives him a sad smile. "I told myself it was too much of a reach," he says. "I was so desperate to find Faith, or a reason I couldn't find Faith, I was grasping at anything. Forging connections out of straw. I wanted it too badly."

"Ian."

"I made notes in my book," he continues, patting the tattered composition book fondly, as one would a beloved dog. Probably just as faithful, really. "I didn't make the files, though, because I couldn't convince myself it was real."

"*Ian,*" Bran grits out.

"And then this summer, I finally let Connie nag me to the doctor for the headaches I've been having for a while now." Two fingers tap the ridge of bone over his eye, where his bushy eyebrow nearly hides a healing scar. "Malignant glioblastoma. Out to take us old men, I guess."

"Incurable," I murmur.

"Not too treatable either, if I go that route."

"*If?*" Bran asks sharply.

"The most it can buy me is a few extra months, Brandon. I don't know if that's worth it. Connie and I are still discussing it."

Which means they've decided against treatment but have gotten grief over it from others. If he was diagnosed this summer, why didn't he tell Bran sooner?

"I was out in the studio last night, just sitting. Don't feel comfortable working the kiln without Connie there now. Going back through Faith's file, through the book. News playing in the background. Then I look up and see a little blonde girl on the television. Brooklyn Mercer. And there behind the reporter, your girl Ramirez talking to an officer. Started wondering when I decided being desperate meant I must be wrong rather than investigating it properly. So here I am." Tears track down his weathered cheeks. I'm not sure he's noticed them. "Six little girls," he says again. "Look at them. How can they not be connected?"

Muttering curses under his breath, most of them not in English, Bran shoves back from the table and stalks out of the conference room. I watch him go, but if I try to follow immediately, he will bite my head off. Then, later, he'll feel bad about it. Feeling guilty will make him snap and snarl, and he'll bite my head off again. Not just me, to be fair. Anyone. But it's best to give him some space to get through this first flash of . . . fear? Fury? Grief?

All of them, and more.

I look down at my lists from last night. I can filter my tagged files, I think, to show just October and November disappearances. We'll have to set the program on both ViCAP and NCMEC, though; Caitlyn Glau wasn't in ViCAP. Police investigating her disappearance concluded that she was likely a runaway, though I can't imagine they had evidence to support that. Yvonne should probably set the filters. Me being fairly confident in my computer skills doesn't stack up against her doing this for a living.

We'll have to put together file requests, transition local cold cases to federal jurisdiction . . . once we figure out which cases actually belong to federal jurisdiction, if any of them do.

Sharp, fleeting pain flares between my eyes. "Ow!"

Vic settles back into his chair.

"Did you just flick me?" I demand.

"You were spiraling."

"I was *thinking*."

"You were thinking so hard you didn't hear three different questions directed at you."

Ian scrubs his knuckles against his cheeks. "Brandon mentioned you do that sometimes. It's impressive to see."

"Less so after the third or fourth time," Vic mutters.

Gala grins, but it fades quickly under the weight of the tension in the room.

"What were the questions?"

"Never mind. What do you think?"

"I don't know that I'm entirely convinced," I say slowly, "but I do think it's worth looking into properly. We passed forty-eight hours; the investigation is shifting. If there's something to this, it could help us find Brooklyn. Maybe even find these other girls. If there isn't anything to this, it's part of something we were already trying to cross off. I think we should go through this with Watts and Dern in the morning."

"Why Sam?" asks Vic.

I'm pretty sure he's one of less than a dozen people in the Bureau comfortable with referring to Agent Samantha Dern—the Dragonmother of Internal Affairs—as *Sam*.

"There's already concern about Bran being on this case right now. And of course you already know that because you're the unit chief."

He grimaces but nods.

"If this is connected, he can't work the case as an agent. Material witness, maybe, but not as an agent. Not if his sister is in the mix."

Bran's—no, Eddison's—phone buzzes with a series of texts. Vic's follows suit. I grab Eddison's and punch in the unlock code that I'm really not supposed to know, given that it's his work cell, and see a string of messages from Ramirez.

"They're coming back," I announce.

"So early?" asks Yvonne.

"The night-shift captain doesn't want them there," Vic elaborates, scrolling down the messages. "He's giving Captain Scott some issues. He seems to think Brooklyn just got lost on the route she's taken every day for three years, and she'll turn up."

"He doesn't really."

"Probably not, but he also doesn't like the FBI or Captain Scott, apparently. Ramirez says, and Watts concurs, it makes more sense to come back and get one decent night of rest than to stay and argue with him when there's a limit to how much they can do at night anyway."

"So we could probably loop Watts into an early meeting without her swearing at us too vehemently," I muse.

"Let me call Sam and make sure she doesn't have any reviews scheduled in the morning."

As Vic leaves the room, lifting his phone to his ear, Yvonne and Gala start shutting down their computers. Yvonne has to get home if her husband's going to have any chance to get some grading done after dinner. Gala's already given up her entire weekend; I'm not going to ask her to stay without an experienced analyst nearby to help. Within a couple of minutes, Ian and I are alone in the room.

"Physically, how are you doing?" I ask, manually copying the names, dates, and pertinent information from the printed files onto my notepad. It's the kind of question Bran is most comfortable answering when no one is looking at him. I don't know if Ian is the same way, but I do know he was a career cop, so pride and stoicism are going to play their part.

"The headaches are the constant problem," he says slowly. "They can be better or worse, but they're always there. Vision's declining sharply. Blurring, doubling."

"That's why you didn't rent a car."

"Not safe to drive anymore. Turned in my license so I wouldn't be as tempted. Nausea has a way of striking out of the blue."

"Any seizures?"

"A few. None terrible. No clusters."

"Anything we can do—lights, sounds, smells, temperatures—to help?"

He chuckles quietly, a far cry from the deep belly laugh he looks like he should have. When he plays Santa each December for the police toy drives and at hospitals, then the laugh booms out of him, but the rest of the time it's this low, dry sound, rough like it scraped across pavement on the way out. "You, Eliza Sterling, are a wonder."

My pen hovers over the page, motionless. After a moment, I set it down and turn to look at him. "Sorry?"

"I have sunglasses I can wear when the lights start getting to me," he says, which does not actually clarify his comment. "Smells only bother me when I'm already sick. Temps . . . I'm a Florida man, born and raised; any place that isn't broiling is in air-conditioning. I've been avoiding the heat where I can. That's as far as I've noticed."

"Did you tell your doctor you were coming up here?"

He shakes his head. "Didn't know for sure myself till this morning. Connie will tell him tomorrow."

"Let me guess: When she calls to reschedule your next appointment?"

He chuckles again, which is basically a yes.

"Why didn't you tell Bran?"

His smile doesn't fade so much as shift, turning small and fond and faintly proud.

And sad. So very sad.

"I should have told him as soon as we knew," he admits. "We were discussing treatments, though, and then whether or not we should, and if declining treatment meant being immediately referred to hospice. I told myself I'd sit down with him once we'd made some decisions.

Once we knew for sure. Then it was October." He looks down at his hands, wide and strong and large-knuckled from age and use. "If I had a choice, Eliza, I wouldn't have told him now. I would have waited a few weeks, get past this anniversary."

"But Brooklyn went missing."

"I would have waited," he repeats. "Life has a way of mocking our choices."

"Sometimes, yes. Did you book a hotel when you got your flight, or do you need a place?"

"You offering?"

"Don't do it, Ian," Bran says from the doorway. He's still pale, a muscle in his jaw jumping from the tension, but he's there, and sooner than I would have expected. "You'll drown in frills and ruffles."

"Yet somehow you've all survived," I retort.

"It's like being in a bottle of Pepto-Bismol," he continues, pretending to ignore me. "It's everywhere pink and delicate and untouchable."

"Slander and lies."

Ian's smile grows as his gaze flicks back and forth between the two of us like it's a game of tennis.

"Her table is perfectly set with linens even when no one eats there."

"As opposed to yours, which was rescued from the trash?"

"Hey, Priya gave me that table."

"Someone had to; it's the only bit of color you have."

Ian laughs and leans against the conference table. "Did he do the whole house in the black and glass his apartment had?"

"That would require doing something to The House," I tell him with a wink. "Right now it's one bedroom and a living room."

"Still?"

Bran flushes and mumbles something I can't make out. Then he clears his throat. "Vic, who has an actual guest room with a bed and a door and its own bathroom, has offered to put you up. The living room and kitchen will be a bit stuffed because the girls are here, but you'll have the room and bathroom to yourself."

"I thought his girls were all off at college?" Ian replies.

"They are. Inara, Victoria-Bliss, and Priya arrived today."

Crap. I'd completely forgotten they were planning to come down. Normally Inara and Victoria-Bliss—survivors of the Garden and the sociopath who tried to make them as beautiful and ephemeral as butter-flies—spend Halloween, and thus the anniversary of the explosion and subsequent madness, with Keely. Her kidnapping and rape ultimately proved the impetus for the Garden's violent end, and all of the survivors are protective of her, Inara most of all. Priya was never connected to the Garden, except that she became friends with Inara and Victoria-Bliss through Eddison and the team.

This year, however, Keely Rudolph is a freshman at Stanford University, and while the girls would gladly have schlepped to California for her, she told them not to. She said she was ready to face it on her own. I have no doubt they'll all spend the next few days glued to their phones and texting like crazy, but it's a really good sign that she feels up to this. Being so young, and her plight being made so very public, Keely was victimized once by the Gardener and again by everyone else.

In the meanwhile, though, the girls already had the week off from work, so they decided to come down here, and Priya decided to join them. They live and work up in New York, and Priya splits her time between their apartment and the house she and her mother share in Paris. It means all three of them visit frequently.

Some families shatter with trauma, and some families shatter with-out it. Either way, Inara and Victoria-Bliss didn't really have anything to go back to. So the team adopted them instead, and something about the combination of Vic's warmth and compassion, Mercedes's understand-ing and endless kindness, and Bran's prickly protectiveness made them feel at home. It'll be good to see them, despite everything going on.

Vic clears his throat to draw our attention; he stands in the doorway with a pair of women's shoes in his hand.

The three of us look at him, baffled, then at the shoes, at my bare feet, and back at him.

Whoops.

"You left these in my office; you might want them for when you leave the building," he says mildly, and walks closer to set them at my feet. "It's probably best if we all head out," he continues once he straightens. "Ian, if you'd rather stay with Eddison or Eliza, I won't be offended, but the offer is there, and my wife and mother live to feed people."

Ian absently combs his fingers through his beard and gives Bran a considering look. "Few years back, you came for a visit with a box of pastries," he says.

"His mother made them."

"Agent Hanoverian, I'm your grateful guest."

Vic chuckles, and even Bran manages to smirk. "Then let's all head out, and we'll get you settled in. You two, go home. Shower. Change. Take a nap if you can. Dinner won't be for three or four hours yet."

"Yes, sir."

"Stop that," he chides, as he has for the last four years.

I shrug. I know he doesn't like being called sir, but bad habits have a way of resurfacing in fatigue. "Okay?" I ask Bran.

"Good enough."

Which means he wants some time alone. I can do that.

They wait for me to finish cleaning up and follow me out to the garage to make sure I leave. I suppose I can't entirely blame them, obnoxious as it is.

Three hours was not enough sleep.

I'm not quite too tired to drive, but I'm tired enough I don't feel entirely comfortable doing it. It's the state of over-attention, where everything feels a little too real but also not-real. Liminal space, as Shira likes to call it. Points of transition where the sense of time and reality skews, making us more open to new experiences.

Speaking of Shira . . .

Up in the apartment, I drop my bag on the table, dig out the pack of cigarettes from the cabinet over the fridge, and grab my lighter from the coffee table drawer on my way to the sliding glass door that splits my apartment from the tiny balcony outside. The entire balcony is filled with a sturdy cloth hammock on a stand, and I collapse down onto it, lighting a cigarette.

Shira and I both picked up smoking in college, more out of defiance than any better reason. It was the same time I dyed my hair red and she went from ginger to brunette. Neither of us actually liked smoking all that much, but it was a habit, and college was stressful enough that it didn't seem to be worth the hassle to quit. We cut ourselves back after college, holding each other accountable to one smoke a day. And then four years ago, not long after I moved here, she and her husband discovered they were expecting, and neither of us smoked for a while.

Which is when I realized there are some times, thankfully few and far between, when the cigarettes are actually useful. The times when I'm too over-trained to give into a panic attack but am also not really okay, when it feels like everything's about to claw out of my skin and I need to stuff it back down into my bones where it belongs—then the act, the ritual of smoking a cigarette, is queerly calming.

And the feeling afterward, of needing to scrape my tongue raw with a toothbrush, is a good reminder to deal with my shit in more mature, healthy ways before it gets this bad.

After the first involuntary taste-bud spasm of "oh shit, what poison are you giving us?" the ritual starts its work, and I resettle into the hammock in a more comfortable position, reaching for my phone to call Shira.

"*Ima!*" is the childish shriek that answers the phone. "*Ima*, is *doda* 'liza!*"

"*Erev tov*, Noam," I greet with a laugh. "How's my favorite nephew today?"

"*Ima*, *doda* 'liza!"

"Noam, what is . . . oh, dear," I hear in the background. There's a shuffle and a *meep* sort of sound, and a huffing breath. "*Erev tov*, Eliza. Have you gotten rid of The Dress yet?"

"And suddenly I'm wondering why I called you."

Her warm laughter eases something that even the familiar ritual of the cigarette can't touch. "I'm keeping my promises. You told me to hold you accountable for getting rid of the damn dress."

"Damn!" I hear Noam chortle happily, because of course he's at the catch-and-release stage of verbal development.

There's a muffled conversation between Shira and her husband, Asher, then footsteps and the sound of a door opening and closing. "Sorry, I'm on the porch now. We're still working with Noam on understanding that the phone isn't just the game and picture thing. So I'm guessing that means it's still lurking in your closet."

"Yes, damn you."

"It's going to become sentient and eat you in your sleep."

"Death by wedding dress? Isn't that a show on TLC?"

"You're smoking, aren't you?"

"Yes."

"Bless you, I've been fucking desperate." Two seconds later, there's the snick of a lighter and a deep, relieved inhale.

"What's wrong?" I ask.

"You're the one calling with a cig already in hand; shouldn't I be asking you that?"

"Shira."

She sighs, and it's so easy to imagine her sitting on her porch, perched on the thin rail because furniture is for people who don't know better, the thin plume of smoke wreathing around her as she shivers in the October evening. She doesn't allow herself a coat while smoking; it's her self-punishment. The location of the porch has changed over the years, different places in and around the greater Denver area, but the threads of it always remain the same. "*Ima* got a call from the prison on Friday. Hadn't told you yet because I'm still working my way through it."

When Shira—or any of the Sawyer-Levy family, really—says "the prison," there isn't a question of which one. They only ever mean one: the Coleman Correctional Facility in Florida. Her father has been a prisoner there since we were in middle school. We came home from school one day to find her house swarmed with police officers and FBI agents, her father arrested for a string of murders over nearly two decades. Women raped, murdered, their bodies thrown away like so much garbage, while he had a loving family at home.

I practically grew up in that home. Shira's mother, Illa, and my *ima* were sort-of friends, and part of the same mothers' group at our temple. As an only child with an *ima* who makes Elizabeth Bennet's mother look sturdy and well adjusted, I adored the noisy, chaotic, warm Sawyer-Levy home. They were my family as much as my parents were. Her father used to take us to the park and teach us baseball, because he didn't think it was a game only for boys. He cheered at all our Little League games and walked us through neighborhoods and office parks, keeping an eye on us as we used devastating cuteness and sincerity to sell Girl Scout cookies, and then he drove us around when it came time to deliver them. He used to watch us fall asleep in the living room after we swore we were old enough to stay up late with the big kids, and then carry us up to Shira's bed and tuck us in together, kissing our hair before he left us to dream.

We studied his case in the academy, and I learned all the details Illa had protected us from, details she may not even have known, and fuck, they were awful. What that man did to those women, some of them only a few years older than his firstborn . . . Strangely, perhaps, those details never crept into the nightmares that started in middle school and got significantly worse for a while in the academy. Rather, it was the literal blood on his hands. I used to dream—still dream, sometimes, certain times of the year or when a case comes too close—that he carried us up to bed and tucked us in, kissing our foreheads, and through all of it, his hands were coated in blood that never darkened, never washed away, spilling over our hair and skin and the lavender-and-white gingham sheets.

All the pain and suffering Shira and her family went through afterward is a big part of why I joined the FBI. A part of me wanted to understand *why*. Why did he do it? Killers were bad men. They were supposed to be noticeably bad men, not my second father. They were supposed to be scary and evil and alone, not laughing and cheering as the girls outhit the boys at the local Little League home run derby while the rest of his family laughs along with him.

That desire to know and understand, to make sense of it, got me to the academy. What got me through it, and what's kept me in the FBI since, is realizing how many other families go through that trauma. We help the victims.

That includes the families of the perpetrators. Some know, or suspect. Some very, very few don't care. Others are too scared to leave or tell anyone. The rest are blindsided, shattered, and left with the consequences, with the abuse from neighbors and friends and media, even from law enforcement and courts.

How could they not know?

Because someone good enough to avoid suspicion for twenty years didn't manage that by showing his evil to his family. He gave them all the good in him and then went a safe distance away from them to let that evil out against others.

It can be hard for law enforcement to have sympathy for the families of murderers and rapists. We tell ourselves *we'd* know. *We'd* suspect. As if our loved ones don't exist in an enormous blind spot.

Mercedes is amazing with child victims. Bran will always be a shoulder for their siblings. Cass has a background in forensics and is usually our best liaison with other law enforcement. I'm the one who talks to the families of the people we suspect or arrest.

I'm the one who says it's not their fault.

"A call from the prison?" I ask when she doesn't continue. "Not from him?"

"Right."

"Ma kore itakh, Shira?"

"He's in the hospital. Massive stroke. Hasn't woken up yet." She takes a slow, deep breath, releases it even more slowly. "They think he's going to die. They need to know if we want to see him, so they can put us on a list of approved visitors for the guards."

"Shit."

"Yeah." We sit in silence for a while, save for the creak of the gently swaying hammock and a couple of my neighbors arguing by the hot tub and grill two stories down. "So," she says eventually, "what's wrong with you?"

"Mamá? *May I put some candy in my lunch today,* por favor?"

Xiomara Eddison looked down at her daughter, her hands still in Faith's lunchbox. She examined the contents—juice box, apple, sandwich, tiny baggie of carrot sticks—and nodded. "I think we can do that."

Faith cheered and bounced in place, clapping her hands.

Smiling, Xiomara reached for the bag of candy above the fridge. Less than a week after Halloween, it was still bulging with offerings. "Three small things," she instructed, holding open the bag. "And no gum at school."

Faith dropped the gum back into the bag. After a minute or two of rooting through, she found what she wanted and gave them to her mother for her lunchbox. "Is Stanzi going to be back at school today?"

"Not today, sweetheart. She's still contagious."

Faith sighed and draped herself against her mother in a way she seemed to be learning from her big brother. "She's been contagious forever," she complained.

"I know it feels that way."

"And Amanda's gone too. Why do they have to be gone at the same time?"

"Amanda's abuela *died,* mija; *she didn't plan this."*

Faith sighed again. "I know. I just wanna whine about it 'cuz it's unfair."

Xiomara laughed and leaned down to kiss her daughter's head. "Now where did you learn that?"

"Stanzi's papá," she answered. "He says sometimes it just feels good to whine and get it out, even if you know it's not going to change anything."

"I suppose that's true. Now, Brandon has cross-country after school—"

Faith's nose wrinkled.

"—yes, he'll come home smelly, and we'll shove him in the shower before dinner." She laughed along with her daughter, then continued. "But the practice means he won't be there to walk you and Lissi home after, and Rafi can't do it because he's got football."

"Could Manny do it? He doesn't have anything after school yet."

"Manny is suspended for fighting, so his tío is putting him to work today."

Faith's nose wrinkled again.

"So you and Lissi have to promise to stay together, all right? Don't wait around talking to anyone or trying to play a little longer at the playground. Go straight to Lissi's. If you don't have any homework, you can read during her piano lesson, okay?"

"Okay."

When Xiomara walked her daughter over to Lissi's house, Manny was there, waiting. His eye was still puffy and swollen and multi-colored from the fight that earned him the suspension. He gave Xiomara a sheepish wave.

"Morning, Tía Xio," he mumbled.

"Manuelito."

He cringed. "Tío isn't coming until close to nine. Mamá said I could walk the girls to school."

"And if I call Angelica, is she going to tell me the same thing?" she asked.

"Sí, Tía. Promise."

"All right then. Girls, as you're walking, make sure you listen to Manuelito."

The two eight-year-olds giggled over Manny's long-suffering sigh. At fourteen, he was sure he was too old to be called Manuelito anymore.

Xiomara kissed all three of them, ignoring Manny's teenage squirm, and headed for her car. Normally all four of the girls walked together, with one or more of the older boys escorting them. Today, though, it would be just Faith and Lissi walking home. She wondered if she should arrange to leave work early.

"We're going to be just like the big kids," she heard Faith tell Manny, her voice bright with excitement.

Or maybe not, Xio thought with a sigh. Maybe she was just having a hard time letting her baby girl grow up.

12

Two hours later, I'm showered and wrapped in a pale pink bathrobe that is the softest thing I have ever felt in my life, when my personal cell buzzes with a text from Bran. *Cass went home. We're heading out to Vic's. Want a ride?*

I text back *yes, please,* grab a shirt off a hanger, and leave the closet, closing the door on The Dress.

Like it's that easy.

Every time I tried to talk about my hesitation or reluctance to marry Cliff, every time I tried to give voice to my doubts, he or one of our mothers would shush me and tell me it was just nerves. That I was being unreasonable. That I needed to be grateful for the time and money going into all of these preparations. Or Cliff's version: I thought you loved me, Eliza.

My *aba* worried. He tried not to be too obvious about it, but once, just once, he pulled me aside and said that if I wasn't sure, he didn't care about losing the deposits. He just wanted me to be happy.

And I was not at all happy.

I was miserable. I just wasn't strong enough, or brave enough, or *something* enough to stand up for myself and say NO. And then, two thousand miles away, a grieving father shot at a child murderer who'd just been arrested, and Victor Hanoverian did his job and protected the man in his custody, taking the bullet in his chest. After a while, when it became clear that Vic would never be fully field-fit again, I was offered the transfer to Quantico to join one of the best CAC teams in the country. Finney sat me down and explained that I'd been requested specifically, and that it was a great opportunity if I was interested.

I was interested. I was very, very interested.

Cliff, on the other hand, was baffled. After all, why would I accept a transfer if I was just going to be resigning after the wedding? What, did I really think I was going to be working after we got married? Don't be silly, Eliza. That wouldn't be appropriate, and with such a dangerous job. So unladylike too. I'll provide you with everything you need, Eliza; all you have to do is ask.

Three hours later, I gave notice to my landlord that I was breaking my lease and called Shira to come help me pack my apartment. Cliff wouldn't accept the ring back, claiming that I would come to my senses and he'd be waiting for my apology, so I gave it to Shira to return to him at some point after I left. She tried all the polite ways, and when those failed, she made sure he got the message in spectacular and inimitable fashion.

It involved a jumbotron and an entire Major League stadium of baseball fans laughing at him.

My mother hasn't spoken to me since.

The ring, it turned out, was a lot easier to get rid of than The Dress. I couldn't return it to the store, but donating or reselling it felt a lot like shoving my bad luck off on someone else who certainly deserved a lot better for their own wedding. I hate everything about The Dress, everything it reminds me of. And yet there it sits, like Shelob on her web.

I'm dressed but not completely ready when Bran texts again to let me know they're downstairs. I bundle my wet, unbrushed hair into a knit cap because it's just cold enough outside for that to matter, toss a few things from my work bag into an actual purse, and run down.

Mercedes has the nerve to laugh at me. "You got home before we did. What have you been doing all this time?"

"Talking to Shira. Her dad had a massive stroke."

Mercedes grimaces. Three years ago, her father—also in prison, though not the same one and not for the same crimes—was diagnosed with pancreatic cancer, and her family tried to guilt her into asking a judge to release him on mercy. It wasn't just that she was an agent and they thought that might have extra influence. She was also his victim. After he died, still in prison, the family that hadn't stopped trying to bring her home—whether she wanted to come home or not—finally turned away, and Mercedes was . . . relieved, I think. Like the weight of the world lifted off her shoulders. So she understands the situation the Sawyer-Levys are facing now.

Next to Mercedes in the backseat, her girlfriend gives a small wave. We met Ksenia Rozova a little over a year ago when we worked a child trafficking case. Ksenia is an international human rights lawyer and anti–sex trafficking activist, and she stepped in to represent the victims we rescued. Mercedes was instantly smitten. Utterly professional, but to those of us who know her well, so smitten. A week after the case wrapped up, Ksenia sent an email asking Mercedes to dinner.

They're wonderful together, even if Mercedes can get a little reserved sometimes. Her previous relationship ended badly, and it's hard not to expect everything to go tits up again. It took all of three group dinners for Ksenia to become family, mostly because of Vic. He adopts daughters like some old women adopt cats; he can't help it.

Our team, minus Cass, who lives over in Fairfax, forms a strange sort of triangle through our part of Manassas, each leg about fifteen minutes long. It used to be me and Bran at one point, our apartment complexes only two streets separate. Now it's Bran and Mercedes, but there's something weirdly comforting about all of us being roughly equidistant from each other.

Vic lives in an older neighborhood, the houses settled and maybe a little saggy. The kind of neighborhood that has parties together, and a semi-annual yard sale day, and people make arrangements with each other to help with yards or pools or repairs. About halfway down the long street from Vic's house, there's a little park with a playground and a couple of benches where we sometimes gather to share a cigarette after a particularly tough case.

We park on the street and head up the fairly new ramp to the porch. Vic and his brothers, plus a handful of nieces and nephews, got together to build it after Marlene had to admit she needed her walker more often than not and the ramp would be easier than stairs. We helped, too, and afterward we laughed and watched all the grandkids carefully dip their hands into trays of paint and press them against the side of the ramp. It's one of a number of small changes around and in the house, most of which started not long after her strokes.

They're not serious strokes—not like Shira's father's—but they're small and somewhat frequent and have a way of clustering together. Marlene is in her nineties, but she's always seemed twenty years younger, healthy and active and still teasing her children at every opportunity. Now she's slowing down, her age growing more apparent. Anything Vic can do to make things a little easier or more comfortable for her, he's going to do. And with the ramp already in place for the walker, it's also there for the wheelchair she has to use the first week or so after a stroke, and increasingly more often as time goes by, however much she fights it.

Jenny Hanoverian, Vic's wife, greets us at the front door, a Virginia hostess to her bones. She thanks us for coming, asks us how we are, kisses us all on the cheek, tugs Bran down by his coat for a second round when he squirms the first time, and scolds me for going out with wet hair in this weather, all in one breath. We peek into the kitchen first, with the coat closet right beside it, and find Marlene sitting on a high-backed stool near the long counter, guiding Victoria-Bliss through shaping a raw pastry shell. Victoria-Bliss has the tip of her tongue pinched between her teeth in concentration, eyes narrowed . . . and her feet planted on a step stool so she can comfortably work on the counter, because she's all of five-foot-nothing when she swells with fury. Even Cass is taller by an inch or so, which cheers Cass immensely.

Bran eyes the step stool and visibly decides not to comment. Instead, we put away our coats and hats and retreat to the living room.

Vic is in his comfortable armchair, the leather faded in places from years of regular use, Ian next to him on a matching chair, while Inara and Priya press together on the loveseat. The girls—women, really, they're twenty-five—look up and grin in greeting. Priya's added more color to her hair since the last time we saw her in person, leaving only about half of her hair black and the other half swirling through four or five different shades of blues. A blue-and-clear crystal stud set in silver glitters at one nostril, matched by a similar bindi between dark eyes lined with perfect black wings and soft silver-and-white shadows. As always, her mouth is a bold slash of red, a challenge and a snarl no matter what the rest of her face is doing. A thin silver band loops over the center of her lower lip, something she picked up from her mother.

Inara is nearly the same height, with pale brown eyes and the golden-brown skin of her mother's Polynesian ancestry. She doesn't have Priya's expressiveness, but rather sits back to watch and observe before deciding what reaction she's going to allow to show. That trait softens somewhat here in Vic's house, in the suite he built for the girls over his garage so they would always have someplace to stay, but it's always going to be a part of her. Her dark hair is long enough for an inch or two to pool around her thighs on the cushion.

They're a striking pair, a striking group when Victoria-Bliss is with them, with her frost-pale skin and a mass of curls so deep a black they look nearly blue in some lights, her eyes so blue they almost look violet. The Gardener did so love to collect lovely girls. These three are beautiful and fierce and fully capable of savaging anyone who thinks to know them by those looks alone. They're formidable, wonderful friends to have.

"Rush out to see us, did you?" Priya asks, biting back a snicker.

"I needed to wash my hair but didn't have the time to dry it." I sprayed it with detangler when I pulled it out of the towel, but I wish I'd thought to throw that in the bag with the brush, because I'm pretty sure the knit cap just leeched it all out. I attack the ends and barely get an inch in when Bran takes the brush from my hand and sits on the arm of the long couch where Ksenia and Mercedes are sitting.

He points in front of him, using the brush.

"I can brush my own hair."

"Not if you're doing that to it."

Inara and Priya lean into each other to muffle their giggles. They're fully grown adults, hard-working professionals, but here with this cobbled-together family, they act more like the teenagers they never really got to be, too shaped by their experiences to be young.

I give up and stand in front of Bran. If he needs to take care of someone right now—even if that means being a little smothering—okay. I can deal.

"He used to be the best hair braider in his neighborhood," Ian says, and the girls pop up like meerkats to regard him. They can always smell a story. "I'd come to pick him up on a Saturday morning and there'd be a line of little girls on the porch."

I don't even have to look behind me to know that Bran's blushing. Of course he is.

"Did he charge them?" asks Inara.

"Just a hug and a thank-you."

"Sometimes the *mamás* would send along food," Bran mumbles. As if braiding hair for food was more macho than doing it for affection.

Inara smiles slightly, sadly—more at the sight of Bran doing the work than at the braided crown that forms the end result. All the Butterflies in the Garden used to have to keep their hair up so the massive wings the Gardener tattooed on their backs wouldn't be covered, and they got very good at doing each other's hair. Simple when they just needed it up, intricate when they were bored, which was often.

Sometimes, when the memories are raw and more painful than usual, the survivors can't stand to have anyone touch their hair, can't have it up at all.

We heal, mostly, but even scars can bleed. The young women adopted by this team know that better than most.

Then again, I think, as Bran's fingers move over my hair, tucking away or smoothing down stray wisps like he used to do for his sister and her friends, so does this team.

13

Dinner is lively, and the careful avoidance of so many uncomfortable subjects is so practiced, so smooth, it doesn't even seem awkward when someone brushes up against the boundary of one of those forbidden areas. Mostly. I head into the kitchen to make some tea—I've gotten two of Vic's three daughters hooked on it when they've been home from school—and hear heavy footsteps follow me. "Would you like some tea, Ian?"

He chuckles, moving to sit on the almost-circular bench in the breakfast nook. "Thank you, yes."

Vic's tap is old and a little slow, so it takes a while to get enough water into the kettle. Once it's on the burner, I pull down one of the tins of tea. There's an entire drawer of novelty tea infusers, many of them gifted by Priya, who frequently pops across the Channel to England when she's home in Paris. I sort through them, pulling out one that links via chain to a floating rubber ducky, and another with a flailing astronaut that clips over the edge of the cup. The filled infusers go into two mugs, and I set them by the stove to wait.

"My first time meeting Inara and Victoria-Bliss," Ian says as I sit across from him.

"You've heard about them, surely."

"Often." He laughs again. "Haven't heard Brandon so aggrieved since he was a teenager. They have a gift for pushing his buttons, so I hear."

"They really do. They mostly mean well, anymore. They sort of broke each other in."

"The girls? Or Brandon?"

"It was a mutual experience, from what I hear. It took him and the girls a while to decide they actually like each other."

The kettle shrieks and I get up to turn off the burner. A minute later I return to the table with the mugs, setting the one with the astronaut infuser in front of him. "It'll need a few minutes."

He looks morosely into the mug. "Doc wants me to cut the caffeine. Switch to tea."

"A lot of teas have caffeine, some of them more than coffee, even. Did the doctor give you a list?"

"No, he didn't."

"I can write one out for you if you like."

"Thank you. There's no hurry."

He's followed me into the kitchen to say something, to have some particular conversation, but he doesn't seem ready to start it. I tap the floating ducky, watching it bob on the surface of the slowly darkening water. Three and a half minutes of silence later, laughter and conversation drifting out from the living room down the hall, I pull out the infusers and set them on a folded paper towel.

"I wasn't sure I believed him at first when he told me you two were dating," he says finally. "Just about everyone had given up hope that 'Brandon' and 'dating' would ever be said together."

I swirl my tea in the mug, then take a sip.

"Even his mother didn't ask him if he was going to settle down and get married. He was always going to drift through flings and bar meets and things that didn't ask anything of him. And then, thirty-eight years old, he suddenly has his first girlfriend. A teammate, no less."

"Someone who, at first glance, looks enough like his missing sister to be unsettling?"

He nods, eyeing me appraisingly. "You're good with connections, Eliza, with connecting the dots. Seeing the pattern. Valuable skill for an agent."

"Not always a valuable skill for a girlfriend."

"Heh, no, I'd imagine not," he chuckles. "It can seem a bit like mind-reading."

Mercedes's ex-girlfriend used to yell at her about "using her agent voice" to calm her down when she was freaking out about something. No matter how separate we keep our lives from our work—and no one on this team is very good at that—some things simply bleed through, whether by training or by instinct.

"And now that the impossible has happened, everyone wants to know when he's getting married and having kids."

"Xio and Paul don't push," I protest.

"No, his parents don't, but the rest of the family does, and half the neighborhood. They can't see the miracle that's him dating in the first place. Three years together. It's impressive."

That's when it clicks. "Ian Matson, are you giving me a shovel talk?"

He at least has the grace to look sheepish, and takes a giant gulp of too-hot tea to mask his flush.

"You are. That is absolutely what this is."

"It's nearly what this is," he manages. Then he sighs and scrubs a hand over his face, and just like that, he looks as old as when he stepped into the conference room this afternoon. Older than he is, maybe as old as he feels. "Connie and I never had children. Never tried to find out why, because neither of us wanted the other to feel guilty. Brandon's the closest thing we've ever had to a son. And I'm not afraid you'll hurt him. People hurt each other, especially when they love each other. What matters is why, and what you do after."

"You're worried about him."

"What if this is as far as he can get?" he asks quietly. Bran's outside, well beyond hearing range, but it's still not something to share with everyone in the living room. "He made such a big step, and now he's just stuck there."

"You realize that's not inherently a bad thing, right?" I ask carefully. "If this is as far as he goes, that's okay, as long as I understand that."

"And do you?"

"His issues aren't the only things keeping us where we are, Ian."

He actually looks surprised at that. I know I've never told him about it, but I really thought Bran or Xio would have.

"I was engaged for a while. Before I came to Quantico. I was bullied into it, didn't know how to get myself out of it."

"What happened?"

"I got myself out of it." I smile, but it's tighter than I'd like. "On what was supposed to be my wedding day, Bran and Mercedes took me to a bar and spent the entire day pouring drinks into me. That was only a couple of weeks before he got shot in the leg."

"And you two started dating."

"After we clarified some of the things he'd said while on painkillers."

"Hell of an origin story."

"I was terrified. I'd come to like him a great deal, in a completely different way than I liked Mercedes, and what if everything went wrong? What would happen to the team, to my standing and reputation in the Bureau? What if . . ." I swallow hard. "What if I lost myself again?"

Ian watches me gravely, and one of his callused hands comes to rest over mine.

"In some ways, saying yes to him was even harder than saying no to my ex," I admit for what may be the first time. "Mainly because I liked Bran a hell of a lot more, even then. It wasn't a marriage proposal; he wasn't asking me to move in with him. He was just asking me on a date. But it was Bran, and it felt like even more of me was at risk."

"You said yes."

"I said yes, and despite some lingering fears, I haven't regretted it. Some of those fears are still there, though. He's not the only reason we stay as we are, Ian. He bought a house."

He nods slowly. "I'd wondered. I thought there'd be an announcement."

"His bedroom and his living room look exactly the same as they did at his apartment, right down to the framed black-and-white photos Priya took of Special Agent Ken's worldwide adventures. He's shown those to you, surely, the Ken doll in the FBI jacket? The ones he keeps over the television? He hasn't put anything up in the hallways or other rooms, hasn't even furnished any other rooms, much less decorated. I don't think he can."

"Why not?"

"Because before he can do anything to a room, he has to know what it's going to be. Guest room? Office? Man cave?"

Ian snorts.

"He can't furnish The House because he doesn't know what its future is. Is it his place? Could it be ours? But he's so determined not to push me into something I may not be ready for that The House is just frozen in place. He's the reason he can't call it home; I'm the reason he can't make it one."

"Your ex . . . you say he bullied you into the engagement?"

"Not just him. Our mothers too."

"But he bullied you."

"Not . . . not like that. Cliff never hit me. Never threatened to. When he was angry, he'd either ignore me or lecture me like a child."

There's a thought, an impression of some sort, lurking behind his eyes. He doesn't share it, though.

"Do you know why Brandon was so resistant to the idea of dating anyone?" he asks suddenly.

I shake my head. We've talked about the fact of it, never the facts behind it. Even then it was mostly from the stance of "I've never been in a relationship before, so I'm going to screw things up sometimes and badly," which was a bizarre conversation for the two of us to flounder through when he was still intermittently on Vicodin.

"He couldn't protect Faith."

I blink at him, open my mouth to speak, and realize I have no idea what to say. "That . . ."

"Wasn't his fault," he agrees. "There is not a thing in the world he should have done differently that day. But it made him more protective of Faith's friends. He got offered a full ride to the University of Miami, and he wasn't going to accept it because it meant being too far away to protect Lissi, Stanzi, and Amanda. We had to talk him into it."

"He didn't date because that was someone else he might fail to protect."

"First time I saw a picture of you, I nearly lost my mind. What the hell was he thinking? To have shaped so much of his life around his missing sister, and the first time he dates someone, you look enough like Faith to need a minute and a third and fourth look. Thought I'd need to dig back into the psychology books. Took him a while to convince me that he liked you in spite of your looks, not because of them."

Closing my eyes, I slump against the table and laugh helplessly. "Er . . ."

"Oh, Ian. If I didn't understand the context of that statement, my perfectly healthy sense of vanity would be mortally offended."

He's blushing so hard his cheeks are practically glowing above his beard. "I didn't mean that the way it came out."

"Yes, you did," I giggle.

"Yes, I did," he sighs.

"And here I thought all the laughter was in the living room," Bran says, walking into the kitchen.

Ian looks up at him and freezes, wide-eyed, and I burst out laughing again. Bran looks between the two of us, clearly curious, but I'm laughing too hard to talk and Ian's blushing too badly to ever want to talk.

Shaking his head, Bran absently kisses me on the temple on his way to the coffee maker on the counter. "I am not asking," he mutters.

That sets Ian off into his great big Santa laughs, belly-deep and loud.

Still shaking his head, Bran walks back out of the kitchen without another word.

14

We don't stay particularly late at Vic's, even with the lure of the girls' arrival. It's been a long few days, and with no real leads, the next few days will likely be worse. And then, too, there's the meeting in the morning to walk Watts and Dern through Ian's suspicions. On our way out, Priya grabs me and hugs the absolute stuffing out of me.

"I know you can't talk about the case," she whispers into my ear, "but is he going to be okay?"

"Okay-ish," I answer, using the word she introduced into the team's vocabulary. I squeeze back and kiss her cheek. "Just be you. That'll help more than you know."

"This sucks."

"Yes, yes, it does."

She laughs softly and gives me a small push out the door. "I'm glad he's got you, you know."

"He has all of us. You know, in whatever way doesn't make that sound like he has a harem."

She just laughs harder and turns away.

Priya Sravasti is a profoundly sneaky person. It's not a bad thing, certainly I'm not making moral judgment upon her, but she is very, very sneaky and uses it the most for the people she loves. Knowing how long it takes Bran to drive between Vic's house and my apartment, granting time for both a general farewell and a private goodbye, getting up the stairs, changing to pajamas, and settling onto the bed or couch, she sends a text exactly at the moment that I'm comfortable enough to try to let the day go. I'd call it coincidence, but it's happened too often to be accidental.

The message has a link, no context. I click it, reading through the article that pops up. A woman's fiancé and his best man—her brother— were on their way to the church for their wedding when they were stopped behind an accident. A school bus on a weekend field trip got hit by a semi. They got out of their car to help get the children off the bus, some of them injured, all of them scared, and were still on the bus when the gas tank the rig was hauling exploded. The bride had just gotten into her dress when they got the call from the state trooper on the scene. She was a widow barely an hour before she was actually a wife, and she lost her brother as well.

It's a long article, focusing on her grief and the ways she slowly began working through it, the things that held her back or tripped her up along the way. And she talks about the dress, how she hated the sight of it but couldn't get rid of it.

Like I said, Priya is sneaky.

Eventually, on what would have been her fifth wedding anniversary, this woman went to town on her dress. She cut the dress into strips, took nonpuff 3-D fabric paint, wrote a message on each strip, then dropped them all into a punch bowl to be drawn at random.

You can be sad today; go through the photo albums.

Make cupcakes and give them away.

Sand and paint the splintering bench.

Buy two bouquets. Keep one—you deserve it. Give the other to someone who looks like they need it.

Unwrap the last wedding gifts. It's time.

There are dozens of strips with instructions ranging from silly and sweet to heartbreaking and hard, but all of them have a common theme: mourn and move forward. Be kind to yourself.

Barely two minutes after I finish the article, there's another text from Priya. *What is it that's holding you back?*

I don't know. Not really.

Every time, I try to understand, and I don't. I just don't. I don't know why I can't get rid of the fucking dress, why I think keeping it will stave off some disaster.

But Priya knows that, so she doesn't push it further. But as I fall asleep next to a teddy bear in an FBI windbreaker sitting on what's long since become Bran's pillow, I think of the first strip of instructions. *You can be sad today.*

How many of us allow ourselves to just sit with a feeling like that rather than try to conquer it or push it out of the way?

Too few hours later, my alarm brings me out of bed with uncomfortable fuzziness in my head. I end up drinking half my carton of orange juice before the sugar high flings me into something like wakefulness. It also makes my hand twitch and shake as I try to button up my shirt. Yes, today is off to a wonderful start.

When I arrive at the conference room, bakery box in my hands, Gala is already there, adding a third monitor to her set-up. No, not a monitor; a television.

"Morning," she says, mumbling around the two cords between her teeth.

"You're here early."

"I couldn't sleep," she sighs. "I kept thinking of Detective Matson's files. I gave up and came in to scan what he had so I could throw together a presentation for the meeting." She takes the cables out of her mouth and plugs them into the new monitor. "We can cast it to the TV, and this way everyone will be looking at the same thing at the same time while he's walking Agent Watts and Agent Dern through it."

I plop the box of cupcakes on the table. The bakery lady looked at me askance when I asked for them, but yesterday's leftovers were still fresh enough to sell, and maybe the article from last night was still on my mind when I was deciding on breakfast. I grab one that's supposed to be strawberry-lemonade and carefully peel away the paper. "Understand, before I say this, that I'm well aware I'm being somewhat hypocritical and that it's something I and every person on this team is still struggling with, but that it has to be stated as a goal and piece of advice regardless."

She looks at me and blinks.

"Cases do this. Especially when you're new. They get in your head and don't want to let go, and you find yourself trying to give everything you have to it even when you're not here."

"Yeah. That's what it feels like."

"It takes time to find that balance. Sometimes you'll get it better than others. This was a good idea, and it will probably help, but it's not something you're always going to be able to do."

"What do you do?"

"You mean when I don't accidentally stay up all night working on it?"

She laughs and sinks down into her chair. "Sure."

"I keep a book of crossword puzzles beside the bed. If, after five puzzles, the urge to come in hasn't subsided, I give up and come in. Maybe sixty percent of the time I can manage to stay put, get it out of my head at least enough to rest, even if I can't sleep. Ramirez does the same thing with logic puzzles. Eddison DVRs every baseball game he can find in the listings. Kearney watches the really gross forensics documentaries they don't show until after normal people are sleeping."

That makes her giggle, and some of the shadows leave her eyes.

I bite into the cupcake, or try to. The frosting is taller than the cake portion, and it smears across my nose. I barely pull it away in time to sneeze.

"Bless you," says Gala, eyeing the cupcake. "Alternate bites?"

"Between what, mostly sugar and all sugar?"

"You're the one who brought them."

"I did not properly anticipate the difficulty of actually consuming them."

She grins and reaches for one frosted with a skyscraper swirl of cotton-candy pink and blue. "Is there an occasion?"

I shake my head. "I'm being kind. Or something."

That earns me a queer look, but she doesn't ask for clarification.

Yvonne is the next one to come in, and she scolds me for the cupcakes, which are Not, as she informs me, peeling back the wrapper on a triple chocolate one, Breakfast Food. She finishes with a groan and a smear of frosting on her nose, because the cupcakes really are that good.

Watts brings Dern in with her. Agent Samantha Dern is probably a decade or so Vic's senior, a stately, straight-backed older woman who makes no attempt to hide or soften her age. Her hair is silver-white, edging over into the kind of yellow bleached bone that age brings, but her eyes are clear and bright. I've never been scared of her like most of the other agents I know, largely because I haven't done anything to piss her off before, but also because she reminds me a great deal of Marlene Hanoverian. The Dragonmother of Internal Affairs doesn't roar or flame unless it's required. Up until that point, you are her agent, and she will protect you and support you with everything in her.

She's who I'd very much like to be in forty or fifty years.

She smiles at the cupcakes and selects one that's raspberry and white chocolate, using the baking liner to twist off a good three-quarters of the icing. That she places back in the box for anyone desperate for a sugar rush, leaving herself with a cupcake that can manageably be eaten.

Watts puts another box of protein bars on the table. "There are not enough eggs in cupcakes to count as proper protein," she informs us. She does, however, take a cupcake.

Vic, Bran, and Ian arrive together. Bran doesn't look like he slept at all. His jaw is dark with stubble, and his grey-streaked curls flop around without any attempt at taming.

Looking at the bakery box, Vic sighs. "Eliza, you do not give me hope that I can talk Holly out of pizza for breakfast."

"She's twenty-five and paying her own bills; it's an efficient use of leftovers."

"It's no worse than Brittany's cake-in-a-mug breakfasts," Yvonne points out.

"Holly's older; I'm working on them in order." He shakes his head and takes his seat. "Cass and Mercedes and the rest of Watts's team are on their way up to Richmond, with the exception of the Smiths, who are still with Brooklyn's grandparents."

"They really didn't get anything out of them yesterday?" I ask.

"Bluster and outrage," Bran replies, sitting down between me and Ian. "They should have better luck today."

"Any particular reason?"

"We got a notice from TSA," Watts says. "A couple of weeks ago, Brooklyn's grandparents bought three plane tickets to Orlando for today's date."

"Three?"

"Three. They have a winter home in Kissimmee. And the third ticket is listed for Brooklyn Mercer."

I blink at her. "Are you serious?"

"As a heart attack. We called Alice and Frank Mercer; they confirmed that his parents had not approached them about taking Brooklyn on a trip. The Smiths should be able to lean on them more firmly with this information."

"But we still can't arrest them?" asks Gala.

"It's suspicious, certainly, but it's not proof that they took Brooklyn. Or arranged to have her taken, I should say, as the Smiths verified their whereabouts all day Thursday. They'll keep us updated."

Agent Dern delicately clears her throat. "Shall we begin?"

When Gala said she put Ian's files together into a presentation, she was definitely underselling her work. She also pulled the addresses for each girl's home and where she was last seen, with the usual routes marked out, included descriptions of the neighborhoods, and noted that each girl lived in a house in a mid-middle-class neighborhood rather than an apartment, mobile home, or mansion. It's solid work, and I can see Yvonne fairly glowing with pride. Dern and Watts listen intently, their attention fixed equally on Ian and the PowerPoint. Dern also glances at Bran from time to time.

Realistically speaking, Agent Dern is the deciding vote here. Vic is not impartial when it comes to Eddison, and Watts is the one whose investigation could potentially be derailed if we pursue this. "Agent Sterling?"

"Yes, ma'am?"

Vic shakes his head, mouth silently forming *ma'am*.

"If we proceed in this direction, what would be your first action?"

"Get the full files for the other four girls and see what other commonalities jump out. Obviously, if the same person or people are in multiple cases, that's a solid jump point, but the more information we have, the tighter we can filter the search to see if there are other victims."

"Do you think there are other victims?"

"There would almost have to be."

"Meaning?"

"Erin Bailey disappeared twenty-seven years ago, Faith Eddison twenty-five." I can feel Bran's habitual flinch against my knee. "But then Caitlyn went missing twenty-one years ago, Emma fifteen years ago, Andrea seven. If they were the only ones, why such a staggering difference in time between abductions? I'd also want to contact Agent Sachin Karwan."

"He's stationed in Omaha now," Bran murmurs.

"Erin was his little sister's best friend," I continue. "If he's looked into it on his own as an agent, using Bureau resources, he might have more information than what's in the investigation file we can get from

Chicago PD. It might not be enough to find Erin on its own, but it could help in combination with other things we discover."

Gala, looking somewhat awed and terrified, looks over at Yvonne, who nods encouragingly. She gulps but sits up straight and squares her shoulders. "We can organize the data mining into rounds of searches," she says, her voice a little squeaky. But she's a brand new analyst brave enough to speak up in front of two team leaders, the unit chief, and the head of Internal Affairs. Only being a little squeaky is damn impressive. "It'll be faster and more accurate than trying to create one cohesive algorithm."

"How do you mean?" asks Watts, sliding Gala a protein bar.

I'm pretty sure Watts uses protein bars to give reassurance and demonstrate affection.

"Agent Sterling already has a national search on the physical descriptions," she explains. "From there, we can filter it by time of year, keep everything in October and November, and discard the rest. Then we can sort out the middle-class neighborhoods of houses. By that point, the list should be more manageable, and we can start filtering by the details we're not as sure of, like the fact that so far they've all been two-parent homes."

"Why eliminate apartments or trailers entirely?"

"Apartments are too close together and it's a lot harder to hide someone," I answer. "Depending on the way the lease is written, the property owners could potentially give permission for police searches when a life is in imminent danger. Trailer parks, kids tend to form packs of a sort. They look out for each other, and they regard strangers with more hostility than kids with houses and yards and safe areas to play are going to. Even good trailer parks have a bit of us-against-them mentality. Kids would notice if there were people who didn't belong. It's also hard to hide someone in a trailer when people are searching for them. Upper-middle-class neighborhoods are often gated or security conscious, frequently with posted cameras. Lower-middle-class are likely to be in declining areas, where kids walk in groups because of their parents' anxieties."

Nodding slowly, Dern studies Gala over the top of her rose plastic-framed glasses. "That was very good work, Miss . . ."

"Andriesçu," Gala supplies, blushing.

"Miss Andriesçu. Very well done."

"So what do you think, Sam?" asks Vic. "Kathleen?"

Watts props her chin in her hand and looks at the screen, where the final slide of the presentation has the photos of all six girls in a two-by-three grid. It looks like the casting call for Heartwarming Blonde Girl in Hallmark Christmas Movie #6. "Our team has been down an analyst," she says eventually, "but Rick's back today from medical leave. He's on half-days for the first month as he's still recovering, so if we can steal a couple of analysts from the pool for him to direct, he can take over the Brooklyn-specific searching. Gala, Yvonne, and Eliza can head the research into the possible links, and as soon as we get proof it's all connected, we reunite the cases."

"And me?" Bran asks quietly.

He already knows the answer, his dark eyes flinty and challenging.

The Dragonmother meets his gaze without flinching. "If you'd like to work with Rick and his junior analysts on Brooklyn's case, you're welcome to do so for now, but the moment we have proof that she is in any way connected to your sister, Agent Eddison, we have to pull you off the case entirely. And I would prefer, for your own well-being, that you be on paid leave rather than paperwork duty. Or—"

He shifts and resettles in his seat, waiting.

"Or you assist Detective Matson. Be his gofer, the point of contact between him and the teams."

He still looks mutinous.

"Agent Eddison, I am not unsympathetic," Dern says calmly, "but I am thinking of both you and the Bureau in this. As much as the inactivity chafes, as much as you want to be working on this, it will take very little for a defense attorney to claim, convincingly, that you were emotionally compromised through the course of the investigation. If your sister is connected to Brooklyn, if the same person kidnapped them, if I allow you to continue working on this case, then everything you're feeling right now, everything you're going through, will be for absolutely nothing when the court has to release the man who abducted Faith because your presence as a bereaved family member compromised the case."

Bran goes very still, hardly breathing, and across the table, Vic winces.

The Dragonmother isn't roaring or flaming, but she has sharp teeth and claws, and she'll use them out of love even faster than out of fury.

Once it becomes clear Bran isn't going to say anything, Dern turns to Watts. "Give your instructions to Rick, and steal whoever you need from the pool. No more than three. Have your team funnel information through Rick and the juniors. Agent Sterling, help Yvonne and Miss Andriescu set up their searches. Vic will establish the shift in jurisdiction and get you the full case files. Agent Eddison, I will ask you to be the one to contact Agent Karwan. The subject will be understandably painful; it will likely be best coming from you, as we reopen old wounds."

"I'm going to impose a gag order on the departments I contact," Vic tells us. "I don't want this leaking. As soon as the media gets a whiff of what we're thinking, it's going to be a zoo, and our ability to investigate will drop significantly."

"My team will have to be told, but they'll be under strict orders not to speak about it where anyone else can hear them. Last thing we want is this getting to the Mercers." Watts stands and shakes her head, her grey-streaked bob shifting around her face. "Eliza, you know what I'm going to say?"

I sigh and pick up my phone, programming alarms in every hour to keep me from disappearing down the rabbit hole.

"Atta girl."

"Faith, we have to go," Lissi urged. "We promised. Straight home."

"I know, but—"

"I have my piano lesson. If I'm late, my teacher will tell my mamá."

Faith looked down at the pair of books in her arms. She hadn't meant to finish both of them already. She'd been closer than she realized to the end of the first one, and during assigned reading she finished and started the second one. And then during recess it was raining, so she read, and now . . . Now she wasn't going to have anything to read while Lissi was doing her piano lesson, and she wasn't allowed to watch TV with the sound on during the lesson, and she was going to be bored.

She'd already read all of Lissi's books at home.

She hesitated, then looked back up at Lissi. "I won't even be five minutes," she said. "I promise! You start walking. I'll switch these out at the library, and I'll run to catch up!"

"You never spend less than five minutes in a library," Lissi reminded her. "You never spend less than twenty!"

"But—"

"Faith, I have to go."

"I'll catch up," she said again. "I will, Lissi, you know how fast I run. Like Brandon! I'll catch up before your teacher ever sees us."

"We're not supposed to split up."

"I won't be long!" Faith called, already jogging for the library. She knew exactly which books she was going to check out. She'd catch up with Lissi before her best friend had even gotten into their neighborhood.

Only, the books she wanted weren't there.

By the time she found new ones that sounded interesting, it had been a lot longer than she realized. Lissi might even be home by now. Faith shoved the books into her backpack and ran, waving at the crossing guards as she passed them. She got into the neighborhood, still running, but it was harder to breathe, and her side was stitching up.

Her brother made it look so easy to run and run forever. Was that something you figured out how to do as a teenager?

But no, Rafi was the same age as Brandon, and even though he was really fast, it was only for a short distance at a time, and then he'd huff and puff and turn funny colors if he tried to keep going.

She slowed down to a walk, holding her aching side. Lissi's lesson had definitely already started. Maybe she could go sit on the back porch and read? And if the teacher said anything to Lissi's mamá, *well, maybe she and Lissi could say she'd been out back the whole time?*

"Faith? You're not out here all alone, are you?"

She stopped on the sidewalk and looked up. "Umm . . . that depends," she hedged. "Are you going to tell my mamá*?"*

The man smiled. "No, I won't tell her anything."

15

"Let's get the big-picture data up on the board," I say once Dern, Watts, and Vic leave. "As we narrow the searches, we'll add the terms. That way, if we take a wrong turn, we'll know where to go back."

"I've got magnetic clips in my office." Yvonne stands and smooths her blouse, today a pale lemon silk that nearly glows against her dark skin. "I'll be right back."

Ian stands as well, stretching and shaking himself out. "Brandon, before you call your friend, will you help me find the cafeteria?"

Bran and I both turn to stare at him. "Marlene doesn't let anyone leave her house unfed," I whisper. "Is she all right?"

"I want to get something for you ladies," he answers with a wry smile. "Something a little more substantial than cupcakes and protein bars. I doubt Brandon has eaten either."

"Got your visitor's badge?" Bran asks instead of answering.

Gala grins, turning to the whiteboard in order to hide it.

Taking my hand, Bran helps me to my feet. "Any requests?"

"Bacon?"

Yvonne shakes her head from the doorway. "Bacon is not a food group, Eliza."

"But if you pair it with eggs and cheese, it's like a protein super sandwich. Protein is a food group."

By the time Ian and Bran get back with egg sandwiches, hash browns, and fruit cups, the whiteboard that forms one wall of the conference room has been transformed. A panel on the right side has the pictures of the girls hanging from magnetic clips, arranged by year, with their names, hometowns, and dates of disappearance written underneath in Yvonne's careful capitals. On the left side, Gala's blend of lowercase and capital letters, unique but still readable, prioritizes our potential search terms.

Bran flicks through his phone for Karwan's number and punches it into the speakerphone console in the center of the table. He hesitates, though, before hitting send.

"Brandon?" asks Ian.

"We're sure about this? Absolutely sure?"

"As sure as it's possible to be with the information we have," I tell him gently. "I know it's opening old wounds for him. But if he were the one with a potential link . . ."

"I'd want to know." He grimaces, face screwed up with concentration and pain, and then slowly, deliberately, he lets out a long breath. "I'd want to know," he says again. He hits the send button.

I unwrap my sandwich while the call rings through. I've got my notepad at my elbow just in case there's anything particular to add. The sandwiches have been under the warming lights a little too long, making everything just a bit rubbery, but we've eaten significantly worse while working.

"Is this really Eddison?" asks a deep male voice from the speakers. "Brandon Eddison, as I live and breathe, actually making a phone call?"

In spite of everything, Bran huffs a laugh, a smirk lessening the strain on his face. "You're still an ass, Sachin."

"Yes, but I'm an ass you choose to keep around, so who's the greater ass?"

"Sachin . . ." He trails off, looking helplessly at the console.

"Is this a work call or a dear God, this-time-of-year-can-go-to-hell call?"

"It's both."

"Both?"

"I've got you on speaker right now," Bran tells him. "Also in the room are Technical Analysts Jefferson and Andriesçu, Agent Sterling, and Detective Matson, retired Tampa PD."

A long, considering kind of silence greets his words. "I'm not sure which to address first," Karwan says finally, "that you called your girl-friend *Agent Sterling* or that you introduced Ian as *Detective*."

"I've heard a lot about you too, Agent Karwan," Ian says.

"And a pleasure to finally meet you, sir. How can I help?"

"We've . . . that is, recently, we've . . . I've . . . oh damn, Brandon, how do I do this?"

But Bran's eyes are closed, his fist pressed against his mouth. The first time I ever saw that expression on his face, it was a few days after he'd been shot in the thigh and was refusing to take his pain medication. The last time I saw it was this summer when Vic's grand-niece dropped a hammer on his toes.

"Agent Karwan, this is Eliza Sterling."

"Nice to meet you at last, Eliza," he replies. "And please, it's Sachin."

"Our team is one of the two investigating the Thursday disappearance of a Richmond girl named Brooklyn Mercer."

"Saw that on the news. She looks a lot like—"

"Like Erin," I finish once it's clear he won't. "Like Faith."

"Hang on," he says grimly. "Let me get somewhere I can pull over."

"You'd better be on speaker," Bran warns, and gets a rude sound in response.

It's a few minutes before anyone speaks. "All right," says Karwan, "tell me."

"Detective Matson never stopped working Faith's case," I explain. "Over the years, he's noticed several other cases with similarities, specifically in the age and appearance of the girls and when they've gone missing. He wasn't sure they were connected, but with Brooklyn's case hitting the news, he brought them to our attention."

"Similarities."

"Eight-year-old white girls with blonde hair and blue eyes who go missing in late October or early November while they've been walking home from somewhere familiar."

"That's . . . very specific," he says with a precision that hints that what he actually wants to say is not so polite.

"Yes. This morning, we were given the official go-ahead to pursue this lead. Our unit chief is putting in the requests for the official files and establishing jurisdiction, but we wanted to warn you and also ask if you ever looked into Erin's case yourself after coming to the Bureau."

"That would be a misuse of Bureau resources for a personal quest," he says dryly.

"So you still have your notes?"

He lets out a harsh bark of laughter. "Yeah, I've got my notes at the office. Have to keep them there so I don't obsess over them this time of year. Can't say I found much."

"We'll be comparing them to the other cases."

"How many?"

"Including Brooklyn, we're looking at a starting figure of six."

"Starting figure."

"The time between abductions doesn't make sense yet."

"Eddison? Talk to me, old man."

Sighing, Bran sits up straight in his chair only to immediately slump against the cushioned back. "It's not a guarantee, but it's strong enough that we got the go-ahead in the middle of a case with a presumably endangered kid."

"And Erin's on that list."

"Erin's on that list. So is Faith."

"I might have another name for you."

I choke on a grape that I really did mean to chew. Bran puts the heel of his hand against my spine, maybe an inch or two lower than my shoulder blades, and gives a sharp push. I catch the grape when it comes flying out of my mouth and drop it onto a napkin.

"What name?" he asks, looking me over.

Yvonne hands me a bottle of water from her tote bag of doom, which I accept with a grateful nod.

"McKenna Lattimore. She's a cold case here in the Omaha office. Disappeared in ninety-five while walking home from her piano teacher's, two streets away."

"What kind of neighborhood?" asks Gala, already typing in McKenna's name.

"Pretty squarely middle-class houses. Yards, but not big ones."

Gala turns one of the monitors around so we can see a girl with a shy smile, blue eyes almost too big for her face, and soft blonde curls with just a bit of a strawberry tint to them.

I check my ViCAP and NCMEC lists, and there she is on both.

As he watches us, Bran's thumb starts to beat an anxious tattoo against the arm of the chair. Normally he paces when he's agitated, especially when he's on the phone. It's impossible for him to sit still. Now, though, with five of us in the room and with so many computer cables, there's not really enough space. "Can you send us her file too?"

"It was FBI, so you should be able to pull it up. I'll check once I'm at the office to make sure nothing got skipped when they scanned everything in a few years ago. I can also see if the lead detective is still around, see if they've got anything to add."

"Vic's got a gag order to keep this from getting out."

"I'll be discreet. And how is your girlfriend Agent Sterling but your boss is Vic?"

It's not hard to imagine why these two clicked at the academy. Erin and Faith would have been enough to link them, but I've heard stories for years about Karwan's mischief balancing out Eddison's prickliness.

They probably would have been brilliant partners if Vic had been in the market for a full team at that point.

Bran ignores the question. "Sterling's going to be official contact on this one."

"Because you're not officially on this one?"

"Something like that."

"If McKenna proves to belong on your list, that means the Omaha office becomes involved. Specifically, my team."

"We'll let you know as soon as we're reasonably sure," I promise, "and we'll have Vic and Agent Dern draw up a letter for your boss explaining why you have to recuse yourself."

"Text me your contact info; I'll get you the files as soon as I get to the office. And Eddison?"

"Yeah?"

"If there's anything I can do—"

"I know," Bran says softly. "Works the other way around too."

"You'll get something from me soon, Eliza."

"Thank you, Sachin." My nose wrinkles before I can stop it. It's positively strange to greet an agent by first name on the first meeting.

"Talk to you soon."

My work cell dings with an email alert not two minutes later. It's from Vic, though, not Karwan, and I pull it up on the laptop. "Andrea's and Emma's files," I announce. "Chicago PD is promising Erin's in an hour or so, once they finish getting everything scanned into a digital file."

"I'm surprised they haven't done that already," murmurs Gala.

"City like Chicago, that's a huge endeavor, and not a lot of manpower to devote to it. They get files digitized as they can. Atlanta is being resistant, Vic says."

"Because she was classified as a runaway?"

"Because the FBI wasn't involved in the initial investigation, and they don't think there's enough evidence to reopen the case or cede jurisdiction."

Bran growls and thumps his fist against his knee. "Unsolved kidnappings don't close. Technically it's not reopening anything."

"Vic's giving it to the Jackal."

Ian tugs at his beard. "The Jackal?" he asks, clearly undecided if he wants to know.

"Agent Hank Jekyll is a unit chief at the Atlanta office, and a friend of Vic's," I tell him. "He doesn't approve of pissing contests between branches of law enforcement, so if he's forced into one—"

"He pisses to win," Bran says, finishing the joke that floats around Bureau offices the Jackal has never even been to. I heard it in Denver before coming here.

"So we'll have Caitlyn's file within a couple of hours. Twenty-one years ago, they'll probably have to scan it in."

"I don't know if we have enough information yet for this to be significant," Gala says, frowning at her monitor, "but there's something that stands out about some of the dates."

"What's that?"

"Erin went missing in ninety-three. Two years later, Faith goes missing. Two years later, McKenna goes missing. Two years later, Caitlyn. Every other year."

Hmm. I look at Bran, but he's glaring at the table. "Make a note of it, but put a pin in it for now. Until we fill in the longer gaps, there's no way to know if that's a pattern or missing data points."

"Got it."

Yvonne has the proud smile again. I don't know if we're actually allowed to have two dedicated technical analysts—a lot of the teams don't even have one, just rotate through the pool—but I have a feeling she'll be asking for Gala to be assigned to her. Hell, I'll ask for Gala to be assigned to our team when all this is done; she has a solid instinct for this.

The first alarm on my phone goes off, making us all flinch.

"And look at that," Yvonne laughs. "You didn't even need it."

16

A bit after one, Ian convinces Bran to take him to pick up lunch for all of us. Bran argues at first, wanting to be here, and initially Ian patiently uses logic to explain why picking it up is better than delivery. Then he huffs and crosses his arms against his chest, muscles pressing against his sleeves despite his age, and Bran abruptly stands to attention, or near enough to it.

"You need to move around," Ian tells him. "You need air, and space, and the freedom to wear a hole in the damn sidewalk. You and I are going outside. You will pace as much as you need to pace, and then we will pick up lunch for ourselves and the ladies and bring it back."

Bran stops arguing.

"I've got another possible name," Gala announces a few minutes later.

"Tell me."

"Shelby Skirvin, from Louisville, Kentucky. Disappeared three years ago while walking home from her grandparents' house. Same kind of neighborhood, also a two-parent home. Date was November 2."

"FBI involvement?"

"No."

The photo is certainly convincing. "All right. Send it to Vic so he can request her file."

She scribbles the information on a piece of paper and slides it over to Yvonne. "I'm recharging my courage," she explains sheepishly.

"For Vic?"

"In general. This morning was a lot."

"Fair enough."

Half an hour later, we add Joanna Olvarson of Oklahoma City, missing since '07, and Tiffany King of Seattle, Washington, Missing Children's Class of '99.

Ian and Bran bring back lunch just before three o'clock, great big foil containers from the family-style Italian place that hates to-go orders if you're not an on-duty FBI agent. Bran picks at his food despite Ian's stern command to eat.

We're still multi-tasking lunch and research when the table console rings with an incoming call. I reach out and poke it with the crunchy end of a breadstick. "Sterling."

"I'm sorry, no, it's going to have to be Eliza."

"Sachin," groans Bran.

"McKenna's file and my notes on Erin are on their way, and I have some other possible names for you."

"That why you took so long?" he grumps, and looks both scared and intrigued.

"It is. Do you remember Carl Addams?"

"Lurch? He's in White Collar here in Quantico. We get lunch sometimes."

"He's married to my cousin, so we keep in better touch. His father was a detective in Charleston. He died last year and Lurch is going through all his papers, and he found out that his father had still been working a couple of old cases, only one of which was actually his."

"Kidnapping?"

"That's what I called and asked him. He knows about Erin, and he mentioned his dad worked a case like that that he couldn't let go of. He went home and opened up the boxes. First file is Diana Shaughnessy, twenty-nine years ago, Charleston."

Our oldest potential case so far.

Gala's fingers fly over the keys.

"Who else?" I ask.

"Lydia Green, from Houston; Tiffany King, Seattle; and Melissa Jones, Sacramento."

"Tiffany!" Gala squeaks, her hands clapping over her mouth.

"We put Tiffany down as a possibility just a bit ago," I explain.

"Before the car accident, his father had just started looking into Miranda Norvell of Las Vegas, and he printed off a mess of articles about the search for Kendall Braun, Madison, Wisconsin."

Kendall was on my lists. "She was just last year." So how does Brooklyn fit into what seems like a clear pattern?

"Miranda and Kendall both had FBI involvement. They've got files you can access, and Lurch is bringing you his dad's stuff."

"Thanks, Sachin. We'll keep in touch."

"Please do."

"I've got another name to consider," Yvonne says as Bran hangs up. "Riley Young, from St. Paul, Minnesota. Five years ago."

"Add her to the list."

I track down the files for Miranda and Kendall on the Bureau intranet. Miranda went missing thirteen years ago. Her file shows much the same as what we've been digging through. She vanished while walking home from the corner store where the neighborhood kids liked to buy treats with their allowances. I open Kendall's. Something about Kendall feels familiar, like maybe I caught one of the press conferences back when she was first missing, but I can't . . .

A heavy knock hits the conference room door. "Yoooouuu raaaang?" says a slow, artificially deep voice.

Bran rolls his eyes. "Come on in, Lurch."

"For heaven's sake." Yvonne sighs and shakes her head. "Why on earth would you call someone Lurch?"

The door opens, and the man behind it actually has to bend over to fit into the room. He must be over seven and a half feet tall in his stocking feet. Question answered. He carefully sets a plain cardboard file box on a clear spot on the table. Or an almost clear spot, which is as close as it gets.

Bran introduces everyone perfunctorily, eyeing the box.

"I flipped through the rest of Daddy's paperwork just in case," Agent Addams says in a distinct Charleston accent, "but these were the only ones that seemed pertinent. I sorely hope they can help." After the fake Lurch voice, his actual light tenor is almost a shock.

"I'm sure they will," I tell him. "Thank you for taking time out of work to get them."

"If there's anything else I can do, please let me know. And don't fret; Sachin told me about the gag order. I won't say anything. I'd appreciate it, though, if you could see your way to filling me in after. Awful nice if it turns out Daddy's work helped find them after all this time."

Ian stands to shake his hand. "I'll update you myself, Agent Addams. Thank you."

He doesn't linger, and we all dive back into the files. Bran goes into each of the new computer files and sends the headshots to his email, then disappears to the bullpen. A few minutes later, he comes back with printed pictures for the whiteboard.

Frowning down at a handwritten page of notes, Ian sighs and pinches the bridge of his nose.

"Eyes bothering you?"

"Can't tell if it's my eyes or this writing."

I hold out a hand, and he gives me the sheet. "Maybe both."

"He mentions someone before Diana. That's the part that's impossible to read."

Ian's probably never had to try to decipher the notes Eddison takes while holding his Moleskine and walking. I still have to squint a bit where the late Detective Addams accidentally overwrote a few lines. "Karen Coburn, Kansas City, Missouri," I say eventually. "She went missing two years before Diana, back in '87."

Gala promptly does a search. No FBI involvement, so we don't have her file, but there's a memorial website that her family created with pictures of her and links to resources for families of kidnapping victims. She spins the monitor, and we all look back and forth between Karen's and Diana's pictures a few times.

"They look more alike than any of the rest," Yvonne says. "Good Lord, they could be twins."

They really could. They even have the same scrunchie-wrapped high-side ponytail that was so popular in the late eighties and early nineties.

"Her parents spent about a decade traveling and speaking to law enforcement and victim advocacy groups," Gala reports, eyes flicking back and forth across the screen. "They spoke in Charleston six months before Diana went missing."

"Explains why the detective would make the connection. Wonder why he didn't put a file together?"

"Why did he sit on them, like I did?" Ian asks ruefully. "If he had the Coburns on his mind going into the Shaughnessy investigation, he might have dismissed it as bias."

"Fair point." I stare down at Kendall's picture. "Gala, with the exception of Brooklyn, is there anyone who fits all of our factors who disappeared in an even-numbered year?"

"Not yet."

Bran stops pacing back and forth across the far end of the room. "What are you thinking?"

"Gala was right, they're every other year, from Karen thirty-one years ago straight through to Kendall a year ago."

"Except Brooklyn," Yvonne counters. "Does that mean she isn't connected?"

I hold up a finger to ask for patience. "According to her file, the day after she went missing, Kendall's parents gave a press conference explaining that their daughter had a dangerous and unpredictable medical condition. They begged whoever had their daughter to please, for the sake of her life, drop her off at any hospital."

"What was the condition?"

"Inoperable brain aneurysm. Recently diagnosed. She was a ticking time bomb."

Bran stares at me, then turns and leans against the wall, muttering profanities under his breath. In Spanish, from what little I can hear.

"For those of us not on the Eddison-Eliza wavelength?" asks Yvonne.

"Kendall's diagnosis was only a couple of weeks old. Her parents told the lead detective that their extended family didn't know yet, because they were still looking into alternative treatments. Her kidnapper wouldn't have known. Kendall might not even have known."

"How would she not know?"

"Aneurysms are largely asymptomatic until they rupture. They tend to be found while examining other injuries. Like a dodgeball to the head, in Kendall's case. The school notified her parents, parents took her to the hospital just in case, to check for concussion."

"Did the impact cause the aneurysm?"

"No, it's just what helped them find it. But how do you explain that kind of condition to an eight-year-old? 'Hi, sweetheart, you have this thing in your head that could kill you at any time without any actual provocation, okay, go play now'?"

"You and Eddison would have interesting kids."

All of us turn and look at Yvonne. She just shrugs.

"Aneurysms do what they want," I continue after a moment. "Telling her to be very careful when she plays wouldn't have decreased the likelihood of it rupturing. It wouldn't surprise me if her parents didn't want to tell her until there was actually something that could be done."

"But if it ruptured and she didn't know to expect it . . . ," whispers Gala. "She would be so scared."

"Depending on how big it was and how quickly it ruptured, there might not have been time to realize anything was even wrong before she stroked out."

Ian clears his throat. "I'm a little disturbed at you knowing this much about it, Eliza."

"My Theory of Knowledge professor freshman year had a stroke and dropped dead in the middle of class. Turned out he had an aneurysm, and the whole experience was traumatic enough that one of the profs from the UC Denver med school came up and taught us all about it. They didn't want us to think we'd missed any signs or anything."

"That's actually impressive on the part of the university."

"Boulder's full of hippies. They care about feelings."

Yvonne braces her arms against the table, forehead against her wrists. "So you think Kendall . . ."

"As far as we know, not one of these girls has been found, dead or alive," I point out, wincing at the bluntness. "What we have to work off of is that repeated two-year gap. *Two years.* Whoever's taking them, it's extremely unlikely that they're killing or trading the girls right away. Not with that kind of gap. Maybe the girls age out of their abductor's preference, or maybe it's something else entirely. We don't know. But we can reasonably assume those two years are significant. And then they take Kendall Braun, with no idea she has a problem."

"You think she died recently," Bran says hoarsely. "He took Brooklyn to replace her. That's why Brooklyn seems to break the pattern."

"Yes."

He resumes his cursing, thumping the side of his fist into the wall with carefully restrained violence.

What's worse: Not knowing anything about who took your little sister and what was done to her, or learning that she may have been kept for two years, suffering God only knows what, and still not knowing what happened to her after?

Eventually, I clear my throat and look down at my notepad to gather my thoughts. "Gala, for the files we already have, start going through and picking out names in common. Neighbors, teachers, friends, whoever."

"Spreadsheet?"

"Beautiful. Yvonne, can you dig more into the people in Brooklyn's neighborhood?"

"We've already done some digging; how far do you want me to get before we run into the need for a warrant?"

"Who's moved there in the past year? Every one of these abductions is in a different place. This isn't someone who puts down roots."

"Wouldn't this move to the area be more recent?" Ian asks.

"We don't know that. Maybe he kidnaps someone as soon as he's been there long enough to see their habits, or maybe he kidnaps someone just before he leaves for a fresh city to make it harder to get caught. What we can reasonably assume is that the move would have happened after Kendall's disappearance and before Brooklyn's."

"*If* he moved," Gala points out with a wince. "What if it's someone who travels a lot for work? Home base could be anywhere, right?"

"Fuck."

She wilts.

"No, Gala, you're right, and it was good to point that out."

"Check anyway," Bran says roughly. "Just in case."

"I don't need a warrant for DMV," Yvonne says, adjusting one of her monitors. "I can see if anyone in the neighborhood has registered a car from out of state. It's a start, anyway."

Vic and Agent Dern join us around eight, closely followed by Ramirez, Kearney, and all of Watts's team. We've spread out too much for there to be anywhere near enough room to manage it comfortably, but everybody squeezes in enough to close the door, and the temperature in the room feels like it jumps ten degrees.

Ramirez stands behind me, her hands on my shoulders, looking at Faith's picture on the board.

One of seventeen pictures on the board.

"Madre de Dios," she whispers.

"Did you get anywhere with the grandparents?" Vic asks the Smiths.

For what may be the first time since I met them, the Smiths look genuinely angry. Smith the Taller sputters something, cuts himself off, and gestures sharply at his partner.

Smith the Stouter doesn't look any less pissed, but he's more collected. "If you weren't sure how deeply contemptuous they are of their son's life choices, it can be summed up in one sentence: they named their damn dog Brooklyn."

There's complete silence in the room except for the whirr of computer fans.

"I'm sorry?" Agent Dern asks finally.

"They didn't like what Frank and Alice named their daughter, so they got a pure-bred blonde Afghan hound puppy and named her Brooklyn. That's who the third plane ticket was for. They bought an extra ticket so they could put their dog under the middle seat and still have their own space. They gave their goddamn dog the same name as their granddaughter."

Vic groans. "And of course Frank and Alice weren't going to think about that when their daughter is missing and they know the seniors want to take her away from them."

"Are there any actual grounds for the grandparents gaining custody?" I ask. "I mean, it's not like she's abused or neglected; it's not like her parents are scraping by on pennies and going hungry or dressing in rags. She's a healthy, mostly happy kid whose greatest stresses in life seem to be her bullying classmate and her bullying grandparents."

"Frank and Alice's lawyer seems confident there are no grounds, and I certainly can't see any," admits Watts.

Burnside, a laid-back and dry-humored man who has refused four separate attempts to promote him to his own team, reads over the whiteboard. "What is all this?"

"Let's find out," Agent Dern invites. She gestures to Gala. "If you please, Miss Andriesçu?"

Gala flashes me a terrified look.

Then she takes a deep breath, gets to her feet, and walks over next to the pictures. "This is what we've learned so far," she begins, and the briefing that follows may be a little shaky at points, a little rushed and breathless in others, but it's a solid first effort. As soon as Gala drops back into her seat, Yvonne hooks her ankle through the base of the younger woman's chair and rolls it closer so she can give her a hug and a few whispered words. Praise, I expect, and damn but she's earned it.

Ramirez and Kearney are less astonished than Watts's team, but then they had to suspect something. Ian's presence in the middle of a case is an unmissable signal that *something* is going on.

"So what do we do?" asks the last member of Watts's team. Johnson is a little more high-strung than the rest of the team, but her energy also provides a good balance. She loops an elbow around Burnside's neck to stabilize herself as she stands on tiptoe to stare at the pictures.

"We keep looking for Brooklyn," Watts says firmly. "She is our priority. This is a lot of information to winnow through, but it's going to help us find Brooklyn."

Burnside strains around Johnson's arm to see Yvonne's screen. "I've got a DMV filter program I can send you," he offers. "If you get a likely VIN, you can plug it into the program to see every place it's been registered. Little faster than tracking them manually."

"Why are you not a technical analyst?"

"Because I like fresh air."

She spins in her chair and jabs his hip with a finger, then turns back to her work. Burnside prefers fieldwork, but he's undeniably the best with computers on Watts's team.

"We're still waiting for files on a couple of them." I pull up my feet so I can resettle cross-legged in the chair. As a conference room, it's really only meant to hold a team at a time. Two teams plus a few is making me feel a little claustrophobic. "But we've been looking for common names across reports and files, and we'll go from there."

"Do not share this," Vic orders sternly. "This is absolutely hush-hush. We do not want to spark hysteria."

"When do you tell the other families?" asks Smith the Taller.

"When there's something definitive to tell them," Bran snaps. Frustration flares across his face, and he immediately nods an apology.

Smith glances at Faith's picture, immediately linkable to the framed photo on Eddison's desk, and nods in return.

"Go home, get rested up," Watts tells her team. "Right now, this is a lull. Until we have a name, we keep on as we have. But understand that as soon as we have something, we're going to be all-out sprinting to find all the girls."

"How much of a chance—" Johnson shuts her mouth with an audible click of teeth.

"We keep looking for Brooklyn," Watts repeats gently. "She'll lead us to the others."

Her team nods and files out of the room. Ramirez and Kearney stay, anxious and silent.

Agent Dern sighs and pulls off her glasses, letting them fall gently on their necklace chain to rest against her chest. "Agent Eddison."

"I'm on leave."

"Yes." She belatedly folds the arms of her glasses, still regarding him sympathetically. "It wouldn't be remotely fair to ask you to focus on other paperwork while this is happening. There's enough wiggle room that you can remain here with the teams, if you'd like, as someone with intimate knowledge of one of the cases in question, or if you'd like to return home to your family, I'll certainly understand."

For a moment, his lips white with tension, I'm not sure he's even going to answer. Eventually, however, he manages a tight nod. "I'd like to help, if I can."

"All right. Agents Sterling and Ramirez."

"Yes, ma'am?"

Ramirez flicks my ear.

Agent Dern simply smiles. "Technically speaking, I should be pulling both of you off of this as well, but I'm not going to. Be careful with your actions, make good choices, and don't make me regret my decision."

"Understood, ma'am."

Ramirez flicks my ear again.

"With your permission, Sam, I'd like to join them in the field for the duration of this case." Vic holds her gaze when she turns to him. "Let me do this."

She studies him for almost a full minute, then nods. "Provided the section chief has no complaint, I'm willing to hold you to the same terms as your agents."

"Should I say 'yes, ma'am'?"

"Sterling gets away with it because she's sweet. You don't have that to fall back on."

Agent Dern stands and crosses to the door. "Agent Eddison, let's get to my office and get your paperwork sorted." He joins her, and she guides him out with a hand on his shoulder. He stumbles at the gentle pressure, walking beside her, his face caught somewhere between numb and pissed.

Kearney studies the board. "These girls were taken from all over the country."

"That's probably part of how he got away with it."

"Are we assuming he, then?"

"It's more likely, and easier than dancing around it, unless you think we'll cut ourselves off from possibilities."

"I guess it depends on why they're being taken."

"How are we going to do this?" Mercedes asks, her voice soft and scared in a way I haven't heard in a little over three years. Not since blood-covered children started appearing on her front porch with a promise from a killer angel that Mercedes would keep them safe.

"This is a case," Vic says firmly. "It's personal, yes, but this is a case and we work it as a case. If anyone doesn't think they can do that, tell me now. There's no judgment, but we need to not find that out in the middle of things."

We're already in the middle of things.

But Mercedes—and it's definitely Mercedes, not Ramirez—frowns at him. "I mean, how are we going to help Eddison?"

"I'll drive your car back to the cottage, Mercedes," Cass offers. "That way you can drive Eddison's."

"What will he be driving?"

"Nothing. Sterling can take him home. I know he's a terrible passenger, but he shouldn't be behind the wheel right now. I'll stay with you again, and we can come back in the morning."

I press the heels of my hands into my eyes, trying to remember how to breathe. A moment later, Vic's hand is warm between my shoulder blades.

"You should know, Eliza, that whatever he says tonight . . ."

"I know."

When everything is spiraling out of control, no one can dig in and hold steady. Not really. They lash out, desperate to grab onto anything.

They lash out.

Faith had been missing for a week.

Mamá had closed the door to Faith's bedroom on Monday, unable to bear the sight of the empty space. She hadn't been back to work all week, nor had Dad. Brandon missed the entire week of school.

And despite all the fliers and all the news coverage and all the volunteers scouring the city, there'd been no sign of Faith.

Brandon shut his bedroom door and sank back against it, sliding to the floor. His room was its usual state of messy, though not as bad as it was when he was younger. He'd come home from school one day to find his room entirely empty but for a sleeping bag, his alarm clock, and his school things. One day's worth of clothing had hung from his closet door. It took him three months to earn everything back.

His room was maybe a little messier than usual, but neither of his parents cared, if they'd even noticed. They'd all been out looking for Faith at every moment, coming home only to collapse into bed and try to sleep. Downstairs, the kitchen counters and fridge were jam-packed with food the neighbors brought over for them so they wouldn't have to worry about cooking.

Rafi's mamá, Tía Angelica, said Puerto Ricans worry with food. And when Faith was found, and she came home safe, they'd celebrate with food too.

But Brandon could see it in Detective Matson's face, in the faces of the officers and the FBI agents who came to help. A week was too long to be missing and still have hope of finding them again.

Getting to his knees, he crawled over to the pile of dirty clothing at the foot of his bed and started sorting it for laundry. Lissi had barely stopped crying all week, blaming herself. She should have waited, she said; she should have just been late for her lesson or stopped her lesson to call her mamá when Faith didn't come right away.

Brandon couldn't blame her. Faith had promised. Faith broke the rule to always walk together. It wasn't Lissi's fault.

But it wasn't Faith's either.

He stripped the blanket and sheets from the bed, starting a third pile on the carpet. He could remember a time, years ago, when his room was so bad he wasn't even allowed to leave it until it was spotless, except for meals and the bathroom. He sulked for days, refusing on principle to start cleaning because it was his room and he could keep it however he wanted.

Then Faith had started crying. She'd only been two or three then, and already his favorite person in the world. She'd sat on the other side of the laundry hamper blocking the way into his room, bawling her little heart out for B'andy, because she couldn't say his name yet, screaming when their parents took her away without letting her see him. Almost as soon as she started crying, he'd started cleaning his room.

It broke his heart when his sister cried.

"Mijo?"

He stood up too suddenly and swayed, blinking and confused. His mamá stepped into the room to steady him.

"When did you last eat, mijo?" she asked softly.

"This morning, I think."

"It's only just morning," she noted. She looked around, and he followed suit in a daze.

How much time had passed? His room was spotless, everything neatly organized and put away or in a box labeled for donations, his bed made with a clean set. The dirty clothing waited for him in three baskets by the door.

"Ay, mijo," *his* mamá *whispered. "It's not like before. No one's keeping her away because your room isn't clean."*

"Yo sé."

"Do you?" She scratched his dark curls, using the motion to bring him closer against her until his head rested on her shoulder. He was almost too tall for that anymore. "We're not giving up on her, Brandon. Don't you give up on her."

He squeezed his eyes shut against the stinging tears and held on to his mamá. *He didn't notice when his dad came in, only felt his dad's arms wrap around them both.*

17

Bran is silent when Agent Dern delivers him back to us. He's silent while Vic persuades Ian to return to the Hanoverians' to rest, because we can all see how tired he is. He's silent the entire way back to The House, his fist thumping rhythmically against the window of the car. He doesn't respond at all to Mercedes's hushed *goodnight/call me if you need anything* before she crosses the yard to her cottage. For the first time since he bought The House, he doesn't stand at the back door to watch until her interior lights come on.

"We haven't eaten since lunch," I remind him quietly. "Go get changed, and I'll see what you've got."

He walks silently down the hall.

But because this is Bran, the answer to that is almost nothing. The options are ramen, blue box macaroni and cheese, or cereal, and I'm not sure I trust his milk enough for the latter two. It's not like he's going to taste anything anyway. He just needs some food in him, and maybe something hot will help thaw the storm that's building in his eyes.

He slumps into the kitchen a few minutes later, in sweatpants and a long-sleeved Nationals shirt. When I told my *aba* I was dating a Nats fan, he just chuckled about it, but a week later, I received a box full of Rockies merchandise in the mail so I'd remember where I came from. Bran drops onto one of the stools around the island counter.

"Water's still working up a boil, but there'll be soup in a bit." Maybe I should just run out and get him something or get something delivered.

"I gave up on her."

"No, you didn't."

"I did. I gave up on her. Stopped looking." He drops his head to his hands, fingers clenched so hard it must be pulling his hair. I'm not sure if it's helping or if he just hasn't noticed. "Ian kept looking. Sachin kept looking. Lurch's father kept looking."

"And not one of them brought it forward because they weren't sure they actually had anything," I remind him.

"He had her for two years. For two years, she might have been just down the street from me, wondering why we weren't rescuing her."

"Bran—"

"Or maybe you're right, maybe he kidnaps them just before he leaves a city, so if someone sees him with her in a new place, it's just his daughter or granddaughter, nothing to worry about. Maybe it was Erin just down the street from me for two years. Sachin's little sister's best friend, alone and scared and going through—what? What do we think he's doing to them, Eliza?"

"Bran—"

"But I gave up on her."

"You did *not* give up on her. Every person who's ever known you knows that."

"Sachin didn't give up on Erin. He used the Bureau systems to keep looking. He has a folder full of notes and questions because he didn't stop looking for her. He joined the Bureau to help find kids like Erin, and he did not stop looking."

I glare at the water as if that will make it boil faster. Behind me, I can hear the scrape of the stool as he stands, the bang of cabinet doors as he rifles through them, not to find anything but just to move, to make sound.

"Seventeen girls, Eliza. Seventeen."

A cabinet door slams so hard it breaks its hinges, falling to the ground with a clatter.

"Faith was the fourth. The fourth girl, and because we didn't find her, all those other girls got taken. All those other girls—"

Died? But he can't make himself say the word.

Another cabinet door falls to the ground. They've needed replacing since before he bought The House, but he was talking about remodeling the whole kitchen, so it hasn't been done. Now it's getting a remodel whether it wants one or not.

"I walked them home whenever I didn't have something after school. All four of them, Faith and Lissi and Stanzi and Amanda. If I didn't have practice, I walked them home. To keep them safe. I should have been there."

Just a few days ago, Daniel Copernik was thinking the same thing. Probably still is, poor kid.

"It is not your fault Faith walked home alone," I tell him. "And it should have been safe for her to do so, and it wasn't your fault it wasn't."

"Seventeen girls, Eliza!"

"Do you think walking Faith home would have kept him from kidnapping someone else?" I snap back. "If this is something he has to do, he would have taken someone else. Would you still be an FBI agent? Would you still have gotten this case, with this team, with the people to make these connections, Ian and Karwan and Addams? Or would no one have any idea this man was out there?"

"Are you saying my sister needed to disappear so we could solve it now?"

"I'm saying if it wasn't your sister, it would have been someone, and there might not be even the tiny shred of hope we now have of figuring out what happened." The water's bubbling now, but fuck it. "Bran—"

"We were agents when Chavi died. We could have stopped him then, but that fucker killed another four girls and then went after Priya."

"Bran—"

"He killed her sister, and he killed her friend, and then he went after her, and we were agents, and there was fuck-all any of us did about it!"

He paces around the kitchen like a caged tiger, grabbing or kicking at cabinet doors as he passes. Some of them slam shut and bounce back. Others end up on the floor. "Thirteen girls since Faith. Thirteen girls who never would have been taken if I—"

"If you what? If you hadn't been sixteen? If you hadn't been a student? It you hadn't lived in a safe neighborhood with people who trusted each other? If you what?"

"I was supposed to walk her home."

"On days when you didn't have practice. And you had practice that day."

"I should have walked her home."

"So should Lissi. They were supposed to go straight home together. Do you blame her?"

"She was eight!"

"You were sixteen! You, Brandon Eddison, were still a kid!"

"I was old enough to pay attention!" he bellows. "I could have paid attention to whoever was watching her!"

"You had no way to know anyone *was* watching her. She wasn't threatened; there was no note or ominous gift left at the door; there was no rash of kidnappings in the days before. Who were you going to pay attention to?"

"The bastard who took her."

"You mean the bastard who doesn't stand out? The bastard who has done this in multiple neighborhoods and never seemed out of place, never aroused suspicion? That's who you would have paid attention to in the days before the kidnapping no one knew to expect?"

His fist actually goes through one of the cabinet doors, splitting the old, dried-out wood. Fortunately, it's an empty cabinet and he hit too low to break his knuckles on the shelves.

"Faith isn't your fault. Not now, and not then. None of these girls going missing is your fault."

"What the hell do you know about it?" he cries. "You're an only child; you've never had a sibling go missing."

"I—"

"This isn't a time for the textbook bullshit we're all taught to say. You don't know anything about it!"

"I—"

"It would have been better if she *had* been your sister. You wouldn't have given up on her."

"Bran—"

"You wouldn't have let go of her. You couldn't. You can't even let go of The Damn Dress!"

His hand slams down on the edge of the stove. Along the way, he hits the handle of the pot of boiling water. I shove him out of the way as the pot snaps up from the blow, the water flying out. Damp heat sears through my sleeve, but most of the water hits the floor and the island.

I turn off the burner and lunge for the sink to spin on the tap. "Don't move," I snap. "Your feet are bare."

Of course he doesn't listen, but he at least steps over the puddles carefully, coming up behind me as I wait for the water to get to warm. Cold water might feel better, but it'll also blister the skin. Warm water eases the burn more gently. I stick my arm under the faucet as soon as the temp is in the right range, not bothering to pull back my sleeve. If the skin is already blistering, the fabric could stick to it, and that's just not pleasant to deal with.

"Eliza . . ."

I turn to look at him, and his face looks chalky, like all the blood just drained out of him. "It was an accident," I tell him softly. "Bran, look at me."

He does. Sort of.

"Not my arm, at me."

He swallows hard and slowly lifts his gaze.

"Brandon Leonidas Eddison, I swear on everything holy, if I ever have reason to think you've hurt me on purpose, I will put a bullet through your knee. At *least* your knee. In all your rage, you were hitting cabinets. Your fist never came at me. You never threatened me. You didn't see the handle; this was an accident. Tell me you recognize that."

"I . . ." He closes his mouth without finishing the thought, looking sick.

Unbuttoning my blouse, I shrug out of the left sleeve. His hands shake as he helps me carefully slide it down my right arm without moving away from the water. The splash marks are already an angry, deep red-violet, and despite the speed in getting it under the tap, it will probably blister. Burns being the rogues they are, there's no way to guess whether or not it will scar.

"We need . . ." His throat muscles work convulsively as he tries to swallow again. "We need to get you to a clinic."

"It'll be okay. I've got burn cream at home."

"You do?"

"Bran, do you have any idea how many times I've burned myself with water? About one in ten times I cook pasta or rice. Or any kind of liquid that can spit unexpectedly."

"But it's never looked like this," he whispers.

I glance down at my thin tank top, then yank up the hem. It's a little awkward one-handed, especially with him staring at me rather than trying to help, but eventually I get the bottom half folded over my chest. There's a pale pink, hammer-shaped discoloration about an inch below my left underwire. "Remember Mjolnir? It's not a birthmark; it's a burn scar. I got it in college because I was stupid enough to bend completely over a pot of water on the camp stove we weren't supposed to have in our dorm room. It was so bad that Shira named it. I got it twelve years ago, and it's shrunk a little, but it still looks like this."

"Eliza, please . . . please, don't . . ." He tugs my shirt back into place, but gingerly, like he's suddenly afraid to touch me.

"Bran, I mean it. If I ever think it's on purpose, I'll have my gun in hand before you finish the follow-through. I will not let myself be abused again."

His eyes flicker briefly to my mouth, but he still won't look at me properly.

"If you ever hit me, I will never downplay it. I will face it, own it, and explain that to everyone who wants to know why I just shot you in the dick."

Another flicker, this time accompanied by a pained almost-smile.

"This was an accident."

"An accident," he finally agrees, faintly. He stares at the blisters already starting to puff up on my forearm. "We should really get you to a clinic."

"They cannot do anything for me that my first aid kit won't let me do myself. I have burn cream. I have gauze. I have bandages."

"I can't . . . I can't . . ."

I lean back against his chest, forcing him to either put an arm around me or fall. "Breathe," I instruct softly.

"I can't—"

"Yes, you can. Just breathe."

He tries, he does—I can feel him struggling to try—but then he jerks away. "I'm getting Mercedes. Just . . . just hang on." And then he's running out of the kitchen before I can do more than say his name.

18

It's not Mercedes who comes jogging into the kitchen a few minutes later, but Cass. She freezes in the doorway and stares at the destruction in the kitchen.

"Careful where you step," I tell her. "There's water on the floor."

"Eliza, what the hell happened? Are you all right?"

"He didn't tell you?"

"He came running in, seemed like he was about to say something, and then raced for the toilet and started horking up his toenails. Mercedes is with him."

I close my eyes. Now that we're not snapping at each other—now that the slams of the cabinet doors aren't stoking the adrenaline—I can feel my hands start to shake, a mirror tremble in my lungs. "It really was an accident."

"Okay."

"He went to slam his hand on the counter, but he was too close to the stove. He hit the handle of the pot instead. I might not even have been splashed if I hadn't shoved him out of the way. It really was an accident."

"Okay." She steps carefully around the fallen doors and the puddles of still-steaming water, eyeing the cabinet that has very noticeably had a fist punched through it. She stretches up on her toes to get a look at my arm. "Doesn't look like it's going to fall off."

"It won't."

"Then if you don't mind being left alone a minute, I'm going to trade places with Mercedes. She's better with the first aid stuff." There's a question in her eyes, not fully hidden by the glasses she wears only when she's beyond tired.

"Neither of us hit each other. Neither of us threatened each other. He's just . . ."

"It's been a very bad day."

"Yeah."

Mercedes brings her first aid kit with her, whistling at the devastation. "Well, you two scared the absolute shit out of each other."

I blink away the sudden sheen of tears stinging my eyes. Turning off the tap, I hold my hand out for one of the soft, thin kitchen towels draped over her arm. I can't do much more than pat around the blisters without risking tearing.

Mercedes studies the burns, then looks up at me. "You promise me that—"

"I swear to fucking God, Ramirez, if he'd meant it, he would no longer have a dick."

"You realize it's not just for your sake I'm asking this, right?" Her fingers are so gentle as she spreads the cool burn cream—so, so gentle— but it still hurts like a wicked bitch. "He's terrified. Eddison is a furious kind of person. He is never not angry. But for all that rage, he has never once been violent to a woman we haven't arrested, and only then when there wasn't a choice."

"He wasn't being violent to me."

"And I believe you, but he was being violent *around* you, and I know you love him, but you need to step back a moment and realize that. He was being violent around you, and that is not nothing. But I'm asking for his sake, too, because you know damn well he's afraid you're just saying that to calm him down."

Between the two of us, we manage to dress and bandage the burns that are now throbbing, but I haven't eaten since lunch, so I don't trust my stomach to take any painkillers. As I head to Bran's room to grab a shirt, I can hear Mercedes picking up the cabinet doors and muttering in Spanish. I find a soft, long-sleeved shirt, the logo faded from age, back when the Rays were still the Devil Rays, and tug it over my head, adjusting the sleeve carefully around the bandage.

"Do you need me to drive you home?" Mercedes asks when I get back to the kitchen. She's on her knees between the stove and the island, mopping up the water.

"No, I'll be fine." I glance at the back door, think about the timing of her question. "You don't think I should try to talk to him again tonight."

"He's freaking out. And as soon as we can calm him down from this, he's going to freak out about Faith and he's going to get worked up, and then he's going to remember what happened to you when he got that worked up and he's going to freak out more. If you're here, he's not going to feel reassured, he's going to feel guilty."

"He's going to feel guilty anyway."

"Yes, but are you really up for spending the entire night reminding him that it was an accident, given that you've already been a little bitchy to me and Cass about it?"

I scowl at her. "You'd be worried if I wasn't a little bitchy about it."

"Naturally, because then you'd be seriously hurt." She sits back on her heels and tosses the soaked towel into the sink, where it lands with a dull splat.

"You'll call me if I'm needed?"

"I promise. Go on. Morning is going to come too early as it is."

I swing through a Sheetz on the way home, because even though I've got food in my kitchen, I really don't feel like doing anything with it. Especially not if it involves boiling water. Not tonight. But when I get to my building and park, I see a familiar car a few spaces down. "Are you fucking kidding me?"

Sure enough, when I get up to my door, there's Vic, leaning against the wall and looking grim. He eyes me and raises his eyebrows. "Are you pissed at him or pissed at me?"

"Right now I'm fucking pissed at everything," I retort, and slam my key into the lock hard enough for it to squeak worryingly. Calm the fuck down, Eliza. Last thing you need tonight is to call the locksmith. "Which one of them called you?"

"Cass. Then Eddison. Then Mercedes. Then Eddison again."

I glare at him, but he has the nerve to chuckle.

"We check in on each other, Eliza. Now, how bad is it?"

"I'm not in the field right now anyway."

"That is not actually an answer. Do you need me to drive you to urgent care?"

"No."

"Would any of the others say I need to drive you to urgent care?"

"No."

"Are you going to bite my head off if I keep pushing?"

"Yes!"

"Good." He pushes off the wall and kisses my cheek. "If anything happens during the night and you need to go in, have one of us drive you." He sticks his hands in the pockets of his coat and strolls down the hall to the stairs.

By the time I'm inside and have wrestled out of my coat and bag, my food is stone cold. Fuck it, I'm going hungry.

I'm itching for a smoke, but Shira and I have these rules for each other, and one of them is that it must be no less than two weeks between smokes, no matter what's going on. Everything is tidy, I don't have enough dirty clothing to do laundry, and even the grout in the bathroom is clean thanks to a bout of insomnia last week. Once I secure my gun in the safe, there is literally no busy work for me to do.

Nothing to keep me from remembering the strange, flickering look Bran gave me at the sink, after I said . . .

Oh.

I will not let myself be abused again.

Again.

Why did I say that?

Taking off my bra and swapping trousers for comfortable leggings, I settle onto the bed with my personal phone. It's Monday, which means I've got a fifty-fifty chance of my mother being at book club. I brace my throbbing arm against my stomach as I listen to the rings.

Then I hear my father's warm, deep voice. "My Eliza," he greets. In the background, I hear a "hmph!" and the slam of a door, as well as the low murmur of recorded voices. "Your mother just flounced away. Is that the right word? Flounced?"

"Knowing *Ima*? Probably."

"You don't normally call if your mother might be home."

"I couldn't remember if this was Book Club Monday or not."

"Eliza."

"Did you ever worry that Cliff was abusing me?"

I cringe and bite my lip. Surely there was a better way of saying it than that.

There's a long silence over the phone. Eventually, he pauses or stops the D&D podcast playing behind him. "No," he says finally. "I knew he was. I worried whether or not it was physical."

"*Aba* . . ."

"You couldn't see it, Eliza, all the ways he was hurting you." He sighs. "Shira and I were beside ourselves, but you couldn't see it. He was isolating you from people, shifting who you were allowed to be around. He was always making those little digs about your job, the ones that were supposed to come off as jokes but never did. Like the ones he made all the time about what you were eating, and you got so thin. And all that mess about the wedding . . . you were so unhappy, *ahuva*, but he had you so twisted around about everything, you hardly knew which way was up."

"I should have seen it," I whisper.

"How could you? It doesn't matter if you're trained to see it in others; it's different when it's you. He was very good at it. It's not like he slammed into it all at once either. He worked up to it too slowly for you to see. And you were never going to see it, Eliza. Not when he wasn't the only one doing it."

"What do you mean?"

"Your mother's been doing it your whole life."

". . . *Aba?*"

"Eliza Adiah Sterling, you are a woman I am proud to know. I am proud to call you my daughter. You have never deserved the abuse your mother has heaped on you. I should have protected you better." He blows out a gusty breath. When he speaks again, his voice is heavy with pain. With guilt. "I used to think she would stop as you grew. Surely she saw what a wondrous creature you were! So smart, and kind, and quick to help. So lively and bright, like bottled laughter. You were a marvel, a joy, and she had to recognize that. I couldn't understand why she didn't. By the time you were in junior high, I'd begun to seriously consider divorce. I loved her, but she was making you feel so small."

"But then Shira's father?"

"Yes, precisely. You were with Shira and the Sawyer-Levys, helping them, and it was good of you that you were, but I couldn't add to that. I couldn't give you the fear of your being taken away. And the courts, you know . . . they're getting better, but so many still believe the mother is the better choice for custody. If I divorced her but she got custody, I would have just made it worse. And so I thought, in a few years, you would be away at college, and . . ." He sighs. "I should have protected you better. You were so used to it from your mother, of course you wouldn't recognize when that man came in and did the same thing just beyond the charm. You were so vulnerable to exactly that kind of man, because you'd already spent your whole life trying to understand why your mother didn't seem to love you."

"Does she?" I sniff and wipe at my itching face; my fingers come away wet. When did I start crying? "Does she love me, *Aba*?"

"She desperately loved the idea of a daughter, but she's never known you, Eliza. She's never known you for the extraordinary daughter you are."

Which, in my father's blanket of kindness, means no. A sob hiccups out of me before I can clap my hand over my mouth, but he hears it. Of course he hears it.

"I'm so sorry, *ahuva*. But I need you to remember this: you are so loved. By me, by Shira, by all the Sawyer-Levys. Illa has never stopped calling you her daughter, Shira's blonde twin. You are more loved than your mother ever has been, because you love us in return. You are so much stronger than you know. Do you know how proud I was when you dumped him? That you stood up to both him and your mother? Do you know how proud I am that you were brave enough to love again? And with such a good man?"

I can hear my front door opening and closing, and a moment later Priya walks into the bedroom, kicking off her shoes to slide onto the bed beside me. She doesn't say anything yet, just cuddles in close as I'm crying into the phone.

"Why do you stay with her? If you've known all this for so long . . ."

"Because she has no one else," he says simply. "She has driven every-one else so far away, there's no one left. Even her book club can't stand her, but she keeps going because it lets her play the victim, and that's what makes her . . ." He gropes for the word. ". . . fulfilled? She can only be happy by being unhappy." There's silence for a moment, and then he says, "What brought this up, Eliza? Is Brandon all right?"

"It's . . . this time of year . . . but it's . . ." I take a deep breath that's shakier than I'd like. "I can't say much about it, because this case has just . . . it's just this tangle of everything and I can't talk about it yet, but . . . I love him. He bought that ridiculous house because part of him is thinking *together* and *family*, but he can't ask me anything, and I'm scared to death that he will ask something, because . . ."

"Because you didn't realize how much Cliff had done to you until after you walked away," he supplies softly, "and you're terrified you'll miss signs again."

Priya's thumb rubs back and forth against the edge of the gauze bandage, a safe distance away from the burns themselves.

"Of course you're afraid. Oh, my Eliza, who wouldn't be? Of *course* you're afraid. But you have been afraid before and stood the line. You will know when it is time for you to do so again. And then, until then, after then, you are loved. You are so loved, Eliza, and by better people than me."

19

Priya doesn't ask me about what must have been a strange call to hear only my end of, doesn't ask about the bandage or the tears or the bag of food congealing on the kitchen counter. She just hands me some tissues and then trades the used tissues for the FBI bear she gave me when I accepted the transfer from Denver to Quantico. Once she's in pajamas from my closet that fit well enough despite a difference in our sizes, she curls up next to me again.

"You borrowed Jenny's van?" I ask eventually.

"Yeah. Vic got call after call after call, but then he *didn't* get a call from you, and I think that worried him more than the actual calls."

"Did he tell you what happened?"

"Not much. Just that there'd been an accident, a real accident, not a cover-up, an actual accident, but for the love of God don't ask her if it was an accident . . ."

Despite the tears, I can't help but snort at that, and she smirks at me.

"I can't help Eddison by going over there. I can help you *and* Eddison by being here. I don't need to know what happened until you want to tell me. I just wanted to be here."

"You're a wonderful person."

"I try."

I plug in my phone and turn off the light so we can settle in for the night, screw hygiene or routine, and then realize the closet light is still on. I walk over to flick it off and see the dress bag sprawled in its corner, complete with the big pink bow on the hanger just below the ribbon-wrapped hook. Like putting a bow on a leash.

I turn off the light and shut the door for good measure.

Way too early, my alarm goes off, and a grumbly Priya burrows deeper under the blanket. By the time I've showered, dried my hair, put on my makeup, changed the bandage, and dressed, the top half of her head has made its way out of the fabric to blink at me sleepily.

"You can stay as long as you want to," I tell her, my voice soft in deference to the obscene hour. "You've got your key."

"Mm-kay."

I kiss her on the forehead, tuck the FBI bear into her arms, and leave her to it.

I get to Quantico around six, which is still two hours earlier than normal, but Cass and Mercedes are already there. Sort of. Mercedes is present, Cass is curled up on the floor under her desk fast asleep. Mercedes gives me a worried, wary look. "Did you sleep?"

"Actually, I did, a bit. You?"

"Not especially."

"Is he okay?"

"Jenny and Marlene managed to come up with a list of things around the house that someone younger than Vic needs to see to, and then they're giving him over to Ian for the day."

So that's a no, but at least they'll keep Bran busy and make him eat. That will help, somewhat. Maybe.

"Inara and Victoria-Bliss are going to be spending the day at my place," she continues, "just in case. They won't mean to rile him up more, but . . . well. Victoria-Bliss. No one needs her and Eddison sniping at each other today. Eddison feels bad enough as it is. Vic didn't mention anything about Priya."

"She's at mine. I don't know what her plans for the day are besides sleep until daylight."

Mercedes yawns, her fingers twitching toward her eyes before she remembers her makeup. "How's your arm?"

"Painful, but Priya kept me from rolling on it or anything."

"Snuggled you into submission, did she?"

"Yes, yes, she did. I'm surprised you two are here rather than on your way to Richmond."

"Watts wanted us to meet here first. I think she's got some extra cautions to give."

"For instance?"

"We'll find out when she gets here, I suppose."

Gradually Watts's team trickles in, aiming for the conference room, and the general sleepiness vanishes as soon as they see those seventeen pictures up on the wall.

Watts hands everyone a printout and a protein bar. "This lists out the girls' names, where they were taken, and when. Memorize it, because I don't want you taking it with you. As you're talking to neighbors and officers and anyone assisting with the search, keep an ear out for any of these names or cities. If someone mentions them, get us their name straight away. This is not someone who stands out. This is not someone the kids are scared of. He fits in, but if he lives there, he doesn't live there long. He's not necessarily going to look worried or scared if you talk to him. He's gotten away with this for a long time. Depending on his particular pathology, he might even be sympathetic to what the parents are going through. He may be on the volunteer lists. Trust your gut on this one; it's gotten us this far."

After the meeting disperses, Vic brings me a massive breakfast and stands over me while I eat it, then hands me a hot chocolate and some acetaminophen.

"Do I want to ask what happened?" Yvonne asks in an undertone after he's left.

"Nope."

"Eliza—"

"There was an accident. I am fine. And I'm sorry, because I know you're concerned and you mean well, but I really don't want to discuss it yet again."

"But you're okay."

"Yes. Or I will be, and today I'm treating that as the same thing."

"You'll let me know if that changes."

"Yes. Thank you."

The day crawls by. Gala and Yvonne have written a solid program to compare names across all the different files, but it's bogging down under sheer quantity. The problem is that so many people get interviewed when a kid goes missing, there's just a deluge of names, and that's assuming the officers or agents wrote down the name every time. When you're talking to that many people that quickly, with that much pressure on you to hurry and find the kid, names can be the first thing to go.

Which is stupid, because we need the names, but that's what happens.

I text Bran twice to see how he's doing, and get back one-word replies, so I think it's safe to say he's still struggling under the weight of the monstrosity that was yesterday. Over lunch—yes, Vic, an actual lunch that did not have to be put in front of me by someone else—Priya texts to ask how I'm doing.

Can I ask you to run some errands for me? I reply.

Absolutely. I'm at Mercedes's with the girls, and Jenny said I can have the van all day, so just give me a list.

Bless Priya, and Jenny too.

Watts sends Cass and Mercedes back early, or early-ish. Before her own team, at any rate, and Mercedes just shrugs. "We're exhausted," she admits. "I don't know what Vic told her about last night, but it was also pretty obvious we were struggling. How's the comparison?"

"Still working on it. We're manually compiling the names so the program can just run the lists rather than search the files."

"Jesus."

"Or something."

"Come on. My place, pizza."

"Mind the girls staying with us?"

"Of course not. They're there anyway, and always welcome." She glances at Eddison's desk, and the two framed pictures on the cabinet. "We can't—"

"Talk about the case. I know."

"Which means we can't actually talk about Faith either."

"Yeah."

When we get to Mercedes's cottage, The House visible behind it, the girls are sitting on the porch swing finishing drinks from Starbucks. There's a plastic bag of clothing at Priya's feet. "So, it's not too cold tonight," Priya says instead of hello, "and it's supposed to be clear. Can we set up around the firepit?"

"Isn't the firepit Eddison's?" asks Inara.

"It's a joint-custody firepit," Priya and Mercedes answer together. Mercedes grins at her. "I think it's a great idea," Mercedes continues. "We need to change, and we'll get the pizza ordered. Then we can start the fire."

Victoria-Bliss beams in a very discomfiting way.

"Is Eddison coming home anytime soon?" Cass asks.

"Jenny and Marlene said that Ian is feeding him," Priya replies. "Apparently he took Eddison out running for the second half of the day."

"Ian was running?"

"No, just making Eddison run, from what I understand."

Right.

I pull on Bran's Devil Rays shirt again, because it's soft and it smells like him and I'm worried about him, and I want a better memory for the shirt than I had last night. Mercedes insists on checking my burns, slathering on more cream before she does the bandage back up. It'll take the blisters a while to go down if I don't lance them, but if I lance them, they're more likely to get infected and scar. While we're doing that, Cass heads out back to start the fire.

We trudge across the grass as the evening settles into twilight, aiming for the ring of wicker-and-cushion couches abutting Bran's back porch. The pit isn't especially deep, a curved bowl carved out from a single large stone surrounded by other stones to form the porch extension. Cass has the kindling glowing, kneeling next to the pit to slowly add in more fuel as well as some larger pieces.

Some of those larger pieces look suspiciously like cabinet doors missing their hardware.

"Does he know you're cannibalizing his kitchen?" I ask as I settle down onto one of the four curved two-seaters.

"He needed to remodel anyway."

The girls laugh, Priya a breath behind the other two, and I get the feeling she picked up more from Vic's end of the phone calls than she let on.

It's a nice evening, strangely. There's pizza and hard cider, and for a while we all make the choice to leave the more serious topics behind. Things have a way of turning, though. Maybe it's the quiet that comes of night, or sitting around a fire. Maybe it's because tomorrow is Halloween, Inara's birthday, and the destruction of the Garden, and that has weight in this circle.

Maybe it's because we always pair laughter with gravitas, dragging one along with the other.

"Did I tell you I went to temple with my cousins for a while?" Priya asks after the atmosphere has shifted to that hush.

The girls nod, but we agents didn't know.

"Mum and I thought moving to France, being that close to family again, maybe it was time to make the effort. To reconnect." She taps a finger against the stud in her nose, the bindi between her eyes. "Feel like these meant more than just something I did with my mother and sister."

"It doesn't sound like it went well," Mercedes notes.

"It isn't mine. It's the culture I was born to, but it isn't mine, and it doesn't feel . . ." She shakes her head, slumping down in her seat next to the stack of pizza boxes. "I wanted it to fit, or maybe I wanted to fit, but I didn't belong. Instead, I just felt like a fraud for having these visible pieces of the culture without having any of the rest."

"You still wear them."

"They're still mine. They were given to me by Mum, by Chavi, and even if they don't have the cultural ties I wanted . . . it started for the three of us. It was ours. I don't want to put aside yet another piece of Chavi."

"How'd you stop feeling guilty?" Inara asks.

"I didn't."

Inara nods, but then we all understand living with guilt of one kind or another.

Mercedes pops the top off another cider. None of us are planning to get drunk, but two won't hit anyone's limits. "Ksenia met Siobhan a couple weeks ago."

Cass sputters and chokes on a bit of crust until Victoria-Bliss reaches over and whacks her hard on her back. "They met?" she asks. "How?"

"Ksenia came to meet me for lunch, and Siobhan was heading out with some of her team. Everyone's nightmare, right? The girlfriend and the ex meet. I just froze. It was so stupid, but all I could think for a moment was God, this is the moment when my job becomes too much again. This is when I start to lose her."

"Ksenia's not that easily scared off."

"No, I know. I did say it was stupid. There were a lot of reasons Siobhan and I didn't work, but right then, that second, I was blindingly afraid I was going to lose Ksenia, too, and I didn't think my heart could take it."

"And Ksenia said?"

"That I was being foolish, naturally. We've been together a little over a year, and I love her, but I keep waiting for it to go wrong."

"Yeah, that feeling lingers," I mutter.

Mercedes toasts me with her bottle.

"I got a letter that was addressed to the restaurant," Inara offers, staring into the flames. "It was from my father."

Mercedes looks up, startled. "Your father?"

"I haven't seen him since I was eight years old. After he and my mother divorced, neither of them wanted me, so they shoved me off on my grandmother and forgot all about me. And now, suddenly, a letter. Says he heard my name on television, and when he saw a picture, he thought it must be me. I look a lot like my mother used to." Her tone is so very, very carefully neutral, which makes me think the letter probably mentioned that, and not necessarily in a flattering way. "Says he's been so worried about me for all the years I've been missing. He wants us to be a family again."

Victoria-Bliss snorts derisively. "You were never a family. And even if he was worried at one point, that bastard waited seven years from when we were splashed all over the news."

Inara's lips quirk in something that's almost a smile. "He never was any good with money."

"You think he's going to ask you for money?" asks Cass, who knows the girls the least.

"No, I think he wants to connect so he can sell a good story to anyone who'll pay him for it. Get a few pictures together, maybe, to up the price. I shredded the letter. I doubt he's going to come visit if I don't respond. I just . . ." She blows out a sharp breath. "When I was a kid, I was so desperate for my parents to love me. I honestly came to accept that they didn't, and I was fine. Better than fine, I was good. And now he comes trying to trick me for money, and he can't even be bothered to pretend to love me in the letter. I've written form letters with more warmth and feeling. I just look back at myself as a little girl and wonder why the hell I thought it would matter."

"Because it does matter," I answer. "Even once we accept they don't love us, it does matter, because they made us feel like we were wrong to want it."

Priya and Mercedes both give me considering looks.

"What about you, Victoria-Bliss?" prompts Cass. "Has anyone been harassing you? Your family?"

"The folks and I are basically at Christmas and birthday-card levels," she says, unashamed. Her fair skin nearly glows in the darkness and the flickering firelight, and I wonder if that's how she looked the night the Garden went up in flames. "And, you know, I'm good with that. Every now and then my therapist makes some noise about dating, or being less angry, but I'm *happy* like this. I don't want to date. Ever. Wasn't particularly interested in it before I was kidnapped either. I don't want to 'let go of my anger' or whatever fucking bullshit; I *like* being angry. It's not just getting by, I enjoy what I have. I'm a little sick of people telling me it's not enough."

"Do you feel like it's enough?"

"Yes."

"Then fuck them," Cass replies with a shrug, and laughter ripples around the circle.

Inara grins at her, reaching for the last slice of pizza before tossing the empty box onto the fire. The flames billow briefly, then subside to their normal level. "I see they haven't sent you running back to your old team yet."

"Not yet, no," Cass agrees.

Mercedes turns to her in surprise. "Not *yet*?" she echoes.

"Okay, you do realize that this team is deeply weird, right?"

Mercedes looks both shocked and offended, her dark eyes shining with righteous indignation, and it sets the girls off into gales of giggles. I just settle back with the last of my cider, one leg hooked over the arm of the couch.

"Yes, I've been here almost a year now, but I had *twelve* years of *normal FBI team experience*—"

"We're not normal?" Oh, God, Mercedes looks like someone just killed her puppy.

"—before that," Cass continues doggedly, "and I am still not fully adjusted. Sterling, here, at least had Vic's old partner to break her in a little to the weirdness—"

"To be fair," I interject, "my first team had its own weirdness, in the form of Agent Archer."

Priya sighs and shakes her head. "Sometimes I still almost feel guilty."

"Only almost?"

"My plan to catch Chavi's killer wouldn't have worked if Archer hadn't been a complete and utter moron eager to use me as live bait. There's only so much of that blame I can take. Especially when he did it on another case all on his own."

"—but you guys are a lot to get used to," Cass finishes loudly. "It was different when I was on another team. You and I could hang out as friends, and when we worked the occasional case together, we could all laugh at the oddities. Now the oddity is permanent, and I'm worried about things that honestly never occurred to me before."

"Like what?"

"Like what happens when I have to work with another team again? Like what happens if I get transferred? Like what happens the day I wake up and suddenly realize I have zero boundaries? Like what the hell stray are you all adopting next?"

"We haven't adopted anyone in years!"

"Her name is Eliza Sterling, and she is sitting right next to you!"

If it weren't for Inara's hand in her hair, Victoria-Bliss would be in real danger of pitching forward into the fire. As it is, I don't understand how she hasn't passed out yet from lack of oxygen. Priya's laughing nearly as hard, but then she's a large part of how I became a Team Hanoverian stray in the first place. She adopted me, so then they did.

Mercedes's lower lip trembles pathetically.

But then she loses it and cracks up, cackling even louder than the others. Cass stares at her, dumbfounded, and it only makes Mercedes laugh harder.

"You . . ." Cass blinks, her eyes huge with shock. "You . . . you absolute whore! You were *teasing* me!"

"Watts owes us each fifty bucks," I tell her. "She thought you wouldn't give in to that rant until after your one-year anniversary with us. Mercedes and I knew better."

"You . . ."

Snickering, I ease off the couch and head into the kitchen of The House as Cass explodes with hissing indignation. Stacked neatly on the counter are all the things I asked Priya to grab for me earlier. Which, it just now occurs to me, means that she saw the cabinets before Cass started burning them.

It takes a little juggling to get where I can comfortably carry everything, especially with the need to be careful of the burns. As soon as she sees me come back out, Priya stands to help me drop the items onto the empty couch.

"What the hell is that?" Cass snarls, possibly near her limit for the evening.

"Marshmallows, chocolate bars, graham crackers, and metal skewers," I inform her. "We're making s'mores."

"Okay," she says slowly, drawing out the vowels. "But what does that have to do with that?"

I follow the line of her finger. "We're burning my wedding dress."

20

Victoria-Bliss is flat out wheezing now, clutching her ribs in actual pain.

"We're . . . we're burning your wedding dress," Cass repeats dully.

"Yes. To make s'mores."

Priya beams at me as she starts opening packages. "You figured out what was holding you back."

"And that was?" Mercedes asks cautiously.

"I've spent four years saying Cliff was a dickhead, he was an asshole, he was a selfish jerk, but I never named the other thing he was." I take a deep breath. It trembles on the exhale. "He was also abusive."

Victoria-Bliss abruptly stops laughing, even if her breathing is decidedly weak and shaky.

"I couldn't see it because he used the exact same tactics my mother does, that she's used all my life. All this time, I've been afraid that I wouldn't recognize the problems in another relationship because I got so over my head last time. It wasn't an unfounded fear, but I'm done with that now. I got away from Cliff. I got away from my mother. I'm getting away from The Dress, because it doesn't matter how many pounds of rhinestones are on it, a leash is still a leash."

"Can we see it on you?" asks Victoria-Bliss.

I blink. "It . . . well, it probably won't fit," I admit. "I lost more weight than I was happy with while I was with him. I've gained it back, and I'm pleased about that, but it means—"

"Oh, it's okay if it doesn't close. I just want to see you in the dress you picked out."

"He and our mothers picked out."

"Well, now I *have* to see it."

Laughing, Priya drapes the garment bag over the back of the unoccupied couch and unzips it. "Come on, Agent Sterling, fashion show."

This is one of those moments that really shouldn't happen without a lot more alcohol beforehand. But somehow I find myself stripping down in Bran and Mercedes's shared backyard, shivering in the space between the late October chill and the sphere of heat from the fire. I slide my arms out of my bra straps, tucking them into the sides of the band for now, and Inara stands up to help Priya tug the dress over my head.

There really is an entire freaking mountain of tulle, and even with their help, it takes several minutes before we can safely get my arms all the way to the top of the dress. The others are laughing, cracking jokes about giving birth, and it takes both Inara and Priya to get the hips of the dress over my actual hips. I unhook and tug away the bra, and then I'm shrugging into the white lace bolero that I would have worn during the ceremony so I wasn't in temple with bare shoulders.

All five of them cluster together on one couch to get the full effect, and with the firelight dancing over the white satin, it is quite an effect. The strapless bodice is stiff with white-on-white embroidery, beadwork, *and* crystals, tight all the way down to my hips, where it flares out into frankly massive skirts. The top three inches and the bottom half of the first layer of skirt are sewn over with heavy lace to match the bolero, and even more beads and crystals are sewn through the butterfly patterns in the lace.

"Holy fuck, you look like a Vegas cake-topper," Inara breathes.

"There was a tiara with it, but I gave that to Shira's nieces to play dress-up with. And one of her nephews got the veil to use as mosquito netting at Boy Scout camp."

Priya pulls one of her small cameras out of her pocket. It's not one of her serious ones, not any of the ones she uses professionally, but the one for the quick, casual shots, the ones that are taken by the friend, not the photographer. "Strike a pose, Miss Wedding Vogue."

I flip her off with both hands, and from the flash, that would appear to be the shot.

"And now, our special guest . . ." She grins and digs into her bag, pulling out a Ken doll in a suit and navy-and-yellow FBI windbreaker.

"Special Agent Ken!" yells Mercedes. "You brought him?"

Oh, God. For years, Priya has taken pictures of Special Agent Ken and sent them to Bran. Not just on the vacations with her mother, but any time she happened to think of a picture and take it. He got a handful of them printed large and framed, and they're the only pictures he's ever displayed in his apartments, or in The House, for that matter.

I take Special Agent Ken by the plastic hand and hold him far away from me, as if I'm about to drop him, and look the opposite direction. I can hear Priya laughing as she takes the picture.

"This," Cass says, "this is what I was talking about." It does not, however, stop her from wiggling off the couch so she can pull her favorite knife from its sheath inside the waistband of her jeans. "The crystals and beads should probably not go into the firepit, just in case. He already has to remodel his kitchen, and who knows what else inside. Let's not force him to do damage control out here too."

"But a hot tub, Cass."

"We want him to *add* that, not swap it out with the firepit."

"I have scissors inside," Mercedes offers.

"Nope, we're good." Kneeling down, Cass gathers a handful of fabric an inch or so above the top edge of the lace. "Ready for this?"

Tossing Special Agent Ken to Mercedes to hold, I take another deep breath and let it out slowly. "Let's do this."

Her knife is sharp enough you can barely hear the satin tearing, and suddenly there's a gaping hole in my dress, right in front. She starts whistling cheerfully. "Quarter-turn, I think, to your left."

I obey, shuffling around. All that trim drags against the stone as it falls. With Priya busy taking pictures, Inara bends down to pick it up, and for a moment it almost feels like it might have on my wedding day, Shira and my other bridesmaids helping me settle the layers before walking down the aisle. It's a weird feeling.

Once the trim is off, Cass taps my hip with the flat of her knife. "How do you want to do this?"

"Vertical strips, I think. That would be easiest. Start on the top layer, work down through the tulle?"

"This is going to be a lot of s'mores." She stabs through the fabric from the underside, keeping the blade away from my legs even though it would take an act of God to reach them through the tulle, and lets gravity do most of the work of dragging the blade through the thin satin. Every so often there's a flash and click of Priya taking another picture.

Fairly soon, the top layer is in careful shreds, and we move the couches closer to the flames. Inara hands me a skewer with a marshmallow already fixed to the end. After a moment's thought, I push the sweet down a little farther so some of the metal shows through. The first strip of dress rips off easily, and I drape it over the skewer on either side of the marshmallow.

"Huh. It'll cook the ends better that way," Inara notes, and hands me another.

When we move the skewers above the flames, Victoria-Bliss lets out a great whooping cheer as the fabric catches on fire.

There are too many layers of dress for one s'more per strip, of course, even with six of us. So, between rounds, we work one of the layers of tulle off, chop it up, and dump it onto the flames. And possibly, at one point, we position Special Agent Ken around a skewer braced between cushions to make it look like he is also making s'mores.

Maybe.

Priya whistles at the sound of a car pulling into the driveway. "Eddison's home, I'm guessing. So . . . I know *I* didn't tell him we were out here. Did anyone else?"

"No," comes the answer from four mouths. Victoria-Bliss is giggling too hard to say it.

A few minutes later, the back door opens and Bran walks out, holding something in each hand. Eyes dazzled by the flames, I can't actually make out what he has. He approaches us, then stops a safe distance away, head cocked and a baffled expression on his face. As my sight clears, I can make out the path of his gaze: the girlfriend wearing the tattered wedding dress, the s'mores, the bottles of cider, the one pizza box we didn't burn because the grease soaked all the way through, and Special Agent Ken, supervising from the arm of a couch. The path repeats. Several times.

"How's your arm?" he asks eventually.

Even Mercedes and Cass lose it this time.

"It's doing just fine," I tell him. "Mercedes checked it again a few hours ago. S'more?"

"Ahh . . . nooo, I think I'll pass. These are for you, though." He holds out a bouquet of tiger lilies wrapped in pink tissue. "I have a feeling you'll have my balls if I apologize for the accident, but I shouldn't have been yelling at you in the first place. And some of the things I said were over the line."

"Yes," I agree simply, "but that doesn't mean you were wrong."

He glances at the heap of burning tulle still visible in the pit.

"Thank you," I add.

Priya's looking at what's in his other hand. "Is that . . . did you put a pink glitter bow on a pound of bacon?"

Even with the distortion of the firelight, I can see the fierce blush that flares up his throat and into his face. "I'm going to leave you ladies alone now." He turns and hurries into The House without even trying to pretend he isn't retreating.

I smile and bury my face in the tiger lilies. There are three different varieties mixed through, pumpkin-orange and pink, both with the dark spots dotted along the inside of the curled-back petals, but also a variety that's deep sunset purple edged in spotted orange. They're gorgeous.

"Are those your favorites?" asks Victoria-Bliss.

"One of them."

"Her favorites are blue columbines," Priya tells her, "but Eddison won't give her those because they're one of the flowers my stalker used in his murders."

Cass gives me a jaundiced look. "Really?"

"What? That seems perfectly reasonable."

"It does, yes. You people have broken me. Broken me, I tell you!"

Eventually, we run out of dress and I have to put my jeans and coat back on or die of shivers. The bolero, like the rest of the lace, is worked over with Extra! and therefore probably unsafe to burn, so Inara asks to keep it. "Sophia's daughter Jillie is going to prom in the spring, and this seems right up her alley. If it's paired with a plain dress, it shouldn't look so Vegas."

"And if it still does?"

"Jillie likes shiny. She can make it work."

She takes the bottom half of the skirt, too, to see if she can break it down into useful pieces like a belt or hair ornaments.

We get everything cleaned up and troop back across the grass to Mercedes's, dropping the garbage and recycling in the appropriate bins by her driveway. Mercedes pokes me in the side as she hands me my bag. "You're parked behind me, so we'll wait for you in the morning."

I grin at her.

Priya gives me a tight hug. "Do you feel any better?"

"I do. Like I had this giant weight sitting on my chest, and now it's gone."

We both look at the heavy bodice and my chest spilling out of it, and laugh.

I head back to The House, locking the kitchen door behind me, and make my way down the hall to the living room. Bran is sprawled across the couch, jeans traded for flannel pants, wearing the long-sleeved University of Miami T-shirt Mercedes bought him three years ago to replace the one she was wearing that accidentally got covered in meth. We have weird occupational hazards.

An open box of photos sits on the coffee table in front of him. It's strange to see him have personal pictures out where anyone else can see them.

I set my bag on the floor at the end of the couch and the bouquet on the coffee table next to the box. "Hey."

"Hey." He doesn't quite manage to sit up, but he gets his elbows under him to prop himself up a little. He looks so far beyond tired he actually looks drained. Like something vital has been taken away.

I shrug out of the coat, then my shoes, and drape myself over him from shoulder to toe. "There's not a way for you to be okay, but are you doing better?"

"I'm . . ." He trails a hand down my arm, fingers lingering at the upper edge of the bandage. "Better for now," he says finally. "Ian and I spent a couple hours going through my photos. We found some from Stanzi's birthday party just a couple of weeks before. It was open to the whole neighborhood. We can see if any faces appear in other case files. I won't go in as an agent, but as . . . as someone who can answer questions."

"Okay."

"Yeah?"

I snuggle against his chest, his shirt slightly damp from his shower. "I know it could help the investigation, but if it also helps you, I'm good with it."

"I do have a question of my own, though."

"Yeah?"

"If that's just the top, how bad was the rest of the dress?"

I laugh and slide my knee across his thighs so I can sit up without hurting him. "It was bad," I admit. "It was so very, very bad."

"I was always curious. I don't think I envisioned this." His fingers play at my hips and the two inches of skirt that remain.

"You never looked?"

He shakes his head, wet hair curling against his forehead. "It wasn't my place," he says simply.

"It's gone now."

"Mostly."

"Well, as to that . . ." I tug his hand behind me, to the thick, sturdy ribbon in a bow at the swell of my ass. "It laces up the back."

Ian leaned against the door to the school clinic, watching the boy on the cot clean up the abrasions on and around his knuckles. The bruising didn't look like it was going to be too bad, he thought, assessing Brandon with a professional eye, but he'd be wearing a bandage around that hand for a few days. Given the way his tongue kept prodding against the inside of his cheek, he might have had a tooth knocked loose as well.

He'd kept an eye on Brandon over the last three months, regular chats with the school's resource officer that made him cringe with every update. There was some pride there, too, but damn, kid. Less than two weeks back from his most recent suspension and he'd been involved in yet another brawl. Ian had barely gotten off the phone with Officer Gutierrez when he got the call from Xiomara. From her voice, she was barely holding back tears as she asked for his help.

Help me save my boy from himself, she'd asked.

Ian wasn't sure it was that easy.

But here he was, uncomfortably aware that he was wearing his gun in a school full of kids, watching a boy who'd gotten far too good at patching up his own war wounds.

He cleared his throat. "Brandon."

The kid jerked his head up, wide eyed and a little afraid, until recognition dawned. Then the caution was replaced with the glare that had become achingly familiar over the past months. "Detective," Brandon growled.

"Your mother called me. Your principal says you're in danger of getting expelled."

Brandon looked past him through the glass half wall to the attendance office, where another kid sat whining to the not particularly sympathetic counselor sitting with him until his parents got there. Ian had the full story from Gutierrez, knew that this fight was only the latest in a campaign against dickish boys who grew to dickish men.

"Come on," Ian said. "We've got somewhere to be."

"Sir?"

"Vamos, chico."

"You speak Spanish like a gringo.*"*

"I am a gringo, *so I guess that makes sense. Come on."*

Shrugging, Brandon taped the last length of gauze over his knuckles and left the unused materials on the counter for the school nurse, who'd been helping him until she got called to a classroom for an epileptic kid having a seizure. Brandon and the nurse had reportedly become great friends.

Ian led the boy out to the parking lot to his unmarked dark sedan that somehow managed to be unmistakably a police car.

Brandon hesitated, looking between the front and back of the car.

Ian swallowed back a grin. "Bag in the backseat, ass in the front," he instructed gruffly. "You're not under arrest."

The kid stayed silent as they drove, not even glancing at him as they turned onto Dale Mabry. That was fine. Ian didn't need Brandon to talk to him today; he needed him to listen. He turned into the parking lot for the Big Sombrero. There were a few cars parked there, but the lots were quiet. The season was over, and everyone was taking a deep breath before throwing themselves into preparations and training for the next season.

Inside the stadium, Ian handed the kid the gym bag the school's track coach had obligingly retrieved from Brandon's practice locker. He pointed to a bathroom. "Change."

Amazingly, Brandon didn't argue. His coach had nothing but good to say about him, excepting his frustration that the punishments for fighting interfered with his practices. Said the kid had the right headspace for cross-country, that he could start running and not realize for miles how far he'd gone. Ian could see that just the gear was starting to settle him; Brandon stretched as they walked through to the bottom rank of seating and didn't seem to know he was doing it.

Ian gave him time to fully stretch. He didn't want him to get hurt, after all. Once Brandon straightened up and shook himself out, Ian pointed up the steep banks of stairs. "Run."

"Sir?"

"Run. Up and down. I'll tell you when to stop."

He kept an eye on the kid over the next hour while he sat and penned his way through a stack of paperwork he'd brought with him from the station. He didn't stop him, though, until he could see Brandon's knees starting to wobble.

Whistling sharply, Ian motioned the kid to lurch down the steps one last time. He tossed Brandon a bottle of water and started walking, forcing the kid to follow him. It gave Brandon a chance to stretch out and cool down, sure, but it also felt a little like sadism.

This was probably why he'd never felt an inclination to coach anything.

"I can't tell you not to be angry," he said when Brandon's breathing had settled out of wheezing gasps and into something more manageable. "You're so full of rage, and you have reason to be. The world seems pretty intent on kicking you in the balls."

The kid choked on his water.

"Your sister's disappearance is shaping your life, and it always will. Even if she turns up at your door today, the experience, what you've gone through, will always have an impact on you. But, Son, you get to decide how it shapes you. You get to decide how you react to it."

"I don't—"

"I spent some time with your principal before coming to get you. He said every fight you've been in has been in defense of your female classmates."

"Yes, sir."

"You know defending them doesn't magically make Faith appear?"

"That's not why."

"Then why?"

"Because they shouldn't be getting harassed!" snapped Brandon. "These assholes go around pulling on their clothes and touching them and saying shit, and when the girls complain, no one does anything! It isn't right!"

"But why is it you?"

"Because no one else is doing it."

Ian nodded slowly. "Drink your water. Slowly."

The kid gave him a disgusted look, like he'd called him stupid or something.

"That desire to defend?" Ian continued after a minute. "To protect? That's a good thing. And you'll be able to do fuck-all with it if you get expelled for fighting."

Brandon blinked at him.

"Put yourself between the girls and their harassers. Tell those assholes to back off. Document what you see, and give it to the administration. Bring it up at PTA meetings, at school board meetings. You carry on this crusade with your fists and nothing will happen except that you'll get kicked out, and who's going to help those girls then? But you get other boys to stand up for them, you demand a change, and you demand it loudly and of every single person who can possibly effect that change, and then you might actually get somewhere. It's a more frustrating way to go about it," he admitted, clearly startling the kid again. "It'll often feel like you're not getting anywhere. It's nowhere near as satisfying as punching someone out. But if you want a change to last, you do it the hard way, not the way that feels better in the short term.

"Now, you've got a week's suspension. You're spending it with me. I'll arrange for you to have limited off-hours access to the stadium so you can run the stairs. Get out some of that energy you keep channeling through your fists. After the suspension is done, you'll be with me two days a week. The

fighting stops, Brandon. And in return, I'll show you other ways to protect people. Deal?"

Brandon stared at his offered hand, thinking it through. Good. "What if I backslide?"

"Then you backslide. We deal with it as it comes. But I need to know you're working on it."

The kid took his hand and shook it firmly. "Deal."

"Good." Ian started walking back toward their things. "And get rid of the cigarettes in your gym bag. You're sixteen, for fuck's sake, and a runner besides."

The kid yelped behind him.

Ian grinned.

21

It takes me a minute or two to recognize the alarm in the morning. It isn't mine, which is designed to scare me out of sleep and into marginal wakefulness. It's Bran's, a looped recording of Priya chanting "Wake up, wake up, wake up!" getting louder with each repetition. And since it's not my alarm, and I'm warm and comfortable, I nestle back in against him and tug the edge of the comforter up over my ear.

"You know," he mumbles into my hair, his voice rumbling in his chest, "you're the one who actually has to get up."

"Mmm."

"I managed to buy some groceries last night. If you start getting ready, I'll make breakfast."

"Mmm."

"And by breakfast, I mean triple-bacon breakfast burritos."

"I'm up!" Except I haven't moved.

Bran laughs and rolls off the bed, dragging me behind him and catching me at the edge to set me on my feet. "Shower," he instructs. "You smell like smoke."

"Fine."

Once I'm clean and dressed—and have taken a picture of the bodice on the living room floor to send to Shira later—I head into the kitchen. It looks bizarre. Every cabinet—*every* cabinet, not just the ones he damaged—is missing its door, which really highlights just how little he has in his kitchen.

"Mercedes and Cass will be here in a few minutes," he calls over his shoulder from his place in front of the stove. "Mercedes is going to check your arm again."

"If we do that in here, are you going to be okay? Or are you going to go spiraling off into a guilt complex again?"

He gives me an unimpressed look. "I'll be fine."

If he says so.

I grab the flowers from the living room and arrange them in his empty lemonade pitcher, pouring in water and the packet of sugar mix that came with the bouquet. "You're actually cooking."

"I said I would."

"I know, but you get bored halfway through mac and cheese and disaster follows. And here you are managing, what is that, four, five different pans? I didn't know you even owned that many."

He scowls and pokes the spatula in the saucepan to stir onions, mushrooms, and taco seasoning. "It was a set."

And probably a housewarming gift from Jenny and Marlene.

Cass and Mercedes come in through the back door, sniffing the air appreciatively. "Well done, Eliza," Cass says.

"This is all him."

They both stare at him.

"In a minute, you're all going hungry."

I clear my throat.

"Except, of course, Eliza, who is generously sharing her bacon with the rest of us."

"The apology bacon," Cass clarifies. "The bacon you bought her and put a bow on."

We eat, and then Cass and Bran clean up while Mercedes checks my arm. It isn't throbbing anymore, at least, and the blisters are starting to shrink down. When we head out, Bran is back in his jeans and UM shirt to make sure everyone in the bullpen knows he's not there to work.

No one in the office makes a big deal of Eddison being there or about his sister being part of the case. (Even with gag orders, the Bureau runs on gossip, so of course it was going to get out within the department.) He gets a few extra handshakes, some grips on his shoulders, but for the most part, the other agents leave the support unsaid.

We settle into the conference room. At some point in the past few days, I've begun to think of one of the chairs as mine, and I might be a little appalled by that. Bran places the box of photos on the table and opens it.

"There are two events," he says, lifting out the photos and sorting them into stacks. "Stanzi's birthday was not quite two weeks before Faith disappeared. It was at the park just off the neighborhood, and everyone was invited. There are also pictures from Halloween."

Like the framed photo on his desk. Teenage Mutant Ninja Princess Ballerina Turtle.

I take a handful of pictures from the party. When Bran was growing up, the neighborhood was predominantly Puerto Rican. It's still about half Latinx today. Almost everyone knew each other; kids could safely roam in packs from house to house and be welcome. Everyone got together for parties, bringing offerings of food and drink and helping to clean up after. The kind of neighborhood where a wedding or birth is celebrated with gifts of food so the newlyweds or new parents won't have to cook for a month.

The first picture shows four girls crammed together in the way kids will, no sense of personal space or hesitation. One of them looks more like Bran than Faith does, with her brown skin and dark hair, and she's wrapped around Faith like a drunk koala. Trying to keep them standing upright is a girl who's a little darker, kinky black hair in an enormous fluffy ponytail behind her, and the fourth girl, who looks like she's falling into the others, has long, skinny red-orange braids and a galaxy of freckles.

"The one trying to become kudzu is Lissi," he says, mostly to Cass. "Faith's best friend. After college, she married my best friend Rafi's little brother, Manny. They were hit by a drunk driver on their honeymoon, and she was paralyzed from the waist down."

"Jesus."

"She works from home and gives herself strange hours so she can escort the neighborhood kids to and from school every day. We lived too close to the elementary and high schools to get bussed. The carrot-top is Amanda. They called her their token white girl, even though Faith looked as white as she did." A smile starts to crack through his somber expression. "The other three all grew up speaking both Spanish and English at home, so Amanda learned out of sheer stubbornness. She had the worst accent but wouldn't give up."

"Sounds familiar," Mercedes murmurs, giving me a sideways look.

Familiar, my ass. I spoke German, Hebrew, Italian, Russian, and Arabic before being on this team made me scramble to learn Spanish to keep up. *Dime cuántos idiomas hablas y después hablamos de acentos,* I retort.

"Definitely sounds familiar."

"Amanda's family moved out to Seattle when they were all in high school," Bran continues, eyebrows raised to see if we're quite done now. "We all kept in touch, though."

"Even you?" Mercedes asks.

"Even me. I was still . . ." He swallows hard. "I was still their *hermano*. All the guys in the dorms at college and the academy made fun of me because I'd get letters from them every week. They liked to write in glitter and bright colors. Still do. I think they buy them especially for the letters nowadays."

"He bought a pack of glitter pens a few months ago for his letters to Amanda," I tell her.

"Just her?"

"She's sick. Breast cancer. They found it early, at least. She and her wife were making plans to have a baby, so they both wanted to get fully checked out. They found the cancer, and treatments are going well. It's still tough on her. I always wrote in whatever pen came to hand—"

"Black," Mercedes and I say together.

"—but I thought the glitter would make her laugh."

"Did it?"

"She loves it. She's a child psychologist and trauma counselor, at least when she's up for it these days. She keeps boxes of silly pens at work for her patients to use. And then Stanzi."

"Is that short for something?" asks Cass.

"Constanze, like Lissi is short for Ivalisse. Only their *abuelas* call them by their full names, though. Stanzi was accidentally responsible for Faith's only fistfight at school."

"*Faith* got in a *fight*?" I ask, fascinated and appalled in equal measure. "I thought that was your specialty."

"So did we. *Mamá* was so mad at me, thinking I must have taught her how to fight. She was just that angry, though. Our *mamás* grew up together on the island, ours, Stanzi's, Lissi's, and Rafi and Manny's. Stanzi's *papá* was black, and some of the kids at school were mean to her about it. Said she wasn't black enough for the black kids, wasn't Latina enough for the Latina kids. And Faith was so mad, she walked right up to the boy who'd been talking, told him Stanzi was perfect just as she was, and head-butted him right in the nose."

We burst out laughing, and even Bran chuckles along with us.

"Stanzi's in Orlando now. She's an event manager at Disney, does a lot of the Make-A-Wish-type stuff on their end."

All three girls grew into women who dedicated their lives to protecting and helping children. That says a lot about them, but also a lot about Faith, that she inspired that in them.

I set the picture of the four of them aside, keeping it separate just because it's such a joyful picture, and start sifting through the others in the stack. Next to me, Bran goes through the Halloween photos with Mercedes and Cass. The girls were all Teenage Mutant Ninja Princess

Ballerina Turtles, it turns out. Faith was Raphael, Lissi was Donatello, and Amanda was Michelangelo. Stanzi was supposed to be Leonardo, but she was home sick with chicken pox, after being unknowingly exposed to it at her birthday party.

It wasn't a drop-off-your-kid-and-run kind of birthday party. In the pictures, parents are there to help, to play, to mediate, to grill, to stand off on the sides and talk to each other. This was a genuine neighborhood. Everyone's smiling and laughing or bellowing at a kid doing something stupid and/or dangerous. But there's something . . . there's something that's . . . huh.

"Cass?" I interrupt.

"Yeah."

"Look at these."

She gives me a strange look but takes the handful of photos while I reach for my tablet. "What am I . . . oh."

"Right?"

"Oh."

"What is it?" demands Bran.

Leaning over Cass's shoulder, Mercedes frowns at the photos and points to the edge of one of them. "Who is this?"

"That's . . ." He frowns, thinking back. "Mr. Davis? Mr. Davids? He lived a couple of streets over, I think."

"Are any of these kids his?"

"No, his family died."

"How?"

"I don't know," he says slowly, looking between us and the picture. "It was before he moved there."

I spin my tablet around, one of the pictures from Friday filling the screen. "Am I just seeing things?"

Everyone studies the man on the screen.

"It's hard to tell," Cass says finally. "The picture from the party is too small."

"He was passing out fliers on Friday. He was one of the volunteers. We stopped and spoke to him on the way to the school."

"He was the nervous one," Bran murmurs. "The one who looked at you and flinched."

I skim through the rest of the stack of photos from the party, looking for one where he's shown more clearly. Finally there's one where he's standing next to a grill, watching a group of kids shove each other at a picnic table covered in condiments. He looks sad, the way a basset hound always looks sad even when you know they're happy. It's something in the shape of the eyes, the way the skin pouches beneath them. He's dressed neatly in slacks and a light windbreaker open over a polo shirt, medium-light brown hair cut tidily. He doesn't stand out on his own.

"He's looking at Faith in a lot of these pictures," Mercedes points out, making her way through my discards. "At first I thought maybe he was watching the birthday girl, but it's Faith. Look here. Stanzi is on the opposite side of the picture, but he's looking at Faith."

"Mark Davies," Cass announces. I didn't see her get her tablet out, but she has it in hand and open to her notes. "I talked to him a couple of hours after you did, I think. And look." She turns her tablet around to show the picture she took that day, and yes, he's the man I remember. He's aged, certainly, enough that I might not connect the pictures to each other under other circumstances. His eyes, though . . . His eyes are what you recognize first. "He's rented a house one street over and a couple lots down from the Mercers for the past year. He works from home, so we gave him extra attention to find out if he'd seen anything."

"What does he do?"

"Remote technical support. Sunday afternoons he tutors."

"Math," Bran says suddenly. "He tutored math for any kids who needed it. Manny studied with him because he was having trouble with algebra."

Gala and Yvonne walk in, both of them balancing carriers of drinks.

"Good morning, you wonderful ladies, can you please tell us everything you know about Mark Davies?" Mercedes says all in a rush.

Yvonne cocks an eyebrow, but Gala hands her entire carrier across to Mercedes to deal with and plops down behind her monitors. "That's going to be a really common name, you know."

"He rents a house one street over from Brooklyn."

Yvonne hands out the drinks. Bran's has a brownie balanced on top of the lid.

Cass looks at the brownie, then back at Yvonne. At the brownie, back at Yvonne.

"He's having a bad week," she replies pertly.

"DMV says he moved there in January," Gala says. She sounds distracted, her eyes flying back and forth across the screen as she sorts through the information. "Transferred registration of a Subaru Impreza from . . . oh. Madison, Wisconsin."

"Address?"

"Five houses down from Kendall Braun."

Cass worms her way between me and Mercedes and sticks her head out the door. "Watts! I don't have a protein bar to throw at you!"

"You've been off the team too long, Kearney," calls back Johnson. "Watts is the one who throws the protein. We're supposed to catch it before it hits us in the face."

Watts, standing with Vic and Ian outside Vic's office, ignores Johnson and looks over at us. "I was about to check in with you."

"Well, come on then, and bring those two with you."

Watts's eyebrows threaten to disappear into her hairline, but she immediately walks our way.

Gala wriggles in her seat.

As soon as our three newcomers are in the room, Mercedes turns back to Gala. "Go."

"Mark Christopher Davies," she says immediately. "Sixty-nine years old, no surviving close family. Parents died when he was young; he got shuffled around between some distant family members. Started college but dropped out his first semester and applied for a marriage license. Seven months later, he's listed on the birth certificate for a little girl, Lisa. A death certificate was issued for Lisa a little over ten years later, on October 30."

"Cause of death?"

"Leukemia."

"Can you find a picture?"

"Yes," she says after a moment. "Turn on the TV."

Bran reaches out to turn on the screen, as he's closest. Once it's awake, Gala casts the black-and-white photo that looks like it's from a newspaper.

Little Lisa Davies had curly fair hair and light-colored eyes and a shy, gap-toothed grin. Her shoulders are hunched up around her ears, like she didn't really want to be photographed, and her gaze is just a little off-center rather than looking into the camera. A parent next to the camera, perhaps?

"She was diagnosed when she was eight," Gala continues, casting another picture up. It's a scanned-in newspaper article. **Local Girl Diagnosed with Cancer: Best Wishes to Lisa Davies for Her Recovery.**

"Oh, fuck." I sink back into my chair, staring at the screen.

"Eliza?"

"Two years. Holy shit."

"Eliza."

"Oh!" Mercedes claps a hand over her mouth. "Two years. He's trying to replace Lisa. She was eight years old when she was diagnosed, so he takes an eight-year-old girl who looks like her."

"Then why doesn't he just raise the new girl as Lisa?" asks Yvonne. "If he's taken a new daughter . . ."

"Because he lost Lisa. Gala, is he still married?"

"No. His wife, Laura, filed for divorce a year after Lisa died. It was finalized a year later. She remarried a few years later, and . . . from what

I can tell, life got a lot better for her. They're still together, have several kids, adopted a couple of others. She's lived in North Carolina for over thirty years."

Leaning back against the counter, Mercedes skims through my lists of names from the various files. "He's on some of these. Kendall, Riley, Melissa, Joanna . . ."

Yvonne glares at her monitors. "He moved to Madison from Louisville."

"Shelby Skirvin," Vic says, looking at the ranks of photos on the whiteboard. "How long was he there?"

"Two years."

"Which?" Watts asks. "Madison or Louisville?"

"Both," Yvonne answers. "He moved to Madison in January 2016. He moved to Louisville in January 2014."

"Everyone in the neighborhood knew he was only going to be there for two years," Ian says. "I've got some notes about it. Said since his family had died, he didn't like staying in any one place too long. Everyone knew he was moving in a couple of months, so no one thought twice about it when he left. They'd known since he moved in."

"The *mamás* talked about it," adds Bran, a little numbly. "They thought it was sad."

"He moved to Louisville from St. Paul," says Gala.

"Riley Young."

It's amazing how much faster you can find specific information when you have a name and a social security number. It takes less than twenty minutes to definitively place Mark Davies as living in the neighborhood each time one of these girls was abducted.

"That's more than enough for a warrant," Vic announces. "We can absolutely arrest him on this."

"Wait, go back for a moment. Sterling"—Watts looks at me—"explain the two years to me. What is he doing with these girls while he has them?"

"At a guess? They're Lisa. The minute he's able to separate them from their typical surroundings, they lose the identity he knew them by, and they become Lisa."

"But why only the two years? He lost Lisa, but then he gets a new one."

"But losing Lisa was so overwhelmingly traumatic that it's shaped his entire life since then. Losing Lisa is inescapable. Two years of leukemia treatments? In . . . what, the midseventies? He would have watched his daughter go through absolute hell in the hopes of a cure, and then he lost her anyway. He wants that hope of a new beginning. He wants that long and happy life with a healthy daughter, but the trauma might as well be written in his bones. He cannot avoid it."

"But the girls are healthy. You can't *give* someone leukemia."

"No, but you can give someone symptoms. You can make someone sick." I reach out for Bran. He puts my hand on his leg and lays his hand over it, too scared of hurting me again to take it in his. "He makes them sick, and over the course of those two years, they get worse and worse."

"And then they die from it," Mercedes whispers. "Ah, *las pobrecitas*."

"Erin was alive," Bran says, his voice strangled. "For almost two years, Erin was alive a stone's throw from my house, and no one . . ."

"No one knew she was there," Ian finishes grimly. He's wearing sunglasses this morning, and I worry all this stress may be too much for him.

"Bran . . ." I hesitate, which makes him look over at me. "Did you talk to your parents yesterday?"

He shakes his head, lips pressing together so hard they're turning white.

"You should warn them. This is going to break and break hard."

Vic puts a hand on Bran's shoulder, solid and familiar. "You can use my office. When you're ready. Take as much time as you need. Let's get the warrant paperwork prepped."

"How much can we ask for?" Mercedes touches the thin silver crucifix at her throat. It's as much a reassuring gesture for her as it is for me to rub my fingers against the *Magen David*.

"Brooklyn is probably in the house," I point out. "He wouldn't have been able to get away to look in on her anywhere else without attracting attention, especially as he works from home. But we should probably get permission to search the yard, as well."

"The yard?"

"Kendall," I say quietly. "If he left the girls in the houses after they died, an outcry would have arisen at one of the other properties. He would have been caught by now. Maybe he takes them somewhere else, but the yard of the property he rents is the first sensible place to search." Bran looks a little sick, but the rest of them nod. We don't mean to be insensitive; it just kind of happens when you're trained to work through the horror now and deal with the emotional fallout later. "We also need to prep warrant requests for each of his prior residences. It doesn't make sense to file them until we find out what he's been doing with . . . with the bodies, but we should have them ready."

"Sterling, I want you with us when we pick him up."

"Eh?" I glance at Watts.

"I want that flinch. I want him to open the door and see you and be unsettled."

I look at the board, with its parade of missing girls. A picture of eight-year-old me could be slipped in between any of them, and no one would so much as blink. "He has seen me before," I feel obliged to mention. "He might not flinch a second time."

"True. But Brooklyn looks like her mother; that could be comforting until we can get her mother to her."

Suddenly the thing that hampered the investigation could help us now.

Bran's hand presses against mine, and I can feel his full-body tremble. He stares down at a picture of his sister playing with her friends, Mark Davies's sad eyes watching from the background.

22

The conference room and bullpen become a carefully contained flurry of activity, everyone jumping to a task. Each address Mark Davies has lived at needs a separate warrant, all of which need approval from a judge, and it'll go a lot faster if we can get one federal judge to sign off on all of them. We also can't tell Richmond PD yet, because sometimes, even with the best of intentions, the local officers can entirely fuck up a Bureau operation by moving in without us. If they did that, they'd get Davies, and maybe they'd rescue Brooklyn, but they wouldn't have the full chain in mind when questioning him, and their arrest warrant wouldn't have all the information.

"Sterling!"

I jump and spin around to see Watts back in the doorway of the conference room. "Yes?"

"Do you have a curling iron in your go bag?"

"No?"

She grimaces, then sticks her head back out to the bullpen. "Anyone have a curling iron we can use on Sterling?"

Someone answers in the affirmative.

"Watts?"

"All the girls have had curly hair," she says at a normal volume, "including Lisa. If we're going to yank the ground out from under him, let's do it properly. Soft and sweet, Sterling. With curly hair."

"Roger that."

Bran is in Vic's office with the door closed. Ian is in there with him. I don't know if he's psyching himself up to talk to his parents, talking to his parents, or recovering from talking to his parents. Or perhaps he hasn't gotten there yet, and he's still talking to Ian. Unless and until he opens that door, I'm not asking.

"Priya's on her way," Mercedes tells me as I grab the go bag from under my desk. "She's got a blouse and sweater for you to go with that whole softer thing."

"I do still need to look like an agent."

"You will; she's modeling it off Agent Dern." She hands me a curling iron from God only knows who.

I tug at the strap on my shoulder, adjusting the weight of the bag, and tuck the tool into one of the side pockets. "When did she even meet the Dragonmother?"

"At my reinstatement party three years ago."

"Right. Did she say what color the top was?"

"Gala has managed to find three pictures of Lisa, and she's wearing pink in two of them."

Well, I've definitely got makeup that goes with pink. Once in the bathroom, I dump the bag on the counter and root through for my spare brush and clips as well as the cosmetics bag. It feels strange to completely scrub down my face and immediately reapply, but soft and sweet is an entirely different kind of face than serious professional. To try to hit both of those marks is challenging.

The curls, thankfully, don't have to be perfect. They just have to look natural. They don't have to be even, or tidy, or carefully shaken out. It is the fastest I have ever curled my hair in my life. When I get back to the bullpen, Priya is there with an FBI visitor's badge clipped to her collar, watching all the activity with wide eyes.

"They're your own things," she tells me, handing me a large Sephora bag. "I wasn't sure exactly what you needed, so I grabbed anything I thought might fit the bill."

I rifle through the shirts. "This is perfect. Thank you."

"Good luck." She glances up at Vic's window—someone must have told her Bran was there—and then heads off the floor.

I pull out one of the blouses, a deep berry that still leans more toward pink than purple, and a three-quarter-sleeved cardigan in a soft carnation. The sleeves of the shirt are longer than those of the sweater, but I roll them back in a way that both hides that and looks kind of trendy, despite the presence of the bandage. I leave the curling iron sitting on my desk for whoever owns it to reclaim it.

Ian's sitting at Eddison's desk now, silently watching everything around him. He's less wide-eyed than Priya. He's seen full-scale operations before, albeit in uniforms rather than suits.

I walk over and lean against the edge of the desk. "Are you okay?"

"Of all the questions to ask me right now, Eliza, you've picked the one I can't begin to answer."

"That's fair."

He looks at the edge of the bandage under my sleeve and sighs. "How's your arm?"

"It's doing better."

"It's been a very long time since I saw the boy that distressed."

"What did you do back then?"

"Took him to the stadium and made him run up and down the stairs for a couple hours."

I grin in spite of myself. Explains where he got his love of running stadiums, then. "What did you do yesterday?"

"I was going to make him find me a stadium, but apparently he's not allowed to do that anymore."

"No, his doctor wasn't too thrilled with him when he tried to keep doing it. There's some lingering damage around his knee from the bullet three years ago."

"So I made him run laps along the battlefield paths."

Wow. I've run the paths on some of the old Civil War sites with Bran and Mercedes. Once through is already a lot of running. Laps?

"Don't let him off easy, Eliza. We both know he didn't mean it. You can forgive the act, but don't try to absolve the consequences."

"I really will try, Ian. I promise."

"Good."

"First warrants got approved!" Watts calls across the pen. Everyone immediately hushes to listen except for one person on the phone with the Central District Medical Examiner's office; she holds up her arms in apology, a sheepish expression on her face. "Ramirez, Kearney, Sterling, let's go."

Vic gives her a sideways look. He's supposed to be in the field, too, on this one anyway. He even asked permission beforehand.

"Sorry, Vic," Watts tells him, not looking sorry at all, "but as soon as we find Kendall, or Davies indicates the girls are buried elsewhere, we're going to be flying on those other warrants and wrangling the local field offices to get out there and find them, and somehow keep it all reasonably secret. You've got the authority and experience to do that."

He considers that and nods, acknowledging the point even if he doesn't look happy about it.

"Look on the bright side, Vic. You've got Yvonne prepping the information. Let's roll!"

"I'll meet you at the cars," I tell Ramirez, handing her my tablet.

She glances up at Vic's office with the door still closed, and kisses my cheek.

The blinds are closed, so I knock on the door, softly in case he's still on the phone. "It's Eliza."

The door swings open, framing a haggard-looking Bran. "I haven't called them yet," he says, his voice rough and tight.

"We're about to head out."

Ignoring the fact that we're in full view of the madhouse that is currently the bullpen, he wraps his arms around me and presses a kiss against my temple. "Find that girl, Eliza. Give one family a better ending."

I breathe him in, my lips against his jaw, and nod.

We ride with Watts, the rest of her team hustling into another SUV. Gala calls and Watts puts it through the car's Bluetooth, the fledgling analyst's voice tinny with speaker distortion. "Davies was arrested once for public disturbance almost forty years ago, but charges were never filed. From the report, it looks like he had a bit of a breakdown in a bar when his wife served him divorce papers. No property damage, no one was hurt, but the bar manager called the police when he wouldn't stop howling."

"Howling?" Kearney echoes.

"Apparently he was crying rather spectacularly? The report says he was in severe emotional distress. They held him overnight, let him go once he was calm. Aside from that, just a couple of parking tickets here and there, a speeding ticket about four years ago."

"What can you tell us about Lisa?"

"One of the warrants got us her medical records, and St. Jude's was eager to help. In addition to the records, they went through her original file to send the nonmedical information. At least during that time, they had the kids fill out questionnaires so the medical staff and other kids could get to know them. She said she was good at math and science and wanted to work at NASA someday. She wanted to be the first ballerina on the moon."

Bless the dreams of children.

"The psychologist's notes indicate she was mostly pretty calm about her treatments and prognosis. She had outbursts from time to time, when it all got too much, but for the most part she was quietly upbeat. Both her parents worked like hell through her childhood to cover all the bills and still give her some nice things, so she was used to quietly entertaining herself. She liked pink and yellow, didn't like green. When asked what her favorite music was, she said the Irish stompy kind."

"She sounds sweet," murmurs Watts.

"According to her records, she never really had a sharp or sudden decline. It was a pretty steady progression of symptoms and disease that the treatments slowed but couldn't reverse."

I clear my throat. "Gala, can you copy over her strongest symptoms and get them to the hospital in Richmond closest to the Mercers' neighborhood?"

From the driver's seat, Watts gives me a curious look. "Sterling?"

"He might not have had time yet, but there's a chance he's already making her sick."

"To contain her?" asks Kearney.

"No, to recreate Lisa."

"Right," she says, looking queasy.

"He can't give them leukemia, he can't take them to a hospital for treatments for a disease they don't have, even if he gives them symptoms. This is all done at home. But Kendall's aneurysm threw off his timeline. He lost her after one year, not two."

"So either he's resetting and treating this as a new beginning, or he's going to make Brooklyn very sick very quickly to match up to where Kendall would have been on that scale," Ramirez says.

I nod. "My guess is the latter. Part of how he's gotten away with this is that he leaves town a couple of months after the kidnapping, in a way that everyone expects, and moves to a new town where he could come up with some sort of explanation for a sick girl if someone were to accidentally see her. His pattern has kept him safe; he has to try to stick with it."

"So the hospital needs to be aware of what those symptoms are so they can quickly look for the things that can cause them," Watts finishes. "Gala, have you been able to access his financials yet?"

"Yes, but nothing's really sticking out," she answers. "No medical supply stores or anything, and no reported thefts from hospitals or clinics that follow him from place to place."

"Maybe not, but he's probably got a number of purchases at home improvement stores. Gardening centers, too, maybe."

"Yes . . . how'd you know that, Sterling?"

"Fertilizers, industrial-strength cleaners, varnishes, pesticides, rat poisons, you can buy all these things without raising any eyebrows, especially if you're known in the area for gardening or helping out your neighbors. Depending on how far he goes to recreate the look of the treatments, you can cobble together homemade IV tubing too. To spread out over two years, the poisoning would be slow and cumulative, so he would never have to buy so much at once that it looks suspicious."

"So . . . do you *have* to have a terrifying and twisted mind to succeed in the FBI, or does it just help?" Gala asks.

Despite everything, we chuckle at that. "Little A, little B," I reply. "A lot of it is training."

"Just think, padawan," says Yvonne, joining the conversation from Quantico, "this is what you have to look forward to."

"'Look forward to' seems like a poor word choice."

Watts shakes her head. "Steal more help if you need to, ladies, but as you're prepping the warrants, try to find out if all his previous residences are still standing. Also, see if anything has been discovered at those addresses over the years that couldn't be identified."

We get to Richmond in just over an hour, because Watts is driving nowhere near the speed limit. She slows down once we hit the city, though, and that's when Mercedes calls the day-shift captain directly to let him know what's about to happen. He promises to meet us there himself, with just a couple of officers and their dogs in order to keep it discreet.

My heart thumps erratically as we pass the school and pull into the neighborhood. It's a Wednesday, and despite the panic of the weekend, life doesn't stop. The kids are back at school, the adults are back at work, with the probable exception of the Mercers and possibly the Coperniks. One of them may be home with Rebecca, as she's likely still sick. All the frenetic activity of the first few days has faded in the face of bills and schedules.

I hate it, but it's reality. And we do it too. The first few days are all-out, sleep-is-for-the-weak endeavors, because that's our best chance of finding a missing kid. But once that period passes, once it turns into an endurance case, as Vic calls them, we have to rest. We have to step away for bits of time, because we're not going to find anyone or anything if we're hospitalized after a collapse. Common sense wars with need and leaves you feeling guilty for taking care of yourself.

Agent Burnside parks the second Bureau car a few houses down, across the street from the K-9 unit's vehicle. The captain's car is a couple houses down on the other side of Davies's house. Nothing to cause alarm; nothing to hint at a trap.

Watts parks just in front of the house, leaving the driveway empty. Davies's Impreza must be in the garage.

I nervously fluff my hair and check my makeup. Soft and pretty and fragile, all the things I worked so hard not to resemble after I joined the Bureau.

"Get us in the door," Watts instructs. "This will be a lot easier if he lets us in. Stay soft, open, be aware of your body language. Be deferential. Did you ever sell Girl Scout cookies?"

"For years," I answer, thinking of Shira's dad taking us around to keep us safe.

"Think that, but dial it back a little. You're not trying to sell him anything, but you do want that impression of opening the door to unbearable cuteness. Once he opens that door, don't let him close it. Ramirez will be next to you. I'll be right around the edge of the garage with Captain Scott."

"Ramirez gets all the fun," Kearney sighs.

"He won't have to look down to see Ramirez," Watts replies with a smirk.

Kearney huffs but doesn't retort.

I take a slow, deep breath, then another. And one more for luck. "Let's go."

23

Ramirez stands a few feet away as I ring the doorbell, not hiding, precisely, but not in focus for anyone looking through the peephole. After a few minutes, I give four firm knocks to the door, and ring the bell again for good measure. I have my credentials folder in my other hand. Usually I'd be holding it up by my shoulder, ready to flip open and present, but this time I keep it low, near my hip, ready to unfold and offer. It's amazing how such a small detail shifts the tone of an encounter.

It takes another few minutes for Davies to come to the door. He's almost seventy now, according to our information, and his middling brown hair is mostly grey. His sad blue eyes look the same as in the pictures from Stanzi's birthday party. He's dressed simply in a pair of tan slacks and a tucked-in plaid shirt that's mostly blue. He's wearing house slippers rather than shoes.

He startles at the sight of me—again—and I smile back, keeping to the watchwords of the meeting. Soft, sweet, open. "Mark Davies? My name is Eliza Sterling, and I'm with the FBI. We're helping the police search for Brooklyn Mercer."

"Yes," he says, his voice quiet and unassuming. Unprovoking. "I remember you. We spoke while I was passing out fliers. It's such a terrible thing."

"Mr. Davies, may we come in? I know you've already been interviewed, but we're following up with everyone based on some new information. I hope you'll forgive the inconvenience. It's to help us find that sweet little girl."

"I'm sorry, I'm not really fit for company at the moment." He gestures self-consciously at his house shoes.

"That's all right, Mr. Davies. We're certainly not going to judge you for what you wear in your own home."

He stares at me for a moment, and as I shift my weight under the scrutiny, several curls tumble over my shoulder. He watches them bounce, his gaze a million miles—or forty-one years—away. "Of course," he says finally. "Please, come in. I can hardly keep you out here in this chill. Wherever is your coat? You'll catch a cold."

Ramirez manages to slip in just behind me without looking like she's trying to sneak or force her way in, and leans against the doorframe in such a way that he can't close the door. "Agent Ramirez, Mr. Davies. We met this weekend."

"Yes, yes, of course. I don't believe we spoke long, though."

"No, I've mostly been with Frank and Alice Mercer. They're devastated with the loss of their daughter."

He closes his eyes in sympathy.

Which is when Watts and Captain Scott come around the corner. Ramirez discreetly shifts across the doorway to where she's actively holding the door open rather than preventing its close. I step around Mr. Davies so I'm at his back, loosening my gun in its holster just in case. Soft and sweet does not mean unarmed.

"Mark Davies," calls Watts.

His eyes snap open to stare at her in confusion. He doesn't seem to register that Ramirez and I have moved.

"I'm Agent Watts with the FBI; this is Captain Scott of Richmond PD. I am hereby placing you under arrest for the kidnapping of Brooklyn Mercer and the kidnapping and murder of sixteen other girls. Their names are listed in our warrant."

"Wh-what? I'm sorry?"

An ambulance races down the street to park in the driveway, probably held back on the next street so it was out of sight.

"You have the right to remain silent," Watts continues. "Anything you say can and will be used against you in a court of law."

Davies backs away from her, stumbling over the edge of his house slipper. He turns sharply, his back to her, and faces me standing a foot away. He flinches and sways with a low moan. "No . . . you've made a mistake. I'm sorry, I don't have time for this. My daughter . . . my daughter is ill, she needs me."

Captain Scott reaches out to clasp the first cuff around Davies's wrist. He's careful not to cinch it too tightly, and he's visibly holding back strength—and probably fury—as he gently tugs Davies's other arm behind him to the second cuff. Watts nods at me and continues Mirandizing the man while Captain Scott turns him and leads him out of the house. Almost as an afterthought, Watts throws a stuffed puppy over her shoulder for me to catch.

Two paramedics run up to the house, a gurney bouncing between them. "Where is she?" the older one asks straight off.

"We're not sure yet. Now that we're in, we can search."

"Want we should wait here?"

"Please," Ramirez answers. "Trust me, we'll yell."

It's a two-story house, with a living room right up at the front and the bedrooms tucked up over it, a narrow hall leading to the kitchen and dining room on one side and the stairwell and a bathroom on the other.

"I'll take upstairs," Ramirez says, and heads up quickly.

I glance through the downstairs rooms. It's a rental property; he can't make many changes. No secret rooms, no hidden doors. My fingers run over a coat closet in the hallway, kind of a weird distance away from the door, and I open it. Yes, a coat closet. But the next door, set into the wall under the stairs, opens to a dark stairwell. I flick the light switch near the door, and a single, swaying bulb casts more shadows than light across the steep steps.

Pulling the flashlight off my belt, I carefully descend. Technically I should have my gun out, but there's no indication that Davies ever worked with a partner, and if Brooklyn's down here, I don't want her first sight of me to be with a gun in my hand.

At the base of the stairs, floor-to-ceiling heavy fabric divider panels block off all but the narrow path leading to the laundry room. My high school had those in the band and chorus rooms to absorb the sound and save the other classes from being driven mad by the cacophony. Near the middle, there's a narrow crack of light.

"Brooklyn?" I ask cautiously. "Brooklyn, are you down here?"

I hear a muffled sniffle, then a quavering "Hello?"

I clip the flashlight back to my belt and get my hands into that crack, shoving the panels apart. More fabric sections line the walls to create a basically soundproof room. The insides of the dividers have pictures and posters pinned in place. There are even curtains around a window frame that has a galaxy poster behind the narrow crossbeams. There's a light pink toy chest spilling over with stuffed animals, a child's desk with boxes of crayons and markers lined against the back edge, and a white dresser with pink drawers.

And there, on the pink-and-yellow bed, a wide-eyed, pale Brooklyn Mercer shakes in fear. A bucket nearby smells unpleasantly of vomit, but all the tubing of the homemade IV stand is dry and draped over thin hooks.

"Brooklyn." I walk forward, sitting down on the edge of the bed, and slowly reach a hand to her clammy forehead. "Oh, Brooklyn, sweetheart, we have been looking for you. I'm so glad we found you."

She starts crying and struggles against the weight of the blankets over her. I help her fold them back and suddenly find myself with an armful of sobbing little girl. I hold her close and gently rock her back and forth.

"I have to let the others know you're down here," I tell her after a minute. "I'm going to pull away just for a second so I'm not screaming in your ear, okay?"

At her nod, I lean back, covering her exposed ear with one hand for good measure. "Down here!" I yell. "She's down here! Down in the basement!"

Footsteps thunder down the stairs, and Brooklyn tenses, her hand closing hard around my arm.

My bandaged arm. I swallow against the flare of pain and the unpleasant squish of blisters bursting.

"It's okay," I murmur. "They're here to help. It's okay, Brooklyn, we took him away. He can't keep you here anymore."

She twists her head to look up at me. Her eyes are a little glassy, which could be shock, and there are two angry blotches of pink high on her cheeks.

Trying not to jostle her too much, I slowly shift my grip until one arm is free and I can offer her the stuffed puppy. This one is mostly dark brown with tan splashes, making it almost a negative of the one I gave her best friend. "You know, while we were looking for you, we gave Rebecca a puppy a lot like this one."

She sniffs and touches the puppy's nose, but doesn't take it. "Rebecca's sick," she croaks, her voice hoarse. From crying, maybe, or from vomiting?

"She is, so we gave her one of these to hug and throw and worry into. She's been so worried, just like your parents."

Tears spread in a damp patch against my chest. "I wasn't supposed to walk home alone," she whispers. "We were always supposed to walk together, but she went home sick, and my parents weren't there, and I didn't know what to do."

"That's not your fault, Brooklyn. You didn't do anything wrong."

"Mr. Davies said I could wait with him until my parents got home. Rebecca needed a doctor. He was worried, because there wouldn't be anyone at her house to help me if something happened."

Ramirez and the paramedics peek through the hole in the acoustic panels. At the sight of Brooklyn, awake and responsive, Ramirez closes her eyes and crosses herself. She holds out a hand to keep the paramedics back for a moment.

"It's okay, Brooklyn." I gently rub her back. "You're safe now. Your parents are going to be so happy. They're not going to be angry, sweetheart. You didn't do anything wrong. And you and Rebecca can look out for each other, okay? You're both going to need a lot of rest to get better."

She touches the stuffed animal's nose again. "Rebecca wants a real puppy. She wants to name it Hamish."

"Hamish! You know, that's exactly what she named the one we gave her." I wiggle the puppy on her knee, making its ears flap adorably. "Do you think this little guy has a name?"

She considers it for a moment, blinking rapidly. "Hubert," she announces.

"Hamish and Hubert?"

"They're two of Merida's brothers," she informs me around a yawn. "From *Brave*. I'm going to be an archer someday. Dad says I'm not old enough to play with anything pointy yet."

"That might be fair."

Her hand curls into the plush fabric, and she draws it to her belly so she doesn't have to lean away to cuddle it. "We have to find a Harris. They were triplets."

"Maybe you can talk Daniel into it."

"Okay." She yawns again and snuggles deeper into my chest. "I don't feel so good," she confides.

"We're going to get you help for that, Brooklyn. These nice paramedics"—both of the men standing by Mercedes smile and wave—"are going

223

to give you a quick check here while someone's getting your parents, and then we're going to take you to the hospital, okay?"

She nods sleepily.

"You don't even have to let go."

"Okay."

The older paramedic walks forward slowly, his hands already gloved. As he comes to stand next to us, he glances into the vomit bucket to one side. I am very sure he gets more information out of that look than I would, and more power to him. He asks her a few questions, then holds up his stethoscope. "Do you know what this is?"

"It lets you listen to my heart," she says. "The nurse at school has one."

"Do you think you could sit up a little for me and let me have a listen? You don't need to let go, just sit up."

She looks up at me, and at my encouraging nod, lets me help her sit upright.

Ramirez catches my eye and points upstairs, then to Brooklyn, then points her finger down at the ground and moves it in a circle.

The Mercers are here.

After a brief look at my bandage, the paramedic gives Brooklyn another warm smile. "Sweetheart, we brought a board downstairs to carry you, but I don't think you need it. I think you can be carried up by one of us, and it won't be as scary. Is that okay with you?"

She eyes him uncertainly, then looks at me again. "You?"

I start to answer—of freaking course I will carry her—but the paramedic speaks before I can. "Do you mind if it's me, sweetheart? The agent has a hurt arm."

Brooklyn follows his pointing finger to my bandage, and her mouth opens into a perfect little O of surprise. "Are you going to be okay?" she asks earnestly.

I give her a hug; I can't help it. God bless this child. "I'm going to be just fine. You know how your parents don't let you boil water on the stove without an adult?"

"I could get burned," she answers solemnly.

"I might need an adult too," I whisper, and she giggles.

It takes her another moment or two to think through it, but she finally nods. "Okay. He can carry me. Mr. Davies put my backpack over by the desk."

I can see it tucked between the desk and the legs of the chair. "We'll get that to you later, Brooklyn. We need to leave it there for pictures."

Without putting too much pressure on my blisters, Brooklyn and I manage to transfer her into the paramedic's arms. He hoists her up comfortably, then bounces her twice, just a little, to make her laugh. She tucks in close against him, her forehead to his neck. His partner goes up ahead of us, Ramirez and I following behind.

When we get outside, Franklin and Alice Mercer are standing there, clutching each other for strength. "Brooklyn!" gasps Alice. "My baby!"

"Mommy?" Brooklyn lifts her head and twists around to see better. "Mommy! Daddy!" She wiggles excitedly, but the paramedic keeps a good grip on her.

"I'll put you down right next to them," he promises. "But you don't feel well, so I don't want you to fall down." He keeps his word and sets her down on the back end of the ambulance, a hand around one of her arms in case she loses her balance.

Alice throws herself at her daughter, sobbing hysterically, and cuddles the girl close, rocking her back and forth. Her husband wraps his arms around them both, crying silently but just as hard.

Ramirez drapes her arms around my shoulders. "This is a good day," she says quietly.

It's a good moment, but the day is far from over. There are a lot of parents who are about to get the other kind of news.

But this *is* a good moment, so I lean into Ramirez and we watch the Mercers fuss over their daughter.

24

Ramirez splits off with Johnson from Watts's team to follow the Mercers to the hospital and get the full evaluation of Brooklyn's condition. Kearney finds a set of houses without fences and goes through to the next street so she can tell the Coperniks. She dutifully promises to tell Rebecca what Brooklyn named her stuffed puppy. We don't have one for Daniel—we don't usually give the toys to teenagers—but I'm sure we can get our hands on one if Rebecca and Brooklyn ask him to adopt one to round out the triplets.

I have a feeling there's not much he won't do for a while for his little sister and her best friend.

Once more police officers arrive to secure the house and basement. I head to the backyard with Burnside and the locals, who introduce themselves as Officers Wayne, Todd, Maximus, and Cupcake.

Maximus and Cupcake, it should be noted, are the dogs.

"Maybe start in the corner," I suggest, pointing to the area in question. "The dirt's been recently turned over."

If I didn't know we were looking for a body, it wouldn't seem ominous. It's one of several areas along the fence line or the back of the house marked off with short brick borders meant to delineate flower beds or vegetable patches. This is the only one that's had recent attention, however.

The dogs sniff eagerly at the command, and in the middle of the quarter-circle-shaped bed, both of them suddenly lay down, their chins between their paws.

"They've hit," Officer Wayne explains.

Burnside pulls a camera and three sets of neoprene gloves from his bag. "We'll get shovels when we need them. For now, we don't know how deeply she's buried."

Officer Todd calls both dogs to him, and they sit next to him without hesitation, watching us keenly. While Burnside snaps photos to document the process, Wayne and I pull on the gloves and kneel down to scoop away handfuls of earth. It hasn't been cold enough to harden the soil in the patches. Here, where it's been worked, it moves easily. We mound it against the fence to keep it out of the way. My hand hits plastic not quite a foot down.

"Hit," I say quietly.

Wayne nods and moves his hands to the same place, and we gently push the soft dirt away, moving outward from that spot. It doesn't take us too long to completely uncover the tightly wrapped bundle of plastic sheeting. There's a blanket within the sheeting, obscuring Kendall from view.

"There are no bugs," he notes.

"The plastic is bound tightly enough to slow decomp, so it hasn't attracted any yet. You can ask Kearney for the details if you're interested," I tell him.

"Yeah?"

"She studied forensic entomology before the academy."

Burnside shudders. "Not around me, please, and not after you've eaten."

A moment later and he won't even have to remember to ask Kearney. From the other side of the back fence, there's a *sproing* and an *oof* as Kearney's head and arms appear over the fence. She heaves herself over the fence and drops to the ground. "I lost track of which yards to go through. The people behind here have a trampoline, so I—oh." She catches sight of the sorry bundle. "No smell of decomp. Must have a good seal." She walks over, pulling a small film canister from her pocket. Inside are a pair of gloves, several Band-Aids, and a folding set of tweezers.

"That's clever."

"It's actually a mini first aid kit. They taught it to us in Boy Scouts, and I never lost the habit." Tugging on the gloves, she kneels down next to me and examines the wrapping. "Thick, but not a full-on tarp. Probably intended for gardening or house painting. Sturdy. See these pleats?" she asks, drawing a finger along them. "There are probably half a dozen layers over the quilt, and those pleats get the plastic in close over the more awkwardly shaped bits like feet and neck. There's sealant over the outside edge too. We need to warn the field offices before they serve the local warrants."

"Warn them?"

"If he prepared them all this way, they're not going to find the expected rate of decomposition. Most of the graves could be expected to have only or mostly bones, but some of them—the most recent ones—will be, um . . . well, let's say 'fleshier' than planned for."

"In case you're wondering, Kearney," Burnside says with a sigh, "this is why we haven't tried to steal you back."

She gives him the evil eye. She does not, however, try to argue with him, so I'm guessing they were more grossed out by science-over-meals than we are.

Officer Todd pulls out his phone. "I'll call the ME to come retrieve the body. Best we leave the wrapping in place, yes?"

"Yes," Kearney replies firmly. "By measuring each layer, they can calculate a pretty close estimate of how much the wrapping retarded decay, and get a date of death from there."

"She was barely a foot down," I point out. "If the others were buried that shallowly, they should have been found a long time ago."

"Maybe he panicked? Kendall's death was unexpected; it threw off his routine. He didn't expect to need a new Lisa for another year, and he would have left soon afterward. Kendall died significantly ahead of his schedule, so he got her in the ground as quickly as possible so he could focus on finding a new girl. Maybe he would have come back and done it properly once he had Brooklyn settled."

"True. And if everyone's searching the neighborhood for a missing girl, you probably don't want to risk the neighbors seeing you digging a grave in your backyard. It would have been a huge risk to keep Brooklyn here for a whole year with everyone searching for her."

"Think he would have broken his lease and left early?"

"Maybe. Or if he was accelerating Brooklyn's sickness to match his usual timeline, maybe he would have kidnapped another girl before leaving."

"Two eight-year-old blonde girls from the same area a year apart? We definitely would have figured something out then."

My work phone buzzes, and I strip off a glove to get it out of its case, flicking the ringer back on before answering it on speaker. "Sterling."

"It's Gala. A girl's body was discovered in the backyard of Davies's Houston residence about eight years ago. It was never identified. He moved there eighteen years ago, moved away sixteen years ago. I contacted the field office; they're pulling the medical records for both Tiffany King and Lydia Green. Tiffany went missing nineteen years ago from Seattle. Lydia is the one who went missing from Houston itself."

"So the body is probably Tiffany. Did they say how it was found?"

"A year after Davies left, the owners he'd rented from sold the house. Six years later, the new owners sold the house. The third set of owners decided to dig out the backyard to install a swimming pool, and the body was found."

"Any details about the body?"

"It was wrapped in plastic. The construction workers didn't realize it was a body, apparently, so they opened it to find out what was inside. It was summer, and by the time they finished freaking out and called the cops and the cops got there . . ."

"Decomp had already accelerated beyond whatever preservations the plastic had offered," I finish with a sigh. "They weren't able to assess a time of death. What did the investigation look like?"

"That's the thing: there really wasn't one. Not much of one. The middle set of owners had a reputation for being a sort of halfway house for undocumented immigrants, so when the police found the body . . ."

"They assumed it was an immigrant child and that the parents hid the body rather than report the death and risk deportation."

"Bingo."

"Did they determine a cause of death?"

"No. Like I said, they weren't looking very hard."

"Okay. We've got a warning for you to pass on to the other field offices, but it's pretty gross. You ready for it or do you want to hand the phone off?"

Officer Wayne looks startled until Kearney leans over and mutters, "Brand new analyst. We like this one. Don't want to break her."

Gala sighs gustily into the phone. "I have to get used to it at some point, right?"

"Atta girl." I pass on Kearney's caution about the decomp, and to·her credit, Gala doesn't sound like she's going to vomit when she acknowledges it. "Is Vic nearby?"

"Umm . . . I can see him in the bullpen. Hang on." There are muffled footsteps, the sound of blinds swaying against an opening door, and a yelled "Unit Chief Hanoverian! Call for you, sir! It's Sterling!"

"I think my phone just blew out," I say.

"Sorry, I forgot I was wearing the headset. Give me a second and I'll transfer it to the speaker while he comes up."

"Sterling?" Vic asks a moment later, huffing slightly. Vic is pretty fit for his age, but he's not field-fit anymore. Every now and then it shows. "What have you got?"

"Kendall Braun, most likely. We need her medical records sent to the Richmond ME, Gala, while I'm thinking on it."

"Roger that."

"Vic, do you think it would be possible to ask Tampa and Omaha to delay executing their searches until we can get there?"

"Why those two specifically?"

"He takes a new Lisa just before he moves to a new place. That means each girl is going to be buried in the next city down the list, not the one she was taken from. Faith is almost definitely buried in Omaha, and if you bar Bran from being there when his sister is found, he may honestly never forgive you."

"Fair point. Do you really think he should see her that way?"

"I think it should be his choice. I also think we both know what that choice is going to be. He'll shield his parents from that, but he's not going to protect himself from it."

"So why Tampa?"

"Because his parents deserve an in-person warning of what's about to happen *before* we go dig up a neighbor's backyard. The whole neighborhood remembers Faith, whether they actually knew her or not. Some of their childhood friends, including their best friends, still live on that street. It's going to be a Big Thing, and I think we should make sure, before we pull a little girl's body out of the ground, that they know it won't be Faith. They need to know she hasn't been two streets over this whole time. Also . . ." I frown as the thought hits me, wondering why it didn't before. "Also, I think we should ask Agent Karwan if he wants to be there. Erin Bailey is buried there, and she was his sister's best friend. He's already had to recuse himself from the Omaha portion of the case because of Erin's place in the chain, and I think he'd be grateful to be offered the choice."

"All right. I'll check with Eddison and Karwan, then call the field offices and arrange flights and cars. But you're going to have to move fast, Eliza. We want all the bodies exhumed before the news breaks nationally."

"We can be in Tampa tonight. Local police will need to be out against Halloween mischief, but we can execute the warrant first thing in the morning, then fly to Omaha and be there by afternoon. Karwan can meet us in Tampa and fly back to Omaha with us."

"Just remember that you're the only active agent going. Eddison and Karwan are both on leave, and if the local agents or police tell them they have to leave the scene, they cannot argue."

"Understood. What about Ian?"

"Same rule will apply for him, if he goes. I'll ask him. You should also understand that Omaha is already likely delayed. Douglas and Sarpy County sheriffs' offices are arguing over who should be with the FBI on this one."

"Why?"

"Because the property Davies rented is only sort of in Omaha. It butts up against the road they use as the county line. It's technically unincorporated and part of Sarpy County, but Douglas is arguing that because it's basically part of the greater Omaha area, they should be handling it."

"That's beyond stupid. The house is where it is, and unless there's actual contestation of the county line—"

"There isn't, but the two sheriffs aren't the best of friends. This is how they snipe at each other."

"Can you tell them to schedule the dick-measuring contest for another time?"

Gala and Kearney both snort, and there's a soft laugh that might be Yvonne in the background of the call. Todd and Wayne both look startled and a little embarrassed. Burnside just rolls his eyes and gives Kearney a meaningful look.

Because she traded to the weird team.

"Watts called," Vic continues after a long silence. Kearney bites her lip to keep from laughing at his less-than-subtle change of direction, because it's not the most appropriate moment, given what she's got her hands on right now. "They're taking Davies to the hospital."

"The hospital?"

"They got him to the station and tried to begin questioning him. He started panicking. Kept saying his daughter was sick, that she needed him. He had a full-blown attack, difficulty breathing, so they're taking him to the hospital to make sure his heart is all right and so he can be sedated if need be. Once the doctors release him, he'll be brought down to Quantico."

"When do they think that will be?"

"Honestly? Probably tomorrow. He's not young."

I could point out that he's only five years or so older than Vic, but I don't. Age isn't the only factor in his health.

"Priya has volunteered to be the home-base gofer today, as she's the only one of the girls that drives. If there's anything you want from home that isn't in your go bag, text it to her. She'll drive Eddison and Ian and pick you up on the way to Richmond International."

"I'll text her."

"After you check the weather in Omaha?"

"Damn straight."

"Eliza . . ."

"Yes?"

"Don't linger in Omaha. We may need you to talk to him."

"I'm not sure how many times we can keep unsettling him with how I look, Vic."

"You might be surprised. The psychology . . ."

"Oh, right. Yeah, okay. We'll overnight in Tampa, catch a red-eye from Omaha."

"Keep me posted."

"You do the same."

"Oh, and Eliza?"

"Yes?"

"Is there any particular reason the girls came home last night smelling of smoke?"

"We burned my wedding dress to make s'mores," I answer blandly.

Yvonne cheers in the background.

In the second long silence of the conversation, Burnside sighs and shakes his head at Kearney, and the officers look well beyond confused. Kearney hides her grin against her hunched shoulder.

Finally Vic says, "Keep me posted."

Coward.

I end the call and look at Kearney, but it's Officer Wayne who speaks.

"What did he mean, 'the psychology'?"

"Davies has been reliving his daughter's illness and death for thirty-one years," I say quietly. "Right up until the moment that he got Brooklyn downstairs into that room, he could probably recognize her as Brooklyn, as someone else's daughter. As soon as she was in Lisa's environment, though, she became Lisa. He became incapable of recognizing her as anyone else. It's how he could be genuinely worried about Brooklyn and help search for her; the girl in the basement was Lisa, not Brooklyn. She was his daughter. And now we're threatening that delusion, trying to force the rational part of his mind beyond the compulsions."

"So if he's that fixated on his daughter . . ."

"Precisely. He'll remember me, but my resemblance to his daughter will be shocking all over again. Like a goldfish finding its castle in the bowl again."

"My girlfriend keeps pushing me to train up for the detective's exam," Todd says. "Next time she brings it up, I'm telling her this is the reason I won't."

Officer Cupcake barks, as if in agreement.

I text a wish list to Priya, which includes the request that she take the rent check off my fridge and drop it off at the office for me tomorrow. The residents have been begging the office to let us pay early, or pay online or have a drop box or *something* that doesn't limit us to office hours on the first three days of the month, but no such luck. There have been a number of months where I've been out of town and Jenny Hanoverian has delivered it for me.

I have a feeling Priya is already driving, because the response is garbled into incomprehensibility, which is what tends to happen when she uses the dictation feature. The London-born, Boston-raised Paris resident has a drifting accent anymore, and it confuses the hell out of her phone.

"Once the ME gets here, we should get you to a clinic," Kearney informs me, standing and stripping off her gloves.

"Huh?"

"There's grave dirt on your bandage, and it looks like your burns are seeping through the gauze. It's not a great combination."

Right. "Brooklyn accidentally popped some of the blisters. And does it really count as grave dirt if there's no decomp?"

"Probably not, but you know why I'm not going to care about that just this minute?"

"Because dirt is dirt and it doesn't belong in open wounds?"

"Good girl."

Burnside reaches out to pat Kearney's shoulder. "Our little Kitten. Right where she belongs."

She tries to hiss at him, but because she's laughing, it comes out as a sneeze.

I look at the sad bundle of what was once an active little girl. Given the aneurysm, it's entirely possible she would have died within the last year no matter what. But she wouldn't have spent that year scared and sick and locked away. She would have been buried properly, with her family and her own name, not hidden away. She would have died as Kendall.

Not as Lisa.

"We'll get you home soon, sweetheart," I whisper.

25

It does not surprise me in the least that when Jenny's minivan pulls up outside the hospital, it is Bran, not Priya, behind the wheel. He'll deal with it when it's Vic driving, but he really is a terrible passenger.

"Tampa is in the high seventies and low eighties, and Omaha might get snow," Priya reports, waving at Kearney through the window as I slide into the middle row of seats. Ian is stretched across the back, fast asleep and wearing his sunglasses. "Accordingly, you have a bizarrely packed bag."

"Sounds about right."

"I'll take care of your rent check tomorrow. Stupid of them to make it so difficult."

"Thank you." Before buckling in, I lean forward to tug on one of Bran's curls. "How are you holding up?"

"Stubbornness is a useful tool. Why are we picking you up from the hospital?"

"Cleaning out the blisters that popped and changing the bandage that got dirty."

He gives me a long look in the rearview mirror but doesn't comment.

"Are Inara and Victoria-Bliss going to be okay tonight?"

Priya wriggles in the seat until she can see both me and Bran. "I think so. Before this year, the get-togethers were mostly for Keely's sake. They're sad about the girls who died, of course, and angry, and any number of things, but it's also the night that saved their lives. The memories have weight, but they're not suffocating under them. With Keely stretching her wings, they came here, because why wouldn't we come here when we can? Actually, I think they're excited to hand out candy to the kids. They've never done it before."

"They don't get trick-or-treaters in New York?"

"No, all the kids in their building have an event at their school, for safety."

Brooklyn's school was discussing doing that tonight. I wonder if they are, or if Brooklyn being found will make them feel safe enough to let the kids out.

"A couple of weeks ago," I tell her, "I ordered Inara a birthday cake from that bakery Marlene uses if she can't bake for something. I can call and tell them you're picking it up, if you'd like."

When we park the car at the drop-off, Bran comes around to wake Ian up. I rummage through my bag to make sure my certification for flying armed is still tucked in its usual pocket. Except when I'm at my desk, I'm required to carry my gun while on duty, and that includes while I'm flying. We all have to complete an additional certification through TSA. Bran, officially on leave, is unarmed.

Priya wraps her arms around Bran in a long hug, and he leans his cheek against the top of her head. Neither of them says anything. Priya gives the squinting Ian a hug of his own, then comes to me. "If there's anything you need from us," she begins, and kisses my cheek rather than continue.

"I'll call," I promise. "Take care of Inara and Victoria-Bliss, whether they seem okay or not."

Our flight is in an hour, which would normally be cutting it too close for getting through security, but it's a quiet afternoon. Getting my paperwork verified takes most of our time in the lines. When they finally wave me through, my gun still at my hip, Bran and Ian are waiting, cups in hand.

I gratefully accept the one Bran holds out to me and breathe deep from the steam rising through the lid. Mmm, zebra hot chocolate. Watts and Ramirez agreed that my look was softer without my coat, so most of my morning has been spent straddled between chilly and cold. As we pass the coffee shop, the barista looks at Bran's cup with frank concern.

I'm not going to ask how many shots of espresso he put in there.

"I'm guessing that's not coffee," I say to Ian, judging from how he's scowling at it. I take care to keep my voice soft in case his headache is making him sound-sensitive.

"You gave me a good tea the other night. This isn't a good tea."

"Places like that never have good tea. If you can't have caffeine, the trick is to get half decaf, half hot chocolate. The chocolate drowns out the nastier notes of the decaf but leaves enough flavor that you still feel like you're drinking coffee."

Bran gives me a queer look. "How did you learn that trick?"

"Shira's pregnancy gave her a strict caffeine limit. She learned all the tricks."

"I'll have to remember that," Ian rumbles. Despite the ferocious glare he levels at the cup, he keeps drinking.

"Did you tell your parents we're coming?" I ask Bran quietly.

He nods. "Sachin too. He'll get in late tonight, stay at a hotel near the airport. One of the local agents offered to swing by and pick him up in the morning."

"How's he doing?"

He thinks about his answer for a moment. "Coiled," he says finally.

Much like Bran himself, really.

In the last few minutes before boarding, I duck into one of the shops and buy an overpriced magazine of crossword puzzles. I've got two in my bag already, one nerd-themed and one variety, but there's only a handful of puzzles left to solve in each of them. I can deal with airplanes. I don't like them, but I can deal with them. It just works a lot better if I can bury my head in puzzles and not have to pay attention to the fact that we're tens of thousands of feet in the air in a metal tube with safety precautions that are going to do precisely fuck-all if we actually crash.

Generally, if we're flying out somewhere, Bran is looking over our case file, and on the way back he gets a start on the paperwork or looks over the next case. Both options are unavailable here. He doesn't have the focus to read anything right now. The games on his phone will just piss him off if he tries to play them when he's worked up already.

I drop the new magazine into my bag, pull out my nerd puzzle collection and a couple of pens, and settle into my seat while he shoves our bags into the overhead bin. Ian sinks into a seat in the row in front of us, closing the window shade and leaning against it. I really hope his wife can talk him into taking something for the pain tonight so he'll feel better for tomorrow. "One across," I read aloud. "Father of modern fantasy, seven letters."

"Are we pretending you don't know that already?"

"Are you saying you don't want to help me with my crossword?"

Bran gives me a long look, then sighs and drops into the aisle seat, drawing his knees uncomfortably close in order to fit in the narrow leg room. Hopefully, no one will be in the window seat so we can shift over and he can stretch out. "You couldn't find a baseball one?"

"I'm sure they're out there."

He laces our fingers together against his knee and leans into my side. "Tolkien, then."

I fill it in using all caps, the way my father taught me when I was little and we'd sit together in the rocking chair out on the porch, slowly working through the crosswords together. "The character on the side of the Ecto Cooler box, six letters."

"Slimer."

"Ecto Cooler?"

"It was a Hi-C thing. They made it green to promote *Ghostbusters*. I can't even think how many of those things Rafi and I drank one summer. We were addicted to them."

When the two-hour flight touches down at Tampa International, the book is done, with a bonus collection of hangman games in the margins. I drop it in the first recycle bin we pass.

Bran's eyebrows lift. "You spent how long on that, and you're just throwing it away?"

"Is there a benefit to keeping them when they're already filled in?"

"Bragging rights?"

"Not worth the clutter."

"Now I wish I'd taken the chance to see your apartment," Ian notes, adjusting his sunglasses.

An agent from the Tampa Field Office meets us outside at the pick-up area, holding up a piece of paper with my name on it and looking barely weeks out of the academy. I have a sudden memory of meeting Bran and the team in just this way, waiting for them at the Denver airport so I could take them to the hospital where Priya was being treated after she was attacked. From the sudden spasm of his hand around mine, I think Bran's got the same memory on his mind.

Before we deal with the agent, though, we stop at another car. The slender, elegant woman standing there bends down to hug Ian. Connie Matson is one of those women who, once she hit middle age, seemed to stop growing older, and through no artificial means. She's also an inch or two taller than Bran, even in flats. She and Ian have probably always made an odd-looking pair, but they've also been happily married longer than Bran has been alive.

Connie gives Bran a long hug as well, and kisses my cheek. "Oh, Brandon, I'm so sorry."

He gives her a tight smile.

Fortunately, she knows him too well to be offended. "I'll bring Ian by your parents' house in the morning. Try to get some sleep tonight, dear."

We stand and watch until their car has safely pulled out of the pick-up lane and joined the flow of traffic, then head over to the baby agent. I have to let go of Bran's hand, though, or look very silly pulling out my credentials. "I'm Sterling," I greet him, holding the folder open. "This is SSAIC Eddison, here off-duty."

"Yes, sir. I mean, ma'am. Um, ma'am-sir."

"Sterling," I repeat firmly.

He just nods.

I am thirty years old; I have only been in the Bureau eight years; I am not allowed to feel old. But damn. Is this how Vic feels when I accidentally call him sir?

The baby agent leads us down the row of cars to a pair of black SUVs, because if you can get the fleet discount with the manufacturer, why go for variety? Another agent, probably about midthirties, leans against the hood of the one in front, smoking. The car, I notice, is parked four inches from the **No Smoking Beyond This Point** sign. When he sees us, he exhales a rush of smoke and rubs out the cigarette on the bottom of his shoe, dropping the butt back into the package.

"Agent Wilson," he says, offering his hand to shake. "Puppy is Agent Rogers, if he forgot to mention that."

He did forget, but I wasn't going to say anything about it. I remember being that new and nervous.

"Your analyst got us the medical records for the morning; the ME's going over them now. I know you've got a tight schedule trying to organize all this mess, so unless it's an issue, we figured eight o'clock tomorrow, get an early start. We'll have the ME waiting, and a tech with the ground penetrating radar. Meet right at the house. Just you two?"

"Four of us, in fact," I answer. "Retired TPD Detective Ian Matson was the lead on Faith Eddison's disappearance and the reason we were able to link the cases. Also Agent Sachin Karwan out of the Omaha office; Erin Bailey was his sister's best friend when they were children."

"Right. The one Rogers is picking up in the morning. Here are the keys," he continues, dropping them in my hand. "One of us will give you a ride back here tomorrow so you don't have to worry about handing the car off again. I figure you've got things to do tonight."

"Thanks."

He hands me a business card with a phone number scrawled in green ink across the bottom. "Call if you need anything. Otherwise, we'll let you get to it. Puppy, come."

Bran automatically reaches for the keys, then stops, his hand still outstretched. "I'm not allowed to drive if I'm off-duty, am I?"

"Nope."

"Damn." He sighs and takes our bags to the back. I adjust the seat a few inches, and the mirrors, and try not to smile when Bran settles into the passenger seat with a glower. "Do you remember the way?"

"Spruce, Dale Mabry, Ehrlich," I answer proudly.

He gives me a sideways look.

"I like the name Ehrlich," I say with a shrug. "It's fun to say. Ur-lick."

"Just drive, Jeeves."

"Want to rephrase that, Wooster?"

". . . now I do, yes."

Rush hour in Tampa, as in most larger cities, is somewhat of a misnomer. Rush *hours*, on the other hand, sums it up quite nicely. Despite it being almost seven, the roads are slammed.

Bran's parents live in a neighborhood just far enough off a main road to be reasonably quiet. I don't know what it was like twenty-five years ago when Faith was kidnapped, but now it's a full mix of families, from college students cramming themselves four and eight into rentals to retirees with craft or memorabilia rooms. The houses show their age, not in the sense of being run-down, but in the way they sag a little. Comfortably settled, my dad would say. We have to drive slowly and carefully once we turn into the neighborhood, because the kids are out in force.

It's wonderful to see all the creative Halloween costumes alongside all the store-bought ones, but it's a little nerve-wracking to drive around so many children who may or may not have a firm grasp on why they shouldn't dart out in front of cars.

It's with a genuine sigh of relief that I pull into the Eddisons' driveway and park beside Paul's station wagon. I cut the engine, click off the seat belt, and wait.

Bran stares at the house, a muscle jumping in his jaw. "I told them we were coming," he says eventually. "I didn't say why."

I touch the chain at my throat, fingers rubbing against the cool gold of the *Magen David*.

We sit in the car for several minutes, long enough to see a group of girls walk up to the porch, clustered together in a moving patch of giggles. They're probably on the upper edge of the socially acceptable trick-or-treating age range, maybe eleven or twelve. There's a Wonder Woman, and a Gamora and a Nebula, who, even with the paint, look enough alike to probably be twins. They've got a Black Widow with them, as well, and a Poison Ivy, both of them wearing identical wigs, and a Captain Marvel wearing a yellow hijab rather than a wig. They push against each other as they jostle for space, laughing and teasing, and they sing out "Trick or treat!" when the door opens to a spill of warm light.

I glance over at Bran. He's facing them, but I don't think he's seeing them.

I rather suspect he's seeing three girls in Teenage Mutant Ninja Princess Ballerina Turtle costumes, dutifully collecting candy for the sick member of their quartet.

The girls pass us, eagerly comparing their haul, but the door doesn't close. Instead, the silhouette of a woman leans against the frame, looking back at us.

Xiomara Eddison.

Bran's mother.

26

"Ready or not?" I murmur.

Bran nods, takes a deep breath, and opens his door.

Ignoring the bags in our hands, Xiomara yanks us both into a hug as soon as we're close enough. "Oh, *mírate*," she fusses. "I knew something was off when you called."

"You did?" Bran asks.

"I'm your *mamá*," she tells him sternly. "*Claro que lo sabía.* What is it?"

"Let's go inside, *Mamá*."

She gives him a long searching look, her hands on his arms. "All right. Go on in. Let me go get Bertito to man the door." She walks briskly down the drive and across the street.

"Bertito?" I ask in a whisper.

"Rafi's oldest boy, Alberto. If she's calling him Bertito again, he's either pissed off the *familiá* or done something sweet."

We set our bags safely out of the way near the base of the stairs, and I text the others to let them know we've arrived.

Bertito—when Xio brings him back—is probably nineteen or twenty and looks distinctly harassed. I've seen that expression on Bran's face when dealing with the women in his life. When he sees Bran, he throws his hands up in the air. "*Tío*, I just made some costumes. I didn't save the world. *Haz que paren!*"

"Sorry, *chico*. Nothing escapes the gratitude of the *mamás*."

The young man grumbles, but he also looks pleased and proud. Taking up the massive bowl of candy from the table by the door, he heads out to the porch and settles on the railing.

"He's studying costume design at USF," Xiomara informs me. "He spent half the summer making Halloween costumes for his siblings and cousins, beautiful things, too, and kept it all a complete secret. We're very proud of him." She ushers us into the living room full of worn, comfortable furniture and bookcases, framed pictures taking up most of the leftover wall space apart from a large television. Paul is in his armchair, long needles and yarn in hand, frowning at the knitting pattern spread across his lap.

Bran looks like his mother, mostly—the same grey-mottled dark hair, the dark eyes, the brown skin. The curls, though, came from his father. He got Xio's height but Paul's build, her sneaky dimples and his long nose. Paul's hair is mostly white now, his blue eyes faded a bit, but it's easy to see where Faith got her coloring. Faith's face, though, the shape of her features, that was all Xiomara.

Paul looks up, does a double take at his son, and sets his knitting aside. "Something's wrong."

"Yes and no. We have . . ." Bran looks at me, helpless in a way I've almost never seen from him until the past few days.

"You might want to sit," I tell Xiomara. "There isn't a graceful way to give this news."

"Are you sick? Was there . . ." She swallows hard. "Was there a baby?" she whispers.

What?

"No," I say slowly. "No, we're both healthy, Xio. This is about Faith."

Xiomara pales and sinks down into the chair next to Paul's, her hand automatically reaching out for her husband's. His meets her halfway, and they lean into each other. "You learned something? After all these years?"

"Ian did, and what he gave us led to the rest." I perch on the edge of the couch, not particularly wanting to be comfortable for the conversation to follow. Bran settles beside me, knees propped wide, his hands clasped between them. "Not quite a week ago, a girl named Brooklyn Mercer disappeared on her way home from school in Richmond, Virginia. We weren't called until the next morning. She's eight years old, blonde, with blue eyes."

The Eddisons' eyes flick to me, track to one of the pictures of Faith up on the wall, then back to me.

"Ian saw her on the news and brought us information on several other disappearances he'd been researching, where all the girls looked alike and vanished the same time of year."

Bran's knuckles gradually turn white with tension as I walk his parents through a very sanitized version of our discoveries. I'm not sure if they're speechless or just choosing not to say anything yet, but without interruption they let me get all the way through to why we've come to Tampa.

"This girl, Brooklyn—she's okay?" Xiomara asks as soon as I've stopped. "She'll recover?"

"Completely. She'll be in the hospital for a few days, and they'll be monitoring her blood work for a while even after she's home, but the doctors are confident she'll have a full recovery."

"Good," she says with a nod. "Good."

Paul scrubs a hand across his face, a gesture I've seen so many times in his son it's almost eerie to see it in him. "And Faith is . . ."

Dead, but somehow I can't bring myself to say the word. There's something about how hard those *d*'s are, the sound that makes the word so harsh.

"We believe she's buried in Omaha," I reply. "We'll head there tomorrow, and they've agreed to wait until we're present."

"We?"

"The two of us, Dad," Bran clarifies, speaking for the first time since we sat down. "Plus Ian and Sachin."

"Sachin? Why—oh, dear," Xiomara murmurs. "His sister's friend."

"Erin Bailey," Bran says. "We think she's buried here in Tampa. He's coming here for her, and then flying up to Omaha with us. But we wanted . . . we thought . . ."

"We're trying to make sure all the girls are located and identified, and the families notified, before it breaks to the news," I finish for him. "Tomorrow morning, we'll be executing a search warrant on the property Davies rented while he lived here. Very likely we'll be digging up part of the yard. We wanted to make sure you knew what was happening before that started, especially given what we expect to find."

"Erin Bailey," Paul says softly. "Someone's little girl."

"Yes."

"And this man, he . . . what does he do with them?" asks Xiomara. "Does he . . . does he touch them?"

"As far as we can tell, he does not. They're replacements for the daughter he lost to cancer."

"Replacements," she echoes. "Then why—why does he kill them?"

"*Because* he lost his daughter to cancer. He wants to do it over, do it better, have the happy life with his daughter they should have had, but she died. The trauma of her illness, of losing her, has completely reshaped him. It's literally rewritten his brain. He can't escape it."

"Do you feel sorry for this man, Eliza?"

"Yes," I say simply, and I feel Bran's knee knock against mine as he shifts and resettles. "It doesn't excuse what he did. It absolves him of nothing. I don't know that it earns him any forgiveness, and I don't know that it should. But yes, I feel sorry for him. His daughter's death shattered him, and he couldn't piece himself back together into a life of anything more than sorrow. That incites pity."

Tears stream down Paul's weathered cheeks, perpetually sunburned because he never remembers to put on sunblock before running yet can't ever manage to tan. Xio isn't crying, but her eyes are bright.

"I know it's not the answer you hoped for—"

But Xio cuts me off with a brisk shake of her head. "It is an answer, Eliza. At long last, it is an answer, and our daughter is coming home. We hoped," she continues ruefully. "How could we not? But it has been many years since we truly believed her to still be alive."

Paul hiccups, burying his face in the hand not clinging to his wife.

"At least . . . at least she has not been suffering all this time. There's mercy in that. *Esos pequeños consuelos.*" Her lower lip and chin start to quiver. "My baby. My baby girl."

Bran shoots off the couch, stumbling to his knees in front of his parents. They fold into him, his arms around their backs. I can see Xio's shoulders shaking as she weeps.

I silently excuse myself and head out to the porch, where Alberto sits with the candy. He grins at a clutch of boys, probably just old enough to cross from sidewalk to porch without their parents. I can see three adults talking together at the end of the yard, watching them. As soon as the boys are gone, though, Alberto turns to me with a solemn expression. "Is everything okay?" he asks anxiously. "*Tío* Brandon never comes back for this week. He's not sick, is he?"

"He's not sick," I reassure him, hopping onto the rail next to him and turning so my back is against a post. "I know you're family, but I can't really talk about it yet. You'll know soon."

His eyes fall to the gun at my hip, the badge at my belt. "It's about *Tía* Faith, isn't it?"

"You call her *tía?*"

"*Papá* said we don't stop calling someone family just because they've died or gone away. *Bisabuelo* died years ago, but he's still *Bisabuelo, sí?*"

"*Sí. Eso me llena de amor.*"

"You didn't answer."

248

"I know. I can't answer that yet."

Which is an answer, in its way, and he nods slowly as he absorbs that. "I can't tell my parents, can I? Or *Tía* Lissi?"

"Xio and Paul will probably tell them tomorrow, or the day after."

He seems to take that in as the no it is, and slaps a smile on his face for the next group of kids.

Around nine-thirty, the flow of kids finally stops. It's mostly been just the older ones for the last hour or so. When twenty minutes have passed without a single trick-or-treater, I send Alberto home with thanks. We've spent the time talking about his studies and where he wants to go with them, and a bit about the FBI and Bran. Then we hit on baseball, and I think I've finally found the source of the shit-talking texts Bran gets every time the Rays have a good series.

He hands me the bowl and slides off the rail, then turns back. "I won't tell my parents," he says. "Promise."

"Thank you. I know it's a lot to ask."

"But it won't be for long, right?"

"Not long at all."

He nods and heads toward home, which turns out to be across the street and three houses down.

The bowl is still a third full of candy. I sift through the variety of mini chocolate bars until I reach a layer of tiny Nerds boxes. I'm in the middle of pouring an entire box into my mouth when the door opens, and I choke.

Bran just stands and watches, the asshat, though one hand does float out in my direction in case I fall, I suppose. "All better?" he asks when I've stopped coughing.

"Sure," I croak.

"Feel like a walk?"

I glance back at the house. "Your folks?"

"Just went up to bed. Thank you, by the way, for, uh . . ."

"Leaving?"

"Giving us space."

"Your nephew's a smart kid. Lamentable taste in baseball teams, but a good kid." I hand him the bowl—resisting the urge to tuck a few boxes of Nerds into my pockets for later—and hop off the railing. He puts the candy back inside and locks up. Before we're even down the driveway, he reaches for my hand.

"We didn't really believe we'd find her," he says halfway down the street. Some of the houses are dark, but even the rest are quiet, save for one house with a roaring party and a yard littered with cars and red Solo cups. "Eventually, anyway. It had been so long, there was nothing new. We didn't think we'd find her, but we couldn't give her up."

That isn't rare. It's not even uncommon. But he doesn't need me to point that out; he already knows. This isn't Eddison the agent; this is Bran the son, the brother.

"You know my parents started a reward-for-information fund all those years ago? They wouldn't ever touch it, not even when the house was falling down around them. They'd just make things work and make things work, even when they weren't working. Then I'd call up Rafi."

"Because he's in construction."

"*Sí.* He'd bring over new employees, or kids he was mentoring through community service or whatever, and tell my parents he needed to train them in something."

"That happened to be whatever needed to be fixed."

"Yes. And because they were only students, it wouldn't be right to charge full price."

"You made up the difference?"

"As much as he'd let me. We've been doing it for years, because the thought of putting the money to any other use meant giving up. But I couldn't just send them the money either. They have their pride."

"They know."

"No, they don't. We've been careful."

"Bran, the last time we were here, when you and your dad were out running? That's when the banister broke all the way through on the stairs. When they sent you out later for groceries, they made bets on when Rafi would suddenly show up with ducklings who needed to learn how to repair banisters and rails."

"Are you serious?"

I lean into him just hard enough to tilt his next step a bit sideways. "I guess they figure you have your pride too."

He huffs a sound that's almost a laugh, and shakes his head again. "All these years, we thought we were getting away with it."

"What is it she told you when we arrived? She's your *mamá*, so of course she knew."

We wander out of the neighborhood, then down Ehrlich a half mile or so to a gas station. I'm only a little surprised when he picks out a pack of cigarettes and a lighter. It was Priya who told me of the Eddison who went through half a pack a day most of the time. According to her, he'd sort of been trying to stop for a couple of years, without any real incentive to do so. Then she saw him reaching for one and told him he smelled worse than the boys' locker room at her school. Somewhere in trying to find out why she knew what that room smelled like, he forgot to finish reaching for the cig.

Rather than comment on the purchase, I pull out my phone to text Shira. *I move to suspend rationing for the next few days.*

Fuck yes, thank you.

Holding up?

Family meeting. Ima said anyone who wanted to go visit has her absolute support, and she'll even go to Florida with them if they want, but for herself, she's choosing not to go to either the hospital or the prison.

Anyone going?

No. We talked about it. The only reason to go would be some sort of obligation. What virtue is served by reluctance? We'll probably sit shiva when the time comes, but mourning what he was to us is different than visiting what he turned out to be.

Has he woken up at all?

No. He probably won't, according to the doctors.

Let me know if you want me to come home.

I've seen the case on the news; you are where you need to be.

Bran hands me a cigarette before we're even out of the store. We walk back even more slowly than we came, trailed by wispy curls of smoke.

"You know, if you want to stay . . . ," I say eventually.

He nods. "I need to be there."

"I know. But you also need to hear that you have the option to stay. No one will judge you for it."

He squeezes my hand and we walk the rest of the way in silence, sitting on the porch and smoking till nearly sunrise. Sleep isn't possible, but this stillness, this quiet . . . it's restful in its own way.

27

Xiomara is normally a morning person, one of those people who fills a house with literal song too early in the day. This morning, however, she's subdued and pale, sitting at the kitchen table and staring down into a mug of milky, cinnamon-laden coffee. She looks up and frowns at the plastic wrap I put around my bandage so I could shower. "My son did that?"

"Not in the way that makes it sound." I sit across from her and hold out my arm for her to inspect. Xiomara was a nurse at the same doctor's office for decades, and when that doctor sold his practice and retired, she retired as well. She lasted fewer than four months before she picked up a part-time job as a school nurse, working on a rotation with several other semi-retirees.

She gives me a rather severe look before bending to the task of peeling away both plastic and gauze. "Whether he intended to harm you or not, Eliza, he hurt you. I believe that it was an accident; that doesn't mean it isn't his fault." She traces carefully around the intact blisters, fingers hovering over the raw skin where the popped blisters were carefully cut away to prevent infection. I produce the antibiotic cream the hospital gave me and she accepts it with a nod. "Brandon always had something of a temper. He got that from me. After Faith . . ." She trails off, her lips tight as the news hits her afresh. "It got worse after," she says simply. "We bear responsibility for our tempers, most especially when someone is harmed by accident. Shorter tempers require greater care from those burdened with them."

Rubbing the cream in gently, she checks the padded strip for any leaked fluid and efficiently redoes the bandage. "It speaks well of you that you want to apologize for him, but be careful. By trying too hard to excuse him, you diminish your own well-being."

I nod rather than try to say anything. This is his mother. And maybe . . . maybe my realization of just what happened with Cliff has made me a little more aware of slopes and warning signs. Do I believe Bran would ever be abusive? Fuck no, he'd cut off his hand before that happened. But maybe Xiomara is right and even accidents need to hold their full weight of consequence.

"There's something I'd like you to do for me, Eliza, if you can. To try, at any rate."

"What's that?"

From the seat next to her, she pulls out a folded quilt and stands to shake it out. Against a pale blue background with swirls of white stitching marking out the suggestion of clouds, two many-pointed stars fill the middle, one set within the other with a small gap between them. They're both done in a beautiful rainbow, several different sizes of triangles paired in such a way that you can see both the stars and the spiral shapes. A wide band borders the quilt, the colors arranged to bleed in a constant spectrum through the rainbow.

"The main shape is called a Mariner's Compass," she tells me. "It's from a combination of the maritime compass and the wind rose charts the sailors used to use. How they used to find their way home again." She shakes it again and folds it up with a few quick motions, faster and smoother than I've ever managed. "Sachin Karwan was the first actual friend Brandon made after Faith disappeared. They had this terrible thing in common." She strokes a hand over the fabric, absently tracing a line of stitching. "For two years, that little girl was alive just two streets over, and none of us knew." She takes a deep breath. "I know there is evidence to be examined, even if you were kind enough to shield us from just what that will be. But soon, they're going to let that little girl go home, and coffins are . . . coffins are so . . ."

I lay my hand over hers, and she gives me a tremulous smile.

"I want to send her home with this, if you think that will be possible. It was Faith's company quilt. Her *abuela* made it for her before she was born. It was too big for years, and then too nice for every day, but whenever family came from far away, we'd put this on her bed."

"You couldn't have known Davies had a kidnapped child in his house."

"No, I know. If he'd been obvious, he would have been discovered long before this. I can't blame myself for ignorance that's shared so widely. But Erin has been there all this time, just the same. She's gone far too long without a kindness."

"I'll ask the medical examiner. I can't imagine they'll say no."

"Gracias, mija."

"Is there one you'd like me to take to Omaha? For Faith?"

Her smile grows a little strong, even if her eyes are still bright with tears. "I'll give that one to my son to carry. He'll need a task to help anchor him."

A knock sounds against the front door, firm enough to carry but soft enough not to wake anyone sleeping.

"Ian or Karwan, I'm assuming."

"Probably, yes. You know that from the knock?"

"It's a very distinctive knock." Finney made me practice that kind of knock—and the same kind of voice—for weeks when I joined his team.

She gets up to answer it. When she comes back in, Ian and Connie Matson are both with her, with another man trailing behind them. He looks around Bran's age, though a little less grey; he's just starting to silver at the temples of his dark hair. His skin and eyes are both dark as well, and he's wearing all black save for a yellow ribbon on his lapel. The Missing Children Awareness ribbon.

Agent Karwan.

"The famous Eliza," he greets, summoning up a smile on his previously grave face. It doesn't quite succeed. "A pleasure to meet you, despite the circumstances."

"Same. I'm glad you're able to be here."

"Wouldn't miss it for the world. Thank you for making sure of it."

Realistically that was Vic, but I'm not going to quibble.

Connie and Ian both have travel mugs, steam drifting out of the lids. Xio moves to the coffee machine on the counter. "Sachin? Coffee?"

"Thank you, Xiomara. That would be appreciated."

She pours the cup and hands it to him, then roots around her cupboard for a box of tea sachets. "It's Earl Grey, Eliza. Is that all right?"

"That's fine, Xio."

Shira thinks Earl Grey tastes like stewed gym socks. I don't love it, except occasionally in a lavender London Fog, but I don't hate it either.

"I remember Mr. Davies," Karwan says, staring into his coffee. "He helped me study for my math tests. I would never have guessed that he . . ."

"No one guessed, Sachin," I tell him gently, still feeling strange at using his first name. "No one guessed, and over the course of thirty-one years, there have been an awful lot of people who could have. You were fourteen."

He nods absently.

It doesn't matter how often the words are said. He—and Ian and Bran and so many others—will only accept them when they can, and not a moment before.

When Bran comes down, cleanly shaven with his wet hair curling against his forehead, he puts a hand on Ian's shoulder, gripping tight.

Ian covers the hand with one of his own. "You sure you want to be there for all of this?" the detective asks bluntly. "Either of you."

"We need to be."

"Fool boys," he says, voice gruff. But his other hand reaches out to Karwan, bracing his shoulder. He's worried, yes, but proud, too, it's plain to see.

Paul comes down in most of a suit, looking a little dazed. "Routine," he explains almost sheepishly. "I'm just so used . . ." He trails off, looks around the kitchen, and sits down abruptly. "Today is just . . ."

Bran moves away from Ian to stand behind his father, both hands on the man's shoulders. Paul takes a shuddering breath.

"Will you two be okay?" I ask. "If you want to call someone . . ."

"Connie is staying with us," Xio replies, "and Lissi will join us as soon as she's back from taking the kids to school. She'll be discreet."

We sit in tense silence until the time comes to leave. Bran heads out first to put our bags and Karwan's in the SUV, and I carefully gather up the quilt. Xio pulls a large, brown paper Cracker Barrel bag out of the pantry and holds it open for me.

I drive us to the house Davies rented all those years ago, two streets over from the Eddisons'. The ME's van is backed into the driveway. Two more black SUVs are parked along the curb on the side of the street, a handful of police cars sprawled along the other side, leaving just enough room for one car to pass between them. I recognize Agent Wilson; he stands near the end of the driveway with a slim, steel-haired woman anxiously clutching her elbows. Probably the current owner or resident of the house.

Bran, Karwan, and Ian join the cluster of law enforcement at the end of the driveway. They're dressed to blend in, more or less, looking official enough that no one questions their presence. Ian shakes hands with several of the officers, asking after families or people at the station. He's been retired about ten years now, if I remember correctly, so he's worked with some of them. Trained most of them, by the looks of it.

One of the officers, in the suit and tie of a detective, holds a hand out to Bran and uses it to pull him into a tight, unself-conscious hug. "I'm so sorry, man."

"At least we know, right?"

"I guess so. Lissi's on her way back from the school. She'll stay with your folks for a while."

"Manny, this is Sachin Karwan," Bran says, beginning the introductions. I tune it out and wait for the ME to finish his conversation with a K-9 handler there in case the backyard proves too difficult for the GPR. Manuel, or Manny, as he usually goes by now, is Rafi's little brother and Lissi's husband. And, I suddenly recall, one of the kids Davies tutored here in Tampa.

No wonder he looks like he's clenching his jaw.

The K-9 handler moves away, so I step in and introduce myself to the ME, who gives me a startled look. His suit is rumpled, and he looks a little like he stuck his finger in an electric socket. "Oh my, you do look so much like young Miss Bailey!"

"Yes."

At this point it's not even worth arguing that a second look would disprove most of the resemblance.

"Agent Sterling. I actually have a request, if I may." I open the bag to show him the quilt, explaining Xiomara's wish. Almost as an afterthought, I highlight Karwan's connection to Erin.

He takes the bag from me carefully, almost cradling it against his chest despite the handles. Scattered, but compassionate. "Of course. An amazing woman to do this in the midst of her own grief. Yes, we'll keep this safe until Miss Bailey is ready for transport. Her brother shouldn't have to see that."

It's on the tip of my tongue to say that she isn't Karwan's sister, but I keep it back. Of course she is. Family's more than blood. Shira and Mercedes and Priya are as much my sisters as any I might have had if my parents had had more children.

He calls over his assistant and gives him the bag, along with strict instructions not to lose it or set it down.

With everyone ready, half of us troop through the fence to the backyard. Manny and two of the uniformed officers join us, the others staying near the vehicles to ward off any curious onlookers who may arrive. Wilson leaves Rogers with the property owner and follows us back. There's a large oak in one corner of the backyard, almost exactly where the various fences would meet if they weren't truncated to allow the tree to grow naturally. Within the tree's shade, an old swing set creaks with slightly rusty chains. The yard looks maintained but largely unused.

"Any place in particular we should start?" asks one of the FBI techs, draped partially over the handles of the GPR.

They're all looking at me. Right. Being part of the original team, I'm technically ranking at the moment, aren't I?

"Not really," I answer. "Kendall was in a corner, but that doesn't mean Erin will be."

It feels strange to simply stand there and watch, and I don't know why. We're not usually the ones finding the bodies anyway. We may locate them in unfortunate circumstances, but there are reasons we have forensic techs. Or maybe I'm just feeling wrong-footed in general. I want to reach for Bran's hand, but he and Ian are focused on Karwan, each with a hand on the agent's back.

Erin is not in a corner, but rather parallel to the back fence, about a third of the way along the property line and a few feet in. The tech whistles when the bones take shape on his screen. His partner scurries over with small flags to stake out a digging perimeter.

Karwan stares at the wire-mounted flags, unconsciously straining against the other two men to try to see the screen. Tears stream down his ashen face.

"Sachin?" I ask softly. "You know it's okay not to look."

"Erin . . ." He shakes his head. "I need to be here for Erin."

"You *are* here for Erin. Do you think she needs you to see her like this to know you're here for her?"

He blinks and turns his head slightly to look at me.

"It's okay not to look. It's okay to keep the memory of her as she was instead of what you'll see here."

Swallowing back most of a sob, he spins on his heel and faces the back of the house. Ian and Bran both turn toward him, bookends in profile, supporting Karwan but still watching the techs. Erin was in this house for almost two years, but she was here in the ground before Faith went missing. No one knew to look for her here.

The techs are experienced; it doesn't take them very long to unearth the plastic-wrapped bundle not quite four feet down. The plastic sheeting is intact enough to lift, but the bugs have been at it over the years. The GPR was only going to show bone, stone, or metal, not flesh. I think, though, from the sound as they move the bundle and from too many of Cass's lectures over lunch, that bone is all that's left. Through the discolored plastic, there's a little bit visible of a heavily stained and decayed quilt.

I can hear Bran speaking urgently in Karwan's ear, distracting him from the sound of the moving bones.

"The skeleton looks about the right size," the ME says quietly, giving Karwan a look to make sure he can't hear. "I'll know more once I unwrap the remains, but it's within the range of likely growth for that age. If he was making them ill, it very likely stunted their growth. Do you see here, with the skull?"

I lean over to look at the still image captured with the GPR.

"Some of the teeth have fallen out. There was bone loss while she was still alive. Once the root nerve decayed, the teeth weren't well seated enough to stay in place. And here, and here," he continues, his finger tracing along ribs and arms, "there's significant loss of bone density, some curving."

"Any signs of external harm?"

"No breaks recent with the death, it looks like; they'd be obvious even like this. Once I can examine the bones themselves, I'll be able to give a rough date to any knits or scars. I can say this is more likely to be Erin Bailey than not."

"How?"

"See the knee? Just here?"

"Is that metal?"

"Her records state she was in a car accident when she was five. Her knee was badly damaged, requiring some hardware to be put in." He pulls the file from under his arm and flips it open, turning pages until he gets to a reproduction of an X-ray. His square, somewhat stubby finger points to the surgically installed hardware. The proportions seem completely different, a close-up X-ray of the knee versus the significantly smaller, still image. It's compelling, though.

"How long do you think it will take to make a solid identification?"

"Not long. Not when we have the records in hand to compare. We'll extract DNA from the marrow, if we can, and run it if you have something to compare it against."

"Her mother and sister both contributed samples. They don't have anything left that's hers."

The techs are gentle as they move the remains into a black body bag and lift it to the waiting gurney. While there's a general attempt to be respectful with every body, this is their job. They see a fair number of bodies, and the . . . well, awe, for lack of a better word, wears off after a while. There's something about children, though, that demands extra reverence.

Ian has tears sliding down his cheeks into his whiskers. He makes no effort to wipe them away or turn his back. "All this time."

Karwan stands, back straight and rigid, and weeps into his hand. Twenty-seven years ago, his little sister's best friend, the sister of his heart, disappeared. Today, she was finally found. Someday that knowledge will help and comfort.

The ME takes the paper bag back from his assistant, and then, glancing at Karwan, turns to me and holds the bag open. "Agent Sterling, if you please?"

I nod and pull out the quilt, beautiful and pristine. Holding it carefully in my arms, I walk around the knot of men so Karwan won't have to turn and look at the excavation site. "Sachin? Xiomara has a quilt for Erin. Is it okay if we tuck her in?"

He scrubs at his face with both hands, though it doesn't stop the tears. "Is she—"

"She's covered."

He's shaking as he takes the quilt from me, but he squares his shoulders and walks directly to the gurney off to one edge of the yard. Manny joins me at the far side, Bran and Ian staying on either side of Karwan, and together the five of us carefully unfold the quilt. The gurney is narrow, barely half the width of the quilt, so we fold the edges under to preserve the rainbow Mariner's Compass. We gently tuck the quilt around Erin, Ian and Bran making sure it's slid neatly under the bag on that side so that Karwan doesn't have to. The rest of us back away, but he stays a moment longer, hand floating over the quilt where her head is.

I shake my head, trying to clear the sense-memory of Shira's father smoothing back our hair and kissing our heads after he tucked us into bed.

When Karwan steps away, Manny and his officers, and the ME and his assistant, step to the sides of the gurney and carefully, solemnly, roll it over the grass and through the fence, looking rather like an honor guard.

Bran catches Karwan in a hug, his eyes wet as he braces his friend against a fresh onslaught of grief. He looks afraid.

I can't fault him for that.

"What time is your flight?" Wilson asks in a hushed tone at my shoulder.

"Eleven-thirty."

He checks his watch. Quarter to ten. "Do you have more you need to do here?"

I glance at Ian, watching the gurney disappear around the corner of the house. "No, not really. We already made our farewells with his parents. They have people with them, and Manny will update them with what we found."

He nods slowly. I follow his gaze back to Bran and Karwan. "Poor bastards," he says, barely loud enough for me to hear. "I can't even imagine."

"No one should have to."

"Good luck in Omaha."

"Thanks."

28

Detective Matson calls his wife to check in with her, let her know that Manny will be coming by later with information. I can make out her tone but not her words; she's worried about him. I don't think anything's going to keep him from being there for Faith, though. Wilson promises me regular updates before handing us off to Agents Spencer and Parker for the ride back to the airport. We break a handful of traffic laws of varying importance, but at ten twenty-four we're in the line for security.

Bran hasn't said a word since we walked out of the backyard.

I glance between him and Karwan. "Okay-ish?" I ask.

He smiles slightly, because that's Priya's word, and nods. Karwan just blinks at me, eyes still bright and damp.

Good enough.

Our three-hour flight to Omaha takes off at eleven-forty and lands at one thirty-two central time. It is, in fact, snowing in southeastern Nebraska, here on the first of November. We make a bathroom stop to change into the warmer clothes Priya packed us, draping our coats over our bags until we get closer to outside. Eppley isn't a large airport, but why sweat before you have to?

Karwan leads us to the exit. He flew out of this airport barely twelve hours ago to join us in Tampa.

Just before the outside doors, an Amazonian redhead in a suit and heavy navy blue peacoat raises a hand in greeting. "Holding up, boss?" she asks.

"I'll keep," he says, his voice still rough from tears. "Agent Fisher, this is Agent Sterling; she's on the ranking team. This is Agent Eddison and retired Detective Matson. They're here off-duty."

"Like you were in Tampa off-duty," she clarifies.

He nods.

"Welcome to Omaha," she says, and I could love her a little for leaving it there. "County squabbling match got sorted out this morning. Sarpy's got the win, no surprise, and the deputies and some of our agents have secured the scene. Car's this way, if you're ready."

"How likely is the snow to interfere with the search?" I ask once we're in the car and moving.

"Not that much. It's a slow build. Overnight is when it'll start complicating things, when the temp drops to freeze it. We've got the equipment staged at the house already. The owners are in hysterics."

Bran squeezes my hand between us. Grateful, I think, that neither Fisher nor I are trying to involve the men in the conversation.

"Has anyone tracked down the current location of McKenna Lattimore's family?"

"Her parents are still here. Still in the same house, in fact, in the cul-de-sac at the end of Emiline, about six houses down from Davies. We sat down with them last night. They've agreed not to tell the rest of the family until tonight, and keep them quiet until the news breaks, but we got confirmation from the Atlanta office: the body in Atlanta was definitely McKenna."

It's all moving so fast. It needs to, but damn. So much information flying about from city to city, and so much work to keep it as secret as possible.

I'd never realized that Omaha is smashed up against the state border. The road from the airport to downtown actually crosses into Iowa for a few minutes. From there we hit 480, Fisher flying comfortably through a construction-laden interchange to 80 westbound. "Harrison is the county line," she tells us as she takes the exit off the interstate. "The house is right against the road."

Bran stares out the window, holding his brown paper Cracker Barrel bag closer. I don't know what this quilt looks like, the one his mother chose for Faith. I do know that he hasn't let go of it since we went through security in Tampa. Not that Bran is ever especially *chatty*, but this silent figure is unfamiliar, unsettling. Understandable, but still foreign.

Fisher parks in the street, not quite blocking the mailbox but making it awfully hard for another car to get to it. "Owners decided not to be present for the search," she says as we climb out of the SUV. "Can't say I'm torn up about it."

"Sterling? That you?"

I look for the voice, and find the agent it belongs to in the doorway. "Langslow? What are you doing in Omaha?"

She bounds down the steps and sweeps me up into a hug, literally lifting my feet off the ground. "My husband got transferred last year. Took me till a few months ago to follow."

The others are giving us overly patient looks.

"Langslow and I worked together in Denver," I explain. "Haven't seen each other since I went to Quantico."

"Ambitious little hussy," Langslow says fondly. "So hey, we searched the interior of the house a little last night, found something of interest."

"Inside?"

"The basement is partially unfinished. We figured that was the logical place to keep someone. We found some loosened particle board against one wall." She holds up an evidence bag with several pocket-sized notebooks in it. The pages are yellowed, the edges curled and crumbling, but the patchily faded blue cover of the one in front has a name written large in black marker.

Faith Eddison.

Bran chokes, and fuck on-duty professionalism, I lean into him and wrap one arm around his waist as he sways. On his other side, Karwan presses into him as well, returning the favor.

Fisher drapes herself over Langslow, using the top of her head as an armrest; Langslow is not particularly short. "Agent Eddison is here off-duty, to stand witness for his sister."

"Ah, fuck. I'm so sorry." She changes her grip, cradling the bag rather than dangling it. "We only did a cursory skim. At a glance, though, it seems she accepted play-acting Lisa for Davies but kept this hidden so she could still cling to her identity as Faith. Real smart girl. I'm sure . . . I'm sure they'll release these to you at some point. If you wanted. Um, hey, boss."

I nod. "Is everything ready out back?"

"Yes. Gate's just this way." She ducks out from under Fisher's arm and hurries ahead of us, probably to warn the others that there's family present.

Close to the elevated back porch, there's a metal swing set braced up against a plastic two-level playhouse. Just past the post for the swings, the yard slopes sharply down to the fence, and there's Harrison Street, just beyond. Considering the angle of the slope and the height of the fence, there's a significant chance that Faith is buried where the GPR is going to have a hard time moving. The only flat ground in the backyard can be easily seen from the road during daylight, and even the most incurious neighbors will notice you digging in the middle of the night. To avoid rousing suspicion, Davies had to have buried her lower on the short hill.

Agents and tech greet Karwan as we approach, giving respectful nods to the rest of us. These are his people here in Omaha. Given the frank concern with which some of them regard him, I'm pretty sure they all know why he's not working the case.

He reaches around Bran to put a hand on my shoulder and give me a small nudge. "Go on, Eliza. To work. We've got him."

I look at Bran, who nods.

Fuck, I hate this.

As I walk away, Ian steps in to take my place, speaking softly to Bran. I head over to the dog handler, stopping a respectful distance away so as not to crowd or startle the German shepherd at her side. "Hi, I'm Agent Sterling."

"Lieutenant Waterston, and Officer Furiosa."

I look down at the dog, who gives a huge, tongue-lolling yawn. Her paws are wrapped in dark blue booties for protection against the cold and damp. "I like the name."

"She used to bite the hell out of the male trainers who came near her. Never so much as growled at me. Seemed fitting."

"Is she bone-trained?"

"Yes, ma'am. When they told us how long the body's likely been there, we were chosen special."

"And it's not too cold for her?"

"Not yet. There's almost no wind chill, it's a small yard, and it's warm for snow yet. As long as we're not out here for hours, she should be just fine to scent."

"We should probably start along the back fence where the GPR can't go. It's out of sight of the road."

"That's what we'll do then. Up, Furiosa."

The dog obeys, shaking the snow off her rump and tail.

I don't have to call to the others; as soon as they see Waterston and Furiosa moving, they fan out into position. I return to the men, standing in front of Bran so I can lean back almost imperceptibly against him. Peeling off my leather glove, I take his hand. From the corner of my eye, I can see him look down and frown, and then he pulls his hand away to strip off his own glove so he can lace our fingers together and shove our clasped hands deep in the pocket of his coat. The handles for the quilt bag hang from his other arm, crushed between him and Ian. Together, we stand at the crest of the slope and watch.

To stand witness, as Fisher put it.

About seven feet this side of the fence, roughly halfway across the width of the yard, Officer Furiosa barks, drops to her belly, and crosses her booted paws over her nose. "She's hit," Lieutenant Waterston announces. One of the techs hurries forward with flagged stakes, and they move through a kind of hot-or-cold routine with Furiosa to mark out a rough boundary. Once it's flagged, Furiosa bounds to her paws and noses at Waterston's hand.

Waterston leads her away from the spot first, then pulls out a treat. "Good girl, Furiosa. You did a very good job."

The techs and three of the officers start to dig.

Bran's hand tightens around mine, starting to get painful. Given the circumstances, I'd usually just grit my teeth and bear it, but I think of my arm, and his mother, and instead I rearrange the grasp so I can curl and uncurl my fingers within his, like a heartbeat. He loosens his grip and kisses my hair in apology.

"Do you want to turn around?" I ask softly.

He squeezes my hand twice, a field response for "no" when we can't speak.

It takes longer to dig than it did in Tampa, the ground colder and harder, the soil different, though thankfully not frozen. Waterston brings Furiosa behind us to the porch to keep her a little warmer on the wood than she would be on the ground. Just in case it's a false hit and Furiosa needs to scent again. Slowly, the dirt moves away to reveal achingly familiar plastic sheeting.

Bran trembles against my back.

Despite being buried two years later than Erin, the plastic is more tattered, at least from what I can see from eight feet away. One of the techs takes pictures as they work. All of them are sniffling, and not just from the cold. As they gently lift the wrapped bundle, something falls from the plastic and catches on the edge of one of its tears, glinting in the weak sunlight.

Agent Fisher lunges forward, yanking a pair of neoprene gloves from her pocket and snapping them on. The techs freeze to let her carefully pull away whatever it is so it doesn't get lost. She stares at her hand for a long moment. The tech's camera flashes to document it. Curling her fingers over the object but not closing them into a fist, Fisher walks back to us.

I gently pull my hand out of Bran's pocket and take a wide step to the side, almost in front of Ian, so that I don't block Bran's sight.

Wordlessly, Fisher uncurls her fingers.

There on her palm rests a necklace. The chain is discolored and the clasp is broken, but the pendant . . .

A pink, yellow, and blue glitter enamel rainbow, the arc ending in two white stars.

29

Bran stares at the necklace, his face bloodless and pale. He saw that necklace every day for ten months and twelve days, bouncing against his sister's brightly colored shirts and getting tangled in her hair. He clasped it around her neck on Christmas morning and she never took it off.

And neither did Davies.

With a choked-off wail, Bran drops to his knees in the dusting of snow, curling over the quilt his mother gave him to lay over his dead sister. I'm not sure he's even breathing. His shoulders heave with the effort, but those broken, animal-in-a-trap sounds . . .

I kneel in front of him, sinking my fingers into his curls to brace his head against my chest. My fingertips scratch against his scalp. I don't try to say anything. What is there to say? But he's not alone. That's all I can give him, and it isn't anywhere near enough, but I can give him that. He is not alone.

"Al molay rachamim," I whisper, slowly rocking us from side to side, *"shochayn bam'romim, ham-tzay m'nucha n'chona al kanfay Hash'china, b'ma-alot k'doshim ut-horim k'zo-har haraki-a mazhirim, et nishmat* Faith *she-halcha l'olama, ba-avur shenodvu tz'dakah b'ad hazkarat nishmatah. B'Gan Ayden t'hay m'nuchatah; la-chayn Ba-al Harachamim yas-tire-ha b'sayter k'nafav l'olamim, vyitz-ror bitz-ror hacha-yim et nishmatah. Ado-nay Hu na-chalatah, v'tanu-ach b'shalom al mishkavah. V'nomar: Amayn."*

One of Bran's arms wraps around my waist, pulling me closer, and I shuffle my knees across the snow-damp grass as close as he wants me to be, his head shifting to the curve of my neck. Tears burn my eyes and down my cheeks, stinging where the cold air hits the trails.

Slowly, unevenly, his breathing starts to settle.

A moment later Ian kneels beside us, his arms around us both, and Karwan follows, bracing both Bran and Ian.

"You found her," I murmur into Bran's hair. "You and Ian found her, and you'll bring her home as soon as they release her."

He shakes his head.

"Yes, you did. All those things had to line up to arrive at this moment, but they came together around you and Ian. You found Faith, and you're taking her home."

Gradually he straightens, not pulling away so much as inching higher, until he gently presses our foreheads together, his ragged breaths warm against my face. I lift the end of my scarf—bless Priya for packing the softest one I own—and wipe his cheeks. He huffs in response.

"Let's give her your *mamá*'s quilt, *sí*?"

It takes a minute or two, but he nods and digs a travel pack of tissues out of one pocket to mop at his face and blow his nose. He offers the package to Ian and Karwan, both of whom avail themselves, and then he pulls out another tissue and wipes my cheeks. When we sway to standing, I wrap Ian in a massive hug just as Bran turns to do the same to Karwan.

I pull away to give Bran access to Ian. They both start weeping again in the embrace, two men whose lives and families have been shaped by the little girl they've searched for so long.

To give them a moment, and because I have something I need to do, I walk over to the gurney standing at the side of the house where it's blocked from sight of the road. Faith's body is zipped away in the black body bag and strapped to the gurney on safely level ground.

I place both hands, one gloved and the other cold, at the head of the gurney a few inches from the edge of the bag. "Hi, Faith," I whisper. "They've been looking for you a long time, sweetheart. I'm sorry it wasn't in time. But there are some things I think you'll be happy to know."

I tell her about Bran, about his career trying to rescue children and bring the people who hurt them to justice, about the strange little family he's formed around him. About her parents, and how they've waited and hoped and loved. About her friends, and the way they've charted the course of their lives by trying to help children. Lissi keeps them safe, Amanda helps them after they've been hurt, and Stanzi gives them joy when they're sick. All of that for her sake.

"I don't know what you would have done had you been able to live, Faith, but you've been extraordinary anyway. I'll do my best to take care of your brother, okay? Just a little longer now, sweetheart; you're almost home."

Bran, Ian, and Karwan join us a few minutes later, eyes red and raw, but there's something else there too. Not peace, exactly—not yet. Acceptance, maybe. The long nightmare is at an end, even if they're still suffering from it. Bran reaches into the paper bag and pulls out a white-banded block quilt in eye-searing bright colors. Together, we shake out the blanket and drape it over the bag. Four of the blocks have paint handprints on them, with the names clumsily finger-drawn on each: Faith, Ivalisse, Constanze, Amanda. Other squares have what were probably meant to be embroidery samplers before four girls decided to veer off the stamped path. In the center block, four flat, twenty-strand friendship bracelets are sewn onto the fabric, starting at the corners and meeting in the middle, where the individual strands explode into stitched daisies and spirals and hearts. A second white band wraps around the central square, the girls' names separated by pink, yellow, and blue hearts, and on the bottom leg of the band, in purple, BEST FRIENDS FOREVER.

"It's perfect," I whisper.

Bran nods. His hand floats for a moment over the fabric, then withdraws, much like Karwan did with Erin. He's spent twenty-five years wanting to hold his sister again.

But not like this.

We tuck the edges of the blanket under Faith, or at least under the bag, and fasten the black straps to keep her in place. After a collective moment to just breathe, we walk beside the gurney as it's wheeled over the grass and snow to the front yard and the ME's waiting van. A tiny woman, probably not even five feet tall and reed-slender, stands next to the van, faded blonde hair up in a messy knot that adds almost three inches to her height.

"Anica Lattimore," Fisher says softly from near my shoulder. "McKenna's mother."

She walks briskly up to us, her eyes pink and red rimmed but steady. "You're the agents from Quantico. The ones who found our girls."

Bran opens his mouth, then closes it again, shakes his head, and points to me.

I step forward to take her hands. "Eliza Sterling, and this is Agent Brandon Eddison and retired Detective Ian Matson. We started making connections based on the research Detective Matson brought us. And this is Agent Sachin Karwan, who gave us your daughter's file as a possible connection."

She glances at the quilt-covered gurney, then up at Bran's face. "You're family."

He nods.

Mrs. Lattimore steps past me and wraps her arms around him, squeezing tightly enough to make him *oof*. "She must be so proud of you."

Bran looks to me, but I shake my head and point to Faith. I'm proud of him too, of course, but she means Faith. He looks about as comfortable as he ever is with strangers hugging him—which is to say, not at all—but after a minute he manages to pat her shoulders without being too awkward about it.

When she releases him, Mrs. Lattimore turns and does the same for Karwan, and then for Ian. "Thank you," she says, her voice tight with fresh tears. "Thank you for finding our girls."

Fisher clears her throat, holding up her phone with a frown when we all turn to look at her. "Weather's going to get worse in a few hours," she says.

"Bad enough to close the airport?" asks Karwan.

"Possibly. I know this is shitty timing, but I also know you three"— she points to me, Ian, and Bran—"were planning on flying out tonight. Do you need to get back soonest, or are you able to hang around a day or two in case they close the runways?"

I know the correct answer; I'm not sure I know the right answer. I need to get back as soon as I can. We still need to talk to Davies. Vic's last update relayed no progress on that score. I need to check on all the other locations, make sure there haven't been problems with official identifications of the remains. Make sure the families have all been notified. Should probably help Watts put together the press release so she can break the story. With so many people aware of it now, it's going to happen sooner than later.

But if Bran needs to stay, if he needs this time with his sister . . . I don't want to leave him.

He gives one last look to his sister as the gurney is tucked into the back of the ME's van, then gives me a small, pained smile. "Let's go home."

"Will you promise to let the girls fuss over you?"

"Are you calling Marlene and Jenny girls?"

He'll be okay. Eventually.

"Ian?"

275

"I'd like to be there for the announcement," he says quietly. "I need to rest, I know that, and I will. But I'd like to be there for the announcement."

"All right."

Karwan, however, is going to stay. This is home now, and I suspect as soon as Erin's body is released, he'll be flying down to Tampa again to escort her back to her parents in Chicago. He leaves his bag in the trunk to retrieve later but gives each of us a hug.

"Well, Eliza," he says when he gets to me. He laughs helplessly.

"Take care of your sister," I tell him. "It's going to be hard on her."

"Yes. But after the first pain . . ." He smiles, and generous lines curve around his mouth. "At least we know. We will always mourn them, but at least now they can all be put to rest among family." He glances at Bran, who's helping Ian into the car. "I'm glad he has you, Agent Eliza Sterling. You're good for him. And if he's not just as good for you, let me know. I'll transfer to Quantico and kick his ass."

I grin and shake my head. "Not necessary, but thank you. We're good for each other."

Fisher drives us back to the airport. We fly out almost immediately, connecting to Richmond through Dallas–Fort Worth for some unfathomable reason. Omaha is a regional airport, so okay, fewer options, but going due south and then along the diagonal when we could have just gone due east? Not sensible.

None of us have eaten today—and we should have been taking better care of Ian—so we grab some fast food and shove it in our faces. A conversation with the gate agent while Ian and Bran are finding a bathroom produces a cot, pillow, and blanket from the stash kept around for canceled flights or weather-stranded passengers who can't leave the airport overnight. I set it up against a bank of windows where there's a little more space available.

He gives it the stink-eye when he returns, but it's a sign of how poorly he feels that he stretches out on it without actual protest and falls asleep almost immediately. He hasn't admitted it, but I suspect his headache has been raging for a couple of days, and he hasn't taken anything for it so he can be clear headed for the searches. That kind of constant pain is immensely draining.

Bran and I spend the first two hours of the layover on our phones, him with his parents and me with whatever combinations of Vic, Watts, Gala, Yvonne, Ramirez, and Kearney happen to be in the conference room at that moment. At one point even Agent Dern is in there and asks how Eddison is holding up.

Around the two-hour mark, he wanders off to find a barista willing to sell their soul to make his eldritch coffee, and comes back with his demon drink and a hot chocolate for me. We settle down on the floor of our gate, at Ian's feet, and set our backs against the windows. Bran holds up his arm to let me curl in close.

"The *hermanitas* had to learn how to sew for one of their merit badges," he says after a while. "They were so excited about it too. They were going to sew like *Mamá*. Only *Mamá* had years of practice and they didn't."

"They were bad?"

"Terrible, and heartbroken about it. They were ready to give up entirely. *Abuela* Cecilia was about to come for a visit from Puerto Rico. *Mamá* asked her to bring a box with her. Day after our *abuela* arrived, she sat down with the girls and this small box and brought out piece after piece of cloth. The sewing was terrible, the embroidery even worse. The pieces of cross-stitch actually had the patterns pinned to them because it was the only way to tell what they were supposed to be. They were awful."

"Your *mamá*'s first pieces."

"*Sí. Abuela* told them all about how frustrated *Mamá* was, how ready she'd been to quit. And after a couple days, when she'd had time to calm down, she tried again. And was still awful. She practiced and she asked for help and she got better with every piece. Over the next few weeks, the girls practiced and practiced. By the time our *abuela* left, she'd helped them piece together the quilt top, and *Mamá* had it on her table to finish. They were all so damn proud. And the quilt was so damn ugly."

I laugh and twist to drape my legs over his so I can see his face.

"A few years later, the other three signed up to do some community projects with the troop. Each group was randomly assigned a project. The girls got quilts for the brand new babies at the hospital, little things to send home with them. Simple ones, just twelve-block tops with a fleece bottom and a ribbon band, and yarn ties instead of actual quilting. I was home for the summer, already accepted to the academy and just waiting for it to start, so I drove them to every fabric store in town to make a stash of cloth that was both cheap *and* baby friendly."

"No blinding pink?"

"No neons, no Lisa Frank, was how their troop leader put it. We took over the living room and I helped them cut out all the squares. So many squares. We pinned them all together, set the girls up at the table with sewing machines. Lissi's *mamá* sewed, and so did *Tía* Angelica, Rafi and Manuelito's *mamá*, and they let us borrow their machines. They got them threaded and ready, and Stanzi burst into tears."

"Because Faith wasn't there."

"So *Mamá* got down the quilt from Faith's room and hung it up in the dining room so they could see it as they worked. After the tops were all done, they ironed and stitched a tiny rainbow patch into a corner of every blanket before they joined it to the backing. They made box after box of these baby blankets, dozens of them. When they gave them to the hospital, they said the blankets were from Faith."

The rest of the layover and all of the flight home is filled with stories of Faith, tales from those first angry, terrible weeks. All kinds of stories and moments he's never told me because Faith was a pain too deep to speak of. He talks himself hoarse, until it's impossible to tell when the rasp in his voice is from overuse or emotion. Lancing the wounds. I settle in against his shoulder and listen.

30

Cass and Mercedes are waiting for us when we arrive at the Richmond airport. Mercedes immediately pulls Bran into a long, swaying sort of hug, her fingers digging into his shoulders. "Watts sent us home," Cass informs us, without waiting for us to ask. "Said we needed to get some sleep."

"So you decided to add three hours of driving time to pick us up?"

"It's only an hour and a half."

"Oh? Are we staying in Richmond?"

"Fuck off, Sterling," she sighs.

Mercedes pulls away from Bran and leans down to kiss Cass's cheek in sympathy. "Have you lot eaten?"

"There was a Wendy's in Dallas," Bran tells her, lifting our bags into the trunk. He eyes the driver's seat, then shakes his head. He helps Ian into the back row of seats where he can stretch out a bit after the cramped flight, then sits down in the middle row. It pretty much forces the other two to join us in the car so we can leave. Mercedes looks at Bran, tucked on the left side, and hands her keys to Cass.

Because Cass is the only one short enough to give Bran enough leg room while driving.

"What's the state of the state?" I ask.

"Are you okay with hearing this?" Mercedes replies bluntly.

Bran winces, nods.

"Okay. Use a safe word, if you have to."

Cass snorts. "What the hell *is* his safe word, Eliza?"

"Nationals," I say blandly. Cass isn't the only one to choke on that; Bran does too.

From the backseat, Ian lets out a long, grumbling sigh. "There are some things, Eliza, I do not need to know about what you and Brandon do together."

"Sorry?"

"No, you're not."

"No, I'm not."

Mercedes just shakes her head and smiles. "Assuming Karen Coburn really was his first, we've found and formally identified all his victims. They finished the ID on Joanna Olvarson a little over an hour ago."

"Why so long for her?"

"It took them longer to find the medical records. Oklahoma City never folded them into the initial investigation. Her pediatrician's office closed some time ago. When her parents finally found their box of records, they accidentally sent the wrong ones."

"Wrong ones?"

"Her twin sister, Joanie."

"Huh. None of the other girls had twins. I wonder . . ."

"How he decided which one to take?" At my nod, she shrugs. "Fraternal twin. Her sister was a redhead."

"That would do it."

"Agents are with the Olvarsons now, which means all the families have been notified. Vic sent out a fresh gag order to every field office to be shared with the partnering local troops: no one is to share the information until after the press conference in the morning. Yvonne and Gala set up alerts in case anyone breaks it tonight."

"It's not like we can revoke the information if anyone does."

"No, but it at least lets us scramble to get the facts out."

"Thirty-one years ago, about three weeks before Karen Coburn went missing, a girl named Barbara Wagner died in KCMO from leukemia," Cass says. "She was ten years old, blonde, blue-eyed. She'd been the focus of a couple of profiles on local news stations while she was in treatment. After she died, her parents took out a few ads asking that, in lieu of flowers or cards, well-wishers should donate to children's medical research."

"That was his trigger?"

"A week later, it was the tenth anniversary of Lisa's death."

"So that's a yes on the trigger."

"According to his records, his moving every two years predates Karen's abduction. He started doing that after his divorce was finalized. Just couldn't seem to stay in one place for any longer than that."

"Is he still under sedation?"

"No, they were able to ease off that this afternoon a bit. He's not . . ." She shares a look with Mercedes, who shifts in her seat as she tries to come up with an appropriate description.

"He's not all there right now," Mercedes decides eventually. "He's going to be getting a pretty significant battery of tests in the near future."

"Incompetence?"

"Safe bet it'll hold. We'll see what happens when the initial shock wears off."

"What do his doctors think?"

"That he's a very sick man."

Bran reaches for my hand.

"How tired are you?" she continues.

"How not-tired do I need to be?" I reply.

"With his relative calm this afternoon, they transferred him to a hospital in Quantico. He was appointed a lawyer to protect his rights. So far, though, no one has tried to question him since his initial panic attack."

"Vic and Watts wanted to wait for me."

"Yes. If you'd like, we can stop by your place on the way, let you get a shower and some fresh clothes."

"Manassas isn't on the way. I can shower at the Bureau and freshen up my hair, change into one of the extra outfits Priya brought to the office. Oh, wait, no. Ian."

"I'm going with you to Quantico," he grumbles from the backseat.

"Ian, you're exhausted and in pain. If we take you back to Vic's, you can sleep on a real bed. We will absolutely make sure you're back in the Bureau in time for the press conference."

"Quantico," he yawns. "You've all got things you need to be doing, and they don't include going out of your way for an old man."

"They were about to go out of their way for me."

"And you don't need them to, so neither do I."

"Stubborn ass," Bran says fondly.

"Insubordinate jackwagon."

"Ah, the beauty of male friendships," sighs Cass.

Mercedes and I both give her queer looks. "You say that like we don't do worse with each other."

"Fuck off, Ramirez."

"Atta girl."

Was it really only yesterday? Or two days ago now, given that it's just after midnight. Cass restrains herself to about fifteen over the speed limit most of the way down. I can feel the week catching up to me, though, and it's not long before I click off my seat belt so I can pillow my head in Bran's lap. His hand runs over my hair, then rests, warm and strong, between my shoulder blades.

I'm asleep before the next exit.

The next thing I know, his thumb is rubbing behind my ear in a way that makes me just a little crazy, a way that is not conducive to working. "Wake up, Eliza," he says softly.

"M'wae," I mumble.

"If you can't pronounce *awake*, you are not actually awake," Mercedes points out helpfully.

I lift one arm enough to flip her off.

Bran helps me up to sitting, sort of. It's a slumping sort of sitting.

More and more light suffuses the night beyond the car. Huh, we're back in Quantico. We pull into the garage, not quite deserted but certainly not as crammed as we're used to during office hours. "We're going to install Ian on Vic's couch, whether he likes it or not, and let Watts know we're back so she can scold us," Cass says. "Follow us once you're a little more awake."

"Mm-hmm."

We help Ian out of the back. He winces at the glare of the garage lights and pulls on his sunglasses. I really wish they'd just driven to Manassas or that I'd kept my mouth shut when they suggested it. He needs to get actual rest tonight, and probably take some painkillers.

Bran sits back down in his seat, bringing me with him across his lap. I bury my face in his neck, ignoring the scratch of stubble, and his thumb and index finger dig into the tense muscles at my nape. "I don't think I've said thank you," he murmurs after a while.

"Don't you dare."

"Not for the case, Eliza."

"Oh. Huh?"

He huffs an almost laugh, the sound rumbling in his chest rather than escaping. "For what you've done for me. I'm always a moody, prickly asshole, but even I can recognize how I've acted this past week. I don't think anyone would have blamed you for needing to step away. But you didn't. You stepped closer, kept me standing. *Te amo*, Eliza Sterling, and I do not ever want to take you for granted. So whether you think you need to hear it or not: thank you for everything you have done for me in this terrible week. *Te lo agradezco de todo corazón*."

I'm definitely awake now, and blurry-eyed with tears. I don't ever doubt that he loves me—he shows it in a thousand different ways—but he doesn't often say it. Neither do I, for that matter. We spend so much of our lives at work, or with our team/family, it feels strange to say it more frequently. It means it carries more weight when we do say it, never glib or accidental.

I sit up straight so I can drop a kiss on the end of his nose. "I love you, too, *H'aim Sheli*."

My work cell rings obnoxiously loudly in the vehicle. At my string of muttered curses across five different languages, Bran just laughs and pulls it out of the case for me. "Sterling," I say.

"So Kearney and Ramirez are clearly incapable of taking care of themselves," says a female voice. It takes me a moment to identify it as Watts. "I'm assuming that means you are too."

"You told Ramirez to draw up a schedule for taking me on walks."

"Get in here. We're feeding you after your shower." And with that, she hangs up.

If I were inside, she'd be shoving a protein bar into my hands, I think.

We haul our bags in with us. Bran drops his at his desk and goes up to the conference room to check in with Vic. I grab the bag Priya brought me for the meet with Davies and head off to the showers. Mercedes follows me with a box of cling-wrap for my bandage. I pin up my hair and take the fastest shower of my life outside of Girl Scout camp, and when I'm out and dressed in fresh clothing, Mercedes changes out my bandage. The remaining blisters are shrinking rapidly, which is heartening.

"You do your face, I'll do your hair," she instructs, plugging in the curling iron that's been borrowed from God only knows which agent again.

Fifteen minutes later, we get back upstairs just as a massive amount of Chinese food arrives. As everyone else heads to the conference room, I detour to my desk to put down my bags. When I join the others upstairs, Vic stands and wraps me in one of his famous Hanoverian

Hugs, warm and strong and just the right side of suffocating. "You've done well, Eliza," he says quietly. "So very well."

I squeeze back rather than answer, and he lets me go in order to hand me a plastic tub of wonton soup.

"We need to talk to Davies," Watts says once everyone has had a chance to stuff their faces a bit. "Whether we can get any sense out of him or not, we need to at least be able to say that we've talked to him since his arrest."

"His lawyer okay with that?" asks Burnside.

"As long as she's in the room while it's happening, and it stops when she or a doctor says stop. Sterling, you up for this?"

I nod and swap my empty soup tub for a container of beef and broccoli. Bran scoots a smaller box of rice between us to share. "I'm not pretending to be Lisa, right?"

"No. Actually, we're hoping your appearance will have the opposite effect from yesterday."

"Two days ago," the Smiths correct in unison.

She gives them a minatory glare and continues. "He's not actively hysterical, but he is still agitated. I'm not sending you to interrogate him. I want you to evaluate if we can interrogate him. The first round of psych evals are already scheduled, and we don't need to interrogate him in order to charge him, but let's make sure we've got all the boxes ticked before we break this."

"What time is the press conference?" asks Bran, scooping three mushrooms from his meal into mine.

"Ten. We wanted to do it earlier, but seven is about the earliest we can expect the West Coast to tune in broadly. All of the local law enforcement agencies are prepared to run interference for the families for a few days. Sterling, I know you're tired, but I'd like you to take the lead at the briefing."

"No."

She blinks at me. "Pardon?"

I swallow the mouthful of broccoli that prevented me from getting out more than the single word. "Sorry. I just think that's a really bad idea."

"Turning shy on me? This is essentially your break. You, Gala, and Yvonne took the detectives' research and ran with it to form a solid case. We're all working it, but you're the one who basically held the reins."

Which is not at all how I would put it, but it's also not the most important point.

"If I go out as the lead, the talking points are about me being young and pretty and looking like the missing girls. It takes focus away from the investigation and the discoveries. And then, because the focus is on me, eventually it shifts to my relationship with Bran, and from that point on, the talking points become Bureau fraternization and compromised agents and the legality of the investigation. We haven't done anything wrong, but defending that will take attention away from the victims and the case and the good work that agents and LEOs in seventeen different cities and states have accomplished. It's not worth it. I appreciate the honor, I do, but it's not a good idea."

She studies me for a long moment. Eventually she nods. "All right." She looks down at her hands and sighs. "Goddammit."

Cass sneezes a laugh into her sleeve. The press conference at the Mercers' house was bad enough for Watts. This morning's conference? Every law enforcement office in the country is going to be tuning in for this one.

Watts sighs again and pegs a protein bar at Cass's forehead, connecting solidly. Cass yelps and sneezes out another laugh.

31

Davies's appointed counsel is a sleek but tired-looking woman in a tailored pencil skirt, blazer, and beat-up pair of running shoes. "Moira Halloran," she introduces herself. "Sorry, the heels come off at eight whether I'm done for the day or not."

"I respect that," I reply, shaking her hand. Her dark hair is still mostly in its pins, a few strands fighting loose here and there. "Agent Eliza Sterling and Agent Cass Kearney." Ramirez and Burnside are down the hall, talking to the agents on guard duty. Vic and Watts are still at the Bureau to work on the language of the press conference. Hopefully Vic will be able to break into someone else's office to find a couch for Bran to sack out on for a few hours.

"So that we're not dancing around each other here, how much are you actually hoping to get out of him right now? Because I'll be honest, trying to get clarity from him is damn near impossible at the moment."

"If that's what we establish, so be it. We're not here to push or to otherwise endanger his health."

"Would you mind if one of the doctors is in the room with us? The hospital in Richmond did some tests; his heart's not the strongest. If he gets agitated, it's best to calm him as quickly as possible."

"That's just fine."

She gives us an odd look before heading to the nurses' station to arrange it.

"I don't think she expected us to be so agreeable," Kearney says quietly, leaning against one wall.

"Brooklyn is safe, and the other girls have been located without his help. There's no particular urgency to make us assholes."

"I prefer emphatic."

"All right, there's no particular urgency to make us emphatic assholes."

"You look too sweet to be so evil."

"It's the foundation of my arsenal, yes."

"At least people stopped asking you if it was Take Your Daughter to Work Day."

"This is why no one feels sorry for you for being on our team now."

"A draw it is, then."

"How long have you two worked together?" asks Halloran.

Kearney flinches at the unexpected voice, loses her balance and slides down the wall to land on the floor with an *oomf*. "Ten months," she wheezes.

"I would have thought longer."

"We assimilate quickly." I hold out a hand to help Kearney up. "Are we ready?"

A tall, rail-thin man steps up next to Halloran and stops, bobbing his head affably. The lawyer nods. "Yes, we're ready."

I anxiously fluff my hair, still feeling out of place with the curls down around me rather than out of my way. "Let's do this."

Halloran introduces us to the doctor, who leads the way into the private room. Davies is on the bed, his left wrist handcuffed to the guardrail. His right hand plucks restlessly at the blanket. His head is turned to the window when we enter, but at the sound of footsteps he looks over. He shows no recognition of Halloran or the doctor, or Kearney for that matter. As I close the door behind me, his eyes light up. "Laura?" he asks in a quavering voice. "Laura, they won't let me leave. My heart . . . But how is she? How's our little girl?"

The lawyer glances at us. "I thought his daughter's name was Lisa," she notes in an undertone.

"It was," Kearney answers. "Laura is his ex-wife. I assume their daughter got her looks from her mother."

I cross the room to stand on his right side, my hands folded over the raised guardrail. "I'm not Laura, Mr. Davies. My name is Eliza Sterling, and I'm an agent with the FBI."

"FBI?" he echoes. "I don't understand."

"Mr. Davies, do you remember coming to the hospital?"

"I . . . no. I passed out, I think. My heart . . ." He shakes his head and lifts his left hand to gesture until the cuff stops him. He stares at it in confusion. "I don't understand. My wife, my daughter, are they okay? My baby girl is sick, she needs us both. You . . . you look so much like them."

"Mr. Davies, do you know what day it is?"

"It's . . . it's Wednesday. Anita came over to give Lisa her piano lesson. She doesn't have much energy for it anymore, but the doctors said the normalcy would help as long as we don't put any pressure on her."

It's Friday, and his daughter's last piano lesson was in excess of forty-one years ago.

"What's the year, Mr. Davies?"

He chuckles, then falls still when he realizes I'm serious. "Are you a doctor?"

"No. My name is Agent Sterling, and I'm with the FBI."

"The FBI? Has something happened? My wife, my daughter . . ."

I glance over at Kearney, who's leaning against the door to watch. Beneath the professional mask, she looks a little sad and a lot frustrated. Halloran looks a little sick, to be honest, but the doctor seems unsurprised.

"Tell me about your daughter, Mr. Davies."

His whole face softens with his misty smile. "Lisa. She's nine, you know, and so smart. So very smart. She loves math."

"You said she's sick?"

"Leukemia," he says with a nod. "The doctors . . . they're not sure . . ."

"They're not sure if it's helping?"

He shakes his head. "We had to move her bedroom down to the basement when she's not in the hospital. It's quieter there. Helps her rest. She's fighting, though. My little girl's a fighter."

I pull my tablet from the back of my waistband, flipping it open and around so he can see the picture. "Mr. Davies, do you recognize this girl?"

"What kind of sick joke is this?" he demands. Pink and red splotches mottle their way across his cheeks and nose. "That's my Lisa!"

I swipe Brooklyn's photo away for Kendall's. "How about this one?"

"Why do you have pictures of Lisa? Is she okay? Is she safe? Answer me!" The cuff on the guardrail rattles with his movement.

"Mr. Davies, neither of these girls is Lisa. The first is named Brooklyn Mercer. We found her in your basement."

"I just told you, *Lisa* is in the basement. It's her bedroom, to help her rest."

"This girl is named Kendall Braun."

He sinks back into the pair of flat pillows. "I don't know that name. But she looks so much like my little girl."

"We found her body in your backyard."

"What?" He looks genuinely shocked. "Oh, God, what happened to her? Are Lisa and Laura all right? Lisa . . . if they're searching the yard, they can't come into the house. Lisa's too sick; she catches almost anything. You'll tell them to be careful, won't you? Tell them they can't come into the house."

"Mr. Davies, this is the year 2018. Lisa isn't nine years old anymore. She isn't sick anymore."

"I don't know what you think you're pulling, but I demand to see my family. Let me see them. Let me—" He drags at the cuff, yanking so hard that it digs into his wrist. "Why is this here? What kind of hospital is this?"

"Mr. Davies—"

"This isn't funny in the slightest, young lady. Help!" he yells. "I need a doctor! I'm being held against my will!"

I back away from the bed and circle around to the door, to Halloran and Kearney. The doctor is already at Davies's side, trying to calm him. Davies gets increasingly agitated, pulling at the cuff and chain, trying to slide out of the bed. With a sigh, the doctor pulls a capped syringe out of his coat pocket.

"Try to relax, Mr. Davies," he says in a soothing, unexpectedly deep voice. He flicks off the cap and inserts the needle into a port on the IV tubing, compressing the plunger. "Take a deep breath."

After a few minutes of struggling, Davies slumps back into the bed, eyes glassy in his flushed face. The doctor remains by his side, one hand on his patient's shoulder, the other at his wrist, as he watches the monitor. We wait in silence, and in less than ten minutes, Davies is asleep, his heart rate mostly back to resting. When the doctor motions us out, we obey. "Thank you for not pushing past that point," he says in the hallway.

Halloran shakes her head. "Not an ounce of recognition. I've been in with him all day, even rode down from Richmond with him, and not a glimmer to suggest he's seen me before."

"When are they starting his battery?" asks Kearney.

"They'll do a few tests this afternoon," the doctor answers, "but most of them will be kept for next week. Psych prefers not to start them on weekends simply because of the amount of time involved. They're harder to do with a smaller staff."

Knowing precisely fuck-all about the process, I'm not going to try to argue. "How bad is his heart?"

"Without this kind of upset, not too terrible, honestly," he admits, hooking his ankle around a portable charging station to drag it over.

"He should probably be on beta blockers to help with intermittent arrhythmias, but it's not the end of the world that his primary care hasn't recommended it."

"But the stress goes right to his heart."

"Yes. So the more agitation he suffers, the more likely it is to lead to cardiac arrest."

Kearney looks up from her phone. "Watts says not to hang out and try again later. We can honestly say that we tried but he's in no condition. With the exams scheduled, it should build a bit of a shield around him."

"How long will you have agents guarding him?" asks Halloran.

"As long as he's in the hospital," I reply. "Standard procedure, if anyone asks about that. Not that he's much of a flight risk or danger, but it keeps him in place and also protects him from anyone who's curious or pissed off. Doctor, do you have a set rotation for which medical personnel are allowed to enter his room?"

He bobs his head, looking a bit like a heron. "In addition to myself and the other doctors, he's assigned to the care of the charge nurse on each shift. They'll draw the labs and deliver his meals, as well, to limit the number of people in and out."

Halloran walks with us down the hall to where Ramirez and Burnside are waiting, to let the agents on guard know they can return to their post. "I'm no expert, of course, but it doesn't seem like he's faking it."

"Doesn't seem like it, no," I say carefully. "That's what the tests will determine."

"I wanted to say thank you, to both of you and the Bureau in general. You've been extraordinarily sensitive about all of this."

"I'll admit, if we were still looking for the girls, it might have been a different story," Kearney replies. "Not that we'd be cruel, of course, but . . . we wouldn't have the space to give him this. It's for the best that we weren't relying on him to find them."

"The story should break around ten this morning," I tell the lawyer. "Do you have a preferred method of contact we can give to the media?"

She pulls a business card from her blazer pocket, flipping it over to show the phone number and email penciled on the back. "It's not a wild guess that this is going to get a lot of attention," she sighs. "A case like this is going to incite a lot of emotional responses. Do I believe he's guilty? Yes. The trail of bodies over the decades eliminates any possibility of coincidence. But I also believe that he's entitled to the best legal defense I can provide him. It's easy for people to forget that a fair trial is a constitutional right."

"Good luck," Kearney says, extending a hand.

It is half past five in the morning, and the only good thing about that is the coffee shop in the hospital lobby is opening its gate. We drain the first round standing there in the shop, then get a second round for the office from the concerned barista.

Our arrival back at the bullpen with caffeine is greeted with a wave of moans. Ramirez kicks the chair out from under Anderson before he can even make the filthy comment promised by his leer. With my cup of tea in one hand, I lift Bran's jet fuel out of the carrier and head over to his desk. He looks like he actually slept a bit. Not much, but some.

He's also not the only one at his desk. He's got my chair rolled over for a guest, a woman in her sixties with blonde hair cut short and styled around a face that's aging gracefully. There's enough grey in her hair to make it look ashy rather than golden, but her blue eyes are clear and alert. And shocked.

"You must be Laura Davies," I greet her, handing Bran his cup. I can see an empty mug at his elbow and a mostly full one beside Ms. Davies.

"I used to be," she says ruefully. "I'm Laura Wyatt these past thirty-some years."

"Of course. My apologies, Mrs. Wyatt."

She shakes her head. "It's just . . . this is all so hard to believe. Mark really killed all those girls?"

"The Wyatts got in about twenty minutes ago," Bran says, answering the questions I'm not quite sure how to ask. "So they haven't really been told much yet. The Smiths took her son down to the cafeteria."

I step away long enough to steal Ramirez's chair and push it over so I can sit. An hour of sleep in two days is not enough. "You must have a lot of questions."

"Probably," she admits. "Hell if I know what they are yet." She rubs at her eyes, her plain gold wedding band worn with time and care. "We just . . . we were married so young. Too young. We hadn't even been dating all that long, and suddenly I was pregnant. I wanted to get an abortion, but he convinced me to keep it. I don't . . . I don't *regret* that, precisely."

"But it was hard."

"Impossibly hard. We had to work all the time just to keep a roof over our heads at first. Things got better financially, allowing us to spoil Lisa a little."

"Didn't do much for your marriage, though."

"If I hadn't started throwing up every day, I doubt our relationship would have lasted the rest of the semester," she says with a pained laugh. "Our marriage was actually better when we were too busy to see each other. We tried to make it work for Lisa's sake."

"And then she got sick."

"I have a neighbor whose little boy was diagnosed with leukemia a few years ago. It's amazing how the treatments have advanced. Still terrible, of course, but they've gained so much ground in the past forty years." Her eyes are bright with tears, but none fall. "Thank God for St. Jude's. We had Lisa home whenever possible, but they took such good care of her. It just . . . it wasn't their fault it wasn't enough. And after she died . . ."

"There was nothing holding you and Mark together."

"I waited for a year to see if I could stick it out, if things would change. And . . . well. I wasn't going to be the woman who served him papers at our daughter's funeral. But it was so much worse than it had been. It was like I was drowning all the time, without ever breaking the surface. I'd managed to keep in touch with one of my best friends from high school. She offered me a place to stay so I could get back on my feet."

"When was the last time you heard from Mark?"

"We finalized the papers two years after Lisa died. He had his lawyer keep pushing for counseling, for couple's therapy. It slowed things down. He sent letters for a few months. I didn't answer them. I moved out of my friend's into a place of my own a few states over, and finally felt like I could breathe. I haven't seen or heard from him since. I should have stayed."

Bran looks up sharply, his whole body tensing up.

"Why do you think that, Laura?" I ask gently.

She shakes her head, looking lost. "If I'd stayed . . . those girls would all still be alive."

"You don't know that."

"But I would have—"

"You don't know that," I repeat, gently but firmly. "After another ten years of being that miserable, how do you think you would have been? If he'd brought home a new Lisa, would you have been in a mental or emotional condition to tell him no? And even if that answer is yes, it was never your responsibility. You are not—were not—responsible for his actions. Laura, this is not your fault."

"Tell that to their families," she says bitterly.

Putting down his coffee, Bran leans forward to take her hands in his. "Laura, I didn't fully introduce myself earlier. My sister was Faith Eddison. Mark took her from Tampa, and just yesterday we found her body in Omaha. I am family. Please believe me when I say no one with any sense is going to blame you. You had no way to know or prevent this. I'm sorry for what you're going to go through as this breaks, for the harassment that will invariably occur. It shouldn't happen, and it is undeserved. My sister's death is not yours to carry."

Laura folds herself over their joined hands, her shoulders heaving in great, wracking sobs, and Bran—who would be fairly happy if handshakes were outlawed so he didn't have to touch strangers—wheels his chair closer so he can pull one hand free to drape his arm across her back.

From the walkway outside his office, Vic looks down on them with a small smile, simultaneously grieving and proud fit to burst.

A few hours later, true to our word, we wake Ian up with time to refresh himself before the press conference. He's still visibly in pain, and light-sensitive enough to need his sunglasses even inside, but none of us are going to try to keep him from this. He brought us to this point. He made this possible.

The press room is crowded, representatives from dozens of news outlets filling the seats, camera operators bristling across the back of the room despite the presence of the Bureau cameras. More press line the far side of the room. On our side, agents line up respectfully. Vic stands on my left, one hand on my shoulder. Bran and Ian stand to my right, Ian in front. Partly that's to respect their height difference, but it's also to keep Bran a little out of view of the reporters. Like Watts, Bran is out in front of those same people and cameras on occasion due to being team leader. Mercedes stands next to Ian, helping to put Bran in a bit more shadow, and Cass next to her. A few agents down the line, Agent Addams stands against the wall, towering over everyone around.

Bran links his fingers through mine, carefully out of sight of everyone.

The conversation and shared questions abruptly silence when Watts walks into the room and centers herself behind the podium to begin the briefing. She doesn't show any of the flustered terror she was swallowing back only moments before.

Burnside had the balls to pat her shoulder and offer her a protein bar.

"Thank you all for coming," Watts says. The room is silent but for the rustle of clothing and the creak of chairs. "I'm Agent Kathleen Watts of the Quantico-based Crimes Against Children division. We've asked you here to make two announcements. The first you may have heard already, but good news always bears repeating. Two days ago, on the thirty-first of October, Brooklyn Mercer was found alive and is expected to make a full recovery from her ordeal."

Murmurs and exclamations sweep across the room, and just as suddenly cut off as people remember the second announcement to come.

"One thing every law enforcement officer learns over his or her time of service," she continues, "is that there are some cases that are harder to let go of than others. This is true at every level of law enforcement. Unsolved cases capture the imagination of the public, and when you have been one of the agents, officers, or detectives on that case, it demands your attention long after any hope of solving it seems to have faded. There are many who continue to work those cases regardless of the odds, and it is because of the work of two of those dedicated, persistent public servants—retired Detective Ian Matson of the Tampa Police Department and the late retired Detective Julian Addams of the Charleston Police Department—that we're able to announce that Brooklyn's kidnapping was not a one-off occurrence, but rather the latest in a chain of eight-year-old girls taken across a thirty-one year period by a man named Mark Davies." She holds her hands up against the swell of noise, pleading a moment's continuance. "Mr. Davies is in custody. By partnering with field offices and local police departments in seventeen different cities and states, all of his victims have been identified, their bodies located, and their families notified."

The room is lost to a blinding array of flashes from the still cameras, the reporters shouting over each other to be heard. I turn to look at Ian, standing with a soft smile, tears tracking slowly down his cheeks, and at Agent Addams beyond, eyes bright and proud, his father's final case closed at last.

Bran gives my hand a squeeze and shuffles a little closer, and Vic, Cass, and Mercedes all draw in closer as well. Together, our team stands, half hidden in shadow, and listens to Watts concisely relay the past week of hell. Taking a deep breath, she lists each girl by name.

By the time she comes back to Brooklyn, there isn't a dry eye in the room.

32

November 30 dawns with a uniquely Florida kind of weather. Despite the overhang of grey clouds and the slow, misting rain, the sun is brightly shining, sparking rainbows off of everything, the light looking golden and alive. It's beautiful and contradictory, and a bit perfect really.

Today is Faith's funeral.

It's a quiet drive to the cemetery, with as many people packing into the cars as is legally and safely possible. Spilling out into the parking lot has something to the effect of a fleet of clown cars. The cemetery is a little ways outside of Tampa, on slightly higher ground because grave-yards aren't really the kind of place you want right at sea level. We walk in clumps along the winding paths to the small hill Xiomara and Paul chose for their daughter's final resting place. The whole team came down, as did Jenny and Marlene Hanoverian, and despite it being nearly finals week, all three of Vic's daughters took a few days off school to be here as well. Bran has been a part of the family nearly all their lives, after all. It took only a little grumbling to convince Marlene that her wheelchair would be a better option than her walker. To keep her from getting stub-born, Vic told her it was because the ground would be slick with rain, which is true. It's also true that Marlene had another cluster of small strokes just a couple of weeks ago, and we're all worried about her.

Inara, Victoria-Bliss, and Priya are here. Deshani, too, Priya's mother, looking as fierce and gorgeous as ever. Priya has mellowed somewhat since I first met the two of them, a little less likely to set the world on fire just to dance in the flames. Deshani is unchanged, and perhaps unchanging. Both Sravasti women are dressed in white, because no matter how divorced Priya feels from the culture and religion of her ancestors, some things carry through. Inara and Victoria-Bliss never wear black to funerals—none of the former Butterflies do, not after they were forced to wear black every single day in the Garden—but Inara wears a dress in a deep cranberry that flatters the golden tones in her brown skin, and Victoria-Bliss is in royal blue only a shade or two brighter than her eyes. Sometime during the year of funerals they attended for the girls who died in the destruction of the Garden and the survivors who took their lives after, this became their ritual.

Paul is all that's left of his family, an only child of only children who have since passed, but a significant portion of Xiomara's family has come. Some of them have resettled in Florida over the past year, as Puerto Rico struggles to recover from the effects of Hurricane Maria. Others already lived in Florida, and still others have traveled from the island, bringing the love of those who remain behind. Mixed in with them are people from the neighborhood, friendships that have spanned the decades. There's Rafi and Alberto, with a tiny spitfire who looks to be Rafi's wife, along with a small swarm of other children who answer to any number of parents. Some of those kids look to be Manny's, from the way they cling to him as he herds them and the others along. Behind him, two older women carefully guide the remaining kids out of the way of the wheelchair that follows. I hadn't met Stanzi until last night, but she pushes Lissi's chair, a toddler perched in Lissi's lap, and alongside them walk a man and two women. The man is Stanzi's fiancé. The woman with the rainbow-patterned scarf wrapped around her head, her face sunken and thin from illness, is Amanda, and her wife is beside her.

Ian is there, of course, wearing his sunglasses and looking a little shaky, his wife keeping a hand on his back as they walk. When anybody asks, they say they're still discussing whether or not they want to pursue treatment. It's an easier answer, I think, than trying to explain why declining treatment is not the same as giving up on life. He may only have a few months left, but he's determined to live them as much as possible. He's not giving up on anything. Sachin Karwan walks beside them, the yellow ribbon still looped on his lapel. Where the ribbon crosses over itself, he also wears a tiny rainbow pin.

Shira and her *ima* Illa are here too. Bran looked startled at that, especially since the funeral for Shira's father was only three weeks ago near Coleman Correctional, but she swatted his shoulder and told him I was her sister, which makes him her brother, and of course they were going to be here. Illa just put a hand to his cheek and welcomed him to the family. My father was going to travel out with Shira and Illa—Bran's never actually met him—but he slid across a patch of ice on his front walk and fractured his femur, so he'll be in a rehab facility for a little while.

No mention was made of my mother joining us. No one asked. She hasn't spoken to me in years.

Bran hesitates at the base of the hill, leaning back against a tree. Water pools in the leaves before dripping down. I wait with him, waving Shira and Illa on. Somewhat to my surprise, it's Inara, rather than Priya, who stays back with us.

Bran gives her a sideways look. "You don't *have* to be here, you know."

She just smiles serenely. "I really do."

"Careful, Inara. Someone might hear and think you almost like me."

"Almost."

He chuckles and turns his attention back to the mass of family moving up the hill. "We'd stopped hoping this day would come."

"No, you didn't," Inara corrects softly. "You stopped expecting this day to come. If you'd stopped hoping, you wouldn't be in CAC."

"How's that?"

"Because if you'd stopped hoping, you wouldn't work so damn hard to give this day, or better days, to others." She stands on tiptoe to drop a kiss on his freshly shaven cheek and walks off to rejoin the others.

"Hope is such a strange thing, Eliza," Bran whispers.

"Yes."

He reaches for my hand and I lace our fingers together, and we follow after Inara.

Faith was actually buried two weeks ago, with Bran and his parents and Lissi present, but Xiomara didn't want that kind of funeral for her baby girl. She wanted something more joyful, without the sight of the too-small coffin. Today, therefore, is the unveiling of the tombstone. When they learned who the marker was for, the memorial company refused to accept payment for it and promised it in half the usual time. They said Faith had waited long enough.

It's been almost a month, and I'm still struck by the extraordinary kindnesses people are capable of, not just for the Eddisons but for all the families. There have been cruelties as well, and harassment of all sorts, but the sincere kindness of strangers has been unfathomable in many ways. I know Illa reached out to Laura through the Wyatt family's lawyer to extend a sympathetic shoulder. After all, Illa was married to her husband through much of his atrocities and never knew about them until after his arrest. She knows better than most what it is to feel that shattering responsibility even when it isn't yours to bear.

"Listos?" Xiomara asks once we're at the top. Without letting go of my hand, Bran threads through the gathering until we're standing with his parents. *"Bueno."* And with that, she and Paul take hold of the heavy lavender sheet over the marker and whip it away.

Lissi, Stanzi, and Amanda all let out startled giggles, clapping their hands over their mouths sheepishly. "It's pink," Lissi mumbles helplessly. "Oh, *Tía,* she'd love it."

It is pink, a mottled sort of rose and carnation, with Faith's name in large letters just below the curved top. There's a circle cut out of the stone beneath her name, all the way through, and below that, the years of her birth and death. We don't actually know what day she died. The journals she managed to keep—and keep secret—ended some months before her probable death. Whether she ran out of notebooks or simply got too sick to continue writing is something we'll never know. They haven't been released from evidence yet; I don't know if Bran will ever read them, to be honest. Some things are better left unknown. Underneath the years is an elegant inscription in English, the Spanish version just below it.

"Is that . . . is that *The Lord of the Rings*?" I whisper.

Bran nods. "From one of Sam's songs. I read to her every night. We'd already worked our way through *The Hobbit* and most of the trilogy. Sam was her favorite. She said of course he'd go to Mordor with Frodo. They were friends."

Looking at her best friends wrapped around each other for comfort and support, I think she was in good company with that belief.

Ian comes forward, carefully kneeling in front of the stone with a cloth-wrapped something in his hands. He folds back the layers of fabric to reveal a small suncatcher, a nonglittery version of Faith's necklace. They've been packing up his studio, aware that it would quickly become too dangerous for him to work the glass and kiln, even supervised. Very likely, this is Ian Matson's last creation. With Bran's assistance, he attaches it to tiny hooks within the open circle of the tombstone.

Oh, that's perfect.

Ignoring the spitting mist, the extended family spreads out tarps and blankets and unloads the army of picnic baskets. Amanda settles next to Lissi and Stanzi, Lissi's toddler on her lap, and opens a can of ginger ale. "Do you remember when Mrs. Santos was out on maternity leave and we had that horrible substitute? The one who was always so mean to the girls?"

"And Faith got all the boys to agree not to raise their hands, so he'd have to call on girls," laughs Stanzi. She sprawls out across one end of that blanket, draped over her friends and fiancé in equal measure. "He called on the boys anyway."

"And every time they said they didn't know the answer." Lissi grins, leaning back against one of the wheels on her chair. "It only took us, what, three weeks to break him? The librarian came to watch over us until Mrs. Santos returned."

"I remember the night Faith talked us into letting her watch a horror movie while we were watching her," Rafi offers, handing Bran a beer, even though it's barely nine in the morning. "There's Brandon, me, Manuelito, scared out of our minds and jumping at every sound and shadow, and little Faith is sitting there shaking her head, bored out of her mind. Wasn't scared at all."

The hilltop is alive with laughter and chatter, a mixture of Spanish and English. One of Xiomara's cousins converted to Judaism to marry her husband, and she and Illa settle happily into a comparison of Yiddish and Ladino. Shira gloms onto Cass and Mercedes, who she's met a few times and heard of endlessly, and Mercedes's girlfriend, Ksenia. They sit with a handful of cousins telling stories about one of Faith's trips to Puerto Rico, and how frustrated she got at strangers assuming she was a tourist, asking where her family was, and how quickly her frustration turned to mischief. Shira follows along with the English, watching wide-eyed during the frequent drifts into Spanish, but Ksenia speaks softly in her classroom-classical Spanish with a Ukrainian accent.

Nearby, Deshani and Jenny sit with Marlene and *Abuela* Cecilia, listening to the women trade recipes. Priya, Inara, and Victoria-Bliss have absconded with Vic's girls and descended on the blanket holding Alberto and the boy cousins around his age. There's a lot of blushing going on in that direction, and the girls are doing precisely none of it.

Vic sits with Paul and Xiomara, the Matsons, and Karwan, watching everyone with delight as the stories fly by. Tears follow laughter, chased by food and more laughter. After a month—a lifetime—of grieving, this is a celebration.

Pulling me back against his chest, Bran rests his chin on my shoulder and laughs, helping Rafi pin a squirming Manny to the floor with a story from a middle school dance that has Lissi in stitches.

It isn't until we're getting ready to leave hours later, when the rain is finally looking to get serious, that I see the back of the tombstone.

Karen Coburn

Diana Shaughnessy

Erin Bailey

Faith Eddison

McKenna Lattimore

Caitlyn Glau

Tiffany King

Lydia Green

Emma Coenen

Miranda Norvell

Joanna Olvarson

Melissa Jones

Andrea Buchanan

Riley Young

Shelby Skirvin

Kendall Braun

Extraordinary kindnesses.

The Quantico contingent flies back the next day, and Bran comes with us. He's been off for most of the month, staying with his family and working through all the arrangements. Helping his parents close the reward account, which was an emotional day for them all. Except for a flight to Chicago for Erin Bailey's funeral, he's been in Tampa since shortly after the press conference. He just shakes his head at Vic's reminder that he can stay longer if he wants to. His extended family has been in town for a couple of weeks, for Thanksgiving and the masses, and he's developed a bit of a twitch whenever a *tía* or *prima* asks him when he's settling down and having children with his *gringa*.

It's possible the extended family doesn't know that I learned Spanish.

Shira and Illa are at the airport with us, their flight to Denver a couple of hours later. Shira and Ksenia have become fast friends, somewhat to Mercedes's surprise, and they exchange contact info in the security line. When we settle into our seats on the plane, Bran pulls a book of baseball-themed crosswords from his messenger bag and hands it to me.

"Really?"

"I'm out of paperwork."

"I can fix that," Vic says from the next row up.

"Please don't."

Given that Vic and Jenny are housing not just their own Hanoverians but also the Sravastis, Inara, and Victoria-Bliss, they've got too many for even Jenny's faithful minivan to hold. We help ferry everyone back to their house, and it's a shock to precisely no one that Marlene uses that to gently bully the rest of us into staying for dinner.

All in all, it's almost midnight before we leave the Hanoverians. Bran's car is at The House, but when I get to the light where our paths home usually diverge, he points straight ahead in the direction of my apartment.

Works for me.

We trudge up the stairs, bags bouncing behind us. There's a plain white envelope taped to my door. I pluck it off, unlock the door, and drop both envelope and keys on the kitchen counter.

Bran pokes at it. "Shouldn't you open that?"

"I already know what it is."

He pokes it again.

"It's a renewal reminder," I laugh. "I have to tell them by the end of the month whether or not I want to renew my lease."

"Ah."

"I'm going to go shower the airport off of me."

It's still strange to go into my closet and not have my old wedding dress hulking in the corner like a clown with a knife. Good strange, but strange nonetheless. I'd never realized how much like an obnoxious roommate The Dress was, taking up space and causing problems and never paying rent. I shower quickly and brush my teeth, then change into leggings and the "Female Body Inspector" shirt that was a gift from Mercedes, intended purely to make Bran choke, back when he was still just Eddison. When I come back out, he's already in bed, the renewal notice in his hand.

I move the FBI teddy bear to the nightstand and slide in beside him.

He flutters the paper. "What do you think?"

"I like the apartment, but I'm sick of having to scramble to pay rent because they refuse to allow early payments or use an online payment system. I don't know."

He takes a deep breath. "What if you move in with me?"

"Into The House?"

"Are the capitals really necessary?"

"Probably not, but I've been saying that about hockey for years."

He thwaps me gently with a pillow, and I retaliate with the knowledge that I am absolutely never, under any circumstances, to share with Mercedes or Priya: his one and only ticklish spot. He squirms away, laughing, and wraps his arms and one leg around me to pin me to the mattress. "Enough, woman!"

"Never."

The kiss that follows is slow and bone-melting and very, very thorough.

"Move in with me," he whispers against my lips.

"You're sure?" I ask, giving that question the weight of everything that's been holding both of us back.

He grins and kisses me again. "I'm sure. Move in with me. I'll even let you decorate."

"Well, with that offer, how can I refuse?"

His indignant laughter is absolutely worth the second pillow to the face.

Brandon watches Mercedes pause in the middle of setting a framed picture on one side of her ofrenda, staring at the rubies and diamonds in her silver band and the way they glitter in the candlelight.

Cass snorts and pokes her in the rump with the butt of her beer bottle. "We get it, you're still shocked she agreed to marry you. Maybe finish your task and then goggle?"

"I'd say vete al infierno, but not tonight." She arranges the newest picture on the shelf, fingers lingering on the frame. Marlene Hanoverian had any number of small, annoying strokes over the past years. About a year after Faith's funeral, however, a much more significant stroke had left her hospitalized for nearly a month. In the two years since then, the larger strokes had become a little more common, taking a bit more from her each time. Just a month ago, she passed in her sleep. She smiles out from the photo, surrounded by grandchildren and great-grandchildren in her kitchen, everyone coated with a thick dusting of flour from the kind of accident that can only happen with that many small hands in the room.

Kissing her wife of only a week, Ksenia leans forward to arrange brilliant orange and gold cempasúchiles around the base of the frame. "I have to take my ring off at work," she admits. "It keeps distracting me when I type."

Eliza toes off her shoes and settles back into the couch, propping her swollen feet on the ottoman. She's had a year and a half to become accustomed to wearing a wedding ring on her hand, only to have to recently adjust to wearing it on a chain around her neck as her fingers swelled.

Brandon thinks she'd be a little less grumpy if men could get pregnant, too, or at least have all the same symptoms.

He adjusts the small offering plates on the left side of the ofrenda, making sure the food isn't obscured by the flowers. For Chavi, who was the reason they'd met Priya, there are yellow chrysanthemums. For Faith, his own Faith, water-dyed rainbow roses. And for Ian, who was the reason they found Faith and Erin and all those other girls, a delicately plaited wreath of forget-me-nots wraps around his photo, taken at a ceremony in which the TPD honored him for a lifetime of service. He'd lived only five months or so after Faith's funeral, and nearly to the end kept saying he was still deciding whether or not he wanted treatment. But he'd died at home, as out of pain as Hospice could make him, and at peace.

Small plates of food sit in front of the frames, as well. Chavi's plate is fragrant with raisin-studded saffron rice, naan, vindaloo, and green curry, along with a tiny bouquet of the root beer Tootsie Pops she almost always had close to hand when she was drawing. For Faith and Ian, Mercedes helped Brandon make tamales from his mamá's recipe, with arroz con pollo, peppery steak empanadas, and a handful of stacked alfajores. The majarete they'd attempted, failed at spectacularly, and then purchased. Ian's also has a shot glass full of the cold ginger beer he'd kept out in his studio to cool him off when his glasswork was done. In front of Marlene's photo, the plate holds pastries and baked goods they all made by hand, just as she'd shown them how to do over the years.

Kneeling in front of Mercedes and Ksenia, almost pressed back against their legs, Priya, Inara, and Victoria-Bliss arrange flowers around a series of frames on the lower two shelves of the bookshelf-turned-ofrenda. Priya has one picture there, a girl with a warm smile and a wreath of amaranth pinned around a dark ballerina bun: her friend Aimée who was killed only three years after Chavi, by the same man. The rest were provided by Inara and Victoria-Bliss, the Butterflies they knew who never made it out of the

Garden, and the girls they knew who never made it out of the Butterflies, from the beaming Cassidy Lawrence to the reserved Amiko Kobiyashi. The girls don't keep their own ofrenda, but Mercedes offered to fold them into hers. They're familiá, after all.

Brandon glances over at Eliza, noting the way she rubs the heel of her hand just above the swell of her belly. He thinks about asking if she's all right, but he has a set limit of how many times a day he's allowed to do that. Does he really want to waste one when she has a smile on her face? She barely showed at all for months, but abruptly, at the seven-month mark, she suddenly looked pregnant, like she glued on a basketball overnight. Without the gradual change of weight and girth to get used to, it's left her off-balance more often than not. Somehow it's hard to believe that just three years ago, he was caged by a house he couldn't claim and questions he couldn't ask, just as she was leashed by a dress she couldn't destroy and a word she couldn't say.

Jenny sits next to her, so he doesn't ask. They're talking about stretch marks and some kind of lotion; he'll have to ask Jenny about it later to make sure he can reliably locate it in a store. Eliza doesn't often ask for the little things that will make her more comfortable.

Vic comes out from Mercedes's narrow kitchen, bottles in each hand. He holds two of them out to Brandon.

He looks back at Eliza.

"They're white birch beer," Vic tells him with a chuckle. "Nonalcoholic, completely safe for her to drink."

"In that case . . ." He accepts them and walks over to Eliza to give her one of the chilled bottles.

She smiles and tugs him half over to run a hand through his curls, nails scratching gently along his scalp.

"So when do we get to find out if we've got a niece or a nephew cooking in there?" Cass asks, flopping onto a chair.

"Oh?" Eliza asks innocently. "Have you been wondering that?"

"Eliza!" comes the protest from the other woman. Vic just laughs and shakes his head.

"You did give in and find out today," Brandon points out. "Even I don't know yet."

"Does that mean we have to leave the room so she can tell you in private?" Cass looks less than thrilled with the prospect.

"Your choice, mi corazón," he tells Eliza.

She reaches for his hand and he gives it willingly, letting her pull him to his knees between the ottoman and the couch. She lifts her Rockies shirt enough to smooth his palm over her warm, bare skin and the life growing within. "There's still a margin of error, even with the blood test," she reminds all of them, "but the doctor says it's a little girl."

A little girl.

For a moment he freezes, fear snaking down his spine. But only for a moment. He's getting better about the guilt that still flares up from time to time at the thought of his sister.

"And I was thinking, for a name . . ."

He looks up at her warily. So many of his family members have asked if he'll name a daughter for his sister, but he doesn't think . . . he's not sure he can have that kind of Faith in his life again.

Eliza bites her lip, watching him closely. "Hope."

Hope. "That's perfect," he breathes, and the knot in his chest loosens.

In the cheerful chatter that surrounds them, she pulls him closer until his cheek rests against her belly. "I know you're still afraid," she whispers. "I know you still worry. But you, Brandon Eddison, are going to be a wonderful father. She is going to love you."

He nods, then backs away with a yelp, rubbing at his cheek. "She kicked me!"

Every woman in the room raises her glass and cheers. "Atta girl!"

Faith and Hope, he thinks in the laughter that follows. The ideas always seemed inextricably intertwined. Maybe now, finally, he understands why.

Eliza struggles to lean forward, and he meets her halfway, their foreheads pressed gently together. "Are you ready for this?" she asks.

He nods and kisses her softly. "Listo."

ACKNOWLEDGMENTS

Holy crow, what a wild ride this has been. As we say goodbye to our team of FBI agents, I want to thank all of you for reading these books, and talking about them, and sharing them with others—your enthusiasm is what's made it possible to continue telling their stories, and I am so, so grateful. Without you, these books wouldn't exist.

All the gratitude in the world goes to the amazing team at Thomas & Mercer. Thank you for your excitement and your celebration for each milestone along the way. It takes a lot of people to bring a book into the world, and even more to make it a series—you've all been amazing, and amazing to work with. I love that each new twisted idea gives you joy rather than scares you off.

Thank you to my friends and family, who never seem to mind when "How's the book going?" gets answered with unnerving laughter. To Robert, who answers some frankly disturbing legal questions without blinking, and to Kelie, who put together a whole file of information on cadaver dogs and sent it to me with the subject line PUPPIES!!! To the Kansas writing contingent, for endless support and commiseration and the occasional drink. To Isabel, who gets deluged with emails and texts with ideas and snippets and moments of pun-induced shame. Thank you all, my lovelies.

ABOUT THE AUTHOR

Dot Hutchison is the author of the Collector series (*The Butterfly Garden, The Roses of May, The Summer Children,* and *The Vanishing Season*) as well as *A Wounded Name,* a young adult novel based on Shakespeare's *Hamlet.* Hutchison loves thunderstorms, mythology, history, and movies that can and should be watched on repeat. She has a background in theater, Renaissance festival living chessboards, and free falls. She likes to think that Saint George regretted killing that dragon for the rest of his days. For more information on her current projects, visit www.dothutchison.com.